Dale Brown is a former US Air Force captain and the author of twenty-three action-adventure, 'techno-thriller' novels, fourteen of which have been *New York Times* bestsellers. Dale's novels are published in eleven languages and distributed to over seventy countries, with sales exceeding 12 million copies worldwide. Dale, his wife Diane and son Hunter live near Lake Tahoe, Nevada, where he enjoys flying his own private jet, a Grumman Gulfstream II.

TIGER'S CLAW

DALE BROWN

corsair

Constable & Robinson Ltd
55-56 Russell Square
London WC1B 4HP
www.constablerobinson.com

First published in the US by William Morrow,
an imprint of HarperCollins Publishers, 2012

First published in the UK by Corsair,
an imprint of Constable & Robinson Ltd., 2013
This edition published by Corsair, 2013

A copy of the British Library Cataloguing in
Publication Data is available from the British Library

ISBN 978-1-4721-0733-6 (B-format)
ISBN 978-1-4721-0730-5 (ebook)

Printed and bound by CPI Group (UK) Ltd, Croydon, CR0 4YY

1 3 5 7 9 10 8 6 4 2

This novel is dedicated to my younger brother Ken, who passed away on July 31, 2011, after a long illness (you might remember the antagonist Kenneth Francis James in my third novel, *Day of the Cheetah,* who was named for Ken, my other brother, Jim, and my dad). Ken was my aircraft mechanic for seven years, a fellow soccer referee, a fellow volunteer for Angel Flight West, and my frequent copilot. He was a rather white-knuckle flier, especially in the bumps and clouds, but he never failed to do an Angel Flight West mission with me and was aboard every postmaintenance flight to make sure everything on the ship was okay after he was done working on it.

His short life only highlights the importance of family—not just the families we're born into but the families we accrue throughout our lives. We all make lousy decisions and catch some bad breaks. But if we celebrate with and support our families when times are good, and aren't afraid or ashamed to ask for help from our families when situations turn bad, we will never be alone.

Keep an eye on the family, bro, and fly safe on your new journeys.

To remind everyone: Angel Fight West is a real organization based in Santa Monica, California, that pairs needy medical patients and volunteer pilots together to provide no-charge air transportation for treatment or other necessary activities. Missions are flown by volunteer pilots and crewmembers who donate their time and the cost of their aircraft and fuel. Learn more about this worthwhile organization at www.AngelFlightWest.org.

CAST OF CHARACTERS

AMERICANS

KENNETH PHOENIX, president of the United States

ANN PAGE, vice president

WILLIAM GLENBROOK, president's national security adviser

HERBERT KEVICH, secretary of state

FREDRICK HAYES, secretary of defense

THOMAS TORREY, CIA director

GERALD MURTH, undersecretary of defense for acquisitions

JOSEPH COLLINGSWORTH, Speaker of the U.S. House of Representatives

DIANE M. JAMIESON, majority leader of the U.S. Senate

U.S. AIR FORCE GENERAL TIMOTHY SPELLINGS, chairman of the Joint Chiefs of Staff

ADMIRAL EDWARD FOWLER, chief of naval operations

GENERAL JASON CONAWAY, chief of staff, U.S. Air Force

DR. HELEN KADDIRI, president and chairman of the board, Sky Masters Inc.

LIEUTENANT GENERAL PATRICK MCLANAHAN, USAF (ret.), vice president and COO, Sky Masters Inc.

DR. LINUS OGLETHORPE, chief engineer and scientist, Sky Masters Inc.

ED GLEASON, XB-1 chief instructor pilot, Sky Masters Inc.

SAM JACOBS, XB-1 aircraft commander, Sky Masters Inc.

LISA MANN, XB-1 Excalibur copilot, Sky Masters Inc.

KAREN WELLS, XB-1F Excalibur ground defensive systems officer, Sky Masters Inc.

GEORGE WICKHAM, XB-1 ground offensive systems officer, Sky Masters Inc.

U.S. NAVY CAPTAIN EDWARD TAVERNA, commander, guided-missile cruiser USS *Chosin*

U.S. NAVY CAPTAIN RICHARD AVERY, commanding officer, Naval Air Station (NAS) Fallon

U.S. NAVY LIEUTENANT COMMANDER CHRIS "NOOSE" KAHN, commander, VF-13 Fighting Saints, NAS Fallon

COMMANDER DOUGLAS SHERIDAN, commanding officer, Coast Guard cutter *Mohawk*

LIEUTENANT COMMANDER EDWARD FELLS, tactical officer, Coast Guard cutter *Mohawk*

LIEUTENANT ED COFFEY, HH-60 Jayhawk pilot, Coast Guard cutter *Mohawk*

LIEUTENANT LUCY CROSS, HH-60 Jayhawk copilot, Coast Guard cutter *Mohawk*

U.S. NAVY ADMIRAL ROBERT LUCE, commander, U.S. Pacific Command (PACOM)

U.S. AIR FORCE GENERAL GEORGE HOOD, commander, U.S. Air Force Pacific Air Forces (PACAF)

U.S. AIR FORCE COLONEL WARNER "CUTLASS" CUTHBERT, commander, First Expeditionary Bomb Wing (First EBW), Andersen Air Force Base, Guam

U.S. AIR FORCE LIEUTENANT COLONEL NASH HARTZELL, deputy wing commander, First EBW

LIEUTENANT COLONEL BRIDGET "XENA" DUTCHMAN, commander, Twentieth Expeditionary Bomb Squadron (B-52H Stratofortress)

LIEUTENANT COLONEL FRANKLIN "WISHBONE" MCBRIDE, commander, 393rd Expeditionary Bomb Squadron (B-2A Spirit)

LIEUTENANT COLONEL JUAN "PICANTE" OROZ, commander, Ninth Expeditionary Bomb Squadron (B-1B Lancer)

LIEUTENANT COLONEL JIMMY "JUJU" MAILI, commander, 199th Expeditionary Fighter Squadron, Hawaii Air National Guard, Joint Base Pearl Harbor–Hickam (F-22A Raptor)

Major Robert "Brewski" Carling, F-22A Raptor pilot

U.S. Air Force Captain Alicia Spencer, intelligence officer, First EBW

U.S. Army Captain Jason Harris, Patriot antiaircraft missile battery commander, Guam

Thomas Hoffman, president, Warbirds Forever Inc.

Sondra Eddington, chief pilot, Warbirds Forever Inc.

Bradley J. McLanahan, instructor pilot, Warbirds Forever Inc.

People's Republic of China

Zhou Qiang, president of the People's Republic of China

Gao Xudong, vice president of China

Tang Ji, foreign minister

Cao Ju, defense minister

Li Peiyan, Chinese ambassador to the United States

Jin Yongkang, finance minister

Shàng Jiàng (Colonel General) Zu Kai, chief of the general staff, People's Liberation Army

Shao Jiàng (Major General) Hua Zhilun, commander, Eleventh Tactical Rocket Division, People's Liberation Army

Shao Jiàng (Major General) Sun Ji, deputy chief of the general staff, People's Liberation Army

Hai Jun Zhong Jiàng (VICE ADMIRAL) ZHEN PENG,
      commander, South Sea Fleet, People's Liberation Army
      Navy, Zhanjiang

Hai Jun Shao Jiàng (REAR ADMIRAL) HU TAN-SUN,
      commander, Second Carrier Battle Group (aircraft carrier
      Zheng He), People's Liberation Army Navy, Juidongshan

Hai Jun Da Xiao (LOWER ADMIRAL) CHEN BOLIN, captain
      of the Chinese aircraft carrier *Zhenyuan*

Hai Jun Da Xiao (LOWER ADMIRAL) WENG LI-YEH, captain,
      Chinese aircraft carrier *Zheng He*

Hai Jun Shang Xiao (CAPTAIN) ZHANG PEIYAN, commander
      of flight operations, carrier *Zhenyuan*

Hai Jun Zhong Xiao (COMMANDER) HUA JI, JN-20 squadron
      commander, carrier *Zheng He*

Hai Jun Shao Xiao (LIEUTENANT COMMANDER) WU DEK
      SU, JN-15 fighter pilot

Kong Jun Shang Jiang (AIR FORCE COLONEL GENERAL)
      ZENG SU, chief of staff, People's Liberation Army Air
      Forces

Kong Jun Zhong Jiang (AIR FORCE LIEUTENANT GENERAL)
      CHEN LI, commander, First Strategic Strike Division (Xian
      H-6)

SOCIALIST REPUBLIC OF VIETNAM

TRAN PHUONG, prime minister

Thượng tá (CAPTAIN) DANG VAN CHIEN, captain of the
      Gepard-class frigate *Cá mập* (*Shark*)

REPUBLIC OF CHINA (TAIWAN)

WU ANASTASIA, president

Zhōng jiàng (VICE ADMIRAL) WU JIN-PING, commander, First Naval District South, Kaohsiung

Shàngxiào (CAPTAIN) YAO MEI-YUEH, captain of the Type 800 attack submarine *Fùchóu zhě* (*Avenger*)

Zun Khong (COMMANDER) CHEIN SI-YAO, executive officer, attack submarine *Avenger*

COMMONWEALTH OF AUSTRALIA

MARK RUDDOCK, prime minister

REPUBLIC OF INDONESIA

JUSUF SALEH, president

REPUBLIC OF THE PHILIPPINES

PATRICIA CRUZ, president

AUTHOR'S NOTES AND CHINESE WORDS

South Sea = South China Sea

Nansha Dao = Spratly Islands

Xisha Dao = Paracel Islands

Wúshēng Léitíng—W= **Silent Thunder**

Hǔ Zhǎo—虎爪 = **Tiger's Claw**

Chinese aviation assault carrier *Tongyi* = **Reunification**

CJ-20 *Changjian* **cruise missile = Long Sword**

Shenyang J-20 *Tiǎozhàn zhě*—挑战者 = **Challenger**

JH-37 *Fēi Bào* = **Flying Leopard**

JH-37 call sign *Qianfeng* = **striker**

JN-15 call sign *Ying* = **hawk**

J-20 call sign *Lǎoyīng* = **eagle**

Xiānshēng = **sir**

Yèyīng = **nightingale**

Baohuzhe—保护者 = **Protector**

Qíyú = **sailfish**

Fùchóu zhě = **Avenger**

Jia = **home**

Yuying = **osprey**

BLU-89E—*Kěpà debō* = **Terrible Wave**

Lóng Dehūxī = **Dragon's Breath**

jī huó = **activate**

Nèizài de dírén—内在的敌人 = **Enemy Within**

WEAPONS AND ACRONYMS

A&P—Airframe and Powerplant Mechanic

ABM—Anti Ballistic Missile

AC—Aircraft Commander

Aegis—advanced shipborne radar system

AGM-86D—Maverick TV-guided missile

AGM-88 HARM—High-speed Anti-Radiation Missile, anti-radar weapon

ALQ-293 Self-Protection Electronically Agile Reaction (SPEAR)—advanced jamming and netrusion system

AMRAAM—Advanced Medium-Range Air-to-Air Missile, radar guided

APR-3E—Chinese air-dropped rocket-powered torpedo

ARCP—Air Refueling Control Point, the rendezvous point for receivers and tankers

AST—Aviation Survival Technician, a Coast Guard rescue swimmer

ASW—Anti Submarine Warfare

ATP—Airline Transport Rating

AWACS—Airborne Warning and Control System

Beak—nickname for the B-2A Spirit stealth bomber

bold-print items—items in a checklist that must be committed to memory

Bone—nickname for the B-1B Lancer bomber (B-One)

BUFF—nickname for the B-52 bomber (Big Ugly Fat F**ker)

C-182—Cessna 182 light single-engine airplane

CAP—Civil Air Patrol

CFI—Certified Flight Instructor

CFI-I—Certified Flight Instructor-Instruments

CJ-20—long-range air-launched cruise missile

CJCS—chairman of the Joint Chiefs of Staff

CNO—Chief of Naval Operations

COO—Chief Operating Officer

DEFCON—Defense Readiness Condition

DFAC—Dining Facility

DoD—Department of Defense

Dolphin-class—Israeli submarine

E-3C Sentry—airborne radar plane

Eagle Eye—unmanned remotely piloted reconnaissance plane

EEZ—Economic Exclusion Zone

EGT—Exhaust Gas Temperature

F-15C Eagle—American-made air superiority fighter

F-22 Raptor—fifth-generation American air superiority fighter

FPCON—Force Protection Condition

GDP—Gross Domestic Product

HARM—High-speed Anti-Radiation Missile

IDAS—Interactive Defense and Attack System, sub-launched attack missile

JASSM—Joint Air-to-Surface Standoff Missile, medium-range cruise missile

JH-37 *Fēi bào*—Chinese carrier-based fighter-bomber

Joint Tactical Information Distribution System (JTIDS)—advanced military data-sharing system

KC-10 Extender—third-generation U.S. Air Force air refueling tanker and cargo plane

KC-135 Stratotanker—second-generation Air Force air refueling tanker

KC-46A Provider—fourth-generation Air Force air refueling tanker

long legs—able to fly long distances

LORAN—Long Range Navigation, ground-based long-range radio navigation system

MAD—magnetic anomaly detector, a system to locate submarines by aircraft

Mjollnr—space-based land or sea attack system

Nansha Dao—Chinese name for the Spratly Islands

netrusion—injecting false code or viruses electronically into an enemy radar

NVG—night-vision goggles

OTH-B—over-the-horizon backscatter ultra-long-range radar

PACAF—Pacific Air Forces

PL-9C—Chinese short-range heat-seeking air-to-air missile

Preppie—cadet entering the Air Force Academy who needs academic assistance

RQ-4 Global Hawk—long-range high-altitude unmanned reconnaissance aircraft

RTB—return to base

SAM—surface-to-air missile

SAT—Scholastic Aptitude Test

SBIRS—Space-Based Infrared Surveillance, new missile launch detection and tracking system

Shaanxi Y-8—Chinese medium turboprop transport plane modified for ASW patrol

shapes—inert practice bomb with the same size, weight, and shape of a real bomb

Shenyang J-20 *Tiǎozhàn*—fifth-generation Chinese jet fighter

sonobuoy—floating air-dropped sensor to detect submarines

StealthHawk—stealthy long-range attack cruise missile

Tank—nickname of the Joint Chiefs of Staff conference room

Thor's Hammer—space-based land and sea attack weapon

Tomahawk—long-range ship- or sub-launched attack cruise missile

UNCLOS—United Nations Convention on the Law of the Sea

UNR—University of Nevada–Reno

Wilco—will comply

XB-1F Excalibur—refurbished B-1B Lancer bomber

XF-111 SuperVark—refurbished F-111 Aardvark bomber

Xisha Dao—Chinese name for the Paracel Islands

Zhongnanhai—Chinese government building complex in Beijing

REAL-WORLD NEWS EXCERPTS

PACIFIC POWER MAY SHIFT WITH NEW CHINESE WEAPON—(*The Washington Times,* August 6, 2010): Nothing projects U.S. global air and sea power more vividly than supercarriers. Bristling with fighter jets that can reach deep into even landlocked trouble zones, America's virtually invincible carrier fleet has long enforced its dominance of the high seas.

China may soon put an end to that.

U.S. naval planners are scrambling to deal with what analysts say is a game-changing weapon being developed by China—an unprecedented carrier-killing missile called the Dong Feng 21D that could be launched from land with enough accuracy to penetrate the defenses of even the most advanced moving aircraft carrier at a distance of more than 900 miles.

. . . The weapon, a version of which was displayed last year in a Chinese military parade, could revolutionize China's role in the Pacific balance of power, seriously weakening Washington's ability to intervene in any potential conflict over Taiwan or North Korea. It also could deny U.S. ships safe access to international waters near China's 11,200-mile-long coastline . . .

THE SIMMERING STRATEGIC CLASH IN U.S.-CHINA RELATIONS—(Stratfor.com, January 20, 2011): ... Beijing is compelled by its economic development to seek military tools to secure its vital supply lines and defend its coasts, the historic weak point where foreign states have invaded. With each Chinese move to push out from its narrow geographical confines, the United States perceives a military force gaining in ability to block or interfere with U.S. commercial and military passage and access in the region. This violates a core American strategic need—command of the seas and global reach.

But China cannot simply reverse course—it cannot and will not simply halt its economic ascent, or leave its economic and social stability vulnerable to external events that it cannot control. Hence we have an unresolvable strategic clash; tempers are simmering, giving rise to occasional bursts of admonition and threat. Yet unresolvable does not mean immediate, and both sides continue to find ways to delay the inevitable and inevitably unpleasant, whether economic or military in nature, confrontation.

LEANING FORWARD, BUT NOT OVERREACHING— (AirForce-Magazine.com, January 27, 2011): Air Force will design its new long-range bomber by leveraging the best of today's technology and not trying to incorporate exceedingly risky approaches, USAF Vice Chief of Staff Gen. Philip Breedlove told lawmakers Wednesday. "One of the cost-savings approaches we have for this bomber is to not lean forward into technology that's not proven, but bring our aircraft up to the current day's standards," he testified before the House Armed Services Committee. For instance, Breedlove said stealth technology has advanced much since the B-2 bomber came along through subsequent work on the F-22 and F-35. "So the new bomber will have better stealth capability, but not [by] making leaps forward that we can't count on," he explained. This same mind-set applies for the bomber's avionics, information-gathering systems, and so on . . .

MORE FOR LESS—(AirForce-Magazine.com, March 3, 2011): Air Force scientists aim to demonstrate a 2,000-pound-class penetrating weapon that packs the same wallop as one of today's 5,000-pound-class bunker busters, said Stephen Walker, who oversees USAF's science and technology activities. This work, occurring under the new High Velocity Penetrating Weapon initiative, is meant "to reduce the technical risk for a new generation of penetrating weapons to defeat difficult hard targets," Walker told House lawmakers Tuesday in prepared remarks. This weapon "will use a higher velocity impact to increase warhead penetration capability," he explained. "Advanced technologies," he continued, "will enhance weapon kinematics, ensure precision guidance in contested environments, and dramatically reduce the size of the overall weapon." In fact, as a result, future fighters "will be able to deliver bunker-busting capabilities currently associated only with the bomber fleet," he said . . .

WHAT WAR WITH CHINA WOULD LOOK LIKE— (AirForce-Magazine.com, March 28, 2011): If China attacks Taiwan in 2015 and the United States comes to the island's rescue, the Air Force would have a tough fight on its hands, predict analysts with RAND Project Air Force. The "significant number" of modern fighters, surface-to-air missiles, long-range early-warning radars, and secure communication links that China is likely to have by 2015, coupled with Chinese capabilities to strike US bases in the western Pacific, would make the air campaign "highly challenging for US air forces," they write in

Shaking the Heavens and Splitting the Earth, a recently issued RAND report. Improving US capabilities to attack China's aircraft on the ground, "may be the most effective way to defeat China's air force," it states.

FORTIFYING GUAM'S INFRASTRUCTURE—AirForce-Magazine.com, April 14, 2011): The Air Force has a number of initiatives planned to bolster the resiliency of Andersen AFB, Guam, one of its strategic hubs in the western Pacific, Chief of Staff Gen. Norton Schwartz told lawmakers last week. For Fiscal 2012, plans are in place to harden infrastructure there, Schwartz told the House Appropriations Committee's military construction panel. "That includes both facilities and, importantly, utilities," such as "making sure that we have some redundancy and resilience in the fuel supplies," said Schwartz. He said there also are plans to disperse Andersen assets "at outlying locations around Guam" in time of conflict . . .

USED USAF F-15S FOR ISRAEL?—(AirForce-Magazine. com, April 20, 2011): Israel may seek to procure a squadron of used USAF F-15s to bridge the anticipated gap until it receives its first F-35 strike fighters . . .

Though Israel inked a $2.75 billion deal with the United States for 20 F-35s last October—with an eye toward an eventual 75—delays in the overall F-35 program may push back the first Israeli deliveries by several years to as late as 2018 . . .

THE LAST GUNSLINGER (by Michael Behar, *Air and Space Smithsonian Magazine,* June/July 2010): . . . The economy is quashing spendy military ventures, and fifth-generation fighters are already suffering the wrath of the red pen . . . The ongoing F-35 development program, a relative bargain at $155 million per airplane, is already over budget and behind schedule, causing Congressional colic. Cutbacks to its $300 billion-plus program are virtually certain . . .

. . . "You don't want to make an airplane be the Swiss Army knife of a fighter," [78-year-old retired colonel Donn Byrnes, who got involved with the F-15 Eagle program in 1969] says. "I'm absolutely not in love with the idea. The F-35 is the worst nightmare of hardware idiocy. It does everything wrong. You need a long-legged fighter, not a short, fat one . . ."

CHINA REVEALS NEW AMRAAM—(by Wendell Minnick, *Defense News,* May 23, 2011): China has revealed a next-generation air-to-air missile (AAM) that the state-run *People's Daily* called a "trump card" and a "secret weapon for gaining air superiority."

. . . The new Chinese PL-12D AAM might use a new active/passive guidance system, said Richard Fisher, a China defense analyst at the International Assessment and Strategy Center, an Alexandria, VA, think tank. "This kind of combined guidance system confers concealment/stealth advantages, while the passive mode also uses less battery power, allowing the missile to achieve its maximum range," Fisher said.

". . . It is a troubling development," Fisher said. "That the People's Liberation Army could field an AAM featuring an active/passive guidance system potentially before the U.S. deploys the AIM-120D is not where we want to be."

CYBERATTACKS CONSTITUTE AN ACT OF WAR—(www.Stratfor.com, May 31, 2011): The Pentagon on May 31 adopted a new strategy that will classify major cyberattacks as acts of war, meaning the United States for the first time can respond to such acts with traditional military force, *The Wall Street Journal* and AFP reported. The Pentagon's first formal cyberstrategy concludes that the Laws of Armed Conflict apply to cyberspace, according to three defense officials who have read the document.

PRICE SMACKDOWN—(AirForce-Magazine.com, June 1, 2011): Boeing on Tuesday challenged Lockheed Martin's recent comparison of F-35 strike fighter and F/A-18E/F Super Hornet prices. Chris Chadwick, president of Boeing Military Airplanes, called a telecon with defense reporters to rebut last week's *Daily Report* entry in which Lockheed's F-35 business development lead Steve O'Bryan said the F-35 will cost about $65 million in 2010 dollars, a figure that he said is "the same cost" as the Super Hornet. Chadwick said the F/A-18E/F actually costs $53 million in 2010 dollars, and that includes an advanced targeting system, APG-79 advanced electronically scanned array radar, helmet-mounted cueing system, and external fuel tanks. He also said the Super Hornet's lower costs for production and sustainment are based on actual data versus "estimates" for the F-35. "Lockheed needs to be a little more true with their facts," asserted Chadwick. Lockheed is assuming volume efficiencies on "aircraft that may never be built," he said. The two-seat Super Hornet F model also offers superior situational awareness compared to the single-seat F-35, Chadwick claimed, adding that the two independent cockpits mean Super Hornet aircrew can assess and attack more targets simultaneously.

CHINESE WARSHIP INTERCEPTS INDIAN VESSEL —(Stratfor.com, September 1, 2011): An unidentified Chinese warship intercepted Indian amphibious assault ship INS *Airavat* in international waters in the South China Sea near Vietnam in July, according to unnamed sources close to the event, the *Financial Times* reported Sept. 1. The Chinese vessel demanded that the Indian ship identify itself and explain its presence. The

Airavat had recently completed a scheduled port call in Vietnam.

LOOMING CUTS CAST CLOUD OVER AFA CONFERENCE—(by Dave Majumdar, Defense News, September 26, 2011): . . . The U.S. Air Force will not push the envelope as it historically has when developing new technology for future weapons because declining defense spending will reshape the military's purchasing priorities.

" . . . Future development efforts will have to be less ambitious because we cannot assume the kind of risk that past acquisition strategies have incorporated in their development plans," Air Force Chief of Staff Gen. Norman Schwartz said Sept. 20. "While the Air Force has historically "advanced the state of the art" of technology, "we now must be more calibrated in pushing the technological envelope," the general said.

". . . We must be ruthlessly honest and disciplined when operational requirements allow for more modest and less exquisite, higher confidence production programs," he said.

CHINA: MILITARY OPPOSED TO INTERNATIONALIZING SOUTH CHINA SEA ISSUE—(Stratfor.com, September 28, 2011): China's military authority reiterated Sept. 28 that attempts to internationalize the South China Sea issue would further complicate the matter, Xinhua reported. Any move meant to internationalize or multilateralize the issue will not help, a Chinese Defense Ministry spokesman said, adding that China's sovereignty over the islands in the sea and the surrounding waters is incontestable.

TIGER'S CLAW

PROLOGUE

KAMCHATKA PACIFIC MISSILE TEST RANGE, EASTERN SIBERIA

SUMMER 2014

"Bridge, Combat, ballistic missile inbound!" the urgent call came. "Altitude six-seven miles, range three-three-zero nautical, closing speed eight thousand!"

The skipper of the USS *Chosin,* captain of an American guided-missile cruiser, activated a stopwatch hanging on a lanyard around his neck. "Sound general quarters," Captain Edward Taverna said calmly. He glanced at the visitor seated beside him on the bridge as the warning horns sounded throughout the ship. Everyone on the bridge already had helmets and life jackets on. "Combat, Bridge, weapons tight, engagement as briefed, acknowledge."

"Bridge, Combat, weapons tight, engagement as briefed, aye," came the response.

"Count it down, Combat," Taverna ordered. He raised a pair of binoculars and scanned the horizon to the north, and the visitor did likewise.

"Impact in fifteen seconds . . ." The skipper couldn't believe how fast this was happening . . . "Ten . . . five . . . zero."

A tremendous geyser of water reaching hundreds of feet in the sky erupted on the horizon, just a few miles away. Through his binoculars, Taverna could briefly see the shape of a large vessel cartwheeling in the air. "Looks like a direct hit," he said. "What's it look like, Combat?"

"Direct hit, sir," came the reply. Taverna knew there were multiple cameras recording this test, both on the surface and in the sky—he'd look at the video later with the Intelligence section, with the Pentagon and probably the White House watching as well.

"What speed was the target going?"

"The target was being towed at twenty-seven knots, sir."

Impressive—and ominous, Taverna thought. He turned to his visitor and said, "Congratulations, Admiral." Then, in the best and oft-practiced Chinese he could muster, he said, "*Gong ji, Shao Jiang.*" Sign of the times, Taverna thought—more and more senior officers in the U.S. military were learning Mandarin Chinese, much like many learned Russian during the height of the Cold War.

This was shaping up to be the new Cold War: America versus China.

One faint glimmer of hope for a nonconfrontational tone to U.S.-China relations was this very occurrence: an invitation for the U.S. Navy to not only observe this test up close and personal, but to have a senior Chinese People's Liberation Army (PLA) officer on board. It had several implications. Yes, China was being much more open about its military capabilities and intentions; it could also imply that, should there be a targeting error, a few Chinese officers would be casualties along with hundreds, perhaps thousands, of American sailors—faint consolation, but something. Also, this test was being run on a

Russian ballistic missile test range, which implied a high degree of cooperation between China and Russia.

But this was obviously a warning to America as well as an olive branch. The message was clear: your warships are no longer safe in the western Pacific.

"Thank you very much, Captain," People's Liberation Army *Shao Jiang* (Major General) Hua Zhilun said in excellent English. The thin, handsome admiral with the seemingly perpetual smile, young for a Chinese general at age fifty-four, bowed, then shook hands with Taverna. General Hua was commander of the Eleventh Tactical Rocket Division, or *Hǔ Zhǎo*: "Tiger's Claw," the special division set up to deploy China's antisatellite and antiship ballistic missiles. Hua's division was part of China's Strategic Rocket Forces, also known as the Second Artillery Corps, the branch of the army that controlled all of China's land-based ballistic missiles, both nuclear and conventional. "I shall prepare a full debriefing and return in the morning to brief you and your department heads on the results of today's test."

"I'm looking forward to it, General," Taverna said. Hua bowed deeply again, then followed his aide off the bridge, escorted by the *Chosin*'s executive officer.

"He's got a reason to smile, the prick," Taverna said under his breath after Hua had departed. It was not lost on Taverna, and certainly not on Hua or his contingent, that the cruiser *Chosin* was named for the Battle of Chosin Reservoir, in which a force of sixty thousand Chinese troops encircled a force of thirty thousand American-led United Nations troops at Changjin Lake in northeast North Korea. Although the Chinese lost nearly two-thirds of their attacking forces in two and a half weeks of fighting, it was the first major defeat of United Nations forces in the Korean War and was the beginning of a massive all-out Chinese offensive that nearly pushed American forces south right off the Korean Peninsula and into the East China Sea.

Taverna also knew that Hua was in command of the forces that attacked American Kingfisher antisatellite and antiballistic missile weapon garages in Earth orbit last year, causing the death of an American astronaut and the eventual suspension of the entire U.S. Space Defense Force program. There had never been any meaningful American response to those attacks or to other antisatellite attacks by Russia, something that really steamed Taverna. Chinese and Russian carrier battle groups were now everywhere, shadowing American warships and shipping—and still no response from anyone in Washington except more cutbacks. It was getting pretty pathetic.

Taverna shook himself out of his reverie and picked up the phone to the Combat Information Center. "Yes, sir," Commander Ted Lang, the operations officer, responded.

"So how did it look, Ted?"

"Pretty awesome, sir," Lang replied. "Direct hit from fifteen hundred miles away. I haven't seen the slow-mo video yet, but judging by the effects it looked like a good penetration angle. Sawed that target ship right in half."

"So you think it could penetrate an armored carrier deck?"

"If they use a nuclear warhead, it doesn't need to, sir," Lang said. "If it's just a kinetic warhead, it has to hit almost perfectly vertical—if it hits at an angle it would probably glance off a carrier's deck, even going eight thousand miles an hour."

"And the missile was directed by satellite?"

"That's what they claim, sir," Lang replied. "The Chinese have several radar and infrared ocean-surveillance satellite systems in orbit. They certainly have the technology. They had lots of aircraft in the area observing the test, and one or more of them could have actually aimed the missile. The missile uses inertial guidance with GPS updates—*our* GPS satellites, by the way—to get within the target area. Then the warhead itself supposedly gets updates from outside sensors—satellites or aircraft, communicating directly with the warhead's terminal guidance package—then uses its own on-board radar to steer itself in for the kill."

"Big question, Ted: Could a Standard SM-3 have knocked it down if it was aimed at us?" Taverna asked. The Standard missile was the carrier battle group's primary antiaircraft missile; the SM-3 was an upgraded version designed to knock down ballistic missiles and even satellites in low Earth orbit.

There was an uncomfortably long pause before the operations officer replied. "Today, we had the advantage of knowing exactly from where and when it was coming, sir," Lang said. "The SM-3's auto-engage system is normally not activated unless we're heading into a fight, so if it's a 'bolt from the blue' attack . . . no, sir, I don't think we'd have the time. If it's engaged, I think the SM-3 would get one warhead. If there are multiple maneuvering warheads . . ." And his voice trailed off.

"Got it, Ted," Taverna said. "Let me know when Intel is ready to debrief."

"Yes, sir."

The skipper hung up the phone. The chill he felt just then was not because of the weather.

"*What do you think you're doing, Basic?*" the cadet technical sergeant instructor screamed. "Get moving, *now*!"

"Oh, Christ," Bradley McLanahan muttered for the umpteenth time that morning. The muzzle of his M-16 rifle had—again—snagged itself in the barbed wire under which he was crawling. He reached out to clear it, but only ended up puncturing his finger with a mud-covered barb. "*Shit . . . !*" he shouted.

"*You will not use foul language on my confidence course, Basic!*" the cadet instructor shouted. He was a tall, wiry, weaselly looking guy from Alabama with thick horn-rimmed sports glasses, and he definitely knew how to shout. "If you are having difficulties negotiating the course, you will resolve the obstruction or request assistance from your cadet instructors. Which is it, Basic?"

"I don't need any help," Bradley said.

"What? I can't hear you!"

"I said I don't need any help!" Bradley shouted.

"Are you dense or just feebleminded, Basic?" the instructor shouted. "When you address me, you will preface and end your reply with 'sir,' do you comprehend? Now state your deficiency to me properly, Basic!"

Bradley took a deep breath and fought to control his anger. This was the fourth week of Air Force Academy Basic Cadet Training, or BCT—known to all as "The Beast," and now Brad knew why they called it that. Six weeks of some of the most intense physical, psychological, and emotional cadet training in the U.S. military, the course was designed to teach military customs, courtesies, and culture to new candidates to the United States

Air Force Academy in Colorado Springs, Colorado, and weed out those who didn't possess the physical conditioning, attitude, or aptitude to make it through the next four years of intense academic training to become career Air Force officers. In just two weeks, he would begin his military and professional education in one of the top ten colleges on planet Earth, completing a million-dollar education paid for by U.S. taxpayers . . .

. . . as some would say: shoved up your ass a nickel at a time.

Brad extracted his thumb from the barb, then shook the muzzle of the M-16 rifle free of the wire as well. Bradley James McLanahan was on his back slithering through four inches of mud and dust, just below several strands of barbed wire arrayed above him. On either side of him were other Basics—candidates for admission to the Air Force Academy—navigating the obstacle course of "Second Beast," the three-week field encampment that preceded the start of the freshman school year. Occasional explosions and firecrackers erupted all around him, especially around the cadets having any difficulties crawling under the wire. Bradley was tall and thin, so normally getting under the mesh of razor wires should be no problem, but for some reason those pesky barbs reached out and grabbed anything they could latch on to—his uniform, his rifle, his thumb, his very soul.

"Sir," Brad shouted, "I have extricated myself from the obstacle, and I am proceeding . . ."

"Don't tell me—*show* me, Basic!" the instructor shouted. Cadet Staff Sergeant William Weber was a second-class cadet at the Academy and a well-seasoned and experienced instructor at Cadet Basic Training, his favorite summer assignment. Rather than going home or doing any other activities during the summer break, Weber always signed up for Cadet Basic Training so he could lock his claws into the very new, raw persons making their way into the Air Force

Academy. No one proceeded past this point without getting past Weber . . . *no way.* Weber stepped over to Bradley and bent down, face-to-face to him. *"What are you doing,* Basic?"

"Sir, I am proceeding on the obstacle course and . . ."

"You aren't doing *crap,* Basic!" Weber shouted. "Get moving! What are you waiting for?"

"Sir, I am . . ."

"Didn't we teach you about controlling your muzzle and your trigger, Basic?" Weber shouted, grabbing Bradley's M-16 before it could swing all the way toward Weber's face. "You are *not* controlling *anything*! You get snagged with your muzzle and then you get snagged when you move to release another snag. Are you *dense,* Basic? Do you want to take all morning to complete this evolution, Basic? I'll tell you right, now, Basic: I'm not going to wait around for you to finish a simple task. Now get your rear in gear and finish this evolution!"

"Sir, yes sir!" Bradley shouted.

Weber went off to yell at some other Basic, and Bradley was grateful for the break, but as soon as Weber was out of the way, some other second-class blasted a fire hose into the pit to maintain a nice deep level of mud. It was late July in Colorado, and even in early morning the air was warm and dry—the afternoon runs with full packs, with temperatures approaching ninety degrees, would be murder.

Bradley knew all about Basic Cadet Training, the Confidence course, and Jack's Valley—all this was no surprise. Once he had been selected for admission—his appointment came from no less than then vice president Kenneth Phoenix, who was now the president of the United States—he had to attend dozens of Academy prep courses taught by liaison officers, listen to guest speakers describing their adventures and problems, have his grades scrutinized constantly and schedule refresher and reinforcement classes with volunteer tutors, pass a grueling fitness test once a month even tougher than the one they would have to take every semester at the Academy, and watch hundreds of videos covering every possible aspect of life as a fourth-class cadet. The Academy and its graduates did everything they could possibly do to prepare a potential cadet for what he was about to face. None of the "Beast" was unexpected—in fact, they had built a "mini-Beast" Confidence Course near the youth correctional facility in Carson City, Nevada, so all the area Basics chosen to attend the Academy could practice.

The first three weeks of BCT were at the Academy, learning how to salute, how to march, how to wear a uniform, and basic military customs, along with intense physical conditioning. Since Brad had spent so many years in the Civil Air Patrol teaching all that to CAP cadets, he was way ahead of most other Basics, and he had a relatively easy time—he had even been asked by a few first- and second-class cadets to help a few of the other Basics. As a high school football player, Bradley knew how to stay in shape, so the long runs, rope climbing, and calisthenics were all second nature.

Maybe that made him feel a little overconfident, even a little cocky—because the second half of BCT, "Second Beast," was in the field. No more dormitories, no more chow halls, no more comfortable PT outfits and clean uniforms—this was down and dirty in the woods and mountains for the final three weeks. Although Bradley was qualified in several CAP field emergency services, his real soul was in flying. Let the nonrated kids do ground searches, first aid, and direction finding—he belonged in the sky.

"State the Core Values of the United States Air Force, Basics!" the guy with the fire hose shouted.

"Sir, integrity first, service before self, excellence in all we do, sir!" Bradley shouted for the umpteenth time that morning.

He finally wriggled clear of the barbed wire, but got his pants caught as he was trying to get on his feet.

"You will state the Core Values *together,* or don't bother saying them at all, Basics!" the cadet trainer shouted. "You will learn to live, work, train, and fight *together,* or you do not belong at my beloved Academy! Now, again: What are the Air Force's Core Values?" Bradley started to respond, but he was hit in the side of his Kevlar helmet with a jet of water from the fire hose and was knocked off his feet again by the blast. He couldn't hear anything except the hammering of the water against his head.

"I think Basic McLanahan here forgot the words to our Core Basics," Weber shouted, materializing as if from nowhere. "Get on your feet, Basic McLanahan!"

That was the first time, Bradley thought as he struggled to his feet, that he had heard his last name here at the Beast while in field training—up until now, they were all simply "Basics." His eyes were stinging from mud, but he dared not try to wipe them clear. He faced in the approximate direction of where he thought Weber was standing and brought his M-16 rifle up to port arms. "Sir!"

"The breech of your weapon is closed, Basic McLanahan," Weber snarled. "You had better clear and check that weapon before you stand in front of me, and do it *now.*"

Now Bradley rubbed the mud out of his face, then made sure the muzzle of the M-16 rifle was pointed straight up away from the cadet instructor, pulled back on the charging handle, and peered into the chamber. He couldn't see that well, so he wasn't sure if there was anything in there, but they had been issued no ammunition so everyone was safe. He let the handle go, then went back to port arms. "Sir, my weapon is clear, sir!" he reported.

"Your weapon is a filthy *mess,* McLanahan, that's what it is!" Weber shouted. He motioned behind him, and a split second later the fire hose was unleashed on him again. "Keep that weapon out of the water, McLanahan!" Weber shouted. "That weapon is your lifeline in the field!" Bradley raised it above his head as the water surged over his body, threatening to topple him in its powerful stream. "What is the Cadet Oath, Basic?"

"Sir, the Cadet Oath is: I will not lie, cheat, or steal . . ."

"*Wrong,* McLanahan!" Weber interrupted. "Try again!"

Bradley swallowed hard. "The Cadet Oath is . . ."

"You had better address me as 'sir,' Basic!"

"Sir, the Cadet Oath is: *We* will not lie, steal, or cheat, nor tolerate anyone among us who . . ."

"McLanahan, you are just plain dense this morning," Weber said. "One more try, McLanahan, and if you screw it up, you go back to the beginning of the Pit to think about it some more. This is the most important phrase in the Academy, Basic, the very basis of who we are, the one thing that every cadet is sworn to uphold and protect. You've had three weeks to learn it. Go!"

Bradley's arms, still holding the M-16 over his head, were beginning to shake, but he took a deep breath and uttered, "Sir, the Cadet Oath is: We will not lie, steal, or cheat, nor tolerate among us anyone who does." Bradley saw Weber's eyes flaring in anger and quickly added, "Sir!"

"About time," Weber growled. He stepped closer to Bradley and said in a low voice, "Maybe you McLanahans have difficulties learning about lying and cheating."

Bradley suddenly forgot about his aching, rubbery arms. He looked up at Weber, who was about a half head taller than Brad. "Sir?"

"Are you eyeing me, Basic?" Weber shouted. "Cage your eyes!"

Brad stared at a spot straight ahead, away from Weber's angry gaze. "Sir, begging the cadet instructor's pardon, sir?"

"What?"

"Sir . . . sir, did you say something about McLanahans, sir?"

Weber smiled evilly, then waved at the guy with the fire hose to turn it on someone else. "Looks like I got a rise out of you, didn't I, Basic McLanahan?" he observed. In a low voice, he said, "Everyone here knows who you are: son of the great General Patrick McLanahan, the hero of the American Holocaust, space hero, the greatest strategic bombing expert since General Curtis LeMay—or so he thinks. You're the guy who got his Academy appointment from the president of the United States himself, served up on a silver platter, thanks to your daddy."

He stepped even closer to Bradley, then added, "But my father told me who your daddy *really* is: a lying, cheating, thieving loose cannon, who flagrantly disobeys orders and does whatever the hell he feels like doing, and screw the chain of command and the Constitution. Now he thinks he can get his stuck-up son into the Air Force Academy with just a phone call to his pal in the White House, and you'll just sail right through because of who your daddy is. Let me be the first to tell you, Basic: that's not the way it's going to work. My mission, and the mission of most of the second- and first-class, is to see you get booted out *soonest*."

Weber stepped nose to nose with Bradley. "I worked my *butt* off for three years to get into the Academy," he growled in a low, menacing voice. "I broke my ass in stupid sports I didn't like, volunteered for the most ridiculous positions in the most ridiculous service clubs, took the SATs *eleven times,* and wrote dozens of letters to congressmen I didn't even know to get an appointment. After all that, I didn't get *one,* and I had to spend a year as a Preppie. And then, here you are. You get to just waltz in here and think you have it made." He lowered his voice even more. "Well, let me tell you, McLanahan . . ."

Weber took three fingers of his right hand and punched them into Bradley's chest, " . . . you're *history* here. I'll see to it, *personally.*"

Now Bradley's entire body began to shake, not just his bone-weary arms. That made Weber smile and nod in satisfaction. "I knew it," he said. "Your daddy never taught you how to deal with the *real* world, did he? That's because he never dealt with it himself. He had his underlings do all the real fighting for him while he just sailed away safe and sound high above the fighting in his supersecret bombers." He chuckled at his own insight, then said with a smirk, "Well, stop your crying and sniveling and go back to the beginning of the Pit. You still have . . ."

And to his surprise, Bradley let the M-16 rifle fall from his hands behind him into the mud.

"*Pick that weapon up, Basic!*" Weber shouted. "Are you *insane? Pick it up, now!*"

"Take it back, Weber," Bradley said flatly.

"What did you say, Basic? Did you just address me by my last name?"

"I said: take it back, Weber."

Weber's eyes were bulging in complete and utter disbelief, and he stuck his face close to Bradley's once again. "*You will address me as 'Sir,' Basic!*" he shouted, louder than Bradley ever remembered him doing so before. "And you will not direct me to do *anything*! *I* give the orders here!"

"I'll tell you once more, Weber: take back what you said about my father," Bradley said.

"Getting rid of you is going to be easier than I thought, McLanahan," Weber said, his incredulous expression replaced by a broad, satisfied smile. Bradley's eyes met his, which turned Weber's expression back to one of red-hot rage. "You're one step away from a board of review, maybe even an on-the-spot dismissal. *Get your eyes off me, Basic!*" But Bradley didn't look away. "How dare you mouth off to a second-class, Basic? How dare you look *me* in the eye? Who do you think you are? You're nothing but a candidate here, McLanahan, a *wannabe*. The only way you survive to attend my beloved Academy is to obey your superior officers, and that's *me*." And he punctuated that last sentence with another punch in Bradley's chest with three fingers of his right hand . . .

. . . except the jab never landed, because Bradley swatted his hand away.

"You just laid a hand on me, Basic!" Weber shouted, his voice just now beginning to grow hoarse. "That's an automatic trip to the squadron commander. You're one step away from going home to your daddy. *Get your eyes off me, Basic!*"

"Take back what you said about my father, Weber," Brad repeated, then added, "or you'll be sorry."

"You're *threatening* me now, Basic?" Weber exclaimed, his eyes bulging in anger and disbelief. "If you want to go home to your daddy so bad, McLanahan, why don't you just ring out? It's easy. I'll take you to the squadron commander, and you tell him you want to go home, and that's it." Bradley said nothing.

Weber moved face-to-face with Bradley. "But if you want to stay—if you're afraid of getting rejected by your own daddy by going home before you even begin fourth class—then this is what you have to do: you apologize sincerely for touching me; you promise to uphold the basic principles of the Academy; and you agree to assist me in all my additional duties for your entire fourth year, in addition to all your other requirements. If you agree to all these things, I'll omit filing a report on you for your breaches of conduct in this evolution, and you can continue Second Beast." Weber nodded. "You did very well in First Beast, McLanahan, and even though your M-16 is lying in the mud right now, you haven't done anything more egregious than what a lot of dipshit Basics do in Second Beast. You can still pull this out of your ass if you choose to do so. What say you, McLanahan?"

Bradley didn't take his eyes off Weber, but looked him straight in the eye . . . for just a few moments, before caging his eyes, looking straight ahead at nothing, then said, "Sir, Basic McLanahan begs the cadet sergeant's indulgence and sincerely apologizes for his inexcusable insubordination. Basic McLanahan was completely out of line, promises never to touch or threaten an upperclassman ever again for any reason, appeals to the cadet sergeant's mercy to allow him to continue the Second Beast, and humbly requests the cadet sergeant's permission to be his undergraduate assistant during the fourth-class year. Basic McLanahan also promises to completely honor, uphold, and defend the principles of the Air Force Academy to the complete satisfaction of the cadet sergeant." Bradley closed his eyes, filled his lungs, then shouted, "*Sir!*"

Weber nodded and smiled with smug triumph. "Very good, Basic," he said. "We might make a fourth classer out of you yet. Now pick up your rifle, then return to the beginning of the Pit. On the double."

"Sir, yes sir!" Brad responded. He turned and stooped down to pick up the M-16 . . .

. . . and as he did he heard Weber say in a low voice, "Now if we can just get your whack-job daddy to apologize for the mess he's caused our country, we'd all be in real good shape."

Brad couldn't describe what he was thinking about at that moment, or why he did what he did. All he knew is in a split second he had tackled Weber and was on top of him in the mud. He remembered getting two good punches in on Weber's face before he heard several whistle blasts and shouts and felt hands reaching for him from behind . . .

16

DALE BROWN

... and he knew those whistle blasts signaled the end of his attendance at the U.S. Air Force Academy, and probably the end of any career in the military as well.

ONE

THE SOUTH CHINA SEA, TWO HUNDRED MILES SOUTHEAST OF HO CHI MINH CITY, VIETNAM

THAT SAME TIME

The American survey ship *Lady Garner* had been at its assigned search area for five months. From its home port in Long Beach, California, the ship had been hired by the Vietnamese oil company Petrolimex to map out an area of its economic exclusion zone and explore the possibility of setting up oil rigs. Displacing almost three thousand tons, the *Lady Garner*'s profile was dominated by the 150-foot-tall oil derrick in the center of the ship, which steered drills and pipes through the hull down through thousands of feet of seawater. Even through thousands of feet of seawater and earth, the bore could be steered by the geologists with incredible precision—one nudge of a joystick thousands of feet away from the objective could mean success or failure. There was also a large helicopter platform on the nose able to recover helicopters as heavy as thirty thousand pounds even in rough seas. The *Lady Garner* was serviced by strings of supply vessels from the United States, Australia, Japan, Vietnam, and the Philippines that carried extra fuel, pipe, provisions, and relief crews for the expected nine-month deployment to the search area.

But the low-tech derrick was not the ship's main tool. The *Lady Garner* was one of the most sophisticated offshore exploration ships in the world, able to perform several different methods for searching for oil, natural gas, and other minerals. Although most of the men and women on board ran the ship, the most important persons were the geologists, chemists, and computer technicians who operated the seismic generators, gravity survey equipment, sonars, chemical analysis laboratories, and other high-tech systems.

The objective of their five months on-site was just being laid out in front of the captain, project manager, chief engineer, and chief geologist and simultaneously transmitted to officials at Petrolimex in Ho Chi Minh City, Vietnam, and the *Lady Garner*'s headquarters in Long Beach. "Good evening, everybody," said Gary Boudrain, the project manager, into the video teleconference camera. Boudrain was a big man from Louisiana with deep wrinkles on his weathered face, the result of over thirty years at sea all over the world. "I'm Gary Boudrain, the project manager aboard the *Lady Garner* survey ship, on station in sector twenty-seven in the South China Sea. With me is the chief geologist, chief engineer, chief chemist, and of course Captain Victor Richardsen. I trust everyone has received the Traffic Light Map."

Heads nodded on the ship and on the video teleconference screen. The Petrolimex officials were smiling broadly, and that made Boudrain feel very good. "We have good news: it looks like we have a good cluster, and my team and I recommend dropping an exploratory well."

He hit a button on his laptop computer, and the image on

the screen changed to a map of a section of the South China Sea with hundreds of green and red dots on it. This was the product of their five months at sea: the Common Risk Segment Map, known as the Traffic Light Map. The green dots indicated a good chance for oil and gas, and red dots for poor areas. There were several clusters of green dots—those were their objectives.

"There haven't been too many surveys of the South China Sea in recent years due to the political and economic turmoil," Boudrain went on, "especially around the Spratly Islands, but I'm pleased to say our mission here is a big success. We are sitting atop one of the largest clusters of good potential oil and gas deposits I've seen outside of the Middle East, perhaps as much as a billion barrels of oil and seventy-five trillion cubic feet of natural gas in this one sector alone." Boudrain didn't think the oil executives' smiles could get any broader, but they did. "We have every reason to believe neighboring sectors contain similar deposits, based on the geography. My project staff unanimously agrees to strongly recommend drilling an exploratory well to verify our findings."

The video teleconference didn't last too much longer—it was clear the Petrolimex executives were anxious to share the news with their superiors in the Oil and Gas Ministry of the Vietnamese Politburo. Boudrain and his staff answered a few questions about their findings and the next step, and the conference was terminated. "I think you kicked a home run, Gary," Victor Richardsen said. The captain was born in Norway, and even though he had lived in the United States for almost ten years as skipper of the *Lady Garner,* he was still getting American cultural references mixed up.

"I usually don't like to use such definitive terms, Skipper," Boudrain said. "Remote geological surveying is an inexact science at best, and dropping an exploratory well in these waters could cost Petrolimex upwards of fifty million dollars. But what we found here is truly extraordinary. Lots of us believed the South China Sea had vast deposits of all kinds of minerals, but this is the first real indication that it could be true."

"*Gratulerer igjen,* Gary," the skipper said. "Congratulations again. I am going to check in with the watch on the bridge, and then I am going to turn outwards. *God natt.*" He shook hands with the rest of Boudrain's staff, then departed.

The *Lady Garner* was one of the most high-tech survey ships in the world, and the bridge reflected this. It took only two men to stand watch on the bridge, and just four when under way. There was still a wheel, throttle levers, and a large compass on the main console, and they were all operable if needed, but steering, propulsion, and all other major functions were now controlled by computer. In the darkness of the bridge, with the only illumination coming from the dimmed computer screens, the captain couldn't make out the faces of the watchstanders, but he knew these men almost as well as his own six children. "How are you boys doing tonight, Todd, Mac?" Richardsen asked.

"Very well, Captain," the officer of the deck, Todd Clark, replied. Clark was a recent graduate of the California Maritime Academy in Vallejo, California; this was only his second cruise in the *Lady Garner,* but he was an exceptional seaman and doing well. "All systems normal. Station keeping is running at twenty-five percent of capacity." The survey vessel used a sophisticated set of thrusters under the ship to keep itself precisely in place—it could keep the massive vessel within a few dozen yards even in gale-force winds and heavy seas. "Weather is forecast to be hot and showery. We might have a small thunderstorm later in the morning."

"Typical summer weather," Richardsen said. "We just received the briefing from the project manager, and I think we will be green-lighted to drill an exploratory well. That means we will be here several more months."

"Great news, Skipper," Clark said.

Richardsen checked the radar display, but the storm was not yet on the screen. Just for curiosity's sake he switched the radar from weather to surface-search mode—and immediately saw a very large ship coming toward them from the north. "We have traffic to the north," he said. "Verify our anchor lights are on, please."

"Yes, sir," Clark replied. A moment later: "All at-anchor lights on, Captain."

That was good, Richardsen thought, but this guy was heading toward them awful fast and not veering east or west. He was a bit less than twenty miles out, but for some larger ships it took that much distance and more to make even a slight turn. "Better turn on the derrick and service lights too—that should make us visible farther out for his lookouts, as long as they're not all asleep."

Just before Richardsen switched the radio to the common ship-to-ship channel and picked up the microphone, they heard in heavily accented English on the 2182 megahertz maritime emergency channel: "Attention, attention, unidentified vessel, this is the People's Liberation Army Navy cruiser *Baohùzhe,* north of your position. You are in Chinese waters illegally. You are ordered to leave this area immediately. Acknowledge."

"*Tull!*" the captain swore. "Mac, verify our position."

"Yes, sir." John "Mac" Portman was one of the most experienced sailors on the ship, serving on the *Lady Garner* almost since the ship first put to sea. The navigator was also the helmsman on this computerized vessel. A few moments later: "GPS position verified with the LORAN, Captain. Dead on the plat, thirty miles inside the Vietnamese EEZ."

Are we going to get grief from the Chinese navy again? the captain asked himself. Chinese patrol boats and aircraft had been shadowing them for days, and other survey vessels had been harassed by Chinese "fishing boats"—more likely old navy utility vessels—trying to ram them. Although they could call on the Vietnamese navy and air force for help, the Vietnamese navy had very few ships that ventured out this far from shore, and very few patrol planes flew at night, so they had little protection. They had a small security detail with night-vision goggles and sniper rifles to protect against pirates, but nothing that could take on the Chinese navy—not that he had any intention of challenging them.

They were adjacent to one of the most hotly disputed regions of the world: the Spratly Islands. The Spratly Islands were a chain of islands and reefs between the Philippines and Vietnam that were claimed by several nations. There was less than four square miles of land above high tide spread out over four hundred thousand square miles, but it had been long assumed—now very much verified—that there were substantial oil and natural gas deposits in the area. Six nations—China, Brunei, Taiwan, the Philippines, Vietnam, and Malaysia—variously stationed troops and conducted patrols through the area. Because the area was so hotly disputed, all parties agreed not to explore for oil or gas within the archipelago until the territorial arguments were resolved, and the *Lady Garner* was careful to stay within Vietnam's economic exclusion zone.

The captain picked up the intercom microphone. "Comm, better send a message to headquarters and to our liaison office in Ho Chi Minh City; tell them we may be getting harassed by the Chinese navy, and ask for assistance. Give them our position." He switched to the ship-to-ship emergency channel. "Chinese navy vessel *Baohùzhe*, Chinese navy vessel *Baohùzhe*, this is the United States survey ship *Lady Garner;* we are not in Chinese waters, repeat, not in Chinese waters. We are well within Vietnamese waters and are operating under a license from the Vietnamese government. Do not approach. We are not under way and are conducting scientific probes of the sea bottom authorized by the Vietnamese government. Over."

"Survey ship *Lady Garner,* this is the cruiser *Baohùzhe,* warning, you are illegally in Chinese territorial waters, and you are ordered to depart immediately," came the reply. "Exploration of this region of any kind is not permitted. Acknowledge!"

"*Dette er gal!*" the captain muttered. "This is crazy! Notify the security detail and have them set up extra lookouts—I want to know if the Chinese send out any small craft to . . ."

At that moment they heard a tremendous *BOOOM!* directly overhead, loud enough to rattle the thick storm windows on the bridge. "*What was that?*" the captain exclaimed. "Did we just get overflown by an aircraft going supersonic?" It was night—there was no way anyone was going to see an aircraft flying supersonic. Richardsen mashed the microphone button. "Cruiser *Baohùzhe,* you are on a collision course with us. We are at anchor in the Vietnamese exclusive economic zone, with permission from the Vietnamese oil ministry. And order that jet not to fly over us again going supersonic!"

"Survey vessel *Lady Garner,* this is the People's Liberation Army Navy cruiser *Baohùzhe;* you are in Chinese waters illegally," the voice from the Chinese cruiser said. "Prepare to be boarded for inspection. Do not resist."

"This is the captain of the *Lady Garner,* and I do not give you permission to board!" Richardsen radioed.

"*Lady Garner,* you are in Chinese waters. We do not require your permission to board any vessel in Chinese waters."

"Officer of the Deck, sound alert condition three, all hands on deck," Richardsen said, using Clark's title instead of his name to emphasize the increasing tension level. On the intercom he radioed, "Comm, notify headquarters and the liaison office that the Chinese cruiser is approaching at high speed and says he means to . . ."

"Bridge, Sellers on the port stern lookout, I hear a helicopter approaching," a security officer radioed. "One or two hundred yards away, maybe less."

"Survey ship *Lady Garner,* this is the cruiser *Baohùzhe.* Our patrol helicopter reports that you have armed men on deck. Weapons are not permitted on civilian vessels without permission from the People's Liberation Army. You are ordered to throw all your weapons over the side. Our personnel are authorized the use of deadly force. Comply immediately!"

"What's going on, Skipper?" the executive officer, Kurt Branson, said as he stepped quickly onto the bridge.

"The damn Chinese navy," Richardsen said. "They got a helicopter on the way and . . ."

Just then they heard on the intercom: *"Bridge, this is Larson; that helicopter is opening fire on the fantail with a machine gun!"* The sounds of heavy machine-gun fire were evident in the background.

Richardsen and Branson raced to the port-side observation wing, a narrow walkway that protruded outboard far enough to see the entire port side of the ship. They saw it immediately— winks of light and tracer rounds zipping out of the darkness, hitting the side of the ship . . . where Sellers the port stern lookout would have been. Sparks flew in every direction from the fantail as the rounds ricocheted off. *"Min Gud!"* Richardsen cried. "My God! Officer of the Deck, sound alert one, all hands to damage control stations!" He got on his portable radio: "Sellers, how do you hear?" No response. "Sellers!" Still no response. "Kurt, get back there and see if Sellers is all right." The exec raced off. Richardsen keyed the portable radio's mic button. "All security details, this is the captain; get your rifles and sidearms out of sight, *quickly*! Comm, radio to headquarters: we are under automatic machine-gun fire from the Chinese helicopter, possibly one fatality. Then broadcast a distress call and request immediate assistance!"

A few minutes later, Richardsen saw it: a large blue-and-white helicopter with coaxial rotors, a large radome under the cockpit, a very bright spotlight sweeping across the deck, the unmistakable red, yellow, blue, and white flag of the Chinese navy—and a crewmember with a large machine gun sticking out a sliding door on the starboard side. The helicopter slowly made its way along the port side of the *Lady Garner,* continued around the bow and down the starboard side, back up the port side, and then set down on the helicopter pad on the bow, the machine gun trained on the bridge.

"Skipper, this is Kurt," Branson radioed. "Sellers is dead, and Larson is hurt bad."

"Survey ship *Lady Garner,* this is the cruiser *Baohùzhe.* You are ordered to lower all waterline docks and gangways. Boarding will commence shortly on both gunwales. Assemble the entire crew on the forecastle deck. Bring your logbooks, manifests, and portable computers. Acknowledge."

"Chinese cruiser *Baohùzhe,* this is the captain of the *Lady Garner;* you do not have my permission to land a helicopter on my helipad, and you do not have the right to board this vessel. This is illegal, and we intend to inform our governments of this unlawful action. Now get off my helipad and . . ." Suddenly they saw winks of light coming from the Chinese helicopter . . .

. . . and milliseconds later the forward windows on the bridge exploded as 7.62-millimeter rounds from the helicopter's Norinco machine gun hit. Clark and Portman screamed as the glass shattered, but the screams didn't last long as the bullets tore through their bodies, and they both collapsed onto the deck in pools of blood. Richardsen hit the deck and raised his portable radio to his lips. "*Stop shooting! Stop shooting!*" he cried amid the thunder piercing the bridge.

The shooting stopped. "Acknowledge my orders, Captain," the voice from the Chinese cruiser said.

"My God!" Richardsen breathed. He crawled back onto the bridge over broken glass and found the body of the navigator, his upper body little more than a mass of blood and tissue.

"Captain, acknowledge my orders immediately."

"All right, all right, *drittsekk*," Richardsen responded on his portable radio. He picked up the intercom microphone on the observation wing console. "All hands, this is the captain. We are about to be boarded by the Chinese navy. Lower the gangways on both rails. All hands, report to the forecastle deck. Medical team, report to the bridge, we have more casualties."

"You had better have an explanation, Admiral," thundered *Shàng Jiàng* (Colonel General) Zu Kai, chief of the general staff of the People's Liberation Army. Zu was short and powerfully built, with a thick neck and large hands. Although a thirty-year veteran of the PLA, his tunic sported no awards or decorations except his shoulder boards. He had reluctantly begun to wear spectacles but refused to put them on unless he needed them to read. "Your orders were to intercept, detain, and inspect that survey vessel and then let it go, not shoot it apart!"

"My apologies, sir," *Hai Jun Zhong Jiang* (Vice Admiral) Zhen Peng, commander of the South Sea Fleet, People's Liberation Army Navy, responded. He was standing before the chief of staff's desk at ramrod attention. Standing beside Zu was his deputy, *Shao Jiang* (Major General) Sun Ji. "The crew of the helicopter that was sent out to the vessel saw crewmembers carrying weapons, and the helicopter commander thought his aircraft was in danger and ordered the door gunner to open fire."

"And shooting up the bridge?"

"The pilot saw a movement just outside the bridge and ordered the gunner to open fire, but instead of firing on the person outside on the observation platform, the gunner fired on the bridge. I am of course fully responsible for this incident."

"You most certainly are, Zhen," General Zu said. "Unfortunately, you will probably not be the only one to lose his stars over this." Zu clenched and unclenched his right fist. "Order a summary court-martial for the captain of the

Baohùzhe, the pilot of the helicopter, and the door gunner. Punishment shall be a year at hard labor for the captain, three years at hard labor for the pilot, and execution for the door gunner. See to it immediately."

"Yes, sir."

Zu looked at the piece of paper handed to him by his deputy chief of the general staff, General Sun. "Before I assign punishment to you, Zhen," he said, "explain what you have sent me. What is this?"

"Sir, that is called a Common Risk Segment Map," Zhen explained. "That is the product that survey ships such as the *Lady Garner* produce. It is a graphical depiction of the scientists' best estimate of oil and natural gas deposits in an area. We pulled it from one of the laptop computers belonging to the project manager on board."

"Why did you send this to me, Zhen?"

"Because, sir, it is the first real proof that there are substantial oil and gas deposits in the South Sea and Nansha Dao," Zhen said, using the Chinese name of the body of water instead of the internationally recognized name "South China Sea," and also using the Chinese name for the Spratly Islands.

"Nonsense. We have known that for decades."

"But it has never been proven before in this particular area because the waters near the Nansha and Xisha Islands have been contested for so long and no exploration has taken place, sir," Zhen said. "This is the first scientific proof that oil and gas are not just present, but present in amounts vastly more than believed."

"Zhen, everyone already knew that oil, natural gas, and probably many other minerals could be found in the South Sea," Zu said angrily. "What is your point?"

"My assertion, sir, is that now is the time to move to occupy and fortify the Nansha and Xisha Dao," Admiral Zhen said.

Xisha Dao was the Chinese name for the Paracel Islands in the northern South China Sea, also long contested by many nations and also thought to have significant mineral deposits. "We have administered the islands for years, and we have fought several small skirmishes over them, but we have never militarily occupied the islands except for occasional patrols."

"Do you remember our battle with the Americans and Filipinos, Zhen?" Zu asked angrily. "How many ships did we lose? A dozen? More?"

"I fought in the Battle of the South Philippines, sir," Zhen said. "I was a junior antisubmarine warfare officer aboard the frigate *Jiujiang,* and I was on duty when the body of Admiral Yin Po L'un was brought aboard." China and the Philippines, assisted by American bombers, had fought a brief but intense war twenty years earlier. Although China was preparing to land several hundred thousand troops in southern Philippines, their naval forces had taken a beating, and a withdrawal was ordered; the overall commander of the operation, Admiral Yin Po L'un, committed suicide on the deck of his flagship. "We did not lose that battle, sir—we were just not permitted to win."

"Zhen, no one cares about the Nansha Dao," Zu said. "Most of the so-called islands are underwater most of the time. The highest point in the entire archipelago is only four meters."

"The importance of the Nansha Dao has been made paramount by what the survey crew found—the oil and gas deposits are substantial," Zhen said. "But what is more important is the strategic location of the islands. With a substantial military force stationed on and around the islands, and a similar force on the Xisha Dao, all reinforced with land-based bombers and missiles, we can completely control access to the South Sea."

"Do you not think the Americans might have something to say about that, Zhen?" General Zu asked derisively.

"The current status of the American military force is precisely why we need to act now, sir," Zhen said. "The American military, especially their navy, is the weakest it has been since before the Great War of Liberation. Now is the time to act."

It was true, Zu thought—the Americans had virtually stopped all major shipbuilding and aircraft projects, while China was building more and more ships and buying ships from around the world that they simply did not have the capacity to build themselves. "I applaud your aggressiveness on this subject, Zhen," General Zu said. "I do not know if the president or central committee is as anxious as you to directly challenge the United States, but circumstances may present an opportunity. I should like to see a plan."

"My staff and I have been working on a detailed plan for many months, sir," Zhen said. "I will finalize the draft and transmit it right away. Thank you."

"And I will leave your punishment up to the minister of defense and the president," Zu said, "but unless it is discovered during the upcoming investigation that you directly ordered the gunner to open fire on the survey ship, I think you are sufficiently distant from the incident to take any blame. You admitted full responsibility to me, which I accept. Direct your commanders to avoid such actions in the future without a clear and unambiguous order from higher headquarters. You are dismissed. Return to your headquarters."

"Yes, sir." Zhen saluted, turned on a heel, and departed.

Zu lit a cigarette and sat back in his chair. "Do you think I was too easy on Zhen, Ji?" he asked.

"Yes, sir, I do," General Sun replied. Sun was a young general officer with very little operational or leadership experience, but he possessed a finely tuned analytical mind and a real talent for playing and manipulating the political aspects of the ministry of defense, something Zu knew he himself didn't have the skill or desire to do—he knew that he had to have a man like Sun on his side to avoid having him as an adversary. "I like Admiral Zhen. He is aggressive and not afraid to go on the offensive. But I do believe he had something to do with that helicopter crew opening fire on that survey ship, and if he escapes any punishment at all, he may be emboldened to do something like that again, without asking for permission. That could be dangerous. A man like Zhen with a weapon like Silent Thunder, who thinks he has unspoken permission to open fire on an American flagged vessel, could be trouble."

"I too like Zhen, and I think his aggressiveness is a great advantage and something that is sorely needed in our military, especially our navy," Zu said. "I am looking forward to reading his plan for Nansha and Xisha Dao."

"The Americans, together with their Asian and Pacific allies, will not stand for China occupying those islands," Sun said.

"I want to see Zhen's plan for taking them on," Zu said. "He was right: America is at its weakest level in decades, and so are all their allies. We could have more aircraft carriers in the Pacific than they in a year or so, if we continue to get the funding we have requested. Look at Zhen's plan when you get it, have the Plans Department look it over, then brief me as soon as possible."

"Yes, sir."

Zu stubbed out his cigarette. "Let us see what President Zhou says about taking Nansha and Xisha Dao," he said. "The president is always saying that the South Sea belongs to China, but he does very little about enforcing it. If he is presented with a plan to do exactly that, will he go forward?"

TWO

NORTHERN NEVADA INDUSTRIAL AIRPORT, BATTLE MOUNTAIN, NEVADA

SEVERAL DAYS LATER

"Looks like you're starting an air museum out here, sir," U.S. Air Force Colonel Warner "Cutlass" Cuthbert remarked. The former B-1B Lancer and B-2A Spirit pilot and bomber wing commander was a short, balding, barrel-chested man, with bright green eyes and a quick smile that Patrick McLanahan knew could turn into a scowl or a bark in the blink of an eye. Cuthbert was commander of the First Expeditionary Bomber Wing at Andersen Air Force Base on the island of Guam, so the hot summertime air in the high desert of north-central Nevada didn't bother him in the least. "They're beauties."

"Thank you, Cutlass," Patrick said. He nodded toward an F-111G Aardvark supersonic bomber, surrounded by scaffolding. "The 'Vark is pretty torn up or I'd take you for a look inside."

"No worries—I've seen plenty of 'Varks in my day, sir,"

Cuthbert said. "Are you sticking that mission-adaptive wing on that one?"

"Actually, we're not," Patrick said, "although we certainly can." The mission-adaptive wing technology, pioneered by Sky Masters Inc., used tiny computer-controlled actuators on the fuselage and wings, in essence making every surface on the aircraft either a lift or drag device and greatly improving both high- and low-speed performance. They had successfully put mission-adaptive technology in a variety of aircraft, vessels, and even race cars. "But that one is still a swing-wing. We're putting in a few electronic displays, the active electronically scanned array radar, upgraded engines, and the pilot-optional stuff, but it's pretty much stock."

"Nice looking Tomcat, too," Cuthbert commented as they walked down the flight line toward one of the main hangars, referring to an F-14A Tomcat carrier-based fighter parked beside the F-111. "What did you do to it?"

"Again, not much," Patrick said. "We put the General Electric–Rolls-Royce F136 engines in this particular bird because we got such a good deal for a quantity of them."

"I'll bet you did," Cuthbert said. "Canceling the alternate engine for the F-35 fighter back in 2011 could have been a disaster for the company." The F136 engine was a dual-source alternative for the F135 primary engine on the F-35-series fighter-bomber, proposed in order to make engines available in case of a major conflict. When the F136 engine was canceled, thousands of workers on two continents lost their jobs virtually overnight. There was talk of the whole branch of the company going down because of it . . .

. . . until one Patrick McLanahan in an obscure little airport in northern Nevada put in a purchase order for several of them.

"They gave us a sweet deal for top-of-the-line power plants––it was a win-win scenario all around," Patrick said.

"Turns out they are real superstars—we get some excellent performance numbers. We have a couple other refurbished planes where we kept the General Electric F110 engines, and they work well, but not as good as the F-35 Lightnings or F/A-18 Super Hornets. We beefed up the structure, put in AESA, a few more electronic displays, the pilot-optional stuff, of course—that's about it. We can go take her for a spin if you'd like."

"I like, sir," Cuthbert said, "but I'm short on time. If you didn't live way the hell out in the boonies, I'd have more time to play. So, the proposal submitted to the Air Force said this project is in support of the AirSea Battle concept. You should know, sir, that AirSea Battle hasn't been implemented because we don't have a large enough air component—there aren't enough long-range platforms to support a carrier battle group."

As commander of the First Expeditionary Bomb Wing at Andersen Air Force Base, Cuthbert was responsible for organizing, training, and supporting the Continuous Bomber Presence for Pacific Air Force, a program that rotated the Air Force's few remaining long-range bombers to Guam for six-month stints. The few B-52H Stratofortresses, B-1B Lancers, and B-2A Spirit bombers at Guam formed a quick-reaction long-range conventional strike force that could reach very quickly throughout the Pacific, as well as provide aircrews a chance to train with the Navy and with foreign air forces. But since the American long-range bomber force had been so badly decimated during the American Holocaust, the bombers and their crews were becoming exhausted, and replacements were needed. Cuthbert had been assigned the task of coming up with solutions to the widening bomber gap from industry.

"I'm well aware of that, Cutlass," Patrick said.

"And you said you can build a fleet of long-range strike aircraft in less than two years for hardly any money at all? How are you going to do that, sir—pixie dust?"

"They're already built and battle proven," Patrick replied. "They aren't flying, but it's not because they're incapable or obsolescent. There are trade-offs. They are not stealthy, at least not twenty-first-century-version stealthy. They don't have antiradar coatings or radar-absorbent materials built into their structures—Sky Masters can add those things, but the cost will skyrocket, and that's not what we want. We want a capable long-range bomber for low cost that can be fielded very quickly."

"So where is this magical aircraft?"

"It's on its way," Patrick said. He glanced at his watch, smiled, then said, "Cutlass, allow me to reintroduce you to the weapons system that we at Sky Masters believe will be the affordable interim ingredient to fulfilling the promise of the AirSea Battle concept: the XB-1F Excalibur."

He could not have timed it better. Just as Patrick announced the name, Cuthbert's attention was grabbed by a sinister-sounding rushing noise, like an oncoming race car, that steadily got louder and louder . . . and then it flew overhead from behind, and the roar of the XB-1's four turbofan engines in full afterburner rolled over them. The sleek gray-green swept-wing bomber flew two thousand feet aboveground, but the immense size of the aircraft made it seem as if it was brushing their heads.

"Holy shit!" Cuthbert exclaimed. "A B-1 Lancer! She's a beauty!"

As the bomber made a steep bank about a half mile away, Patrick began his carefully rehearsed sales pitch: "Not a Lancer, Cutlass. The XB-1 Excalibur looks like the standard B-1B Lancer bomber because on the outside it *is* basically the same—most of the changes are on the inside. We replaced the original F101 engines with the F136 engines, which are more powerful and more fuel-efficient; we retained the two-person crew of the EB-1C Vampire bomber and opted for remotely operated offensive and defensive operator stations and highly automated attack systems; we gave it the same steerable Active Electronically Scanned Array multifunction radar that's been on the F/A-18 Super Hornet for years; and we replaced the older avionics with modern off-the-shelf electronic systems. The only other system we added was the ALQ-293 Self-Protection Electronically Agile Reaction system instead of the ALQ-161 electronic warfare suite."

"What's the ALQ-293?"

"The ALQ-293 SPEAR was developed by Sky Masters years ago in a competitive bid for the F-35 Lightning's radar," Patrick explained. "Our system was designed to not only send out a signal and then listen for the same returned signal for processing, but to listen for signals and then transmit other signals in response at that same frequency. SPEAR can alter the timing of the returned signal to make the enemy's radar think we are farther away or even invisible. We also found that we can transmit just about any other kind of signal to enemy radar, even computer code."

"Computer code?" Cutlass exclaimed. "You mean, like inserting a virus into a computer?"

"Exactly," Patrick said. "We called it 'netrusion,' and it worked like a charm when we sent the Vampires over Iran during the civil war—we were able to spoof radars and even issue shutdown commands to computers and electronics. We installed SPEAR into all the special EB-1D Vampire bombers, but they were all taken out and replaced with APG-77. Sky Masters put them back into production right before Jon was killed, and I decided to put them on the refurbished B-1s."

"Excellent, as long as it doesn't break the bank," Cuthbert said. "But putting that kind of system on a forty-year-old airframe must really crank up the refurbishment time, right?"

"The total time to do a conversion is just a few months—most of that time is airframe inspections," Patrick replied. "But it's also notable for what we did *not* do to the B-1B Lancer. As you know, Sky Masters did the initial research and development on the original B-1B conversion, the EB-1C Vampire flying battleship, and the work was done at Air Force Plant 42. The Vampire used mission-adaptive surfaces for flight control, which greatly improved its performance, and it also had other systems such as active laser defense, pilot-optional control, and StealthHawk attack cruise missile retrieval and rearming. But these advanced systems also added to the cost, which is why only a handful of those excellent planes were created.

"Sky Masters recently purchased all the B-1B conversion tooling, plans, and equipment from the Air Force, and we hired many of the workers and engineers who were laid off at Palmdale when the conversion program was canceled due to budget cuts, so now we're doing the conversion work ourselves," Patrick said. "We can create the Vampire again if the Pentagon wants them. We also have plans to convert a number of F-111 bombers for an even lower cost, and we are planning other conversions such as the F-14 Tomcat fighter. But we think the XB-1 Excalibur has the best combination of range, payload, and speed, and it's the best value as well."

"It's an interesting idea, General," Cuthbert said. "But you don't expect the Air Force to train B-1 crewdogs, do you? Who's going to fly the thing?"

"Our plan is not just to refurbish planes, but to provide everything needed to deploy the force," Patrick said. "We anticipated that the Air Force was not going to want to train active-duty or Reserve crewmembers for a weapons system that might only be around for five or ten years, so we plan on providing all the personnel on a contract basis. We recruit and train the aircrews, maintainers, ground support personnel, and administration; and we deploy the aircraft based on a contract negotiated with the Pentagon. As part of the AirSea Battle strategy, our XB-1 Excalibur crews would perform long-range maritime reconnaissance, and if a strike mission is needed, the Air Force picks the targets and weapons remotely, just like a remotely piloted combat aircraft—our aircrews just drive the bus."

"Just like your deal with reconnaissance operations in Iraq a few years ago, eh?" Cuthbert pointed out. "What was the name . . . Scion Aviation International? How did that work out for you, sir?" The skepticism was thick in his voice.

"I and the other company leaders made some unfortunate errors in judgment and planning," Patrick admitted. "We didn't anticipate Turkey's aggressive military response. But the basic concept of using contractors to do interim jobs for the Pentagon is still sound, especially in this economic climate."

"Yes, sir." Cuthbert's tone and expression told Patrick that he wasn't totally convinced. "You brought in those manned robots and a couple of your rebuilt B-1s to clean that situation up," Cuthbert observed, "except now we're on Turkey's shit list, along with Russia and China."

"I'm not really interested in who has us on their hate list, Cutlass—all I care about is building a military force with some teeth without breaking the bank," Patrick said.

"I'm with you all the way and then some, sir," Cuthbert said. The Excalibur made another low pass, thankfully not in ear-shattering afterburner this time, then maneuvered in the runway traffic pattern to set up for landing—he couldn't take his eyes off the sleek, menacing-looking bird. "So, how many of those things can you build?"

"There were twenty-six B-1s at AMARG in flyable storage, plus another nineteen airframes not flyable and designated for spare parts," Patrick said. "There are just six B-1Bs in

the inventory now—all the rest were lost in the American
Holocaust or the counterattack. We've refurbished two B-1s
that were in storage already, on our own dime. Out of the
twenty-four flyable airframes left at AMARG, we've identified
twenty suitable for refurbishment, for a total of twenty-two
planes—two set aside for training and two squadrons of ten
birds."

"And how long did it take you to refurbish the two you've
done?"

"About eight months."

"*Eight months*? No friggin' way, sir! One plane refurbished
in just eight months?"

"We did *both* planes in eight months, Cutlass," Patrick said,
smiling as he saw Cuthbert's stunned expression. "Assuming
we don't find any major problems with the airframes, it will be
quicker than that for the next batch. As I said, we don't really
do that much to them—the engines, avionics, and AESA radar
are practically plug-and-play, and we have a large staff of some
of the best and most experienced engineers and technicians in
the country. We've already got the engines, and the Air Force
gives us equipment already in their inventory—literally off-the-
shelf—so there's no waiting for suppliers."

The XB-1 had landed and was now taxiing toward them.
While Patrick and Cuthbert donned flying helmets, a ground
crewman in a light blue flight suit with an orange safety vest
trotted out, wearing a headset and safety goggles and carrying
bright yellow marshaling batons, and he directed the Excalibur
bomber to its parking spot. Patrick plugged his helmet-mounted
headset to a portable radio and keyed the mic: "How did it go,
Colonel?" he asked.

"Flew like a homesick angel, General," came the reply.
"Coming aboard?"

"You bet we are," Patrick said. "Keep 'em running. I'll get

the ladder." Patrick motioned for Cuthbert to follow him, and together they walked up to the bomber. Patrick clasped the ground crewman's shoulder as he stepped past him; Cuthbert shook hands with him, then looked at him quizzically as he headed to the plane. Patrick unlocked the entry ladder control lever on the nosegear door, then activated a switch that extended the boarding ladder, and he and Cuthbert climbed up. Patrick opened the hatch to the crew compartment, and they entered the aircraft.

The first area they stepped into, the systems officers' compartment, was incredibly spacious, because the ejection seats and instruments had all been removed. "No offensive or defensive systems operators on a big-ass jet like this . . . pretty amazing," Cuthbert shouted through the noise of the big idling engines. "Those systems are controlled from the ground now?"

"Yep," Patrick replied, "just like the sensor operators do with Reapers, Avengers, and other remotely piloted attack aircraft. The aircraft commander can also do a lot of the en route navigation chores from the cockpit, and the mission commander can control the Sniper targeting pod if necessary. The defensive suite is pretty much automatic. So it wasn't that great a leap—the Vampires switched to just two crewmembers years ago. Datalink technology is so sophisticated now that operating the offensive and defensive suites from the ground are the closest to real-time we can get. In an emergency, the pilots can operate the Sniper targeting pod and locate their own targets and manually fire chaff and flares and activate the jammers. I'll show you the electronics bays after we get back— we've eliminated about three-quarters of the line-replaceable units the jet originally had."

As the two stood aside in the empty systems officers' compartment, a woman appeared through the tunnel connecting the systems officers' compartment and cockpit and maneuvered herself between them. "Colonel Cuthbert, I'd like to introduce you to Sondra Eddington, part of the Excalibur flight test crew," Patrick said. Cuthbert shook her hand. Even wearing bulky flying gear, Cuthbert could see how extremely attractive Eddington was.

"Nice to meet you, Colonel," Eddington said. "Have a nice flight."

"You're not coming with us, Miss Eddington?"

"I don't want to know what General McLanahan is going to do on your hop, sir," she said with a bright smile, "but I know he wants to water your eyes. I'll see you when you get back." She gave him a surprising and alluring wink, then headed through the hatch and down the ladder.

"I'll get in first so I can hold the brakes, and then you switch with the AC," Patrick said to Cuthbert, and he headed up to the cockpit, shook hands with the pilot, then began to strap into the copilot's ejection seat. After he was strapped in, the pilot unstrapped and headed aft. The guy was immense and filled up the narrow corridor between the cockpit and systems officers' compartment. He went back to Cuthbert and shook his hand. "Colonel Cuthbert, I'm . . ."

"I know who you are: Colonel Thomas Hoffman, Operation Desert Fox, the B-1's first operational deployment," Cuthbert said. "You were the one who came up with the idea of launching Bones into 'kill boxes' without preplanned targets, getting target coordinates passed from other aircraft or special-ops guys on the ground. A pleasure to meet you, sir."

"Same, Colonel," Hoffman said in a booming voice that was easy to hear even in the loud compartment. "Have a good one." He started to move past Cuthbert.

"You're not going with us either, Colonel?"

"You're in good hands with McLanahan, Colonel—except

for me and Sondra, he's got more experience in Excaliburs and
Vampires than almost anyone else on the patch," Hoffman
said. "I'll see you later, sir. Have a nice flight." Cuthbert had
to retreat into the vacant offensive systems officers' space so
Hoffman could get by, and even so Hoffman's broad shoulders
brushed Cuthbert's chest as he lumbered past.

After checking that the aft entry hatch was secure,
Cuthbert ducked under the empty systems officers' panel,
past the crew rest compartment—he was happy to see that
the Excalibur still had a relief pilot's bunk, tiny galley, and
chemical commode—then went up to the cockpit and looked
around a bit before hoisting himself up into the aircraft
commander's seat. Both the pilot's and copilot's sides of the
instrument panel had two twelve-inch color multifunction
displays. On the pilot's side, the left one was displaying flight
information, with an artificial horizon on the top half and a
horizontal situation indicator on the bottom; the right display
showed a checklist, with electronic buttons and switches beside
each line on the screen. There were two more MFDs in the
center of the instrument panel between the pilot's and copilot's
pairs with engine, fuel, electrical, and other systems' readouts.
Patrick's MFDs displayed a moving map of the airport and
his own checklist page. The center console between the seats
contained most of the controls and switches he was familiar
with. Rows of standby flight instruments were arrayed below
the crewmembers' MFDs.

Cuthbert strapped in and plugged in his headset cords and
oxygen hose. "Quite a nice job with this instrument panel—it
looks like a bizjet," he said after checking in with Patrick on
the intercom.

"All off-the-shelf stuff that most bizjets and airliners have
been using for years," Patrick said. "The checklists are mostly
automated: you set normal or emergency conditions and phase

of flight, similar to the B-2 bomber, then initiate a checklist at the proper time and just monitor the jet." He swapped checklists with Cuthbert. "Normal, takeoff/land, before taxi," he read. "When each step in the checklist is accomplished, you'll get a green indicator; yellow is caution or wait, and red is a malfunction. Instrument displays will change on the MFDs depending on the checklist being run: engine and aircraft systems instruments for takeoff, navigation for cruise and landing, weapons status diagrams for bomb runs, fuel system for air refueling, et cetera. Pretty straightforward, easy to learn, easy to teach. Again, all off-the-shelf stuff, so it's easy to get stuff repaired, upgraded, or reprogrammed. Parking brake lever is . . ."

"I know where the parking brake handle is, General," Cuthbert said with a smile. "At least you haven't automated everything on my jet." He moved the control stick in a circle, deflected the spoilers and horizontal stabilizers to let the ground crewman know he was ready to taxi; Patrick got taxi clearance from the control tower. Guided by the ground crewman, Cuthbert turned the Excalibur around and headed down the taxiway toward the active runway.

After he had made the turn and gotten a thumbs-up from the ground crewman, telling him he was clear of all obstacles, Cuthbert said, "That linesman looks familiar, General. Isn't that . . . is that your son, *Bradley*?"

"Sure is," Patrick said. "When was the last time you saw him?"

"A year or so after Wendy was killed," Cutlass said solemnly. After a moment of respectful silence for Patrick's ex-wife, murdered by Libyan terrorists many years ago, he added, "Jesus, he's a big kid." He looked at Patrick. "I heard he got an appointment to the Zoo from President Phoenix himself."

"He did."

"So . . . pardon my curiosity, sir, but shouldn't he be in Colorado Springs getting hell beat out of him?"

"He had an . . . unfortunate and ill-advised disagreement with an upperclassman," Patrick said. "They asked him to depart during Second Beast and not return."

"Sorry, sir. What was the disagreement about?"

"He won't say," Patrick said moodily. "I think he was provoked into an altercation, but he refuses to explain his side, even on a direct order from the Academy commandant. The second-classman said Brad refused instruction and correction, misused his training rifle, then attacked him without warning. Doesn't sound like him at all, but he offered no explanation." Patrick's face and tone of voice were stony as he added, "So he's out."

"That's too bad," Cuthbert said. "What's his plan now?"

"I thought I'd give him the rest of the summer to get his bearings and make a plan," Patrick said. "He knows how to operate the power cart, fuel trucks, and tugs, and how to marshal and tow aircraft, so he's helping out on the flight line for a little folding money. But the moment I see him break out the video games instead of working, he's out on his keester."

"Don't be too tough on him, sir," Cuthbert said. "I've got two daughters that both dropped out of college. I was bugged that they didn't seem to do anything much with their lives afterward and I made the mistake of telling them so. The first got pregnant. The second . . . joined the Army."

"Oh, *no*," Patrick deadpanned.

"Actually, it's all good," Cutlass said. "The first is married to a dentist and has given me two grandchildren, and the second is a first lieutenant flying Chinooks. A little friendly advice: nudge, but nudge carefully. Don't be a general officer to your kids."

"Advice well taken, Cutlass," Patrick said. "Thank you."

"Don't mention it, sir," Cuthbert said. He looked around the cockpit and out the forward windscreen at the air refueling receptacle aiming markings on the nose. He punched the "Takeoff/Land" checklist on his MFD, selected several steps, then looked out his left side window to make sure the wing sweep, flaps, slats, and spoilers were set properly. "The bird looks great, sir," he remarked. "What did you do to the skin? It looks brand new."

"Nothing except inspection, minor repairs, anticorrosion treatment, and a little paint," Patrick said. "No stealth antiradar coatings, no structural improvements except to fix minor structural flaws and to add a few features. We didn't consider stealth hardly at all."

"Why?"

"Because we assumed the battlefield would already be consumed with electronic jamming and intrusion," Patrick said. "The Bones' radar cross section—the lowest of the entire world's heavy aircraft until the B-2 Spirit came along—could mostly be neutralized by electronic jamming. Our objective was to field an AirSea Battle attack and antimissile airframe in minimum time and cost. We analyzed the risk and advantage of the B-1B with advanced jammers and low-level flight profiles, and designed an attack profile to match. The B-1's radar cross section is actually about the same as a Super Hornet."

"Pretty good," Cuthbert said distractedly. "Where did you get all the plans and manpower to do these conversions?"

"When the Air Force closed down the B-1 refurbishment project at Plant 42 in Palmdale, we bought all the tooling, design and manufacturing software, tech orders, and plans from the Air Force—much of which was designed and written by Sky Masters—and brought a bunch of the engineers and technicians up here," Patrick said. "We've got the best in the business, all seasoned pros, and they set out to prove we could do it faster and better up here in Battle Mountain."

"A private company doing it faster and better than the government? Who knew?" Cuthbert deadpanned. "So you're not going to put all that fancy drone recovery and rearming stuff and the mission-adaptive wings on your birds?"

"We certainly can—Sky Masters developed both systems years ago, and we put all that technology on a B-1 just a couple years ago," Patrick said. "We did retain the weapon loadout capabilities, software, and data bus of the Vampire bombers, so we can carry every air-launched weapon in the arsenal, including air-to-air missiles."

"Air to air! No kidding?"

"We can put up to eight AMRAAMs on a rotary launcher, and we can carry a max of three rotary launchers," Patrick said. "Although AirSea Battle envisions land-based bombers working with carrier-based fighters, we wanted to keep the capability of long-range unescorted land attack. Just give us whatever weapon you want to employ, and we can carry it into battle for you and let you launch them."

"Pretty cool, sir."

"The idea behind this project was to quickly field a force of long-range bombers to help protect the fleet over the horizon and to validate the AirSea Battle concept in minimum time and money," Patrick said. "It's just an interim solution, but time and money-wise, we think it's the best option until they find more money for a new long-range bomber."

"And I'm sure Sky Masters has a design in mind for that, too," Cuthbert said.

"Of course."

"Thought so," Cutlass said. "So let's talk turkey a bit before we take off, General. What's it going to cost the Air Force to build your little fleet here?"

"Nothing," Patrick said matter-of-factly.

"*Excuse* me? *Nothing?*"

"Sky Masters is making an investment in this project, not just trying to get a government contract," Patrick explained. "We want the Air Force to give us the engines, avionics, radars, weapons, fuel, and access to the other aircraft at AMARG for spare parts—all stuff the Air Force already has in abundance and taxpayers have already paid for. The company pays all the personnel costs—engineering, maintenance, aircrew, support staff, and instructors. If the Air Force cancels the program, you get your hardware back, and Sky Masters writes off the personnel costs."

"Not that an old warhorse like me knows anything about business, sir," Cuthbert said, "but I have to wonder: How do you make any money at this? Sky Masters *is* in this to make money, right?"

"The company's shareholders want to make money, Cutlass—*I* want to support the AirSea Battle strategy and contribute to the defense of our nation by building highly capable long-range reconnaissance and strike aircraft in a short amount of time," Patrick said. "We make our money by employing the Excaliburs after they're built. The Air Force is going to need personnel to fly and service the jets—that'll be Sky Masters's job. Once the bombers are built and the program validated, the Pentagon pays for the labor to build the bombers, and we sign a contract to operate the jets at the direction of the Air Force or theater commander. We'll provide fully qualified aircrew and the datalink technology for Air Force personnel to operate the offensive and defensive systems in the plane, and we'll drive the bus wherever you want. Your folks—or ours, if you prefer—remotely man the weapon systems and do the strikes in case there's an operational need."

"And your board of directors agreed to not getting paid until and unless there's a contract job?"

"It was a little bit of a chore to convince them to make the investment," Patrick admitted. "We got a little help from some local, state, and federal agencies, because we're bringing in hundreds of skilled laborers and their families into one of the poorest and economically hardest-hit areas of the western United States. But I noticed something when I first created this program: like any government program these days, the workers who moved to Battle Mountain from Palmdale and other places to work at Sky Masters know that this whole deal could never materialize, or it could be canceled at any moment even after the contracts are signed. They're still willing to move out here and do the work. That's more than just getting a paycheck, Cutlass—that's being dedicated to the work and the country. I want to support that, and after I pointed this out to my board, they agreed . . . eventually. After they saw the first refurbished Excalibur fly, they were fully on board—they even authorized the funds to refurbish the F-111 and F-14. The F-111 might be a lower-cost solution to the air arm of AirSea Battle, and we can build about fifty of them, a lot more than the B-1s."

They got back to work as they neared the hammerhead area of the active runway at Battle Mountain. Cuthbert pressed the "TTO" switch, which automatically set the trim and spoilers for takeoff, then checked the rows of green dots on the checklist page on the MFDs, indicating that the plane was configured for takeoff, Patrick typed a text message on one of his MFDs. "I told the range controllers at Naval Air Station Fallon that we're ready for takeoff, and they cleared us into the military operating area and low-level routes," Patrick said. "The navigation heading bug is on the range entry point. I'll talk to Battle Mountain Approach after the handoff, then the Fallon range controllers." Patrick made his own scan of the checklist page and the engine instrument page, then fastened his oxygen mask over his mouth, and checked his straps, and armed his ejection seat. "Seat's armed. I'm ready to roll, Cutlass."

"My seat's hot. Ready." Patrick got takeoff clearance, then said, "You have plenty of runway for a rolling takeoff, and we're extremely light, so no need to lock the brakes to run the engines up. Pedal to the metal."

"Coming up," Cuthbert said. He smoothly applied full military power.

"Compressors look good," Patrick said, scanning the engine instruments. "Clear to go into the zone."

"Here we go." Cuthbert moved the throttles past the detent into afterburner zone.

"Good nozzle swings, temps look good."

"Zone five," Cuthbert said, and then he felt it—that satisfying, almost surprising kick in the small of his back as the engines reached full thrust. "Oh baby, that feels good," he murmured seductively.

"V-one, seven thousand to go, continue," Patrick said, using the runway length remaining and their airspeed to determine the go/no-go decision point in the takeoff roll— even though the Excalibur's flight computers automatically calculated that, the human backup kept the crew ready for emergencies. There were two such V-speeds, one to determine the time to abort if there was an engine failure and the other to determine if the plane should continue the takeoff in case of engine failure. "Coming up on Vr . . . now." A third reference speed told the pilot when to begin takeoff rotation. Cuthbert smoothly pulled back on the control stick, and seconds later the Excalibur bomber fairly leaped off the runway. They were climbing at over five thousand feet per minute just seconds later and going faster every second. "Clear of the runway, I got the gear." He raised the landing gear handle, and moments later he raised the flaps and slats as well. "Flaps and slats up, clear on wing sweep."

"Roger. Wings coming to thirty." Cuthbert moved the large wing-sweep handle on his left side back to the thirty-degree setting. He nodded happily. "Wow, this baby really likes those wings swept back. It felt like a B-52 on takeoff with the wings forward, but with them back the controls feel a hell of a lot lighter."

Within the restricted Naval Air Station Fallon bombing and gunnery ranges, they climbed up to thirty thousand feet, and Patrick demonstrated some basic airwork maneuvers—slow flight, stalls, and steep turns—followed by more advanced maneuvers—lazy-eights and chandelles—and finally some simple aerobatics—inverted flight, barrel rolls, and aileron rolls. The Excalibur performed all of them without difficulty, which gave Cuthbert enough confidence to try them on his own. Patrick was pleased to see Cuthbert grinning like a young kid on a Ferris wheel after he was done.

"What do you think, Cutlass?" Patrick asked after the Air Force colonel finished his second aileron roll.

"She handles like a great big fighter jet," Cuthbert said, still grinning. "Just fantastic."

"Of course, we can't do most of this with weapons aboard—but I wanted to show you that this bird is still very solid and has plenty of power to do advanced maneuvering," Patrick said. "But now it's time to show you what the original B-1 was made for." He called up a flight plan on his MFD, and a serpentine corridor drew itself on the moving map, while Cuthbert's MFD showed a series of squares on the synthetic-vision display that they were passing through. He then called up the "Before TFR Flight" checklist. "Now we're going to have some *real* fun," he said. "Terrain-following system checks, radar configured, one-thousand-foot clearance plane set. Engage when ready, Cutlass." Cuthbert pressed the "TFR ENGAGE" button on his MFD, and the Excalibur nosed over into a fifteen-thousand-foot-per-minute descent. "Wing sweep to sixty-seven," Patrick said. "Throttles to keep us from going past the Mach—we have the Rod Pod on, and we haven't tested it beyond point nine five Mach." The AN/AAQ-33 Sniper Advanced Targeting Pod, nicknamed "Rod Pod," was a device mounted underneath the fuselage that allowed the crew to search for and laser-designate targets on the ground from long range and at night for precision bombing. The pod could laser-designate targets for the Excalibur, "buddy laze" targets for other bombers, or spot targets, measure coordinates, and transmit images and data via satellite to other commanders around the world. "If you want to hand-fly the course, just keep the plane inside the squares on your screen and let the TFR control pitch."

In two minutes they had descended to just one thousand feet aboveground. They performed another system check, then stepped the altitude down to just two hundred feet aboveground, traveling over six hundred miles an hour. Cuthbert let the terrain-following radar and computers control their roller-coaster ride over the terrain while turning the bomber to keep inside the squares that depicted their flight-planned course, sometimes having to bank at almost ninety degrees to stay on course because his attention drifted away at the wrong moment. He finally engaged the autopilot so he didn't have to concentrate so hard on flying and get a chance to experience terrain-following flight in the Excalibur. "This is fantastic, Patrick, just incredible," he said. "She feels rock-solid."

"We were happy that the ship's original Stability and Control Augmentation System interfaced so well with the new Active Electronically Scanned Array radar," Patrick said. "But SCAS was ahead of its time. We could also do away with some of the other systems such as the radar altimeter and bank angle fail-safes on the TFR, because AESA performs well at any bank or pitch angle or in situations such as over water, whereas the original radar had severe limitations." They were coming to the end of the low-level route on the flight plan, and the squares on the synthetic-vision display were starting to indicate a climbout. "Want to go through the route again?"

"I'd like to, Patrick, but I've got a flight back to Hickam to catch," Cuthbert said. "But you definitely watered my eyes today. Thanks for an incredible demonstration."

As they were climbing out of the low-level route, with Cuthbert hand-flying the aircraft again as he liked to do, they heard on the Fallon range control frequency: "Masters One, Fallon Range Control."

"Go ahead, Control," Patrick replied.

"Masters One, we have a couple Hornets scheduled for the range in fifteen minutes after you exit, but they're already airborne, and they requested some formation flying for pics. They've never seen a B-1 before except in museums. I can approve MARSA with them if you approve." MARSA stood for Military Assumes Responsibility for Separation of Aircraft and was commonly used for operations such as air-to-air dogfighting practice and aerial refueling.

Patrick looked over at Cuthbert, who nodded with a big smile on his face. "Sure, Control, Masters One welcomes them in."

"Roger that, sir. Masters One, Welder One-Seven flight of two, Fallon Range Control approves MARSA while in the ranges. Maintain block altitudes angels fifteen to angels twenty-one. Report canceling MARSA on this frequency. Masters One, your traffic is at eight o'clock, forty-eight miles and closing."

"One copies," Patrick responded. He switched one of his

MFDs to a radar-warning defensive systems display. Moments later, an icon of a friendly aircraft appeared at the clock position called out by the controller.

"Masters One, Welder flight of two, we're tied on radar, moving in," the lead pilot of the approaching F/A-18 Super Hornets radioed.

"Masters One, roger," Patrick responded.

A few minutes later the Hornet pilot radioed, "Masters, we're tied on visual, splitting up, one on each side for a better shot."

"Masters One, roger."

A few moments later, the Navy-gray Hornet two-seat fighter-bombers appeared out their side windscreens, and they could see the Navy backseaters snapping pictures of the XB-1 with their wingman on the other side.

"She's a big mutha," one of the Hornet pilots radioed.

"Show us what she can do," another said. Cuthbert started a left turn, getting steeper and steeper until they were at ninety degrees bank. The Hornet pilots remained in tight formation as if they were airshow performers.

"Not bad, not bad—for a big ol' dinosaur," another crewmember radioed. "What else does the old girl got?"

Cuthbert glanced at Patrick. "What do you think, General?" he asked.

"I think they want to play." Patrick called up the low-level flight plan again, and Cuthbert kept the turn in until they were headed for the entry point again. Patrick ran the "Before TFR Flight" checklist again, then shook his control stick and said, "I've got the aircraft."

Cuthbert shook his stick in response. "You've got the aircraft."

"How about it, momma?" a Hornet pilot radioed. "Got anything else to show us?"

"They're probably afraid it's going to break if they G it up too much," another chimed in.

"No, we're just waiting for the right spot," Patrick radioed back. "Ready, Cutlass?"

"Go fry their butts, sir," Cuthbert replied, his wide grin hidden by his oxygen mask.

"Here we go," Patrick said. He swept the wings full aft and moved the throttles up to full military power.

"Well, sweeping the wings is cool, like a great big F-14 Tomcat," one of the Navy pilots radioed, "and I see she still has a little oompf left in her . . ."

. . . and Patrick hit the "ENGAGE" button on his MFD and started a hard right turn into the low-level corridor.

"*Hey! Watch it!*" one of the Hornet pilots radioed. "Where in hell are you going?"

"Catch us if you can, girls," Patrick radioed. The two Hornets had disappeared from sight as the Excalibur began its dramatic plunge toward Earth.

"No sweat, momma," a Hornet pilot said. "Welder Two, you're at my three o'clock; join on me in loose fingertip."

"Two," the wingman responded.

The two icons on the defensive systems display showed the Hornets merging and moving higher and farther away. Patrick reluctantly had to pull the throttles back to avoid going supersonic in the steep descent. In less than a minute they had descended to two hundred feet aboveground and were again riding the ridges, now traveling closer to seven hundred miles an hour.

"Hornets at seven o'clock high," Patrick said, scanning his checklist and defensive displays. "TFR system checks." He strained to check out both side windscreens for terrain. "Hang on, Cutlass," he said, and he threw the Excalibur in a steep right turn.

"Hornets at six o'clock . . . five . . . four . . . coming back to five o'clock . . ."

"Not for long," Patrick said. Just before reaching a peak, he threw the Excalibur into a very steep left turn, hugging the peak so closely Cuthbert could see individual cracks on the rocks below.

"You got the dirt, Patrick?" Cuthbert asked a little worriedly.

"I've got the dirt, I've got the dirt," Patrick said.

"Hornets at nine o'clock, eight o'clock, moving away . . . now turning back, still at eight o'clock . . ."

"No fair using radar, chums," Patrick said. He called up another checklist page, this time to activate the Excalibur's defensive ALQ-293 SPEAR system, then made another tight right-hand turn and skimmed over another rocky ridge. "I'll just scramble their radars and radios, not take them out completely," Patrick said. Moments later the icons representing the Hornets disappeared. "Take that, squids."

"Welder flight, knock it off, knock it off," the lead Hornet pilot radioed a few moments later, his voice a combination of anxiety and anger. The radio was a mess of squeals, pops, and static—the pilot's voice was barely recognizable. "Lead is climbing to angels seventeen. Fallon Range Control, Welder One-Seven is canceling MARSA at this time."

"Welder One-Seven, repeat," the range controller replied through the jamming. "Did not copy."

"Fallon Range Control, Welder One-Seven canceling MARSA," the pilot repeated through the haze of static. Then he said, "Hey, Masters, shut the damned jamming off, dickheads." Patrick shut down the defensive suite, and the squealing stopped. "Fallon Range Control, how do you copy now?"

"Loud and clear now, Welder," the controller responded.

"We're canceling MARSA, squawking normal."

"Roger, Welder One-Seven. Radar contact, five-seven miles northwest of the field, passing angels thirteen. Your wingman is at your seven o'clock position, four miles, passing through angels eleven. I have negative radar contact on Masters One."

"That's because the bastard went low-level while we were in formation!" the lead Hornet pilot replied angrily, "and then he turned on his jammers and shut every radar and radio down for fifty miles in every freakin' direction!"

"I copy, Welder," the controller said. "Masters One, are you on frequency?"

"Affirmative, Fallon Control," Patrick replied. "We're ten miles south of waypoint Tango on IR-7, passing six thousand climbing to one-six thousand, on the way to range control point JASPER."

"Still negative radar contact," the controller said. "You were directed to remain MARSA with Welder flight in the block angels one-seven to two-one."

"We still own the range and the IR-7 low-level route for another five minutes, Fallon," Patrick said. "We simply reentered IR-7 and resumed our test flight. If the Hornets couldn't remain MARSA with us, they should've reported that to you and stayed in the block."

There was a long pause on the frequency, then: "Masters One, contact Fallon Range Operations after landing. You are cleared to point JASPER, climb and maintain angels one-six. Upon reaching JASPER, you are cleared direct to Battle Mountain Airport. Contact Battle Mountain Approach upon reaching JASPER, and after arriving at Battle Mountain, contact Fallon Range Control by telephone," and the controller read off a phone number.

"Masters One copies all," Patrick said, adding, "Have a nice day, Welders."

"Bite me," came the reply, and the frequency remained silent until they exited the range and switched to civilian air traffic control.

"So, what do you think, Cutlass?" Patrick asked.

"It was *awesome*!" Cuthbert replied, pulling off his oxygen mask, squirming excitedly in his seat, and clapping his hands. "Man, I'd forgotten how exciting low-level flying is—the heavies haven't done it in years. Sounds like you might get a spanking from the Navy after you get back for turning on that SPEAR jammer thingy and shutting everything down."

"They'll get over it—I'll let the legal beagles sort it out," Patrick said, completely unconcerned. "Feel like making the landing, Cutlass?"

"Damn right I do, sir, damn right I do!" Cuthbert said happily. "I feel like a young butter-bar bomber jock again. *I've* got the airplane!" He shook the control stick to indicate he had control of the aircraft, and Patrick shook his stick to acknowledge. "I might miss my flight back to Hawaii, but it was damn well worth it!"

THREE

SOUTH CHINA SEA

THAT SAME TIME

"Who said it looks ugly? I think it's cute," U.S. Navy Lieutenant Paula "Cowgirl" Caraway commented as she studied the image on her multifunction display from her station in the aviation warfare section of the P-8 Poseidon reconnaissance plane, based in Hawaii but temporarily deployed to Taiwan. Caraway, a trim, athletic blonde with an almost perpetual smile, was the patrol plane navigator/communications officer, or NAVCOM, aboard the aircraft. The P-8A Poseidon was a naval variant of the Boeing 737–800 airliner outfitted with extended-range fuel tanks, a small bomb bay for torpedoes or cruise missiles—they were currently unarmed—electronic intelligence-gathering and antisubmarine warfare equipment, and sonobuoys for detecting and tracking submarines.

"It's kinda sleek," Caraway went on, "with its upturned nose, like a supermodel. Graceful." She had switched one of her digital radar displays so she could see the high-resolution inverse synthetic-aperture radar image from the Poseidon's

AN/APY-10 multimode radar. Even at a range of almost forty miles, the APY-10 produced an image as sharp as a black-and-white photograph—she could easily count and identify the aircraft sitting on her deck. "A little princess."

"I was the one who said it was ugly, and it is," her partner seated beside her, Lieutenant Commander Richard "Beastie" Sykes, said. Sykes, a veteran maritime patrol plane officer with almost fifteen years of service in P-3 Orion and S-3 Viking patrol planes, was the patrol plane tactical coordinator, or TACCO, directing the activities of the P-8's naval warfare crew. "So they slapped some paint on it and gave it some interesting new bulges. It's still an antiquated pig."

Sykes and Caraway were talking about the main subject of the day's surveillance mission over the South China Sea: the *Zhenyuan,* the People's Republic of China Navy's first aircraft carrier. Formerly the *Kuznetsov*-class Russian carrier *Varyag,* it had first been transferred to Ukraine after the fall of the Soviet Union. It was purchased by Iran purportedly to be used as a work platform for offshore oil rigs, but it had been secretly made operational and based in the Persian Gulf and Gulf of Oman as the carrier *Ayatollah Ruhollah Khomeini,* the first aircraft carrier operated by a Middle East nation. After a brief skirmish with American Air Force bombers, where the ship was severely damaged, the carrier was stripped of all its weapons and sensors and sold to China, again purportedly to be used as a floating hotel and casino near Hong Kong. It appeared briefly as the aircraft carrier *Mao Zedong* and was involved in the conflict between mainland China and Taiwan after the island nation declared independence, and then retired once again after being severely damaged. The Chinese announced it was an environmental hazard and transferred to the northern port of Dalian to be scrapped.

Instead, several years later, the ship emerged from dry

dock with newer, more powerful engines and improved digital sensors. It successfully completed sea trials in 2011. According to the Chinese navy, the carrier, renamed the *Zhenyuan,* would only be used for "experimentation, training, and research," and stay near the Chinese mainland. The world was surprised when it appeared in the Gulf of Aden a year later as part of an eight-ship carrier battle group that at first drilled with the Russian aircraft carrier *Vladimir Putin* battle group, then attacked the Yemeni port city of Aden and participated in attacks against pirates in Somalia, using advanced JH-37N fighter-bombers flying off its decks. Few analysts in the world would have guessed that the Chinese would have an aircraft carrier battle group operational before the year 2020, let alone actually use one in combat. When China agreed to withdraw its troops from Somalia in 2013, the *Zhenyuan* and its escorts returned to home waters and rarely left the South China Sea. The Chinese navy began intensive carrier flight operations training aboard the *Zhenyuan* in anticipation of outfitting its second aircraft carrier, the *Zheng He,* planned for 2015.

Although more than twenty miles away, the Poseidon's synthetic-aperture radar provided very detailed images of the *Zhenyuan*. Like British Invincible-class carriers, instead of aircraft-launching steam catapults, the Chinese carrier used an up-sloped forward deck called a "ski jump" to throw fixed-wing aircraft far enough into the sky for them to accelerate to flying speed before they descended and hit the water. It had a very large island superstructure on the starboard side, with light-colored smoke billowing from stacks in the rear. The island bristled with antennas and electronics domes, as well as phased-array radar panels and self-defense missile launchers and gun emplacements; there were more missile launchers and gun turrets midships on both sides along the gunwales. There were six arresting gear wires aft to recover fixed-wing aircraft. Four very large twin-tailed aircraft were parked forward of the island and six more smaller jets aft on the starboard side, plus two large helicopters parked on the port-side elevator and an aircraft waiting to launch from the ski jump. The sensor measured the *Zhenyuan*'s forward speed as twenty-five knots.

"The planes forward of the island look like JH-37s," Sykes remarked as he studied his right-side multifunction display, which was displaying radar images, "but the ones aft of the island and the one getting ready to launch look smaller than the others. Are they JN-15s?" The Shenyang JN-15 was an unlicensed copy of the Russian Sukhoi-33 carrier-based fighter, reported as the original aircraft to be deployed on Chinese carriers until the surprise appearance of the much larger JH-37 fighter-bomber. "Can't tell yet," Caraway said as she made reconnaissance log entries and took a sip of water from a hip flask. "I'd expect to get a visit from one of those JH-37s any time now. I can't wait to see one up close. I hope they . . ."

At that moment they heard on the international emergency GUARD frequency: "United States Poseidon naval reconnaissance aircraft with the unit number of VP-9, this is the combat controller aboard the People's Liberation Army Navy carrier *Zhenyuan* on GUARD channel. How do you hear this transmission, please?"

"*He read off our squadron number?*" Sykes exclaimed. "Unless they got a very high-powered telescope or made a really good guess, they must've intercepted us. Pilot, TACCO, any visual?"

"Negative!" the P-8's pilot, U.S. Navy Commander Renaldo "Nacho" Sanchez, another veteran patrol aircraft crewmember, responded. "Let me try some turns to see if . . ."

"Wait, wait, I see him," the copilot, Lieutenant Helen "Troy" Lister, radioed, her voice high pitched from excitement.

"Four o'clock, high. Boy, that is one tiny plane. It's . . . hey, I think it's a J-20!"

"*What?*" Sanchez exclaimed. He strained forward in his seat to get a better look out the copilot's side window. "I think you're right, Troy." The Shenyang J-20 *Tiǎozhàn zhě*, or "Challenger," was the People's Republic of China's answer to the American F-22 Raptor: sleek and stealthy, reportedly able to cruise at supersonic speeds without afterburners, with internally carried air-to-air missiles, a powerful active electronically scanned radar, and telescopic infrared sensors that allowed it to engage targets without using its radar. "I thought it was experimental only."

"Grab some pictures and I'll upload them to the satellite," Sykes said.

Lister immediately pulled out a digital camera and began taking pictures. "I don't see any external weapons," she commented as she snapped away.

"They're supposed to be internal, like the F-22," Sanchez said. "Do you think it came from the carrier or from a land base?"

"A Chinese carrier-based stealth fighter—that would be huge," Caraway said. "*We* don't even have anything like that yet."

"Pretty good job sneaking up on us like that," Sykes remarked. "Not one squeak on the 'raws.'" The "raws," or Radar Warning Receiver, warned of any ground, ship, or airborne radar that might be tracking them.

"He could be using AESA or IRSTS," Caraway said. AESA was Active Electronically Scanned Array, an advanced radar that shifted frequencies more quickly than most RWRs could identify; IRSTS was Infrared Search and Track System, a sensor that detected and tracked heat sources. Both systems could allow a fighter to track and target another aircraft and guide missiles with a very low probability of being detected.

"Carrier *Zhenyuan,* this is Nickel Five-One-Five, U.S. Navy reconnaissance aircraft," Sanchez announced on the UHF GUARD channel. "We have visual contact on an aircraft at our seven o'clock position. Is that one of yours?"

"That is confirmed, Five-One-Five," the controller responded. "There is another aircraft approaching on your left."

Sure enough, when Sanchez swung around to look out his window, he saw another J-20 flying close formation. "It's another J-20!" he exclaimed. "They have two of those suckers out here? How far are we from a Chinese air base?"

"At least four hundred miles," Sykes said. "How about that? Looks like the Chinese built themselves a carrier-based stealth fighter."

"Are you sending all this to headquarters, Cowgirl?" Sanchez asked.

"I'm typing like crazy," Caraway said. "I'll come up for your camera after I get the acknowledgments, Troy."

"State the purpose of your flight near our ships, please," the Chinese controller radioed.

"Routine reconnaissance flight, carrier *Zhenyuan,*" the pilot replied.

"Are you armed, sir?"

"Negative," Sanchez replied. "We are unarmed."

"Please open your bomb bay and lower your landing gear, Five-One-Five," the Chinese controller said, "so our fighters can visually inspect your weapons bay."

"*What?*" Caraway exclaimed. "He's nuts!"

"We cannot comply, *Zhenyuan,*" Sanchez replied. "That would be unsafe at our current airspeed, altitude, and weight. We are on a peaceful routine reconnaissance flight over international waters."

"It is well known that your aircraft can be fitted with antiship cruise missiles in the internal weapons bay," the Chinese carrier's controller said. "Such aircraft are not permitted to fly within cruise missile range of our vessels or of our petroleum facilities unless their armament status is visually confirmed and your peaceful intentions verified. You must turn north immediately and exit this area. Continued flight in this area will be considered a hostile action and an appropriate response will be initiated without further warning."

"Pilot, TACCO," Sykes called on the intercom, "what do you want to do, Nacho?"

"The ROE says we don't mess around with a couple of Chinese fighters on our tail," Sanchez replied, referring to the Rules of Engagement operations plan briefed before each and every mission. "We briefed the possibility that we might get intercepted—just not by freakin' *naval* J-20s. Cowgirl, send home plate a text and advise them of our situation. Troy, give me a heading back to the refueling track."

"Not completely unexpected, especially since what happened last year," Sykes said on intercom. "After what the Air Force did in the Gulf of Aden to the Russians, I'm surprised they let us get *this* close." Tensions between the United States, Russia, and China following the previous year's skirmishes in the Middle East had decreased markedly, but they were still uncomfortably elevated. "They definitely got the drop on us, sneaking up behind us."

"Steering bug is on the air refueling initial point," Lister said. Sanchez started a right turn to center up the steering indicator. As they turned, Lister turned in her seat to look out the windscreens and make sure the Chinese fighters were turning with them. The last thing they wanted was another midair collision like the one that happened in 2001 when Chinese J-8 fighters collided with a Navy EP-3 Orion patrol plane near Hainan Island, killing one Chinese pilot and forcing the EP-3 to land on a Chinese military base. The crew was detained for ten days and the plane for three months while the Chinese scoured every inch of it for intelligence and engineering information. "Hey, I don't see our little friend anymore. Looks like he went home."

"The one off our port side is gone too," Sanchez said.

"We can expect some more little friends soon—we saw one ready to lift off the carrier," Sykes said.

"What's our range to the carrier, Beastie?"

"Forty-six miles," Sykes replied. "Boy, I'd love for them to kiss my narrow hairy ass," he went on. "Being forced to get jerked around in international airspace is bull. But we wouldn't let them come any closer than a hundred miles from *our* ships, so I guess . . ."

And at that moment, completely without warning, the entire interior of the Poseidon went instantly and completely dark, the engines started to spool down, and the cabin depressurized.

"*Holy shit!*" Sanchez shouted, right after his last breath whistled out between his lips in a loud "BARK!," and air that hadn't leaked away instantly became a thick fog. Sanchez and Lister immediately slipped quick-don oxygen masks over their faces with well-practiced ease. "Troy, can you hear me?" he shouted through his oxygen mask.

"Roger!" Lister shouted back. She was surprised at how calm she felt—this was very much like a scenario they might practice in an emergency procedures simulator session. Strangely, the quiet inside the plane was eerily relaxing—or was that hypoxia kicking in, the sudden lack of oxygen lulling her into a false sense of security? She checked her oxygen regulator just to be sure it was working. "You got the plane, Nacho?"

"I . . . I think so," Sanchez replied. He wasn't yet sure. The full-color MFDs were dark, so he had to search for the standby engine instruments. "Christ, all the engine instruments read zero." He moved the throttles. "No response to throttles, and flight controls feel like they're in 'mechanical' mode."

"The freakin' batteries are off-line too?" Lister asked.

"We've got *squat,* Troy, except for standby pitot-static instruments—altitude, vertical speed, and airspeed," Sanchez said. "Both engines flamed out, no battery power, no generators, no alternators, *nothing*! Let's get the power back on, then do an airstart." While Lister retrieved her paper emergency checklists, Sanchez immediately began doing the first few steps of the checklist by memory, shutting off the aircraft electrical systems, checking circuit breakers—several were popped, an indication that the aircraft had experienced a massive power surge of some kind—and preparing to recycle the battery and generators.

Richard Sykes, the designated message-runner between the cockpit and sensor cabin in emergencies such as this, entered a few minutes later wearing an oxygen mask and carrying a walkaround oxygen bottle in a green canvas sack slung over his shoulder. "Sensor cabin is secure, everything is shut down to shed the load, and everyone's on oxygen and reporting okay," he said. "No injuries." He scanned the instrument panels. "You lost *everything*? Both generators *and* the batteries? Can you get them back online?"

"We'll find out as soon as we reconfigure," Lister said.

"Any idea what happened?"

"No friggin' idea."

"Need an extra hand up here?"

"No," Sanchez said. "Better get strapped in. Tell the crew to run the 'Before Ditching' checklists, in case we can't restart."

Sykes's mouth dropped open in surprise, but he nodded. "What about the classified stuff?" he asked.

Sanchez hesitated, but only for a moment before replying: "Better start destroying it. If we ditch, helicopters from that Chinese carrier will be on us in just a few minutes." Sykes swallowed, finding his throat instantly dry, and headed back to the sensor cabin to order the crew to destroy the classified equipment and documents.

"Okay, circuit breakers reset, all systems in the 'Emergency Power Distribution List' are off, and sensor cabin main power buss is open," Lister said, reading through the items in her checklist. "Ready to recycle the battery switch."

"Here we go," Sanchez said. "Battery switch off . . . battery switch moving to on." He flipped the switch again . . . and nothing happened. "Oh, crap," he muttered, then shut it off again. "Double-check everything, Troy."

Lister swept the left and right instrument panels with a flashlight, confirming that all the switches and circuit breakers were in the proper position. "It all looks good," she said. "What the hell happened, Nacho? What could have knocked out the generators and the batteries all at once?"

"The only thing I know is an electromagnetic pulse from a nuclear detonation," Sanchez said. "If we got hit by one of those, this goose is cooked. Even the standby instruments are out. I'm going to activate the ELT." The ELT, or Emergency Locator Transmitter, was a battery-powered radio that transmitted a coded location signal that could be picked up by rescue aircraft, ships, or satellites. The transmitter was completely separate from the other aircraft systems, and the location signal contained the aircraft's call sign and GPS coordinates to make it easier to find in a search.

"I'll get my survival radio," Lister said. She quickly unstrapped, donned her survival vest, strapped back in, then pulled out a portable combination radio/GPS/satellite messenger unit, powered it up, and waited for it to lock on to satellites. "Heading is steady at south-southeast . . . no, wait, we're in a slight left turn."

"I'll keep the turn coming around and head north," Sanchez

said. He used the ocean horizon to judge a standard-rate turn, counted sixty seconds to himself, then rolled out. "How's that?"

"North-northeast."

"Close enough," Sanchez said. He raised the nose a bit, but he didn't want to risk slowing down below best glide speed. "How's our altitude?"

"Nine thousand five hundred."

"Speed?"

"Two-twenty."

He raised the nose a bit more, which slowed them down and extended their gliding range, then removed his oxygen mask because they were below ten thousand feet, where the air was denser. Lister did likewise. "Let's go over the 'Before Air Restart' checklist again, slowly and carefully," Sanchez said. They rechecked everything, then attempted to bring the battery back online . . . still nothing. "Read off the numbers again, Troy."

"Ground speed one-sixty, altitude six thousand three hundred, still heading north-northeast." She began tapping on the portable unit's tiny keyboard. "I'll text a message to headquarters advising them of our situation. The portable will append our position to the message."

Sykes came back into the cockpit, noticed the pilots were off oxygen, then did likewise. "'Before Ditching' checklists complete, and classified circuit board and memory chip demolition is under way," he said. "Nothing yet up here?"

"Nope," Sanchez said. "We're at six thousand. We'll have time for maybe two more restart attempts before we hit the drink."

"Message received at headquarters," Lister said. "We should be getting a reply as soon as . . ." She looked at her portable unit in confusion. "Oh shit, it looks like it's dead!"

"You're kidding, right?"

"It was working fine a second ago." She tried to turn it back on, but it didn't respond. She tried switching batteries, but that didn't help either. "It's dead."

"I'll see if anyone else has a GPS," Sykes said. A few moments later he returned with a similar unit and powered it up, but a few minutes later it too shut off and wouldn't power back on.

"I don't know what the hell is going on," Sanchez said, "but something is frying all the electronics on this plane." He looked at his watch—it was a mechanical Rolex, and it was still running. "You got a digital watch, Troy?"

"Yes." She glanced at it. "It's dead."

"We got hit by something that toasted our electronics," Sanchez said. "Let's do the checklist again." But the batteries still would not come online.

"Three thousand seven hundred, speed one-sixty," Lister read off.

Sykes came back up to the cockpit. "Nothing?"

"Nothing," Sanchez said. "We'll try a couple more times. Tell the crew to prepare to ditch." Sykes hurried back to the sensor cabin. "Is there anything we haven't tried, Troy?" Sanchez asked cross-cockpit.

"I can't think of anything, Nacho." They ran the emergency checklist twice, but still got no results.

"Okay, screw it," Sanchez said. The standby altimeter said they were less than a thousand feet above the South China Sea, but that could be off by hundreds of feet. "We're ditching. Tighten your straps as tight as you can, Troy." He reached around, grabbed an air horn canister, pressed the button to warn the crew to prepare for ditching, then started to tighten his straps. "Remember, let's get a good read of our attitude in the water before we start opening hatches, and remember not to . . ."

"Hey, *look*!" Lister shouted. There, off to the right of
their nose, was a Chinese JN-20 fighter, flying in very close
formation. "It's back! His electronics seem to be working fine."

"That means ours might work this time," Sanchez said.
"Whatever we were being hit with, they may have shut it off.
Run the airstart checklist, *fast*!" This time, as soon as he cycled
the battery switch, lights popped to life on the instrument
panel. "Hot damn, the batteries are back! Port starter-generator
to start!"

As soon as Lister activated the switch on the overhead
panel, the standby engine instruments responded. "We've
got RPMs and turbine power!" she shouted. "Five . . . ten
. . . fifteen percent power!" Sanchez moved the left throttle
over the detent, and engine power and temperatures steadily
began to rise. "We've got a light! We've got power! Temps are
stable . . . temps are good. Starter switch to generate . . . good
voltages . . . batteries are in good shape, charging normally . . .
avionics power switch on." Moments later, the primary flight
and multifunction displays came to life.

"C'mon, baby, *fly*," Sanchez said, and he slowly and carefully
moved the left throttle forward. The engine gauges responded,
and for the first time in what seemed like an eternity, the
vertical speed indicator moved to zero. They were close enough
now to the ocean that they could see the contours of waves
clearly, but they weren't going down. "Thank you, Jesus," he
muttered. "Troy, get the avionics on, then let's get the right
engine . . ."

At that instant there was a brilliant flash of light from the
left side of the plane, a massive explosion that drowned out all
other sensations, and a wave of searing heat. The P-8 swung
hard first to the right, then to the left so hard that it felt as if
they were inverted. Sanchez mashed the mic button and yelled,
"*Mayday, Mayday, Mayday, Nickel Five-One*—". . .

. . . just as the Poseidon hit the ocean. It flip-flopped end over end for nearly a half mile, shedding pieces of itself in all directions and cracking the fuselage in several places, before coming to rest upside down. In less than five minutes it had slid under the surface, leaving only a few pieces of the wing and tail behind.

President Kenneth Phoenix stepped quickly into the Situation Room, wearing a Marine Corps physical training outfit after the early-morning wake-up call. Tall, trim, and athletic, the former Marine Corps officer and judge advocate, federal prosecutor, U.S. attorney general, and vice president of the United States waved everyone back to their seats. "What's going on?" he asked.

"We lost contact with a Navy P-8 Poseidon reconnaissance plane," said the president's national security adviser, William Glenbrook. "It was over the South China Sea on routine patrol, in the vicinity of the Chinese aircraft carrier *Zhenyuan*."

"Oh, Christ," the president muttered. He reached for a cup of coffee—he knew right then he wasn't going back to bed for a long time. "Were they intercepted or engaged in any way by the Chinese?"

"They were intercepted by two PRC fighters, reported to be J-20s," Glenbrook said. William Glenbrook was a thirty-year Army veteran who rose through the ranks from private to four-star general and was former chairman of the Joint Chiefs of Staff, serving in the same White House as then attorney general Phoenix under President Kevin Martindale. "The P-8 reported suffering a massive electrical malfunction."

"How did they report that with an electrical malfunction, General Glenbrook?" asked Secretary of State Herbert Kevich, who had just arrived at the Situation Room moments before the president. Kevich had been deputy secretary of state under the previous administration, but he was so experienced and knowledgeable in Russian and Chinese affairs that he was kept on by the Phoenix administration. A short, round, impatient-looking man with round reading glasses affixed to the end of his nose even though he mostly looked right over them, Kevich was clearly exasperated by most military officers and high-ranking government officials, even to the point of not acknowledging he was one himself. Kevich arrived quickly when the notification went out to the president's national security staff because he had no other life other than as secretary of state—he would have been perfectly happy to live in the Situation Room, or even in the basement of the White House, if it meant he had speedier access to all the world's events.

"The crew was communicating with their command post via civilian satellite text messages for a short time after the malfunction took place, Secretary Kevich," Glenbrook said.

"Texting while driving? Not a smart move, I think," Kevich quipped.

"A very heads-up move, I think, Herbert," Phoenix said. "I want a search-and-rescue mission initiated immediately, and I don't want the Chinese involved in any way, especially that carrier. If it's in the area of the crash, I want it out of there."

"Yes, sir," Glenbrook said.

"That might be problematic, Mr. President," Kevich said. "The South China Sea may legally be considered international waters, but the Chinese consider it their exclusive domain, as we do with the Gulf of Mexico or the Japanese with the Sea of Japan. The Chinese government will not like being told what to do in their own front yard."

"If the Chinese lost an aircraft over the Gulf of Mexico, I wouldn't mind if they brought search teams or even an aircraft carrier battle group in to search—we'd keep an eye on them, but I'd allow it," Phoenix said. "We're not going to play power politics or geopolitical upmanship with a search, rescue, or recovery mission—China must not interfere, period. I want the crash site located and secured from the air as well as the surface. Warn anyone nearing the area to remain clear."

"And if they don't, Mr. President?" Kevich asked.

"Have the on-scene commander for the rescue report to me if the Chinese won't cooperate," Phoenix replied after a short pause for consideration. "Commanders can do whatever they need to do to protect their forces, but no other action without approval. Tensions are going to be high—I don't want anyone shooting first and asking questions later." Glenbrook nodded and picked up the telephone to issue the orders.

Several minutes later, Vice President Ann Page entered the Situation Room, carrying a secure tablet computer. She was accompanied by Thomas Torrey, the director of the Central Intelligence Agency. Page was a multidegree engineer and physicist by training, but her background spanned the universe, from her years as a U.S. senator from California to one of America's most experienced astronauts and space weapons designers. Slender and energetic, with short gray hair, she was the president's closest adviser. Torrey was a thirty-year veteran of the CIA despite looking no older than forty years of age; in the drastic downsizing of the federal government under the Phoenix administration, the post of director of national intelligence was eliminated and once again the CIA director oversaw all civil foreign intelligence operations in the United States. "Tom just gave me the transcript of the text messages sent by the surveillance plane, Mr. President," Page said, holding up the computer. "The crew believed the J-20 fighters launched from the carrier."

"They obviously wanted us to see those fighters, sir," Torrey said. "The Chinese could even have allowed the Poseidon to come in close enough to see them launch from the carrier."

"But why would they shoot down the Poseidon?" the president asked. "It doesn't make sense."

"Something else happened out there," Page said. "The text transmissions stopped abruptly for some reason. Then several minutes later one of our Asian search-and-rescue satellites picked up a 'Mayday' distress call with the Poseidon's partial call sign. No other transmissions were picked up until the SARSAT received the Poseidon's emergency locator beacon, which is usually activated either manually or after a crash." The SARSAT, or Search and Rescue Satellite, was a satellite dedicated to picking up and relaying signals from aircraft and vessel emergency beacons, providing accurate position data to rescuers. "It was obviously activated manually because the position of the plane changed quite a bit, as if it was still flying. Then the position stopped. But the plane's track was only active for a couple minutes."

"So they didn't activate it manually until just before they hit the water?" the president asked. "Would they do it so late?"

"Depends on what they were experiencing," Torrey said. "If they had an in-flight emergency, such as a fire or flight-control problem, perhaps they were dealing with that right before they crashed."

"We may not know anything until we recover whatever's left of the plane and its black boxes," Page said. "Even then, we still may not know for sure."

"So the Chinese may not be culpable after all," Secretary of State Kevich said. "Sir, do you still want to issue the order to keep the Chinese away from the crash site? They are obviously closer to the site and have considerable resources to conduct a rescue. If they offer their assistance—or if they initiate a search-and-rescue effort on their own, as any nation or vessel on the high seas should—we should welcome such cooperation. After all, China is not our enemy."

"That might be the neighborly thing to do, Herbert," Phoenix said, "but I think it's no coincidence that one of our surveillance planes falls out of the sky near a Chinese carrier battle group. I want the reason why that plane went down determined as best we can before I rule anything out. If this was indeed a deliberate act and not an accident or malfunction, then whoever did it will try to erase the evidence—and if that someone is China, and if they reach the crash site, I think that's exactly what they'd do."

Kevich looked at the president carefully for a few moments. "We've had this discussion before, sir, after the Chinese withdrew from Somalia," he said carefully and directly, "but it does bear repeating: presuming China as an adversary may make it come true, even though they may not be."

"I don't think of China as an adversary, Herbert," the president said. Kevich gave him a skeptical expression; the president paused for a few moments, then nodded. "To be honest, Herbert, I consider them a serious *potential* adversary."

"With respect, sir, I think much of that comes from fear," Kevich said.

"Maybe so, Herbert," Vice President Page said, bristling at the insinuation that Kenneth Phoenix was fearful of anything. "But the Chinese government is not doing very much to lift the unknowns and secrecy that are causing fear to rise. We're not asking them to reveal every secret or strategy. They are more than happy to accept our efforts at openness and cooperation, but it's rarely mutual."

"The Chinese are an old and insular people, Miss Vice President," Kevich said. "They are isolated politically, geographically, and culturally. It is important for us to remember and understand that the nations of the West have done nothing but exploit China from the sea for centuries. Now that China is embarking on a program to modernize and increase trade with the world, we become suspicious. They are looking to the future and willing to wait to become a world power. We think in terms of months or fiscal quarters—the Chinese think in terms of decades or even generations."

"All that may be true, Herbert," the president said, "but it hasn't always been the case. Chinese explorers have traveled half the globe. Isolation has mostly been the chosen method for controlling their enormous population, especially when their maritime provinces became rich and powerful and the agrarian inland provinces stayed in abject poverty. Besides, this is the twenty-first century—no nation, not even China, can remain isolated."

"And when we get reports nearly every day of another computer or network hacking attempt traced back to a Chinese government-owned or controlled entity," Page said bitterly, "I wonder if the war has already started—we're just not engaged in it yet."

"All I'm saying, Miss Vice President, is that it makes little sense to me why a three-thousand-year-old nation would do anything to threaten its own existence, especially versus the most economically and militarily powerful nation on Earth," Kevich said. "Although China is undergoing an economic and military surge, please remember that its economy is still one-third of ours; we have over a hundred years of naval aviation experience, while they have just a few; and we still remain a world power, while China is only on the brink of becoming a regional power."

"But that region is pretty damned important to us and the rest of the world, Herbert," Ann said. "If this incident turns out to be a bid by Beijing to claim sovereignty over the South China Sea region, we need to squash that plan immediately."

"If they were involved in the Poseidon incident, I would expect it to turn out to be an accident or an isolated incident by an inexperienced and misguided sea captain, and we should keep open minds so as to not threaten our strategic relationship," Kevich went on. "Never forget, we rely closely on each other in dozens of areas: trade, finance, investment, education, technology, geopolitical balance, the list goes on. The fate of the entire planet rests on the balance between the West and China. One incident shouldn't threaten to upset that balance."

President Phoenix remained silent for a few long moments, then nodded. "Points well taken, Herbert," he said finally. "Maybe I am jumping to conclusions." Kevich nodded and smiled, satisfied that his arguments seemed to win over the president. But his smile faded when the president went on, "But I still don't want the Chinese near that crash scene. We'll politely but firmly ask them to stay away while we conduct search, rescue, recovery, and investigation activities."

"I reiterate, sir: China considers the South China Sea of the utmost strategic value—sending in a large armada of ships, even to mount a search and rescue, may be perceived as a provocation," Kevich said.

"I understand what you're saying, Herbert," the president said, "but we're not going to get into a philosophical discussion about foreign relations with China when we have American sailors down in the South China Sea." He thought for a moment, then continued: "I'll call Premier Zhou right away and notify him of our intentions, and ask him not to allow any vessels to interfere. I'll also speak with Prime Minister Ruddock of Australia, Tran of Vietnam, Cruz of the Philippines, and Saleh of Indonesia. They should all know what is happening and what we intend to do next. Herbert, contact NATO, ANZUS, and ASEAN and advise them as well." The countries of NATO, the North Atlantic Treaty Organization alliance, were always notified of such contingencies, even though they were not in the region; the other organizations—ANZUS, which stood for Australia, New Zealand, and the United States; and ASEAN, or the Association of South East Asian Nations—were important regional alliances and associations with whom the United States regularly cooperated. "Bill, get together with General Spellings and give me a rundown of the forces in the region and the assets the task force will use for the search and rescue." Air Force General Timothy Spellings was the chairman of the Joint Chiefs of Staff and the president's primary uniformed military adviser. "Give Pacific Command full authorization to start the search."

"General Spellings is on his way over with the order of battle and a search-and-rescue plan right now, sir," Glenbrook said. "He's already sent me the latest disposition of forces, and he said he'd be ready to brief a real-time update by the time he arrives at the White House. I'll get a briefing from him first when he arrives, ask him to fill in any holes, then let you know when we're ready to brief the national security staff."

"Very good," Phoenix said. Now that everyone had their assignments they filed out of the Situation Room, leaving Phoenix alone with Ann Page. "So what do you think, Ann?" Phoenix asked.

"I think I don't like Kevich implying you were acting out of fear of the Chinese," she said.

"I meant about the Poseidon incident," Phoenix said. "Herbert speaks his mind, which is why I have him in the Cabinet. Everyone here is supposed to speak their minds with me, not just you."

"So he thinks he can admonish and even accuse the president of the United States just because he's forgotten more about Russia and China than we've ever known? I don't think so," Ann said perturbedly.

"Let's get back to the Poseidon loss, shall we?" Phoenix asked. "I'm about to tell Premier Zhou that I'm going to send in a number of warships right into the middle of his own private lake, and I don't want any of his ships or planes nearby while they're there. Herbert's right: he's not going to like it. *I* wouldn't like it if he told me he was going to send a bunch of warships into the Gulf of Mexico, and I wasn't allowed to at least monitor their activities, if not be directly involved. I would allow it, but I'd reserve the right to keep close watch on what they're doing. Do you think I should allow China to monitor us, like Herbert suggests?"

"Hell no," Ann said. "We lost a sophisticated surveillance aircraft and several Navy personnel near a Chinese warship and aircraft. The plane was unarmed, on a peaceful surveillance mission, and it was flying in international airspace and went down in international waters. I don't buy the argument that the South China Sea is China's private lake. We're going to conduct a search-and-rescue operation, and then a recovery-and-investigation operation, and we don't want anyone—especially China—interfering. Period. End of sentence. And the definition of 'interfering' is whatever *we* say it is, *whenever* we say it."

Ken Phoenix thought for a moment, then smiled and nodded. "I agree completely, Ann," he said. "Herbert is the geopolitical guru around here, but we're going to put geopolitics aside until we rescue our sailors and find out what the hell happened. If anyone gets in the way, we're pushing back. All the other relationships with China don't matter until our rescue and investigation operations are concluded."

"Sounds good to me, Mr. President," Ann said. "I'll get together with my staff and get ready for a morning press briefing." In the extreme drawdown of the federal government, the vice president acted as chief of staff and press secretary as well as performing her other constitutionally mandated duties; despite the extra workload, Ann Page made doing the extra tasks look easy. "I expect my phone will be ringing off the hook when I get back to the office. You want me to do a few morning shows too?"

"Not until we have more information, Ann," Phoenix said. "I don't want you in front of forty million viewers saying nothing more than 'we don't know anything yet.' Give a statement to the press corps—nothing about our suspicions about the Chinese fighters or aircraft carrier, of course—and that's all for now."

"Yes, Mr. President," Ann said. They discussed a few other important matters over coffee, then they headed back to their offices to continue their day that had started so early with the iconic "phone call in the middle of the night." But before Ann departed, Phoenix called out to her: "One more thing, Ann."

Page stopped at the door. "Yes, Mr. President?"

"It's a 'Ken' question, Ann," the president said. He paused, thought for a moment, then spread his hands. "How do you think I'm doing, Ann?" he asked.

"Doing . . . what, sir?"

"Doing . . . the job. Being president. How am I doing?"

Ann rolled her eyes and shook her head. "Excuse me, sir, but what kind of question is that?"

"Don't give me that 'sir' crap, Ann," Phoenix said. "I didn't pick you to lay the extreme protocol formality stuff on me when we're in private—I know you're not bred for it, which is why I chose you to run with me in a last-second primary and general election blitzkrieg campaign. We lucked out and won, in the narrowest of margins ever recorded.

"But sometimes I feel like I'm spinning my wheels," Phoenix went on. "The economy is still in the tank and there seems to be no end in sight. I've cut the budget and tax rates down to bare bones, but it doesn't seem to be affecting anything very much. At the same time, China and Russia are pushing forward with reclaiming old empires and challenging us everywhere." He paused for a moment, his brow furrowing, lost in thought; then: "Ann, am I presiding over a failed republic? Is the United States . . . done?"

"Done? What do you mean?"

"I mean . . . I mean, we just lost an airplane over the South China Sea, and my most knowledgeable adviser tells me to 'be careful' in deploying search-and-rescue forces in the area," Phoenix said. "Years ago, the United States moved where it wanted, when it wanted, and we never considered other nations' concerns, especially in a crisis situation. Now, even with an absolutely critical and sensitive emergency event such as this, we seem to be hamstrung by caution. We're afraid of offending China. Our own sailors are down, perhaps by hostile intent, but we're still afraid of offending the People's Republic of China. Why? Is this right? How did we get to this point?"

"First of all, Ken, Herbert is an academic and an administrator," Ann said a bit testily, stepping back into the Situation Room with the president. "We hired him because he has an encyclopedic mind, speaks both Russian and Mandarin along with six other languages, and can organize everything from individuals to entire cabinet-level departments better than anyone we've ever seen. But he's just a bureaucrat. He lacks vision. He needs guidance and direction.

"You, on the other hand, are a *doer*, a man with leadership qualities and a vision for the future," Ann went on. "You decided that the best way to fix the economy was to cut taxes, cut the size of government, reorganize the military, and stimulate growth, reinvestment, and hiring by cutting rules and regulations that were squeezing businesses. You made a decision, charted a course, moved forward, and pushed your ideas through Congress in record time.

"But along with vision comes introspection and even a large measure of self-doubt, and sometimes that worries me more about you than anything else," Ann said earnestly. "The presidents I'm most familiar with—Thorn, Martindale, and Gardner—may privately have had doubts, but they never expressed or showed them. You, on the other hand, wear them on your damned chest like a general's ribbons.

"The people of this country, and of the entire world for that matter, don't need or especially expect peace, prosperity, or comfort from their leaders, Ken. They need and expect *leadership*. They want our leaders to *do something,* take a stand, fight for what they believe in, and make arguments about why what they have planned is the right thing to do. So you keep on doing what you do best: lead. You focused in on exactly what the issue here is: search for and rescue our sailors and find out what happened. Kevich advises you to be careful and lectures you about China, but you keep returning to the matter at hand. You're doing it right. Stop worrying."

"A lot of people—a lot of *nations*—will get hurt if I screw up things with China," Phoenix said. "The economy will really melt down if China decides it doesn't want to invest in us anymore."

"Let's worry about that after we get our sailors back," Ann said. "Besides, my economic advisers and the commentators I trust are telling me the economy is doing better than you think. If you want, let me worry about the critics of your economic plan. I listen to dozens of politicians whine and complain about austerity measures, but I also hear thousands of small businessmen cheering about lower taxes and freedom from Washington bureaucracy. Unfortunately, the politicians and the whiners are usually the ones who get the press.

"About Russia and China: they're going to do whatever

they're going to do, and there's precious little we can do about that except keep the lines of communication as open as possible, hope for the best, and prepare for the worst," Ann went on. "It so happens that their economies are on an upswing while ours is in the crapper. That is not going to last very long. Russia's surging economy and foreign policy is based on energy exports and bullying their neighbors into not cooperating with the West—when oil is back to thirty dollars a barrel, Russia runs out of cash. China's surging economy and seemingly stable government is based on cheap exports, a shadow currency and economy, and suppressing dissent. As soon as exports fall, the true market value of China's currency is revealed, and the unemployed and poor agrarian segments of the population start to rise up against the government, China is on the skids."

"You're starting to sound like Herbert," Phoenix said with a wry smile.

"I'm not an analyst, Ken," Ann said. "But I agree with Herbert: unless there's a loose cannon in Beijing or in the Chinese military, I don't think China is a threat to us. I think Beijing will be perfectly happy to wait to see if we collapse on our own instead of choosing to take us on, especially at sea. They can afford to wait, even for fifty years. What's fifty years to a country that's been around for three *thousand* years?"

Phoenix thought for a moment, then shook his head. "I disagree, Ann," he said. "I've felt for several years that something is stirring in Beijing and Moscow. The Chinese invasion of Somalia and the deployment of antiship ballistic missiles all over Southeast Asia confirmed it, and now this suspicious event over the South China Sea reinforces it. Beijing may not want to pick a fight, but I think they'd like to show the world that they are ready to take more of an active role in the world, including militarily. I think if they're waiting for the collapse of the United States, they'd be happy to do whatever they could, short of all-out war, to hasten our demise."

The vice president nodded noncommittally. "No argument from me, Ken," she said. "I'm tired of being surprised by the Russians and Chinese. The Chinese invasion of Somalia, the antisatellite missile strikes from submerged subs, and the quick proliferation of DF-21D missiles all over the Pacific and Indian Oceans were all real eye-openers. We were caught completely flat-footed. Now we lose a surveillance plane near a Chinese carrier battle group, and again we're hunting for answers. It's not a happy place to be." She looked at the president carefully. "What are you thinking about, Ken?" she asked.

"I'm thinking about breaking the damned bank and beefing up the military, especially the Navy and Air Force," Phoenix said. "I can't do anything about the economy more than what we're doing already—doing everything we can to help businesses invest, government standing out of the way so businesses can grow. If we're going to invest in anything in this era of reduced government and reduced taxes, it's defense. I want to rebuild the military. I want to stop the reductions in military spending and show the world that even if the United States is back on its heels in its budget, we will still push ahead with a strong military force."

"You know you're going to get hammered in the press, Ken," the vice president said. "You campaigned on an antispending platform and put together a massive austerity program, promising to balance the budget in eight years—then you want to propose spending more money on defense? That's not going to fly."

"Politically, it'll be a train wreck," Phoenix said. "But no one in the media is looking at what we're looking at in China and Russia: they are surging, and we're lagging. I'm tired of worrying about what we should be doing out there—I want to do something about it."

"But face the facts, Ken—there's *no money. Zero,*" Ann said. "Everyone knows there's no money for new weapons systems, aircraft carriers, next-generation bombers, or space. All that is out the window. Deal with it. We have Armstrong Space Station with antisatellite and antiballistic missile weapons installed, but everyone is thinking it's a huge boondoggle and can't wait for it to reenter and burn up in the atmosphere. No one on Main Street, and especially Congress, will give you money for a high-tech military that might take ten years to put together. No one believes that anymore."

"I'm going to find a way to do it, Ann," Phoenix said determinedly. "I don't know how, but I'll find it. A change in strategy, closing bases, reducing duplication, maybe even doing away with a branch of the service—I'm going to find a way to modernize our military without going back in debt to do it."

"Doing away with a branch of the service?" Ann asked incredulously. "Where in the world did that come from, Ken?"

"I've thought about this for a long time, Ann," Phoenix said. "Each branch of the service spends . . . what, a hundred fifty billion a year? The Navy maybe a little more? But if you combined the duplicated major budget categories of the two services that operate the most aircraft, maybe we could save as much as half that amount, or more."

Ann shook her head in wonderment. "We gotta sit down and talk this over sometime soon, Mr. President—maybe over a glass or two of Scotch," she said. "I think I'm going to need a little alcohol to wrap my head around the monumental challenge of passing a bill through Congress that will pull the plug on the Navy or Air Force. Let's find our sailors and find out what happened to our plane, and then we'll work on doing away with a branch of the service. Good morning, Mr.

President." And she departed, shaking her head with a wry smile.

By the time the president made his way back to the Oval Office, Glenbrook and the chairman of the Joint Chiefs of Staff, Air Force General Timothy Spellings, were waiting for him. Phoenix invited them in, and they sat at the meeting area with cups of coffee. Glenbrook opened a large wall-mounted computer monitor from inside its hidden compartment, and Spellings stood beside it, a wireless presentation remote control in his hand.

"Thanks for getting this information out here so fast, General," the president said. "Please proceed."

"Thank you, Mr. President," the tall, thin four-star general said. He activated the monitor, which showed a map of the North Pacific Ocean region. "This map shows the current deployment of carrier strike groups and Marine amphibious-ready groups in the Pacific, current as of last night—there was no time to bring this morning's updates. As you can see, sir, there's only one carrier group under way in the Seventh Fleet area of operations, the *George Washington,* and one amphibious warfare group, the *Boxer,* which are part of an exercise being conducted in northeastern Australia in the Coral Sea. Of the other four Pacific carriers, only one, the *Reagan,* is available—it is participating in fleet replacement carrier qualifications near San Diego, but it can be retasked fairly quickly. The others are undergoing planned maintenance or complex refueling overhaul. The *Stennis* will be available in about four months; the *Carl Vinson* in about a year, and the *Lincoln* in eighteen months."

"Just two carriers immediately available to cover the entire Pacific?" the president asked, surprised.

"That's been the pattern for the past few years, sir," Glenbrook said. "And Seventh Fleet extends all the way into the Indian Ocean. With budget cutbacks, the carriers spend a lot less time on patrol. Generally, there is just one carrier strike group operating in Seventh and Fifth Fleet areas of responsibility at a time. Extended carrier and amphibious-ready group deployments in Second, Third, Fourth, and Sixth Fleets have all but gone away."

"No wonder China seems to be more aggressive these days—our most potent weapons are all in home port," Phoenix said. "How long would it take to get the two Pacific carrier groups into the South China Sea?"

"The *George Washington* can be on station in just a few days, sir," Spellings replied. "The *Reagan* would take about ten days to arrive after wrapping up its carrier quals. Admiral Fowler wanted me to remind you, sir, that sending the *Reagan* unless it was absolutely necessary would delay working up replacement carrier crews, which would entail longer deployments for crews serving now."

"I'll keep that in mind, General," the president said, "but I'm more concerned about our crewmembers lost in the ocean and finding out what happened to our reconnaissance aircraft. Better get the *Washington* moving up there to assist in the search-and-rescue operations, and warn the *Reagan* personnel that they might be needed. What else do we have?"

"Unfortunately the closest military units aren't well suited to search and rescue, but we'll have a presence and can keep an eye on things until surface units arrive," Spellings went on, reading from a secure tablet computer. "The closest unit we have available is the attack submarine USS *New Hampshire,* on patrol in the southern South China Sea. It can be in the area in about four hours. We can send a Global Hawk from Okinawa and have it on station in about six hours." The RQ-4 Global Hawk was a long-range, high-altitude, long-endurance unmanned surveillance aircraft that could send radar, electro-optical, and infrared sensor images via satellite to bases thousands of miles away. "We also have five long-range bombers and three aerial refueling tankers based at Andersen Air Force Base in Guam that are on thirty-minute alert. They can be over the area in three to four hours."

"Bombers?" Kevich remarked. "Surely you're not thinking of attacking anyone, General? With what are they armed?"

"Day-to-day normal alert: nothing more than chaff and flares for self-defense," Spellings replied. "They have a variety of weapons available, but they are loaded only as the situation dictates. Their real value in this scenario would be as a rapid-reaction forward presence."

"Saber-rattling, General?" Kevich intoned. "I thought we were all beyond that."

"The Chinese have been saber-rattling with their new aircraft carrier all over the South China Sea for months," Glenbrook pointed out. "They've harassed every military or military-related vessel that cruises within two hundred miles of their shoreline."

"I don't think that's a good reason to elevate tensions in the area by sending in bombers," Kevich said. "Armed or not, the bombers are a clear provocation. I would be against sending in the aircraft carriers except if they would participate in the search, rescue, and recovery."

"All the bombers have excellent radar, and the B-52s and B-1 bombers have low-light TV and infrared sensors that can transmit images back here to us," Spellings said. "They wouldn't be there just to saber-rattle, Mr. Secretary."

"Have Pacific Command send a warning notice to Guam, advising the bomber wing of the situation and to stand by in case they're needed," the president said. "But for now, we'll keep them away from the South China Sea. So, how do we proceed with the other assets we have on hand, General?"

"Until the *George Washington* arrives, the surface search-and-rescue task force will be led by the high-endurance Coast Guard cutter *Mohawk,* based in Seattle but on a joint search-and-rescue drill with Taiwanese coast guard vessels in the northern South China Sea near Kaohsiung in southern Taiwan," Spellings went on. "It has a helicopter and an unmanned tilt-rotor aircraft embarked. They can be in the area in about eight hours."

"A Coast Guard cutter? That's the best we have?"

"For a search-and-rescue mission at sea, they're the experts, sir," Spellings said. "We're lucky to have one so close. We could see if there are any commercial vessels in the area, but I don't have direct access to that information. Besides, the Poseidon carried classified equipment and documents, so I think we'd want to keep all civilians and foreigners away, not just the Chinese."

"I'm thinking about the worst-case scenario—our ships tangling with that Chinese aircraft carrier or its escorts," the president said. He thought for a moment; then: "Get the cutter moving to the crash site as well, but find out if there are any Taiwanese, Japanese, or Filipino navy vessels available to assist. Get the sub moving and the Global Hawk airborne, General."

"Yes, sir." Spellings picked up a telephone to issue the orders.

Turning to his national security adviser, the president said, "Bill, I want a detailed analysis of the transmissions—and lack thereof—from that P-8 as soon as possible. The sudden loss of communications indicates some sort of electromagnetic interference—jamming. I want to know if any other ships or aircraft in the area were affected. I also want to know if we have any information that the Chinese are working on any sort of electromagnetic weapons that could have been used on the P-8. I know we'll know more once we recover evidence from the crash site, but I want a list of questions that need to be answered as this thing moves forward."

"Yes, Mr. President." He moved toward another telephone to issue orders, but instead pulled out a vibrating cell phone, looked at the display, and punched in unlock codes for the secure line. "Glenbrook, secure," he spoke. He listened for a few moments. He said, "I'll pass the word. We'll need an order of battle assembled as soon as possible," then hung up.

"What is it, Bill?" Phoenix asked.

"Radio transmissions picked up by commercial vessels in the South China Sea, sir," Glenbrook replied. "Helicopters from the Chinese carrier are headed north toward the suspected crash site, and the carrier itself is also heading north. It appears the Chinese navy is ordering other ships and aircraft out of the area and setting up a search at the crash site."

Battle Staff Room, First Expeditionary Bomb Wing, Andersen Air Force Base, Guam

A Short Time Later

The other staff members were already in the Battle Staff Room when Colonel Warner "Cutlass" Cuthbert entered. "Room, ten-hut," someone in the darkness ordered.

"Take seats," Cuthbert said immediately. "We will suspend military formalities, here and everywhere else on base until the situation is back to normal." He looked at the others seated at the conference table. Three were in green Nomex flight suits; the rest were in desert-gray battle dress uniforms. "Looks like we might have ourselves our first real-world operation, boys and girls. Captain, please proceed."

"Yes, sir," Air Force Captain Alicia Spencer, the wing intelligence officer from Barksdale Air Force Base, Louisiana, responded. She went to the head of the conference table. "Ladies and gentlemen, about ten minutes ago we received an advisory notice from Pacific Air Forces about a situation in the South China Sea. Although the wing has not been issued a warning order, Colonel Cuthbert suggested we respond as if one will be issued soon. We will receive regular updates from PACAF, but we won't be tied into the regular Pacific Command battle network until we are issued a warning order.

"Here is what we know so far: less than an hour ago a U.S. Navy P-8 Poseidon intelligence aircraft went down over the South China Sea. The reason is unknown. Despite requests to remain clear, China's People's Liberation Army Navy has sent helicopters into the crash area, along with their *Zhenyuan* aircraft carrier battle group. One U.S. carrier strike group is en route but it won't be on station for a couple days; there is a second, but it wouldn't be in the area for a week and a half at least. One Coast Guard cutter is nearby and will start the search-and-rescue operation shortly. A Global Hawk and a submarine are en route as well." Spencer nodded to Cuthbert and took her seat.

"That's about it, guys," Cuthbert said. "PACAF says that the White House is afraid that sending bombers would escalate tensions, so we're not going anywhere yet, but I want to be ready. So I requested that we take one BUFF, one Bone, and one Beak, load them with weapons and fuel for what we think we might use if we were alerted, and have them stand by. That'll leave one B-52 and one B-1 unloaded and prepped. I recommended JASSMs all around, with the Bone and the BUFF carrying some Mk-62s." The JASSM, or Joint Air-to-Surface Standoff Missile, was a cruise missile designed to attack heavily defended targets from as far as two hundred miles, well outside most enemy defenses; the Mk-62 was a five-hundred-pound general-purpose bomb fitted with a Quickstrike fuze, turning it into a shallow-water antiship mine. "Not sure if we'll get permission, but that was my recommendation. Thoughts?"

"The South China Sea might be too deep for Mk-62s," said Lieutenant Colonel Bridget "Xena" Dutchman, commander of the Twentieth Expeditionary Bomb Squadron from Barksdale Air Force Base, Louisiana, leading the flight of two B-52H Stratofortress bombers at Andersen. "Depends on where the targets are."

"If we can't use Mk-62s, what else do you suggest, Xena?"

"Harpoons," Dutchman said. The AGM-84 Harpoon was a subsonic air-launched antiship missile with a five-hundred-pound high-explosive penetrating warhead; fired in the direction of enemy ships from as far as sixty miles, it would skim the surface of the ocean, detect a target with its on-board radar, and attack. The Harpoon was much older than the JASSM and had about half the high-explosive punch, but it was still a fearsome weapon against most ships. The B-52 could carry as many as twelve on underwing pylons.

"I'll add that to the order of battle," Cuthbert said. "Anything else?"

"The more JASSMs, the better," said Lieutenant Colonel Juan "Picante" Oroz. Oroz commanded the B-1B Lancer bombers of the Ninth Expeditionary Bomb Squadron from Dyess Air Force Base in Abilene, Texas. "Wish we had the extended-range ones though."

"Maybe we'll get them if this thing escalates," Cuthbert said. He turned to the third lieutenant colonel. "Wishbone? Anything?"

"The loadout sounds good to me, sir," said Lieutenant Colonel Franklin "Wishbone" McBride, commander of the 393rd Expeditionary Bomb Squadron, Barksdale Air Force Base, Louisiana. Since the American Holocaust and the destruction of many of the American bomber bases in the northern half of the country, all the surviving B-52 Stratofortress and B-2 Spirit bombers had been headquartered at Barksdale Air Force Base but frequently dispersed to other air bases, including Andersen and Naval Support Facility Diego Garcia in the Indian Ocean; Wishbone commanded the two B-2A Spirit stealth bombers currently based at Andersen. "When will we find out if we're cleared to load?"

"No idea," Cutlass said, "but unless I miss my guess, it'll be days and days of waiting and not knowing anything, followed by a mad hurried dash to get loaded planes in the air. That's why I'd like to load up at least one bomber from each squadron."

"Can't we call it a munition-loading exercise or something and just do it, sir?" Oroz asked.

"Things are tense enough already at PACAF—I don't want to be playing games with live ordnance," Cutlass said. "We'll play this by the book. I submitted a plan and I've got my crews on the starting blocks—let's see if or when the brass wants to shoot the starter's pistol."

Cutlass again looked at the others around the conference table. Faces were somber—the gravity of the situation was starting to sink in. "Okay, guys and gals, this might be the real thing, so I want you to make sure your crews are situated properly, rested, and completely up to speed," he said. "Like I said, if this happens, I'm betting it's going to be a mad scramble to get planes in the air, and I don't want any avoidable mistakes. When the call comes, let's lean into it and hustle, but let's do it smoothly and professionally. Get ready to do some flying."

FOUR

NORTHERN NEVADA INDUSTRIAL AIRPORT, BATTLE MOUNTAIN, NEVADA

LATER THAT DAY

Late that afternoon, Patrick drove out to his airplane hangar and found Brad inside on a stepladder, wiping bugs off the leading edge of his father's turbine-powered Cessna P210 Centurion's wings. "Hi there, Brad," he called out.

"Hey, Dad," Brad said over his shoulder. He was using a nylon scrubbing pad to remove bugs from a bright metal panel on the leading edge of the wings. This panel had thousands of tiny laser-drilled holes, through which deicing fluid was pumped to keep the wings free of ice in winter—the holes were easily clogged and had to be meticulously cleaned after every flight. "I think I flew through the planet's largest swarm of insects."

"Good Angel Flight West flight?"

"Everything went great." Angel Flight West was an organization that matched up needy medical patients with volunteer pilots to fly them for medical treatment; both Brad and Patrick were command pilots.

"Where did you go?"

"Sacramento Executive," Brad said. "It was a three-leg relay: one pilot flew a mom and her son from Wyoming to Salt Lake City; another flew them to here; and I flew them to Sac Exec. The son was a burn victim."

"No mission assistant?" A mission assistant sometimes came along to help the pilot with the passengers so the pilot could concentrate on flying.

"Not this time. I've flown this family a few times before, so they know the routine."

"Good. Need help?"

"No. Just about done." Patrick waited until Brad finished cleaning the wings; he noted that the windshield, propeller, and stabilizer deicers were already clean. When he was done, Brad put away the stepladder and bagged up the cleaning supplies. "*Finis.*"

"Good. I need to talk with you."

"Sure, Dad." They went over to the desk in the rear corner of the hangar. Brad got a couple bottles of water out of a little refrigerator and handed one to his father. "What's up?"

"I'm really happy with the work you're doing around the airport," Patrick began. "The pilots and techs say the same thing. You're putting in a lot of hours, and you volunteer for lots of overtime. And I'm also happy you're doing all these Angel Flight West missions. I'm sure the patients really appreciate the time you're putting in." He pulled a piece of paper out of a pocket. "But frankly, son, I think you're flying way too much. We can't afford the fuel bill. I hate to say it, son, but it's breaking the bank. The credit card bill is through the roof."

"But it's a charity," Brad said. "Aren't the expenses tax-deductible?"

"They are to a certain extent, son, but we still have to pay the bill, and we just don't have the cash," Patrick said.

"But you run Sky Masters. You're the chief operations officer and a vice president, right?"

"I guess I never explained the situation to you, Brad," Patrick said. "My salary is just enough to pay household expenses every month—that's all. There's no money at the end of the month."

"There's not? Why?"

"Because as CEO part of my job is to make sure the company has money, and every dime past what we need every month is money the company can't use," Patrick explained. "My job is to make sure the company makes money, not me."

"That doesn't sound fair," Brad said. "The company has shareholders, right? *They* make money, don't they?"

"If the company makes money, the shareholders earn dividends and profits when the price of their shares goes up," Patrick said. "*We* are shareholders of the company, you and I. If the company makes enough of a profit, I get a bonus at the end of the year, but most of that is reinvested in the company by purchasing stock or stock options."

"I thought all COOs were rich," Brad said.

"We're not broke, Brad," Patrick said. "But we don't have a lot of spare cash, either. I feel it's important to invest in the company rather than take a big salary. The company directors and shareholders like that, so they're more likely to keep me around."

"'Keep you around'?" Brad repeated, the astonishment evident in his voice. "Dad, you're *Patrick McLanahan*. You're a retired three-star Air Force general. You've commanded bombing missions all over the world and even in space. They're lucky to have you. Why would they even consider not having you as part of the company?"

"Because business is business, Brad," Patrick said. "I get

what you're saying about me, son—and thank you for saying it—and I think the company president and chairman of the board of directors would agree with you, but at the end of the day it really doesn't matter who I am if I'm not doing everything I can to help the company make a profit. If I wasn't doing the job and doing everything possible to make them money, they would politely but firmly show me the door. They might even be nice enough to hold it open for me so it didn't bang my ass as I depart."

Brad just shook his head. "I don't get it," he said. "It's all about making money? You do all this stuff, come up with all these ideas, put in all these long hours, and end the month with *zero* in the bank . . . just to make *other* people rich? It's not right. It's not fair."

"Welcome to the wonderful world of capitalism, son," Patrick said with a smile. Brad wasn't smiling—in fact, he appeared very disillusioned, almost angry. Patrick touched his son on the shoulder to get his attention. "But let's get a few things clear first. The *company's* objective is to make a profit. My *job* is to see to it that I do everything possible to achieve the company's objective. But *my* objective is not to make money for Sky Masters. *My* objective is to raise a happy and well-adjusted son and to produce high-tech systems to help defend the United States of America. The company has the resources to help me meet *my* objective—if it didn't, I wouldn't be here.

"The deal is simple, Brad: I use what skills I have to help the company meet its objective—earn a profit—and the company contributes its resources to help me meet *my* objective—build stuff to help defend the nation," Patrick went on. "There's a simple agreement between the company and me: as long as we're meeting our mutual objectives, we stay together. If either of us feels our objectives aren't being met, we're done, and it's over. We have no written contract. We signed this agreement with nothing more than a handshake. The instant either one of us feels we're not meeting our objectives, the deal is over, and we part ways."

"You mean . . . you could get fired *tomorrow*?" Brad asked incredulously. "They could ask you to leave, *anytime,* and we'd *have* to go?"

"Exactly," Patrick said. Brad shook his head in utter disbelief. "You see why doing everything possible to keep money in the company is so important?" Patrick asked. "It has nothing to do with fairness. It has nothing to do with what you or I feel I *deserve* or might be entitled to. It's not personal. It's the world of capitalism. I think they'd still like and respect me . . . but yes, they'd fire me in a heartbeat if I didn't make them money. But the reverse is true too: if they didn't allow me to build things that I feel helps to defend the United States, I'd go somewhere else that would, and they couldn't stop me."

"It still seems like you're getting the raw end of the deal, Dad, but I think I see what you're saying," Brad said. He took the credit card bill from his father. "I guess I didn't realize how much I was spending on Jet-A," he said. "I'll cut back on the flying." He looked at his father. "If we have no money at the end of the month, how do you pay the credit card bill?"

"I use my Air Force retirement, and if necessary I sell some company stock," Patrick said.

Brad looked embarrassed. "I . . . I'm sorry, Dad, but I didn't realize you were doing that," he said. "I'll kick in for more of the fuel bill, and I'll cut back on the missions."

"A little bit less would be good," Patrick said. "I want you to stay current and proficient, but if you can do that with, say, one or two missions a month rather than three or four, that would help."

"Sure, Dad."

"I'll still help with the fuel bill, don't worry, but a little

smaller grand total on the credit card bill would be nice."
Patrick leaned forward in his chair. "This is a good time to
talk about your plans for the future," he said. "I gave you some
time after you got back from the Academy to think about it.
I'm happy you've stayed busy and productive and haven't been
sitting around idle, but what do you have in mind for what's
next?"

Brad thought for a long moment, then shrugged. "I don't
know, Dad," he said. "I like working on the flight line, and I
need to save up some cash for college, so I hadn't really thought
about it. I'm just getting into the swing of working the flight
line, and I enjoy doing the Angel Flight West missions. That
was keeping me plenty busy."

"I have been thinking about it, and I have some ideas,"
Patrick said. "I do have a little money in a college fund. Frankly,
when you got the nomination to the Academy from President
Phoenix, I stopped contributing to your college fund, so there's
not as much as I would have wanted in there, but there's
enough for four years of in-state tuition at the University of
Nevada–Reno and living in the dorms—no cars, apartments,
restaurants, or spring breaks in the Bahamas."

"Thank you, Dad," Brad said, a bright smile on his face.
"That's awesome. I was afraid I'd have to wait years to go to
college." His smile dimmed. "But I don't know what I want to
study, and classes start up in just a few weeks. I haven't even
been accepted yet."

"You could go to the community college here in town and
knock out some first-year prerequisite courses while you apply
to UNR," Patrick suggested. "Or, I had another thought."

"Not college?"

"I think you would need advanced schooling eventually,
but there's nothing that says you need to get it right out of
high school," Patrick said. "Here's my idea: Colonel Tom

Hoffman runs a company called Warbirds Forever at Stead Airport north of Reno. It's an aircraft repair shop, and he imports and restores all sorts of planes, but he also runs a flight school where he trains his clients in how to fly the exotic planes they buy. He trains pilots in all sorts of planes: foreign jets, restored warbirds, bizjets, commercial planes, experimentals, everything. He's setting up a training program for us to train pilots to fly the XB-1 Excalibur and any of the other planes we might be refurbishing, like the FB-111 Aardvarks. It's an accredited flight school, and you can use your college funds there. You can get a commercial pilot's certificate, a flight instructor license, and get type ratings in some of the hottest jets in the world. Every imaginable plane flies in and out of that place. If you wanted, you could even get an Airframe and Powerplant mechanic and Inspector's Authorization license there."

"Go to flight school?" Brad exclaimed. "Sounds great! I could keep on flying!"

"And with added ratings and experience in jets, you might be able to get a flying job, maybe even right there with Warbirds Forever," Patrick went on. "If you saved up your money, went to college, got enough flying hours, and got a business or engineering degree along with an airline transport pilot certificate, maybe you'd be hired by Sky Masters."

"'Maybe' get hired?" Brad asked. "If you're the COO, couldn't you just get me in?"

"It doesn't work that way," Patrick said. "You have to compete like all the other applicants—and in this economic climate, I get three hundred applicants for every position I advertise."

"*Three hundred?*" Brad exclaimed.

"I'm not exaggerating one bit," Patrick said. "I broke my own rules and interceded with Personnel and Dr. Kaddiri, the company president, just to get you a job parking airplanes and sweeping floors." Dr. Helen Kaddiri was the longtime president of Sky Masters. "But along with having lots of flying experience in different machines, perhaps that mechanic's license and a degree in business or engineering, you'd have a special advantage: everyone around here *knowing you* and knowing your work. That's a big plus: it's usually not just what you know or who you know, but who knows *you*."

Brad thought about it for a moment, then nodded. "It sounds great, Dad," he said. "I still want to look into college, maybe go visit UNR, but Warbirds Forever sounds very cool." "I've already spoken with Colonel Hoffman, and he can get you started at any time," Patrick said. "We'll check out UNR and any other college you might be interested in. Give me your decision as soon as possible." He paused, then said, "There are a few . . . issues."

"Like what, Dad?"

"First of all, there's not enough money in the college fund to get you all the way to an ATP," Patrick said. "Colonel Hoffman is giving us a big break on the cost of the course because he's getting a lot of work from Sky Masters, but you need fifteen hundred hours of flying time, and that's going to take a few years unless you get hired by an airline. But you can get type ratings in a lot of jets, and if you do a lot of flying and maybe some ferrying or instructing, you can build the hours quickly. But there's not a lot of money to pay for training in a wide variety of planes either. So you'll have to work for Colonel Hoffman as well as be a student."

Brad shrugged. "That sounds okay with me. Doing what?"

"Whatever Colonel Hoffman tells you to do," Patrick said. "I imagine it'll be a lot of the stuff you do around here—parking planes, assisting the techs, being a gofer, odd jobs, sweeping floors, fueling planes. After you get your commercial certificate, you could do flying chores for his business, like picking up other students, picking up parts, and so on. If you got your instructor's license, you'd build hours flying students and build your hours even faster. You'll get paid a regular salary based on your hours, but you'll only receive about half the money—the rest will go toward reimbursing Warbirds Forever for your flying training."

"That's cool."

"But remember, you'll also be a full-time aviation student as well as a full-time worker," Patrick warned him. "That means a regular job on top of a lot of studying and flying."

"I can do it," Brad said. "I had part-time jobs on top of football and high school. No sweat."

"I think there will be a lot of sweat, son."

"I can handle it, Dad. What other issues?"

"Warbirds Forever is an accredited school, but it doesn't have dorms—most of Colonel Hoffman's flight school clients are pretty wealthy and stay in hotels or apartments and rent cars, and there's no money for any of that for you," Patrick said. "He also doesn't have dining halls, gyms, or recreation facilities."

"So what am I supposed to do?"

"Colonel Hoffman has offered to let you bunk in a storeroom in one of his hangars, rent free," Patrick said. "I have no idea what it's like. I'm sure you won't have TV or much of anything else in your room, but I don't think you'll have much time for TV either."

Brad was a little more reserved this time, but after a few moments, he still nodded. "I can handle it," he said. "Just a few weeks ago I was crawling in mud over my head at Second Beast—I think I can live in a storeroom for a little while."

"That's the spirit," Patrick said.

"Anything else?"

"One more thing." Patrick paused for a moment, then said: "This is strictly between you and me, okay?"

Brad narrowed his eyes in concern, but nodded. "Sure, Dad. What?"

"Colonel Hoffman can be . . . a real Doctor Jekyll–Mister Hyde character sometimes," Patrick said. "He's a good guy and a great pilot and instructor, but if he thinks you're not working hard enough, he'll turn on you like a rabid werewolf. You do things his way, or *else*. You said you had some tough cadet instructors at the Air Force Academy? Tom Hoffman will be a hundred times tougher. He demands excellence in everything he gets involved with. You will train to nothing less than ATP flight standards the moment you step into any one of his planes, from a piston single to a twin jet. The minimum passing score on all his written tests is *ninety percent,* and on the emergency procedures bold-print items and reference speeds that have to be committed to memory his passing score is *one hundred* percent. Three failed written or flight test is cause for dismissal. The only reason he still works with me and lets me fly the jets is that I'm the boss and I pay the bills—he would have dismissed me from flying the Excaliburs months ago because I couldn't hand-fly it within fifty feet of an assigned altitude. His cadres of instructors are just as tough." Brad was silent again, and Patrick even thought he saw his son swallow nervously. "But we all work with him almost on a daily basis, and no one has tried to strangle the other, so we know it can work. You just do what you've been doing around here: work hard, keep your mouth shut and your ears open, pitch in, and strive for perfection."

Foreign Minister Tang Ji entered President Zhou Qiang's office to find the chief of the general staff of the People's Liberation Army, *Shàng Jiàng* (Colonel General) Zu Kai, already waiting on him. Tang, a longtime foreign affairs official who had served three previous administrations, knew very well how great General Zu's influence was with the president, and he was dismayed but not surprised to see him here before he was allowed to brief and speak with the president first. The feeling he immediately had was that the next decision had already been made. "Good evening, Comrade President, General," he said, bowing to Zhou.

"You spoke with the American secretary of state, Kevich, Comrade Tang?" Zhou asked without preamble or without offering his foreign minister a seat.

"Yes, Comrade President," Tang said, still standing. "The Americans are requesting that we not interfere with search-and-rescue operations for their surveillance plane in the South Sea, what they call the South China Sea."

"I know what they call it, Tang," Zhou spat. A longtime Chinese Communist Party Central Committee member and former president of a shipping company in Shanghai, Zhou Qiang was well educated in business but even more familiar with down-and-dirty Party politics. He wore dark business suits, Western-style shoes shined to a high polish, and preferred silk ties, gold wristwatches, and French cigarettes. He kept his hair dyed black despite being well over sixty years of age, and he even invested in contact lenses to avoid wearing glasses.

"They would *like* to call it the 'American Ignores China Once Again Sea.'" General Zu smiled at the remark. "You told Kevich that movement of Chinese forces in the South Sea is not subject to any foreign powers' authority, yes?"

"I told Mr. Kevich that I would pass along his request to my superiors and return with their reply," Tang said. "Kevich thanked me, reminded me that the lost aircraft contained classified information important to American national security, and asked if I understood the importance of cooperation in this matter. Kevich said that a ship or aircraft lost due to unknown circumstances is a highly grave and important matter for any nation and since America had search forces in the area that we should understand and respect their wishes."

"He said all that, did he?" Zhou asked acidly. "They send a spy plane to snoop on us over the South Sea, which they know to be extremely vital to our national security and closely guarded by China, and then we should be cooperative when their spy plane goes down? Why were they not so cooperative when we ordered them not to continue eavesdropping over China's eastern coast?"

"I told you, sir, the Americans do not care about cooperation or mutual respect—they want us to heel and do as ordered," General Zu said. "No matter if they are a few mere hundred kilometers from our soil, they continue to order China around. Even now, they are sending an aircraft carrier battle group northward, and we believe they will send a second one soon."

"They lost an important aircraft and a valuable crew, General," Tang said. Tang appeared to be Zu's complete opposite: he was tall and thin, almost fragile-looking. "They are understandably concerned. I know Secretary Kevich very well, and I believe him to be sincere, straightforward, and unthreatening. As is customary in maritime accidents involving foreign powers, China should offer assistance before approaching the crash site."

"Is that so, Tang?" President Zhou asked. "You do not seem to be too offended that the Americans freely send their spy planes, ships, and submarines near our shores day after day. We lose more and more control over our own affairs every day. For all we know, the Americans staged this entire episode simply to give themselves justification to move their warships into the South Sea and harass our commercial shipping and monitor our military activities!"

"Down their own aircraft and kill their own soldiers?" Tang asked, disbelief thick in his voice. He glanced at Zu, who was watching Tang closely. "That is not credible, Comrade."

"How do we know it was a spy plane?" Zhou asked. "General Zu says the Americans build their spy planes from civilian airliners and purposely do not use military markings on them so they cannot be differentiated from unarmed civilian planes."

"I do not know about such things," Tang said. "If it is true, we should condemn such practices in the strongest possible terms. But again, sir, why would the Americans bring down one of their own planes and kill their own sailors? They are free to send their warships through the South Sea at any . . ."

"*That* is the attitude I want terminated here, Comrade Tang, *right now* and *forever*!" Zhou interjected, jabbing a finger at Tang and then angrily rising to his feet. "The South Sea belongs to *China,* do you understand? It is not an international body of water that any nation, friend or foe, can traverse on a whim! Free navigation of the South Sea is possible only because China allows it!"

"Excuse me, Comrade President, but that is simply not the case," Tang said. "Seven other nations have borders on the South Sea. Almost half the world's shipping transits the South Sea every year. No nation can claim ownership of the South Sea."

"There is over a thousand years of historical fact and scores of international agreements to back up China's legitimate claims,"

Zhou said. "Most of the countries that claim parts or islands in the South Sea did not even *exist* a thousand years ago—how can they claim ownership of something when they were not even there? And the Americans have absolutely *no* claim to expect free navigation through the South Sea, especially by spy planes, submarines armed with nuclear weapons, and warships carrying cruise missiles that can devastate our country from long distance."

"Sir . . ."

"Tang, I am not saying China wishes to prevent any *friendly* nation from transiting the South Sea," Zhou said. "But if any nation seeks to threaten China in any way via the South Sea, militarily or economically, we *will* take action." He turned directly to Tang. "Kevich wants a reply from me, does he?" he snapped. "Tell him this: We may not have the military might of America—yet—but we will not be frightened away from our ancestral territories. You consider the South Sea international waters and free to do whatever you wish? I am telling you, America is wrong. The South Sea belongs to China—it has for millennia, and it always will.

"China wants nothing but peaceful commerce on the high seas and unfettered access to all the world's oceans and ports," Zhou went on. "We shall continue to allow free transit of the South Sea to all peaceful commerce. But warships and spy planes are another matter entirely. You fly your spy planes and sail your warships through our territory at your own peril. China will employ whatever weapons systems we feel necessary to match or exceed the military might of any interloping foreign power. That is all, Comrade Tang." Tang bowed, keeping his eyes averted, and departed the president's office.

"It is about time someone utters those words and takes that arrogant bastard Tang down a peg, Comrade Zhou," General Zu said after Tang had departed.

"The bureaucrats and foreign industrialists are getting drunk on foreign money and the power they can buy with it, Colonel General Zu," Zhou said angrily, finding a cigarette and lighting up. "And the Communist Party Central Committee and the People's Committee are doing nothing to rein in these fat cats. The foreign industrialists, bankers, and the bureaucrats who support them want nothing more than accommodation with a resurgent American military presence in the Pacific so they can keep on churning out goods and making themselves rich. The industrialists do not want to confront the Americans. They value their balance of trade figures and profits over sovereignty, and they forget basic Communist ideals. The Party is confused about what to do—side with the industrialists who are stripping China of its sovereignty in the name of profit, or repel the outsiders."

"Then nationalize the foreign companies and banks and make the Party toe the line, Comrade President," Zu said. "You have the power to do so. The military will stand beside you. You have shown your commitment to a strong air force and blue-water navy, and the general staff and corps commanders agree with you that we need to get rid of this rampant capitalism and return to our revolutionary roots before yet another generation is corrupted."

President Zhou took a deep drag of his cigarette and stared off into space. "It is not that simple, Comrade General," he said. "The people want jobs, and they are moving more and more to the east where the jobs are. If we do not have jobs, the peasants will rise up against the government. The industrialists guarantee to the bureaucrats that the jobs will be there. The Party committees in each province get payouts in exchange for more factories. It is the infection of capitalism, General."

"Then take command of the situation, Comrade President," Zu said. "The Party and the military have always been successful in controlling both the countryside and the cities by working together. We can retake control of the people and our basic Communist tenets by removing all the corrupt bureaucrats and nationalizing the foreign companies and banks. Take the next step, sir—the military will stand with you, I guarantee it."

"Tread carefully here, General," Zhou said. "If foreign investment dries up, the economy could collapse."

"The world wants Chinese labor, they want us to buy their raw materials, and they want us to supply inexpensive goods from our factories," Zu said. "We will still supply all those things . . . except the Party should control how our resources are managed, not the foreigners and the greedy bureaucrats."

Zhou nodded, staring into nothingness. "Thank you for your candor and insights, Comrade General," he said finally. "It is good to know others share my concerns about the direction our country is heading." He paused again, then asked: "Is there any evidence about what happened to that American patrol plane, General?"

"No, sir," Zu lied. "The P-8 Poseidon is a relatively new system, although the aircraft itself, based on a popular commercial airliner, is very reliable. They chose to mount a great deal of new equipment in a smaller aircraft than the previous P-3 Orion. I would suspect a massive electrical fault crippled the aircraft."

"I am not inclined to pull our own search helicopters away from the area," Zhou said. "I think it is important for China to show a large and dedicated presence when major incidents like this happen in the South Sea. We should offer full and complete assistance in conducting a search and rescue."

"I agree completely, sir," Zu said. "The intelligence value of this incident must not be overlooked. America chose to take the risk by flying one of its spy planes close to our warships, and it lost. We owe it to ourselves to gather as much intelligence information as we can before the American Navy pushes us aside, which they can and will do. If we can recover the fuselage intact, we could gather a great deal of information about the Americans' latest signals-gathering systems. That is the reason they want us out of there, sir, not because they are afraid of a collision. We should make all efforts to gather as much of the wreckage as possible before the Americans move an aircraft carrier battle group in position."

"Then that is how we shall have it, Comrade General," Zhou said. "I do not want a shooting war, but I will not be pushed around by the American secretary of state. Recover as much as you can before the American aircraft carrier arrives. Avoid hostilities unless your forces must defend themselves. Withdraw your forces after the American warships arrive."

"Yes, sir," Zu said. He saluted and departed.

Zu was met by his deputy chief of staff, Major General Sun Ji. Both men said nothing until they were back in Zu's staff car and were on their way to army headquarters, then Sun spoke: "Sir, we received yet another message from the American naval attaché." He handed over a message form. "They are asking us to withdraw our search helicopters from the crash site. They are sending a Coast Guard vessel with its helicopters to start the search, and they fear a collision."

"Foreign Minister Tang spoke with the American secretary of state, stating the same thing," Zu said. "Zhou authorized us to proceed with our own search until the American searchers arrive, and then back off."

"That will be in just a few hours, sir," Sun said. "An American Coast Guard aircraft is already approaching the area, and they have a Global Hawk aircraft overhead. The Coast Guard vessel will be on station in a few hours."

"I want to talk with Admiral Zhen." General Sun activated

the car's on-board secure satellite telephone, waited for a secure connection and a reply, then handed the receiver to Zu.

"Admiral Zhen here, sir," *Hai Jun Zhong Jiang* (Vice Admiral) Zhen Peng, commander of the South Sea Fleet based in Zhanjiang, Guangdong Province, responded.

"Status of the search."

"We have collected a few artifacts, sir, and a few items such as antennae that may have some intelligence or technology value," Zhen said. "Nothing yet of any personnel, the fuselage, or the engines."

"I want to delay the Americans finding out about Silent Thunder or the air attack on the P-8 patrol plane as long as possible," Zu said. "Increase the number of search helicopters."

"Yes, sir. The *Zhenyuan* reports that the American Coast Guard cutter has dispatched search aircraft as well, and that they have a Global Hawk surveillance aircraft overhead. Request permission to use Silent Thunder against them."

General Zu was silent a moment, then said, "You may use Silent Thunder against the cutter's search aircraft only."

"Understood, sir."

Zu passed the phone back to Sun. "A wise precaution, sir," Sun said. "Knocking a helicopter down is one thing, but knocking down a Global Hawk would certainly invite added scrutiny."

"President Zhou is weak and indecisive, but in this case he is probably correct: we can overstep ourselves if too much attention is directed toward our activities in the South Sea," Zu said. "I want just enough activity for the Americans, Japanese, Taiwanese, Filipinos, and Australians to wonder what is going on, maybe even become a bit fearful, but not enough to elicit a response. I want the Americans to be thinking twice before parking their aircraft carrier battle group in the South Sea."

"The Eagle Eye will be on station in about ten minutes, sir," Lieutenant Commander Edward Fells, the tactical officer aboard the United States Coast Guard cutter *Mohawk*, announced. The cutter's skipper, Commander Douglas Sheridan, had just entered the tactical action center to observe first contact.

"Any hits yet, Ed?" Sheridan asked.

"Negative, sir," Fells said. The Eagle Eye was a long-range tilt-rotor unmanned aerial vehicle that carried surface-search radar and infrared cameras to conduct searches from very long range until the cutter got within range of its HH-60M Jayhawk search-and-rescue helicopter and its crew of rescue swimmers. "A few more minutes and we should start picking up debris, if our estimates of where the crash occurred are correct."

Sheridan studied the large tactical display in the center of the room. The tactical display merged sensor data from a variety of sources into one map. The main sensor shown on the display was from an RQ-4 Global Hawk unmanned aircraft that had arrived on station over the crash site just a couple hours earlier. "Those Chinese ships still heading toward the crash site?" he asked.

"Yes, sir," Fells said. "The carrier *Zhenyuan* is already within fixed-wing aircraft range, and the Global Hawk has detected at least three helicopters dispatched to the crash area."

"When will we be within radar range?" The high-endurance cutter—in essence a small frigate, but tasked for search-and-rescue and patrol instead of antiair or antisubmarine warfare—was equipped with the TRS-3D radar, a digital air-and-surface search radar system.

"We'll be at max aircraft search range in forty minutes," Fells replied. The Global Hawk accomplished surface search operations very well but had limited air search capabilities. The Global Hawk's infrared and electro-optical sensors could detect slow-moving or hovering helicopters, but they were only hit-or-miss with faster-moving airborne targets—they needed the *Mohawk*'s radar to map out the air situation in the crash area. "Optimum air search range will be in about ninety minutes."

"Damn," Sheridan muttered. "That Chinese carrier could have fighters covering those helicopters."

"Eagle Eye has radar contact!" one of the sensor technicians shouted. "Large surface radar return, not moving, just north of the suspected crash area."

"Maybe the Chinese will keep on searching in the wrong spot," Sheridan said. "Mark the return and continue to the original search area. I don't want the Chinese to think we found anything. We got a visual image of that contact?"

"Stand by, sir," the tech said. A few moments later, one of the side monitors in the tactical action room changed. It showed a large piece of what was definitely an airliner-sized fuselage. Several other objects could be seen floating in the ocean near the wreck.

"Jesus," Sheridan breathed. "Those look like bodies."

"Eagle Eye will lose contact in sixty seconds, sir," the technician said.

"When can we launch the Jayhawk, Ed?" Sheridan asked.

"We're at extreme range of the -60, sir, even with the external fuel tanks," Fells replied. The HH-60 Jayhawk was the Coast Guard's version of the Army Blackhawk helicopter, optimized for long-range search and rescue at sea. "They would have zero time on station when they reached the crash site."

Sheridan thought for a moment, then asked, "That's with standard fuel reserves, correct?"

Fells looked at his commanding officer. He knew perfectly well what the rules said—what was the skipper thinking? "Sir?"

"It'll take ten minutes to launch the Jayhawk—that's ten minutes on station," Sheridan said. "We can push the normal fuel reserve times a bit because it's an emergency and the weather is decent."

"Sir, the weather isn't a factor when making a decision about launching a helo for a search-and-rescue or recovery," Fells said. "Fuel is life. A million things can go wrong—that's why reserves were built into the program."

"You don't need to lecture me on procedures, Ed," Sheridan said irritably. "I'm more concerned about bringing Americans home than rules and regulations." He paused and went on, "Launch the Jayhawk. I want at least one American or a piece of that aircraft recovered." He picked up a phone that was tied directly to the bridge. "Officer of the Deck, this is the captain. Max forward speed for helo operations, then push it up to flank speed after the helo is away."

"Max forward for helo ops, then flank after the helo is away, aye, sir."

It was a tense several minutes as the U.S. Coast Guard Jayhawk helicopter was preflighted and launched, with two pilots, a rescue hoist operator, and a rescue swimmer aboard. Sheridan watched the launch, then headed forward and strode onto the *Mohawk*'s bridge a few minutes later. "Officer of the Deck, I've got the con," he announced.

"Aye, sir, Captain has the con," the officer of the deck repeated. "We are at flank speed, heading two-zero-zero, ops normal."

"Very good," Sheridan responded. "Radio Pacific Fleet and Coast Guard Pacific Area that we are proceeding at flank speed to suspected Poseidon crash site. Chinese helicopters are in the vicinity." He picked up the shipwide intercom. "All hands, this is the captain. We are heading toward the estimated crash site of the Navy patrol plane. We have already sent the Eagle Eye and Jayhawk out ahead. The Chinese already have helicopters searching the crash site. They've been asked to leave the area but have not responded.

"We still don't know why that patrol plane went down, but we should assume the worst and that China had something to do with it," Sheridan went on. "There are Chinese air and surface forces in the area, and we can anticipate that they will be shadowing us. Hopefully, that's all they do. We also know that they have submarines, maritime bombers, and perhaps long-range antiship cruise and ballistic missiles. We know China considers control of the South China Sea as in its vital national interests, and they have been increasingly aggressive against all foreign military activities there. If the loss of that patrol plane was because China is beginning to actively defend the South China Sea, then we could be cruising into trouble. But an American plane and its crew are down, and our job is to search for any survivors until some heavier hardware shows up. Stay on your toes. I'll keep you advised of the situation. Captain out."

"Bridge, Tactical, the Eagle Eye has reached the original search area," Lieutenant Commander Fells reported a few minutes later. "Numerous radar contacts reported."

"Pick out the largest ones and have it orbit over it," Sheridan said. "I want lots of pictures. What's the sea state?"

"Two to four feet, sir."

That was good news—if they put a swimmer in the water, the sea shouldn't be a major factor. "How long until the Jayhawk is on station on that first Eagle Eye contact?"

"Fifty-five minutes, sir. Time on station will be less than twenty minutes."

"How long can the Eagle Eye stay on station?"

"Another two hours, sir."

"And how long before we're within air search radar contact?"

"About an hour, sir."

Nothing left to do but sweat it out, Sheridan thought. Hopefully, if the Chinese had helicopters and fighters airborne, they'd shadow the Eagle Eye in the original search area and ignore the Jayhawk farther north. They'd find out soon enough.

Several minutes later: "Bridge, Tactical, Global Hawk has a visual on two unidentified helicopters in the original search area. They appear to be hovering."

"Damn," Sheridan muttered. He had nothing to work with to scare the Chinese away from the search box, nothing to threaten or intimidate anyone . . . except the full force and power of the United States of America, even if it was only broadcast on a radio frequency by a lowly Coast Guard cutter. "Have Comm send on all civil, commercial, and military frequencies: advise all parties that the U.S. Coast Guard is conducting search-and-rescue operations and to stay well clear of the search box. Transmit coordinates of the box. Advise that it is illegal to interfere with an active search-and-rescue operation on the high seas. Send in English and Chinese, and make it damned loud and *strict*. Then advise Pacific Fleet and Coast Guard Pacific Area that suspected Chinese helicopters are hovering in the search area and may be recovering artifacts from the crash. Tactical, are you sending images to Fleet and Area?"

"Affirmative, sir." A few minutes later: "Sir, we have video from the Eagle Eye of Chinese helicopters hoisting objects out of the water."

"You're positive they're Chinese helicopters?"

"Positive, sir. Kamov-28 Helix helicopters, red, white,

and blue People's Liberation Army Navy banner on the aft fuselage," Fells said. "Good clear images from Eagle Eye. Positive ID."

The Ka-28s were Russian-made helicopters, transferred when China purchased Russian destroyers, but the People's Liberation Army Navy banner on the side was unmistakable. "Very well," Sheridan said. "Send images to Fleet and Area and request instructions." He hated that phrase "request instructions"—he very much preferred to come up with a plan of action himself and ask for permission to carry it out—but he had no viable options whatsoever until he was closer to the search box. Even then, he had very few options against an armed Chinese warship. "Where's that Chinese carrier?"

"Approaching the southern search box now, sir," Fells responded. "Well within fixed- and rotary-wing range."

"Where's our closest aircraft carrier?"

"The *George Washington* is a couple days away, sir," Fells said. "Well out of fixed-wing range for at least eighteen hours."

"I've got *no* air cover *anywhere* in this entire freakin' area for eighteen hours?" Sheridan exploded. "We've got the most powerful military force in the entire freakin' world, and a lone Coast Guard cutter is completely alone and helpless in the South China Sea against a Chinese aircraft carrier? The United States of America is actually *outnumbered* in the South China Sea?" Sheridan ran a hand across his face, trying unsuccessfully to wipe away the frustration—and yes, the *fear*—he was feeling right now. "Comm, this is the captain, I want you to send a message directly to the Pentagon: tell them to get me some long-range persistent air support out here, and do it *now*, or you might as well pull me the hell out of here, because I can't do shit with the assets I have. Send it *now,* and send it verbatim."

"Say again that last, sir?"

"I repeat, tell the Pentagon I need some heavy long-range

air support out here, or I recommend we withdraw from the South China Sea," Sheridan said. "I'm not risking the lives of three hundred sailors on my vessel because we don't want to piss off the locals. Send it in the clear and *verbatim*. I'm going to lose tactical control of this area because I don't have long-range control, and that is completely unacceptable. Give me long-range air and sea lane control, or pull me out, because I can't do *squat* right now. And keep on warning aircraft to stay out of the area."

It seemed like an eternity, but soon: "Bridge, Tactical, air search contact on the Jayhawk entering the northern search area."

"Any other aircraft in the area, Tactical?"

"Negative, Bridge."

So far so good. Sheridan picked up a telephone receiver and hit a channel button. "Mohawk Zero One, this is Mohawk One. How copy?"

"Loud and clear, sir," the pilot of the Jayhawk, Lieutenant Ed Coffey, reported.

"Any surface contacts, Ed?"

"Affirmative, sir," Coffey replied. "Off our nose, about ten miles, very large surface radar return. Probably too big for us to pick up."

"Survivors or victims are our first priority, Ed, but when you start getting close to bingo fuel, pick up whatever you think you can snag."

"Roger, Mohawk One."

"No traffic in your vicinity," Sheridan said, "but you can expect some company when they start seeing you circle and hover. We'll keep an eye out for you."

"Roger."

FIVE

"Sir, our search helicopter is reporting a medium-sized helicopter approaching the crash site near our helicopters," the controller reported aloud. "The pilot reports that it appears unmanned."

"Acknowledged," Vice Admiral Zhen Peng said curtly, stubbing out his cigarette. He was at the commander's seat in his battle staff room at fleet headquarters on Hainan Island in eastern China, watching an electronic chart of the South China Sea. Thin, with a long angular face, longish jet-black hair, small dark eyes, and jutting cheekbones, Zhen at age sixty appeared to be no older than forty. He had risen quickly through the ranks after graduating from the naval academy in Beijing thirty-five years earlier, serving aboard mostly heavier warships before being given his stars and assigned to the South Sea fleet.

An unmanned helicopter, aboard a simple patrol craft? That was most interesting, Zhen thought. While he struggled every day to find and train helicopter pilots to fly off the aircraft carrier's big deck—let alone do the much more difficult task of landing on a destroyer's or frigate's deck—the Americans were flying *unmanned* patrol helicopters. China needed to start doing that sort of thing right away. It was yet another reminder of the awesome military might of the United States, particularly its navy. Imagine what sort of weaponry a big-deck ship had if a lowly patrol boat embarked an unmanned patrol aircraft! Even though China was pouring trillions of *yuan* every year into new weapons systems, it would probably take an entire generation or two to build a force that could match the United States of America.

Which was another reminder of why China could not and should not try to do so, Zhen thought. China needed to think smarter and not just toss money at a losing proposition like trying to match America ship for ship, like the Soviet Union tried to do during the Cold War. It ended up bankrupting the country and left America as the world's only superpower. China could follow the same path if it was not smarter.

There were other ways of moving the unmovable . . . *always* other ways.

"Where is the *Zhenyuan*?" Zhen asked.

"Forty kilometers south of the search helicopters, sir," the controller responded.

"Tell Captain Zhang of the *Zhenyuan* to see to it that the American helicopter does not collide with our helicopters," Zhen said.

"Captain Zhang reports that the American aircraft is very small, and it does not have a transponder that we can interrogate, sir," the controller said after he made the radio call and received a reply. "He says the radar return is small and intermittent and that separation may not be possible."

"Tell him I do not want excuses," Zhen snapped. After a moment, he said, "The American helicopter is posing a serious hazard to our search helicopters. It is unmanned, does not have a transponder, it is beyond radar coverage of its mothership, and cannot look for nearby aircraft. This is clearly unsafe and is not permitted under maritime law." He picked up a telephone, selected a channel, and waited for the secure satellite link to activate. "Captain Zhang."

"I read you, sir," Zhang, the captain of the aircraft carrier *Zhenyuan* responded.

"Deploy *Wúsheng Léitíng* against the unmanned helicopter in the search area," Zhen ordered.

There was a slight pause on the other end; Zhen couldn't be sure through the squeaks and pops of the secure satellite link, but it sounded as if Zhang was muttering something. It might be time for that old bastard to be replaced, he thought— how dare he question an order? Finally: "Deploy *Wúsheng Léitíng* against the umanned aircraft in the search area, yes, sir. Acknowledged." Zhen hung up.

A few minutes later: "Sir, our search helicopters are withdrawing from the area," the controller reported.

"Maintain surveillance," Zhen said. "I want to know what that unmanned helicopter does."

Yes, Zhen thought, there were many, many ways to move the unmovable.

"Bridge, Tactical," Fells radioed, "Mohawk Zero-One reports he is retrieving what appears to be a victim. He will RTB immediately after hoist is completed."

"Thank God they found one," Sheridan muttered to himself. "Very well," he replied. "Is the airspace still all clear?"

"Affirmative, sir. We can see into the original southern search box, and we have radar contact with the Eagle Eye. It appears the Chinese helicopters have departed the area."

"Excellent," Sheridan said. He was glad they departed, but he immediately became suspicious. Why would aircraft from an aircraft carrier pay any attention to orders from a foreigner aboard a ship a fraction of its size, not even a true warship? "Comm, Bridge, any response from our hails?"

"None from the Chinese, sir," the communications officer replied. "Commercial vessels and a Filipino frigate responded and said they will remain clear but stand by in case they're needed."

Finally, Sheridan thought, some cooperation and a friendly warship to help out. He would've preferred it to be an American frigate, but any friendly help would be appreciated. "Very good. What's the frigate's position?"

"Thirty miles southeast of the southern search box. About two hours' steaming time."

"Request that they move closer to the box but remain clear for the time being, and pass along my . . ."

"Bridge, Tactical, lost contact with the Eagle Eye!" Fells interjected, using the direct "CALL" function of the intercom to interrupt all other communications.

Sheridan swore aloud. "Shit! What the hell happened, Ed?"

"Don't know, sir. No malfunction annunciations. The thing just went dark."

"Crap," Sheridan muttered. All they had in the southern search box was the Global Hawk now. On the radio, he spoke, "Mohawk Zero-One, how's it going?"

"Swimmer's in the water," Coffey replied. A moment later: "Sir, swimmer says the person in the water is *alive*! He's busted up very badly and may not survive the return flight, but right now he's breathing!"

"Sweet Jesus, that's incredible!" Sheridan said. "Head back to the barn at best speed as soon as your swimmer's aboard."

"About five more minutes, sir."

"Call sick bay, tell them we have a survivor inbound, ETE about an hour," Sheridan said to the officer of the deck. "I want this guy alive." He switched channels on the telephone. "Tactical, Bridge, Ed, any ideas on what the hell happened to the Eagle Eye?"

"None, sir," Fells replied. "But from the initial reports I read about the P-8 incident, they reported the same thing: sudden loss of contact, no indications of a malfunction. It's possible that whatever hit the Poseidon hit the Eagle Eye too."

"Hit it? Like what? A missile, fired from a sub?"

"Possible, but unless the missile was some kind of a magical silver bullet, the aircraft would have reported multiple malfunctions before losing contact—engine fire, electrical, hydraulics, so on," Fells said. "Whatever hit the P-8 and the Eagle Eye shut them down in the blink of an eye, before any malfunctions could be reported."

"Mohawk One, Zero-One is RTB," Coffey radioed.

Thank God, Sheridan breathed. With first the Poseidon gone and now the Eagle Eye gone but hopefully automatically on its way back, the South China Sea suddenly felt like a very dangerous place, and the quicker he got his last air asset back on the deck, the better. "You got the Jayhawk on radar, Ed?"

"Affirmative, sir," Fells reported. "He's doing a hundred knots, and his fuel reserves look good."

"Admiral Chen of the *Zhenyuan* is on the phone, sir."

Admiral Zhen picked up the telephone. "Go ahead, Admiral Chen."

"Sir, radar reports another aircraft, possibly a patrol helicopter, heading north away from the search area," Chen said. "It was observed hovering for several minutes in an area just north of the search box."

"A second search helicopter?"

"The high-endurance American cutters embark two rotary-wing search aircraft, sir, one manned and one unmanned," Chen said. "The unmanned aircraft has been neutralized, but the second one is heading north at high speed."

Heading back to its mothership, Zhen thought. And if it was hovering, it means it could have found something—and if that something could implicate China in the downing of the American search plane, his mission would have failed.

"Bring down that second patrol helicopter with *Wúsheng Léitíng,* Admiral Chen," Zhen said. "I do not want that helicopter to return to the Coast Guard vessel."

"Stand by, sir," Chen said. Zhen's anger rose as the seconds ticked by. Finally, Chen reported: "Sir, the helicopter is out of range of Silent Thunder."

"Then order one of your screening vessels to shoot it down."

Another maddening pause; this time, Zhen anticipated the reply: "Sir, we have no destroyers or frigates in position."

"Then launch the alert fighter, Chen," Admiral Zhen said. "Shoot down that helicopter."

"*Repeat that last,* sir?" Chen asked in a high, squeaky voice, obviously not expecting that order whatsoever.

"That is the second time you questioned an order," Zhen said. "I repeat, shoot down that damned helicopter! I do not want that helicopter to get back aboard that cutter! Acknowledge my order!"

"But sir . . . sir, none of our pilots are night carrier landing qualified, sir," Chen said.

"What did you say, Chen?" Zhen thundered.

"Sir, this was a shakedown cruise for the deck handlers and propulsion section crews, not for night flight operations. Our pilots are day carrier landing qualified only!"

"I do not want excuses, Chen!" Zhen shouted. "Get a fighter and your best pilot airborne *now*. I do not care if he has to recover on a land base or if he has to ditch, but I want him airborne *now*!"

ABOARD THE PEOPLE'S LIBERATION ARMY NAVY CARRIER ZHENYUAN

THAT SAME TIME

"Acknowledged, sir," Admiral Chen responded, but the secure connection had already been broken. He immediately selected the telephone channel for carrier flight operations.

"Flight operations duty officer Lieutenant Wu, sir."

"Captain Zhang, *immediately.*"

"*Shì de, xiânsheng,*" the duty officer replied. A few moments later: "*Hai Jun Shang Xiao* Zhang, sir."

"Captain Zhang, launch the alert fighter," Chen said. "Vector the pilot to an American helicopter flying north. I want it shot down immediately."

"*Dui-bu-qi, xiânsheng?*" Zhang replied in disbelief.

"Immediately, Captain," Chen said in a completely toneless, almost dead voice.

"Sir . . . Bolin . . ." Zhang said. He was one of the few junior officers on the entire vessel—in the entire *fleet*—allowed to call the admiral by his first name; they had known each other for years. "Are you damned sure you want to do this?"

"I have orders directly from South Sea Fleet headquarters, Peiyan," Chen said in a low voice. "Directly from Admiral Zhen."

"But you are still the captain of the *Zhenyuan* battle group, Bolin," Zhang said. "You took a chance by complying with that order to shoot down the American patrol plane if it appeared it would not crash. I think you can escape retribution for that. But shooting down an unarmed patrol helicopter?"

"I have my orders, Peiyan."

"I say again, you are the commanding officer of this entire battle group, Bolin," Zhang said. "You have the ultimate authority and responsibility to refuse any order that might endanger your men or your vessels. Shooting down that helicopter will certainly result in immediate American counterattack on this battle group. Their carrier battle group will be within striking range in just a few hours!"

Chen hesitated for several moments, scanning the bridge and noting the duty officer and a few of the watchstanders glancing in his direction, wondering what the captain would do. Finally, Chen straightened his shoulders. "Launch the alert fighter, Captain Zhang. Immediately. Attack and destroy the American helicopter. Acknowledge."

"Acknowledged, sir," Zhang responded in a voice even deader than Chen's had been. "I will fly the sortie myself. Then, if we are shot or imprisoned as murderers, we will do so together." And the connection was terminated.

"It's a real miracle, Skipper," the copilot aboard the HH-60 Jayhawk, Lieutenant Lucy Cross, radioed. "The survivor is a *woman*. She was wearing a flight helmet, so my guess is she was the pilot or copilot. I don't know how she got out alive. She's unconscious, and she's got several broken bones, including a badly fractured neck, but she's breathing."

"How far out are they, Ed?" Doug Sheridan asked on intercom.

"Still thirty-five minutes, sir," Edward Fells, the tactical officer, responded.

"Doctors and medics ready on the helo deck?"

"Medical crew standing by, sir," the officer of the deck responded after radioing down.

"Victim is in cardiac arrest," Cross radioed. "Stand by, Skipper."

Shit, Sheridan thought, but this time he didn't say it aloud. "Do what you can, guys," he radioed. C'mon, darlin', he thought, fight, *fight*! . . .

"Got her back, Skipper," the copilot radioed a couple minutes later, the relief evident in her voice. "I think the ASTs just said she was in arrest so they could put their hands all over her chest."

"Get your head back in the game, guys," Sheridan said gruffly, but inside he was breathing a sigh of relief too, thankful that he had some of the Coast Guard's finest aviation survival technicians serving on his cutter. The ASTs were the workhorses of Coast Guard aviation. They trained as hard as Navy SEALS, knew as much about helicopters as a mechanic, as much about emergency medicine as a paramedic, and as much about . . .

"Bridge, Tactical, high-speed bogey, sixty miles south, low altitude, speed six hundred knots, heading right for us!" Fells radioed.

"General quarters, man battle stations," Sheridan said calmly. He was pleased with how relaxed he felt: just the simple act of talking to the crew about this very eventuality put him instantly at ease. "Stand by on the 76 to repel hostile aircraft." The 76 was the ship's 76-millimeter Otobreda Super Rapid dual-purpose gun, mounted on the bow. The gun could engage surface and air targets as far away as eighteen miles. The *Mohawk* also carried a Phalanx Close-In Weapon System on the stern, a radar-guided twenty-millimeter machine gun that could engage air targets as far as two miles away across the entire rear quadrant of the cutter. "Comm, radio on all emergency frequencies, high-speed aircraft, alter course immediately or you will be fired on. Advise the Jayhawk. Bearing on the bogey?"

"Bogey bearing one-niner zero, heading zero-one-zero, directly for us."

"Helm, steer one-niner zero," Sheridan ordered. He wanted to match the aircraft's bearing in order to present the smallest profile possible to the attacker. "Range from bogey to Jayhawk?"

"Twenty miles, sir. The helo is directly between us and the bogey."

He picked up the radiotelephone. "Mohawk Zero-One, Mohawk One, alter course twenty right to stay out of our line of fire."

"Mohawk Air One, roger," Coffey replied, his voice definitely on edge.

"Range to bogey?"

"Fifty miles."

The officer of the deck handed Sheridan a white Kevlar helmet and streamlined auto-inflating life vest. "The *Mohawk* is at battle stations, sir," he reported. "Weapon systems manned and ready. We are heading one-niner-zero, flank speed."

"Very well."

"Bridge, Tactical, the bogey is altering course!" Fell announced. "He turned hard right! He's keeping the helo between him and us!"

"Why the hell is he . . . ?" And his eyes bulged in fear as he realized what the aircraft was doing: "Damn, *he's going after the helo*!" Sheridan shouted. "Comm, send to Fleet and Area, unidentified high-speed aircraft pursuing rescue helo, request immediate help! Tactical, range from bogey to helo!"

"Eight miles."

Sheridan picked up the radiotelephone. "Mohawk Zero-One, Mohawk One, you've got an unidentified fast-mover about eight miles on your tail and closing fast. Try warning him away on the radio—we tried, but maybe he can't hear us. Make sure your transponder is on."

"Roger."

"Range between the bogey and the helo?"

"Five miles."

Sheridan could hear Cross's radio calls on the UHF GUARD emergency frequency, so there was no doubt she was broadcasting and could hear his instructions. "Range?"

"Two miles. His airspeed is decreasing. He may be closing in for identification. One mile. Radar returns merging."

"Any identification on this guy at all?" he asked. "Is he . . . ?"

"*Mayday! Mayday! Mayday!* U.S. Coast Guard helicopter Mohawk Zero-One, two hundred and sixty miles north of Lincoln Island, catastrophic engine explosion, suspected air-to-air attack, we are going down, we are going down, Mayday, Mayd—"

And that was the last they heard from the Jayhawk.

THE JOINT CHIEFS OF STAFF
BATTLE STAFF ROOM, THE
PENTAGON, WASHINGTON, D.C.

A SHORT TIME LATER

"*We lost two helicopters?*" the chairman of the Joint Chiefs of Staff, Air Force General Timothy Spellings, thundered. "Will someone explain to me *right now* how we can lose two helicopters from one vessel in the same ocean and we're not in a state of war?" He looked around the conference table, fighting to regain his composure; then he said: "Ed, what's the status of our surface forces in the South China Sea?"

"Sir, I ordered the Coast Guard cutter *Mohawk* to exit the area and head for Manila at best possible speed—I didn't want it in the area facing off alone against that Chinese carrier," Admiral Edward Fowler, the chief of naval operations, replied. "If there were any survivors from the crash, we'll have to send out searchers from the Philippines. The *George Washington* carrier strike group is proceeding on course to the Poseidon crash site and is at battle stations, but they won't be in position to launch aircraft for several hours."

"If I was a suspicious guy, I'd say whoever is shooting down our aircraft did it precisely when we wouldn't have any carriers in the area, Ed," Spellings said. "What did the cutter report?"

"The *Mohawk* reported a fast-moving aircraft pursuing their helicopter before it went down," Fowler said. "We believe the fighter came from the Chinese carrier *Zhenyuan.*"

"Damn it," Spellings breathed. "I'll brief the president. Send the latest position data to my tablet. We still have the Global Hawk up?"

"Yes, sir," Fowler said. "It'll be on station for about eight more hours, and another one is standing by at Andersen Air Force Base. E-2C patrol aircraft from the *Washington* should be ready to take over by then as well."

"No aircraft gets near our planes or within a hundred miles of our ships without a Super Hornet on its tail," Spellings said. "I'm concerned about carrier planes attacking that Coast Guard cutter. What other air defense aircraft do we have up?"

"None, sir," Fowler said.

"None? Anywhere?" Spellings asked.

"Not readily available," Fowler said. "We rely on carrier-based planes for much of our fighter air patrol activity because of the distances involved. The one exception is the bombers based on Guam—they routinely patrol all across the Pacific and Indian Oceans. They're the only ones that have the legs to reach out that far."

Spellings turned to the Air Force chief of staff, General Jason Conaway. "But those bombers don't have air-to-air weapons, do they?" he asked.

"No, sir," Conaway replied. "But they do have very long legs as Admiral Fowler said, as well as excellent radars and electro-optical sensors, pretty good intelligence-gathering and transmission capabilities, and of course if the balloon goes up, they'd be one of the best conventional platforms to get our first licks in. At least one stealth bomber is rotated in every six months." He paused for a moment, then added, "The Air Force did have bombers fitted with air-to-air missiles a few years ago, but since the American Holocaust and the economic slump I believe that capability has been removed."

"What fighter assets do you have that we can use now, Jason?"

"We can deploy some F-15 Eagles from Joint Base Pearl

Harbor–Hickam to Guam and set up an air defense zone until the Hornets from the *Washington* arrive, sir," Conaway said.

"How long will that take?"

"Several hours to get them out to Guam, sir, and then a few hours to set up a patrol box."

"What about getting help from the Philippines?"

"The Philippines has virtually no air superiority aircraft," Conaway said. "Their money goes for counterinsurgency light attack aircraft. I think they still have F-5s, but they are day VFR aircraft only and probably don't fly too far from shore."

Just as well—Spellings hated the idea of relying on a foreign air force for air cover over his own forces anyway. "Get the Eagles on their way, Jason, and have them bring an AWACS radar plane with them. Ed, I'll need a recommended comm plan between the cutter and the Filipinos so we don't start firing on one another." Conaway and Fowler picked up telephones to issue instructions. Spellings issued a few more orders, then adjourned the meeting and headed for the White House to meet with the national security team.

Conaway's call was to Pacific Air Forces commander General George Hood in Hawaii. "How are you, George?"

"Fine, sir, thank you."

"The chiefs just met here in the Tank," Conaway said. "A Coast Guard search-and-rescue helicopter went down in the South China Sea a short time ago. Coast Guard believes it was shot down by a fighter from the Chinese aircraft carrier *Zhenyuan.*"

"Oh, shit," Hood breathed.

"CJCS wants F-15s and an AWACS sent to Guam to set up a fighter patrol in advance of the Navy sending a carrier. What do you have available?"

"Stand by, sir." The wait was not long: "I have the tanker support available to drag six Eagles out there, launching in about an hour. That's a fairly routine exercise for us. One AWACS is available, and I can rotate a couple more out there in a day or two."

"Get them moving."

"Yes, sir. The Thirty-Sixth Wing usually handles these deployments, but if they'll be doing regular patrols I'd rather put the fighters over on the First Expeditionary Bomb Wing side instead of with the normal transients. Colonel Warner Cuthbert is the commander out there; he'll take good care of them, and there'll be a lot fewer chances of fighter activity being monitored from outside the base."

"Approved."

"We may want to discuss regularly rotating fighters and AWACS planes out to Guam, like Cuthbert does with his bombers."

"Write up a plan and send it to me right away," Conaway said. "There wasn't money in the budget to permanently station more jets out there, but now I think CJCS will be amenable to that idea, given what's happened out there today. They might even give us back some fighters that were cut in the latest round of budget hack-jobs they did on us."

"Yes, sir. After the alert notification about the Poseidon, Colonel Cuthbert on Guam submitted a plan to load up a few of his bombers with weapons. He's got two B-1s, two B-52s, one B-2, and four tankers in his Continuous Bomber Presence task force. He wants to load up one B-1 and one B-52 and put the crews on alert, and keep the rest of the planes available for training but available to be loaded up on a moment's notice."

"That's all the bombers we have out there?"

"That's a third of the entire fleet that survived after the American Holocaust, sir," Hood said. "The crews are on a pretty busy rotation schedule."

"What does he want to load?"

"It's a mix of JASSM cruise missiles, Harpoons, and mines," Hood said.

Conaway thought for a few moments; then: "I'll have to run it by SECDEF, and he'll probably take it on up to the White House," he said. "If word got out that we were loading up bombers with live weapons, the world will think we're getting ready for war with China."

"If it turns out China did shoot down that helicopter and possibly the Poseidon, too, maybe that's what we should be doing."

"I agree," Conaway said. "But with just a handful of bombers and carriers deployed to the Pacific right now, there's not much we can do if war did break out. It would take us months, maybe years, to gear up enough to take on China, even at sea. But tell Cuthbert I'm going to recommend approval and have his guys leaning forward ready to go. If the shit does hit the fan, I'd want those planes in the air soonest."

"Roger that, sir."

"Those bombers don't have air-to-air capability, do they, George?" Conaway asked.

"I don't know for certain, but I don't think so, sir," Hood replied. "I'll ask Cuthbert when I talk to him."

Conaway shook his head. "Jeez, George, I thought we had more assets out there," he said. "I guess with all the activity in the Middle East over the past decade, we've let things in the Pacific and Asia slide a little."

"Hopefully, if the budget situation improves, that will get fixed before something serious happens out here, sir," Hood offered. "PACAF is very good at doing more with less, but the Pacific is a pretty big pond. We should be thinking about more things to beef up defenses around Guam and Hawaii: putting Patriot air defense missiles and maybe one or two Aegis antiballistic missile ships out there, and doing the same for other bases in the Pacific that we would need to disperse our forces, like Tinian."

"Write it all up and send it in to Pacific Command and me right away, George," Conaway said. "This is definitely the time to be asking for stuff like that." He paused for another moment; then: "You know, George, SECDEF handed me a proposal not long ago from a company in Nevada that says they would refurbish, train, equip, and even operate a fleet of over twenty B-1 bombers in less than two years."

"*What?* That sounds outrageous, sir."

"I thought so too," Conaway admitted. "I think SECDEF just wanted it off his desk—he passed it on without a recommendation. When I read the overview I almost pitched it in the 'bullshit' pile."

"Almost, sir?"

"Almost. The reason I didn't was because of the guy who wrote the proposal: Patrick McLanahan."

"*McLanahan?* You're *kidding*!"

"He's the new CEO of the company that's been building high-tech air and space toys for the Pentagon for years," Conaway said, his recall of reading the proposal improving. "Apparently he got his hands on a couple B-1 airframes from AMARG, some new engines, and AESA radars. He's got one flying now and one almost ready to fly, and he claims he can do the rest in less than two years. I believe your man Cuthbert flew with McLanahan and submitted his own report, and he was impressed. And get this: McLanahan's doing the first two planes on his company's dime—the Air Force hasn't paid him anything yet. All we're doing is giving him the equipment."

"Still sounds too good to be true, sir."

"Maybe," Conaway said. "But you could make use of twenty B-1 bombers out there in your theater, couldn't you?"

"Hell yes," Hood said, "especially if they have air-to-air.

Unless we get access to air bases in the Philippines, Brunei, or Vietnam, fighters are just too short legged to operate effectively in the South China Sea, and that will include the F-35—if we ever get any of those. PACAF relies on the Navy's carriers to do the bulk of the air-to-air missions except for Hawaii, Alaska, and Korea."

"And with the budget cuts, there are fewer and fewer carrier deployments in the Pacific and Indian Oceans," Conaway pointed out.

"Exactly, sir," Hood said. "If I remember, McLanahan was in command of that spooky black bomb wing that employed the high-tech B-1s and B-52s that had AMRAAMs and did everything else under the sun—he even put antiballistic missile lasers on a BUFF. If anybody can pull it off, he can."

"I'll have to dust off that proposal, give it a look, and pass it on up to CJCS and see what he says," Conaway said. "After the shit that's happened today, they might scrape up the money to rebuild some of those old Bones."

THE WHITE HOUSE OVAL OFFICE

A SHORT TIME LATER

"I sincerely apologize for taking so long to return your phone call, Mr. President," the voice of the Chinese translator said, speaking on behalf of People's Republic of China President Zhou Qiang. "I have been attending several emergency meetings regarding this most unfortunate occurrence."

"This is much more than an 'unfortunate occurrence,' Mr. President," Kenneth Phoenix said angrily. With him on the conference call in the Oval Office were Vice President Ann Page, National Security Adviser William Glenbrook, Chairman of the Joint Chiefs of Staff General Timothy Spellings, and Secretary of State Herbert Kevich. Kevich gave the president an anxious glance, silently warning him to remain calm. "Our initial reports from the scene say that the Coast Guard search-and-rescue helicopter was pursued by a fighter launched from your aircraft carrier and was shot down without any attempt at visual identification and without any warning. That is an overt act of war, Mr. President, and I demand an explanation!"

"Please calm yourself, sir," Zhou said. "A war is not what anyone wishes, not at all, the least of all China. I do not have a complete understanding of the situation, sir. Reports are still coming in, and the ones I have received are contradictory and incomplete. If you will please be patient, sir, I will personally brief you when I know the facts."

"I want an explanation *now,* Mr. President!" Phoenix said. "Stalling only makes it apparent that you wish to cover up a serious act of aggression."

"I do not think it is fair to you, myself, or the families of those affected to make any decisions or actions without first obtaining all the facts, Mr. President," Zhou said. Phoenix tried to gauge Zhou's truthfulness and demeanor through his own voice in the background, but could not. "I can only tell you what I have sorted out in my own mind, based on the rather disjointed reports I have been given: that it appears to be a horrible and tragic accident."

"An 'accident'? You launched a fighter after one of our search-and-rescue helicopters and opened fire without even attempting to identify it?"

"Those are not the facts as I understand them, Mr. President," Zhou said. "The indications I have from the battle group commander is that he ordered a fighter to pursue a helicopter that appeared to be retrieving wreckage from the crash of your P-8 patrol plane. After repeated warnings by both the carrier and the pilot of the fighter, hostile intentions were verified, and the pilot was authorized to shoot."

"What hostile intentions were those?"

"Reports are not absolutely clear," Zhou said. "The helicopter refused to comply with instructions, and the fighter pilot reported he observed gunfire coming from a side door of the helicopter. Standing orders authorize our planes to return fire immediately if attacked, which he did, with tragic results. I sincerely apologize for this horrible accident, President Phoenix. This is a disaster of the highest order, and I am solely to blame."

"I don't buy it, Mr. President," Phoenix said. "A Coast Guard helicopter is very hard to mistake, even at night, and our Coast Guard cutter was monitoring many frequencies and heard no such warnings."

"I do not know about such things, Mr. President," Zhou said. "Mine are preliminary reports from the commanders on the scene. A full investigation will be conducted and a report issued to you, I assure you."

"I expect the People's Liberation Army Navy to stay away

from the site of our Poseidon patrol plane crash," Phoenix said. "That aircraft carried sensitive materials that China has no right to recover."

"Our naval forces certainly do have the right to recover anything it finds in waters owned and controlled by China, and that includes the South Sea where your plane crashed," Zhou said. "However, in sincere apology and abject humiliation for the accidental downing of your patrol helicopter, I will order People's Liberation Army Navy surface vessels to stay away from the crash site. We reserve the right to monitor your ships in the South Sea, of course."

"As long as your forces do not interfere with ours, sir."

"We will not interfere with any *peaceful* vessels or aircraft," Zhou said. "But we recognize that with all these warships and planes operating in the waters of the South Sea, mixing in with civil and commercial traffic, accidents can and, as we have seen, do happen. I urge all parties to think and act responsibly. China stands ready to assist your rescue and recovery forces at any time, Mr. President."

"I thank you, but that won't be necessary, sir," Phoenix said. "We will be conducting our own investigations, and then we will see who has been acting responsibly . . . and who has *not*. Good day, Mr. President." And Phoenix drew a line across his throat with his thumb, and the connection was terminated.

"Bastard," Phoenix said. "Tim, are Coast Guard helicopters armed?"

"The MH-60T Jayhawk, which are the ones usually deployed on medium- and high-endurance cutters, have machine guns to fire warning shots at suspected smugglers, and sniper rifles to take out engines of fleeing vessels," General Spellings replied. "I don't know if the Jayhawk that went down was a T-model, but I'm betting it was."

"Is it possible our guys were shooting at something, and

the fighter thought it was being fired upon and returned fire?" Phoenix asked.

"You don't believe any of that load of crap Zhou was spouting, do you, sir?" Ann Page asked. "That helicopter was *deliberately* shot down, and probably the Poseidon patrol plane too. No question."

"Why would the Chinese shoot down a Coast Guard search-and-rescue helicopter, Miss Vice President?" Secretary of State Kevich asked. "That does not make any sense."

"I don't know, Herbert," Ann said. "Maybe they thought our guys found some piece of damning evidence. Maybe they just wanted to do an act that was plausibly deniable, and they found it. Maybe they just wanted to throw some weight around. You heard him: Zhou thinks the South China Sea belongs to China. If he 'accidentally' shoots down aircraft in 'his' ocean, he may think he's completely justified."

"I need to find out," the president said. "If the crew of that helicopter was firing at something in the water—pirates, a ship trying to take a body, classified materials, anything—then it's possible for that fighter to misinterpret it as an attack and open fire."

Ann Page shook her head, not believing it for a second, but she remained silent. "I'll find out for sure, sir," Spellings said, "and I'll find out what the procedures are for the helicopter crews if they did encounter something like what you describe."

"Zhou won't be able to throw his weight around much longer with the *George Washington* carrier strike group barreling down into 'his' ocean," Vice President Page said. "But once the *George Washington* enters the South China Sea, will we regain the strategic and tactical advantage again? Obviously we were surprised and outgunned in this encounter, and it cost us a lot. Will the carrier strike group give us the military advantage again?"

Glenbrook looked exceedingly uncomfortable. "Ma'am, you know the situation as well as I," he said finally. "China has been quickly ramping up its surface, subsurface, and air military forces in the South China Sea, East China Sea, and as far away as the Indian Ocean for almost a decade now, reinforcing their trade routes with military hardware, while the United States either has been diverting the same assets to the Middle East or cutting those forces altogether. They've also been building dozens of ballistic missile and cruise missile bases as far away as Africa. We used to believe that China's navy and air forces were large but qualitatively inferior. No longer. Their quality has increased and their numbers have held steady—numerically far better than ours."

The president turned to General Spellings, silently asking his opinion, and the four-star general nodded agreement with the national security adviser. "Zhou says China 'owns' and 'controls' the South China Sea, and he may be right, sir," Spellings said. "To answer your question, Miss Vice President: it would be very difficult, if not impossible, to keep an aircraft carrier strike group in the South China Sea, within range of Chinese land-based bombers, ballistic antiship missiles, and cruise missiles. We could certainly hold a number of fixed Chinese targets at risk with our own sub- and surface-launched cruise missiles. But keeping a strike group in the South China Sea leaves the rest of the Pacific and the Indian Ocean uncovered. We give up a lot and don't get any benefit. Not to mention the huge increase in world tensions with two fleets eyeing each other in relatively close proximity."

"So let's get another carrier strike group to cover the rest," Ann said. "Let's park a carrier strike group in the South China Sea, right in Zhou's face, and have two other groups patrol the rest of that part of the world."

"I don't want to do that, Ann," President Phoenix said. "I'm angry about what happened out there, and there's no question that China wants to exert more control in the South China Sea. I'm not convinced that Zhou ordered our aircraft to be shot down, but when we lose planes and then he says China 'owns' the South China Sea, I'm nervous.

"But I know the effect putting one of those carrier strike groups has in a region," the president went on. "The firepower it represents is enormous. It's a direct challenge to any nation. A lot of fingers start hovering a lot closer to red buttons when you know there's dozens of bombers and hundreds of cruise missiles right over the horizon."

He thought for a moment, then said, "I need more options, people. As much as I want to, I don't want to get in Zhou's face and challenge his claim that China 'owns' and 'controls' the South China Sea—things are tense enough as it is. I want to keep the carrier strike groups on patrol. The *George Washington* can move into the South China Sea and assist with rescue and recovery, but then they go back on patrol and do a normal rotation. Same with the *Reagan*—when the *GW* moves out, the *Reagan* can move in, but unless something else happens, it resumes its patrol or goes back to San Diego to complete its fleet qualifications." He turned again to Spellings. "What about aircraft, General? What do we have out there that can maintain a presence along with our carriers? What about long-range bombers?"

"As you know, sir, our long-range heavy bomber forces were nearly wiped out in the American Holocaust and the ensuing counterattacks over Russia," Spellings said. "That left us with just a handful of survivors that had been deployed to bases that weren't hit by the Russians. Over the years we de-emphasized manned air-breathing bombers and started to develop the next generation of unmanned bombers and space-based attack, but when the super-recession hit, all funding for new, untested programs went away." Kenneth Phoenix averted his eyes, his mouth a hard line—he knew he was the one most responsible for killing all the expensive, untried defense programs since taking office.

"Nowadays most of the surviving bombers are rotated to Andersen Air Force Base on Guam, the airfield at Naval Support Facility Diego Garcia in the Indian Ocean, and other countries in the Pacific that allow armed attack aircraft to use their facilities, such as Australia," Spellings went on. "But it's a very thin force: usually only five or six bombers are deployed, with the others preparing to deploy or just coming back from a deployment."

"My God," Ann breathed. "We used to have hundreds of bombers; during World War Two, we had thousands. Now we have less than a couple *dozen*?"

"We still have a number of tactical fighter-bombers that can be set up for long-range patrols, but unless we secured agreements from friendly countries that border the South China Sea, our available land bases are just too far away," Spellings said.

"And those countries that border or directly interact with China are very unlikely to allow American strike aircraft access to their bases, for fear of losing trade and friendly diplomatic relations with China," Secretary of State Kevich reminded everyone. "Their relations with China are at least as important, and in some cases *more* important, than their relations with us."

"What would it take to use fighters like the Eagles and Hornets over the South China Sea, General?" the president asked.

"Even with extensive aerial refueling tanker support, an aircraft such as an F-15E Strike Eagle would have to be loaded up with two and perhaps three external fuel tanks, which decreases its weapons load," Spellings went on. "An aircraft such as the smaller, lighter single-engine F-16 Fighting Falcon would be under even more constraints. It would be a monumental task for even a more modern aircraft such as the F/A-18 Super Hornet or F-35 Lightning Joint Strike Fighter."

"But those crews have done it all before, General, haven't they?" Kevich asked. "What about Iraq and Afghanistan? They flew long sorties out there, too."

"They had to do a lot of flying, sir, no question," Spellings replied, "but the distances in the Middle East and Southwest Asia were nowhere near as great as what we're talking about in the Pacific. It's fifteen hundred miles one-way from Guam to the middle of the South China Sea—that's a three-hour cruise just to get to the patrol area, assuming the Philippines gives us overflight permission. Navy and Marine Corps carrier planes used against targets in Iraq during Desert Storm and over Afghanistan in Operation Enduring Freedom only had to fly about one hour or so to get to the target area, and that was a lot for guys who had to tank often, go into combat, tank again, and then land on a carrier deck afterward." Spellings hesitated for a moment, looking at the others, then to the president: "There may be another option to consider, sir."

"What's that, General?"

"I received a proposal from a high-tech firm in Nevada to refurbish twenty-two B-1B Lancer bombers that were in flyable storage in New Mexico and outfit them with modern off-the-shelf avionics and weapons," Spellings replied. "The company would . . ."

"Excuse me, General: 'high-tech firm in Nevada'?" Ann Page interrupted, her entire visage brightening. "Do you mean *Patrick McLanahan*?"

Spellings blinked in surprise. "Why . . . yes, ma'am, retired General McLanahan," he said. "How did you . . . ?"

"I heard he took over Sky Masters when Jon Masters was

killed by those domestic terrorists last year," Ann said, a huge smile on her face. "Boy, that guy doesn't waste any time. One minute he's a retired guy playing Air Force with the Civil Air Patrol—the next minute he wants to build B-1 bombers."

"Twenty-two B-1 bombers, General?" National Security Adviser Glenbrook asked skeptically. "We don't have the money for something like that. Besides, it would take forever to build that many."

"He's not building them, sir: he's *re*building the ones that were retired and are in flyable storage, and he's using existing off-the-shelf components that are already tried and proven," Spellings explained. "He refurbished one and did a successful demonstration recently, all on his company's nickel. Plus, his written proposal claims he can deliver the fleet in less than two years, and he says he can refurbish all of them for about the price of less than ten F-35 Lightnings."

"It sounds interesting and a little fantastical," the president said. "Less than two years?"

"If you don't mind, Mr. President, I'd like to check it out," Vice President Page said. "I'd like to see Patrick again, and I can't wait to see what he's got in mind."

"I need you here, Miss Vice President."

"I can have him come out and give me his dog-and-pony show," Ann said. "I can't wait to see what the corporate life has done to him."

Phoenix gave her a shake of his head and an exasperated smile, but then nodded assent. "Invite him to the residence when he gets in," he said. "I'd like to see him too—and I'd like to find out what mischief he's getting into next."

Office of the President, Zhongnanhai, Beijing, China

That same time

"*How dare he lecture me like a child!*" President Zhou shouted, throwing the receiver back on its cradle and jumping to his feet. "I will not stand being spoken to by a miserable sniveling white round-eyed dog like Phoenix!" He patted his jacket and pants pockets for cigarettes and found none. "Bring cigarettes in here!" he shouted to his outer office assistant. He turned to the chief of the general staff of the People's Liberation Army, Colonel General Zu Kai. "Now what happened out there, General?" he asked angrily. "I authorized you to retrieve pieces of the wreckage if possible, and now the Americans accuse us of downing two helicopters!" He turned to his outer office again. "Where in blazes is that assistant? Bring cigarettes, dammit!"

"I do not care about the American's accusations, Comrade President, and neither should you," Zu said dismissively. With him in the president's office were Vice President Gao Xudong and Foreign Minister Tang Ji. "They are going to accuse us of everything under the sun."

"I asked you, General: What happened out there?" Zhou asked.

"I did as I was ordered to do: I retrieved pieces of the downed aircraft," Zu replied. "What else happened is of no consequence."

"No consequence, eh? Is that your professional political opinion? Where are those cigarettes!" Zhou seemed on the verge of a breakdown. "Were helicopters shot down by Chinese forces, General?"

Zu considered for a moment whether or not he should

answer. Foreign Minister Tang looked at him in some confusion; Vice President Gao seemed intrigued by this confrontation and Zu's hesitancy and actually seemed to want to smile at him. Finally, Zu shrugged his shoulders. "One of my young admirals took some initiative," he said. "He observed that the Americans had sent two rotorcraft, one manned and the other unmanned, to retrieve pieces of the wreckage of the P-8 Poseidon armed patrol plane. If they found any, and if it indicated that China was involved in the shoot-down, it could be bad for China, so the admiral ordered . . ."

"Wait a minute, General," Zhou interrupted, his eyes gradually widening in disbelief. "Are you saying . . . China *was* involved in the downing of that American patrol plane?"

Zu remained silent until he thought Zhou was going to jump up and strangle him on the spot. "Comrade President, you speak of the South Sea as being a sovereign part of China," Zu said. "You speak of wanting to challenge all hostile foreign military forces in the region. If this is true, sir, China needs to act. China should . . ."

"*How dare you?*" Zhou exploded in incredulous anger. "You *deliberately* shot down *three American aircraft*? You will be shot for this, Zu! You will be executed as an insubordinate insane berserker!" He plopped back down onto his chair, staring at his desk, his hands flat on the desktop as if bracing himself. "We must report this to the Central Military Commission and the Politburo," he said in a low voice. "I must admit this to the Americans. We will all be in prison or executed for what you have done."

"We must do nothing of the kind, Comrade President," Zu said. "No one outside this room need know."

"The Americans will find out," Zhou said, his voice almost a whisper now. "They will demand that we be turned over to them for trial—if we are not at war with them! They will destroy all we have built—our navy, our air forces will all be vaporized. China will be the pariah of the entire planet. We will be thrust back into isolation, worse than the Great Proletariat Cultural Revolution."

"You must get hold of yourself, Comrade President," Zu said. "You are not looking well. Perhaps you need medical attention." He then walked over to the office door and opened it. The deputy chief of staff, Major General Sun Ji, was just outside . . . with two armed soldiers beside him. "General, as we discussed, summon the medical support team, and clear the building."

"Yes, sir," Sun said, and he nodded to others behind him.

"What is the meaning of this, Zu?" Zhou exclaimed. "What did you mean, 'clear the building'?"

"Comrade President, this is no time for weak leadership," General Zu said. "China is on the verge of greatness, but you do not seem to understand that and are completely unwilling to lead this country forward. Even with the United States so weak, you refuse to stand up to them. China has attacked one of its colonies with nuclear weapons in the past, and nothing was done—no retaliation. The downing of a few helicopters will be met by nothing but bluster. But this situation that we find ourselves in needs careful and strong leadership, and you are not the man for the job. I have therefore set in place a plan to have someone else take command."

"Someone else? You do not have the power to do that!" Zhou exclaimed, rising to his feet slowly, as if his muscles were wasting away by the minute. "Only the Central Committee can do that!"

"The Central Committee will take charge again once the military and security crisis situation is over," Zu said. "Until then, a replacement will be chosen."

"This is outrageous!" Zhou cried. "This is a thuggish military coup! You will never get away with this! You will be hanged for even speaking those words!"

"That will not be any of your concern, Comrade," Zu said evenly. "You will be secretly taken to a secure medical facility for observation. I will notify the Central Military Commission and the Politburo that you have taken ill."

"*You will not do this,* Zu!" Zhou cried out. "It is illegal! You do not have the authority! You swore an oath . . . !"

"My oath was to protect the people and the country from all enemies," Zu said. "You, sir, are our greatest enemy. You rant about protecting us, then do nothing. I am being true to my oath.

"You will be taken to a medical facility, where you will be kept for a period of time until I have determined that you will act against all foreign military powers in the South Sea," Zu went on, his voice completely under control, almost muted. "If you do not convince me you will act decisively, you will be medically retired after suffering a debilitating stroke that will rob you of most of your faculties . . . or you will have suffered a massive heart attack and died peaceably in your sleep." General Sun reappeared in the doorway and nodded to Zu. "General, take charge of the president."

Zhou turned his flabbergasted gaze to Vice President Gao. "Gao! What in blazes are you doing just standing there? Do something! Call security!"

Gao looked at Zu, who remained silent and expressionless, then at Zhou. Vice President Gao was probably the most Westernized Chinese politician who ever occupied a high office at Zhonghainan—he was educated in the United States in business and government, and he had never served in the military. Zu greatly mistrusted Gao, but he was the first vice president, and he was popular overseas, so he thought of him as someone to possibly be exploited. It was impossible to figure what Gao would do at any moment—it was well known he was an opportunist, but in which direction he would jog was always impossible to gauge.

"But, Mr. President," Gao said finally, "you do look a bit unwell. Perhaps some close observation at a competent medical facility is in order."

"*Why, you traitorous bastard!*" Zhou exploded.

"Take charge of the president, General," Zu repeated. The soldiers stepped forward quickly and took Zhou by the arms. Gao could see that there were medical personnel in the outer office, along with a gurney; a soldier in uniform was preparing a hypodermic injection. The outer office secretary and the security detail that was always present in the outer office and corridors were nowhere in sight.

The door closed after Sun led the president out. "So, Comrade Vice President," Zu said, turning to the others in the room. "Speak."

Gao nodded, and the smile that was before only hinted at grew. "I think it would be better if I contacted the Politburo and Central Military Commission about the president's illness, General," he said. "You should mobilize necessary military forces in order to increase readiness and maintain order during this uncertain time, and be prepared to deploy forces as necessary to keep the peace and secure the nation. With the Americans sending forces into the South China Sea and blaming China for the loss of their aircraft, they are causing tensions to rise throughout the entire region, and we must prepare for any eventuality."

"Some excellent suggestions indeed . . . *Acting* President Gao," Zu said. He turned to Foreign Minister Tang. "Comrade Minister?"

"I never thought I would see the day, General Zu," Tang

breathed. "A military coup by a Chinese general, right in the office of the president, before my very eyes!"

"Did you expect me to roll tanks down the streets, Minister?" Zu asked. "Storm the Politburo? Take over the airwaves and announce a military takeover? This is China, sir, not some third-world banana dictatorship. Decide whose side you are on, Minister."

"Death, or joining your coup, General?" Zu said nothing, but looked directly at Tang, waiting. Tang took a deep breath as if he had stopped breathing a long time ago. "I swore an oath to protect and defend the people, the nation, and the Party . . ." he said finally, then added, " . . . no matter whom the president is, or who may really be running the government."

"Not exactly a ringing endorsement, Tang, but I was not expecting anything more," Zu said dismissively. "But be warned: speak of this to anyone, and your term in office will be terminated even faster than Zhou's. You are dismissed." Tang looked extremely relieved to be leaving that office.

"Do you trust him, General?" Gao asked.

"Not in the least—but I trust *you* even less," Zu said acidly.

"I want to be on the winning side, that is all," Gao said, "and I believe the military is the winning side. And I agree it is time for China to step forward and take her place as the true leader of the world. The old men in our government like Zhou would be content to wait another thousand years while the bureaucrats and industrialists sucked the country dry. Only the military can set China on its proper course."

"You say all the right words, Gao," Zu said, "but your words do not mean anything to me—it will be your actions that decide your fate. Act the part and do as I say, and you will have a smooth and uneventful time as acting president. Betray me, and you will suffer a far worse fate than Zhou. Now return to your office, draft a statement to the Politburo and Central

Military Commission as quickly as possible, see to it that I get it right away, and then prepare to deliver it. You are dismissed."

General Sun Ji returned just as Gao was leaving. "Zhou is en route to the facility," he reported. "He put up quite a fight for an old man before he was administered the sedative."

"The last struggles of a tired old man," Zu said. He looked at his watch. "Schedule a meeting with the general staff for two hours from now."

"Yes, sir," Sun said. "I do not think we will have any trouble with them. None were particularly loyal to Zhou."

"I am not worried about the general staff or the Central Military Commission, Ji—I am worried about the Politburo whipping up the people," Zu admitted. "That is why Gao must play the role of acting president long enough for us to cement our takeover. We will need to prepare the army, independent and local infantry divisions, border guards, and reserves to respond in case the Politburo tries to stir up trouble. And in case we get any trouble from foreign countries when we exert our claims to Nansha and Xisha Dao, we will need a mobilization plan to deploy the navy and marines quickly to both archipelagos."

"I am sure Admiral Zhen has such a plan prepared, sir," Sun said. "And I think he will be very happy to see it put into place."

"It's a real pleasure to have you here, Brad, a real pleasure," boomed Thomas Hoffman. The tall, hulking owner of Warbirds Forever Inc. was carrying a duffel bag for Bradley as they made their way through an immense hangar filled with planes of every description, carefully parked to maximize floor space without creating a hazard. It was just after sunset, and Patrick had just dropped Bradley off in the turbine P210 Centurion. "Sorry you got here so late—I wanted to show you around and get started on some paperwork."

"I didn't mean to be so late, sir," Bradley said. "The guys at Sky Masters threw a little going-away party for me after closing, and I put in a full day at Sky Masters before the surprise party, so it was a really long day. I hope you don't mind."

"Not at all, not at all," Hoffman said pleasantly. "You have a little homework to do before your day starts, and it'll be a busy day tomorrow. We should have a little time tomorrow to show you around, but I think you'll be pretty busy."

"Thank you, sir," Brad said. He looked around the hangar in sheer wonderment. The floor was incredibly clean—it even looked polished enough that the overhead lights reflected off it—and painted with light gray petroleum-proof paint. There were about a dozen large wheeled toolboxes, decorated with every possible sticker, patch, and photograph, but it was all tastefully and professionally done. This had to be the cleanest and most well-organized workshop he had ever seen, he thought.

But the really amazing sight was the planes: Some were in various stages of repair; others looked brand new. There was everything from large bizjets to single-engine two-passenger light-sport airplanes . . . and warbirds. Brad was not a real warbird fan, but he recognized a few from World War Two, Korean War, and Vietnam War movies, and most looked as if they had just come off the assembly line. "Man, I don't even recognize some of these jets," he said.

"You'll become very familiar with all of them and probably get type rated in a few of the more popular warbirds," Hoffman said. He nodded to one of the showroom-quality planes. "That's one of our favorites: an Aero L-39 Albatros. This one was from Romania. For a fraction of what any other single-engine jet costs, guys can pick one out and have it dismantled and shipped here from Eastern Europe. We check them over, rebuild them, paint them, train the owner, and they've got themselves a real nice jet that's easy to fly and relatively inexpensive to fly and maintain. A lot of guys race them at the Reno Air Races." He nodded to his right. "There's the avionics shop, my office, the publications room, and the employee break room. Down that corridor are the company offices. The customer welcome area, pilot store, and Accounting are on the other side of the hangar."

They made their way through the crowded hangar, through a dimly lit corridor, and past several rooms until they came to a door almost in the middle. "I didn't want to put you at either end of the hallway, Brad, because of the smell from the main hangar on one end and the smell from the paint shop and composite layup shop on the other," Hoffman said. "I don't think you'll notice the smells from either side, but if you do, let me know and we'll figure something else out. You can even stay at my place until we get better digs. I have a spare bedroom available, when the grandkids aren't using it." He nodded down the hallway. "The employee locker room and bathroom is three doors down—I hope you brought towels, because I forgot to bring any." He opened the door. "Here you go."

The room was large, but the usable area was very small because the place was choked with boxes, tires, shelving, a large workbench, and aircraft parts stacked to the ceiling. Along one wall was a single bed with spring-and-wire foundation with a roll of thick foam material, linens, and a pillow atop it; next to it was a two-drawer dresser. The room was lit by a single bare bulb affixed to an ancient-looking ceiling fan. There was a simple folding-table desk on the other side of the bed with a desk lamp and power strip.

"I know it's not the Ritz, Brad, but until we figure something else out, it's the best I can do," Hoffman said. "At least you can't beat the price."

"I'm sure it will be fine, sir," Brad said, trying to sound cheerful.

"I don't think you'll be bothered by any smells in here from the tires and whatnot," Hoffman said, "but if you are, let me know. Now, this is still a storeroom, so the other employees will have access to it between seven A.M. and five P.M. or so, so plan on being up and around by then. They won't mess with your stuff, but just in case someone doesn't get the word that I will squish them like a bug if they so much as look at your stuff, I'd secure your laptop in your locker."

"Yes, sir."

"The office manager, Rosetta, brings donuts and makes coffee for the employees at seven A.M. in the employee break room, but the donuts disappear pretty fast, so be warned," Hoffman said. He nodded at the desk. "There's a slip of paper there with the access code to the wireless router for your laptop, and a temporary user name and password to the company's employee site and calendar. Take a look at your calendar, the linesman course, and the employee handbook online before we get started tomorrow morning. We do most of our internal communications on the secure area of the website. If you have any access problems, let me know in the morning. Your course books are all online too." He handed him a cell phone. "Your new phone, all programmed with the important numbers. We use the phone quite a bit around here, especially for last-minute tasks, important calendar changes, and when you're out of earshot of the paging system. Business use only, please."

He stuck out a hand, and Brad shook it. "Welcome to Warbirds Forever, Brad. Your dad tells me you're a good pilot and a hard worker. Too bad about the Academy. I graduated from there in 1970. I can look back on it now and say it was a good experience, but at the time I remember thinking, 'What the hell am I doing here?' But we'll give you an experience here that I think you'll enjoy, and a lot closer to home."

"Thank you, sir," Brad said. "I'm looking forward to it."

"Good to hear. See you in the morning." And he lumbered out of the storeroom, the flimsy plywood door rattling loudly on its hinges even after it closed.

Yeah, Brad thought as he looked around, what in hell *am* I doing here? But then he put things in perspective: the space he had was similar in size to his bedroom in the trailer he lived in for years without complaint; he had a job, and he was going to learn to fly a few of those hot-looking airplanes back there in the hangar. This could be an incredible opportunity. He had no doubts that he could fly well enough to please Hoffman. Plus, the boss seemed like a really nice guy.

Brad set up his laptop, but since it was pretty late—and he had a couple beers at his going-away party—he decided to go to bed and get up early to log in and check his schedule. He unrolled the roll of foam on the bed. It looked like engine or parts packing material, several inches thick and fairly clean. He wedged the corners through the wires in the bed to keep it from rolling itself up again, wrapped it in a sheet, then made his bed.

He did indeed bring towels, so he was all set. He set his watch's alarm for six A.M., which should give him plenty of time to shower, check his schedule, and head out for donuts and coffee. He had brought energy bars and beef jerky, which would have to serve as meals until he had a chance to borrow a car and do some shopping.

He walked down the hallway with his toiletries kit and a towel and found the locker room and bathroom with no problem. He found his locker, already marked with B. MCLANAHAN on white cloth tape and black Magic Marker. About twenty other lockers had names on them. The bathroom and showers were extremely clean. He was actually starting to feel at home here—it was very much like the dorm rooms he had seen at the University of Nevada–Reno, except for the aircraft parts stacked to the ceiling in his room, of course.

The spring-and-wire bed made a horrendous creaking and groaning sound as he settled in. He would have to find a piece of plywood to strengthen it, maybe even find a thrift store or swap meet to get a better bed. But he was too tired to let the creaking bother him, and in minutes he was asleep.

"What in hell is going on here?"

Awakened from a deep sleep, Brad nearly flew straight up out of bed. The light snapped on, and Thomas Hoffman was standing in the open doorway, fists on his hips. "Wha . . . what? Mr. Hoffman? Why . . . ?"

"It's five A.M., McLanahan!" Hoffman thundered. "Why aren't you up?"

Brad checked his watch—it was indeed a little after five A.M. "I . . . I was going to get up at six, sir," he said. "That would give me plenty of time to . . ."

"You didn't log in and access your calendar, did you?"

"N . . . no, sir. I thought if I did that at six I'd have time to log in, check the calendar, and get up and get ready by the time the others showed . . ."

"Son, the other employees get here by seven, they're at work by seven fifteen, and they go home at four thirty," Hoffman said. "You, on the other hand, have several months of preparation, training, and testing ahead of you before you can even think of following their schedule. Your day starts at *five* A.M., mister, and it goes until all your work is done. I assume you didn't review the employee handbook or look at the linesman's training presentation, either?" Brad's expression gave him his answer, and he shook his head in exasperation. "You arrived late yesterday, so you're several hours behind. Your first day on the job and you'll be hustling to catch up.

"Okay, here is what we do," Hoffman said loudly, taking a menacing step toward Brad. "The priority is making sure all the ground vehicles are fueled up and oil checked, but before you do that you have to watch the linesman's PowerPoint presentation to learn how to use the fuel pumps, vehicles, and equipment, and then you have to pass a written test, and *then* you have to inspect the fuel filters in the gasoline, avgas, and Jet-A pumps before you service the vehicles, and you have to do all this in less than two hours, before the mechanics, customers, and clients arrive. Once the mechanics arrive, you help them get parts and supplies, help move airplanes, anything they need. Then Rosetta has employee, airport security, and schoolhouse paperwork for you to fill out. In between helping the mechanics, you need to prepare for your written systems, performance, and procedures test in the Cessna 182. But if you hear your name paged and you don't respond in the blink of an eye, I'm coming hunting for you, and you *don't* want *that,* believe me. Any questions?"

"Y-y-yes, sir," Brad stammered. "How do I know how to inspect the fuel pumps?"

"It's all in the PowerPoint you were supposed to watch last night," Hoffman said, looking as if the top of his head was going to explode. "Besides, your father told me you were experienced on the flight line—I hope he wasn't blowing smoke up my butt. Now, you've got ten minutes to get into your uniform, make me a pot of coffee, and get ready for your linesman's test. The ground vehicles need to be serviced by seven."

"Make coffee? But where do I find the . . . ?"

"Son, I showed you where the break room was last night, and all break rooms throughout the entire *planet* are the same: they have coffeemakers, sinks with running water, refrigerators with coffee, and cabinets with coffee filters, cups, stirrers, sugar, and all the other stuff. I'm sure you can figure it out. If you can't even figure out how to make me coffee, what makes you think you can fly one of my airplanes? Now *get moving*!"

WARBIRDS FOREVER INC.

A FEW DAYS LATER

Brad answered his cell phone on the first ring—he had found out that Tom Hoffman and many in his front office liked to use the cell phones as pagers, and answering the phone on more than the second ring was a big no-no. "Yes, Colonel Hoffman?"

"Brad, it's your dad," Patrick McLanahan said. "I just wanted to check in and see how things are going. Did you have a good day today?"

"I don't know, because it's not over yet."

"Not over? It's after nine P.M.!"

"I know," Brad moaned. "But I have a written test on the Piper Aztec first thing tomorrow morning, and then I'll have a flight review, like a Civil Air Patrol Form 5."

"Getting checked out in an Aztec?" Patrick asked. The Piper Aztec was a light twin-engine low-wing airplane, very easy to fly and economical to operate. "It sounds like great progress. What did you do this week?"

"What *haven't* I done?" Brad exclaimed. "Not only am I doing the flying stuff, but I'm constantly being called away for something else. There are tests for everything around here: linesman, security, aircraft ground handling, safety this and safety that. But I'm interrupted every ten minutes by Mr. Hoffman texting, calling, paging, or bellowing for me to do something."

"Sounds a lot like Civil Air Patrol. Did you pass all the tests?"

Brad took a deep breath, then let it out slowly. "Yes," he said finally. "The linesman and ground handling were actually easy—the guys back at Battle Mountain had already taught me most of the stuff."

"Good work."

"But once I passed the test, I have a bazillion tasks to do, all before the mechanics show up at seven o'clock."

"Seven A.M.? What time do you start every day?"

"Five A.M., if I'm lucky," Brad said. "And I just got back to the room a few minutes ago. But I've got to study for the Form 5."

"You're taking a flight review in an Aztec? What's that for?"

"The multiengine rating."

"Multiengine? You're doing multiengine stuff already? What about single-engine?"

"I already passed the check ride for the single-engine commercial certificate."

"You *did*? Congratulations!" Patrick exclaimed. A commercial pilot's certificate would allow Brad to fly for compensation, a big first step in any aviation career. "Wow, that was quick! You've been there for less than a week and you got your commercial license! Outstanding! Why didn't you call or text me?" Brad didn't say anything. "Man, you must be beat."

"I'm *exhausted,* Dad—'beat' doesn't even begin to describe it," Brad said. "Along with all the studying and flying, I'm running all over this place doing errands. I have to check the calendar online every hour for schedule changes, because if I'm late for anything, Mr. Hoffman screams in my face."

"You were late for something?"

Brad rubbed his eyes in exasperation. "I didn't check the online calendar the first night, and I didn't know I started at five A.M.," he said.

"But you knew about the online calendar, right?"

Brad sighed again. "Yes, Mr. Hoffman gave me all the log-in stuff," he admitted. "But I was so tired after I got here, I just went to bed. He told me to look it all over before we met up in the morning, and I thought he meant we were going to meet up when the employees got coffee and donuts at seven A.M. I was going to get up early to go online—I didn't know I'd be starting at frickin' oh-dark early and have *two hours* of stuff to do *before* work began!"

"I'll bet that won't happen again," Patrick said.

"Everybody is my boss, even the nonlicensed mechanics," Brad blurted out. "I miss out on the donuts every morning because they're gone before I have a chance to get to the break room, I usually miss lunch, and I'm having one of my energy bars for dinner because I haven't had a chance to go shopping."

"I'll put together a CARE package and either overnight it to you or fly it out myself, if I have the time," Patrick said. "What else do you need?"

"Everything," Brad said. "I live on break-room coffee, which *I* make most of the time because Colonel Hoffman drinks it by the gallon and never wants to run out. My bed is a rusty old contraption that looks like it was recovered from a hundred-year-old shipwreck, and my mattress is aircraft flight control packing material."

"I'll bring out an inflatable mattress too—it'll be better than packing foam," Patrick said. "Drop me a text or an e-mail and let me know if there's anything else you need. How's your room?"

"It's a storeroom, which I share with a couple dozen aircraft tires, cases of oil piled up to the ceiling, sheet metal, janitor stuff, and tools," Brad replied.

"But it's okay?"

Brad looked around his room, with its one bulb and

looming boxes surrounding him, and shrugged. "It's okay," he said grudgingly. "It's better than the tents out in the field during Second Beast."

"And you're doing all right?"

Brad hesitated again. "I guess," he said finally. "I am just so friggin' *tired*. Mr. Hoffman has tests for everything—two, three a day on everything imaginable. I'm up and down answering pages and driving back and forth between all the hangars he's got out here."

"But you've already got your commercial pilot's license, and you're going for a multiengine rating! That's great! I can't believe how fast you're going. You must be doing well."

Brad paused again, this time much longer; then, in a low voice: "Dad, I'm not sure if I can do this."

"What?"

"Dad, I know I can do intense flight training, and I can work, but . . . but I'm not sure if I can do *both*," he said. "I mean . . . I'm *really* tired, like crazy tired. I don't have time to eat, and I get maybe four or five hours of sleep a night."

"Mr. Hoffman says that'll all change after you're checked out in his planes and familiar with the routine," Patrick said. "It won't always be twenty-hour days. Besides, you'd have to pull a few all-nighters if you were in college, believe me."

"I feel like I'm being hazed, as if I was back in the Beast," Brad said. Patrick narrowed his eyes—he'd never heard Brad use this whiny tone like this, and he was angry and concerned at the same time. "I don't feel like I'm getting anywhere. Yes, I got the commercial pilot certificate, but I don't see that as much of an accomplishment—there are a lot of people knocking out their commercial license in two or three days around here. I study and take tests all the time, but except for the Cessna 182 I'm not doing any real flying."

"Brad, you've only been at it less than a week—Mr.

Hoffman told me his basic program is a minimum of five months," Patrick said. "You've got to give it a chance."

"I've read those flight training magazines. They say I can get my licenses and ratings in the same amount of time, and I can live in an apartment and don't have to do chores and errands—nothing else but fly and study."

"I know there are plenty of flight schools out there," Patrick said. "I don't know if we could have afforded them, but we could've given it a shot. But remember, the reason we chose Warbirds Forever was because you'd have the opportunity to get checked out in some of the huge array of planes Colonel Hoffman has out there."

"I thought it was because Colonel Hoffman is doing work for you."

"He is, but he offered the opportunity and built a program just for you," Patrick said. "Besides, I know he's a great instructor and aviator."

"I haven't flown with him yet. I fly with a different instructor almost every time." He paused for a few moments, then he said, "Dad, isn't there something else we can do?"

"You don't like it there? Sounds to me like you're doing pretty well."

"I'm really dragging, Dad," Brad said. "I shouldn't have to be everyone's slave just so I can get a few ratings."

Patrick didn't like hearing his son talk like this—it sounded as if he was giving up. After dropping out of the Academy, Patrick was afraid that his son was developing an unhealthy quitter's mind-set. "Here's the situation, Brad," he said in a deep monotone, trying not to sound angry. "You have what's left of a college fund. I wish it had been bigger, and we've already expended a lot of it with Warbirds Forever, but there it is.

"You're an adult and can make your own decisions about what you want to do and how you want to do it," Patrick went

on. "Choice one: you can use what's left of the money on any
school you want. I don't like the idea of borrowing money for
college, but if we have to, we will. Two: you can take the money,
minus taxes and penalties, and use it for whatever else you
want, like flying or travel. I hope you don't do that, but it's up
to you. Or three: you can give Warbirds Forever another shot.
We've already paid the money—you might as well stick it out,
get as many certificates and ratings as you can, then make a
decision when it's time for the next tuition payment in three
months."

"*Three months!*" Bradley groaned. "Oh, man . . ."

"Brad, you made a commitment, and Tom Hoffman has
built a great program for you based on that commitment,"
Patrick said sternly.

"You can ask him to refund the money for the flying I
haven't done yet."

"I could, but I won't," Patrick snapped. "He made a
commitment to you, me, and the folks he hired to train you. Do
you think your instructors just appeared out of thin air? Tom
had to recruit and hire them. Some of them have families that
rely on that income. Do you think it's right for them to get laid
off just because you're *weary*? A lot of those guys have second
and third jobs, and some had to relocate to get the job. If you
quit, they lose their jobs." Brad said nothing.

"So what's it going to be, Brad: stay or quit? I think you
should stay, but it's up to you." Still nothing from Bradley.
"Give me a call when you make up your mind. I'll fly out
this weekend either to drop off your CARE package and air
mattress, or pick you up and bring you home. Talk to you later,
son." And Patrick hung up.

Patrick decided to let Brad think about it over the weekend,
but he hadn't heard anything, so a little before eight A.M.

Monday morning, Patrick landed his turbine pressurized Centurion at Reno-Stead Airport and taxied over to the main Warbirds Forever hangar. He was pleasantly surprised to be greeted by Bradley, who trotted out onto the tarmac wearing ear protectors and an orange reflective safety vest and carrying marshaler's batons. "Hey, Brad," Patrick said after he was led to his parking spot and shut down the engine.

"Hi, Dad," Brad said. They didn't embrace or shake hands. "How was the flight?"

"A little bumpy already," Patrick said. "I needed to speak with Colonel Hoffman, and I didn't hear from you, so I thought I'd bring the air mattress and some goodies for you."

"Thank you."

They stood in awkward silence for a few moments, then Patrick asked, "Made a decision yet?"

"I don't really have much choice, do I?"

"You do, and I'll support any decision you make." Brad's cell phone beeped, and he looked at the display. "You're being paged?"

"For about the hundredth time this morning," he said. "Do you need fuel? Should I top it off?"

"Depends—are you going back with me, or staying?"

The cell phone beeped again. Brad looked at the display with a rather concerned expression, then at his father. "I gotta go," he said. He looked at his father, once, the weariness evident in his face, but he nodded. "I'll top it off for you."

"Okay, Brad," Patrick said. That *should* mean he was staying—the turbine P210 couldn't hold two men, all Brad's belongings, the CARE package, the air mattress, and full fuel tanks, and Brad knew that. Patrick retrieved the CARE package and the air mattress and headed inside.

On his way there, he saw Brad hurrying out of Tom Hoffman's office. "I'll put this stuff in your room, Brad," he said.

"Thanks, Dad," Brad said over his shoulder, then quickly disappeared.

Patrick found Hoffman at his computer, with the TV on in a corner. The office was Spartan, with just a desk, two chairs, and a couple bookshelves crammed with technical manuals. The walls were filled with photographs, plaques, and memorabilia from his twenty-six years in the U.S. Air Force. "When are you going to invest in a real office, Tom?" Patrick asked.

"Don't need one," Hoffman replied. He nodded at his laptop computer. "My entire life and business is right here." He glanced up at the television. "What do you make of the Chinese acting up in the South China Sea, General?"

"I don't find it credible that the Coast Guard helicopter was shot down by mistake," Patrick said. "If they were recovering pieces of that Poseidon, the crew of that Coast Guard helicopter would have seen them doing it. Downing that helicopter bought them several hours to search for wreckage."

"So you think China was involved in the P-8 crash too?"

"I don't have any details, but I don't believe in coincidences," Patrick said. "There's no doubt that China is laying claim to the South China Sea and building up their air and naval forces there quickly. I think we're going to see many more unexplained occurrences, mistakes, and accidents out there. Beijing thinks as long as there's no solid trail leading to them that we won't do anything."

"Well, we're *not* doing anything," Hoffman said, "so it appears their strategy is working. What do you make of the Chinese president laid up and the vice prez taking over?"

"Zhou was starting to get up there, so I'm not too surprised," Patrick said. "We'll see how the new guy does. He's much younger, just a little older than President Phoenix, and Gao was educated in America. Other than that, I don't know much about him."

"I don't like seeing all these Chinese military units gearing up all of a sudden," Hoffman commented, "but I guess with a sudden change in leadership and the uncertainty in the country, that's bound to happen." He nodded at the packages. "Stuff for Brad?"

"He's running short of some things, and he moaned about his bed, so I brought an air mattress for him. Mind showing me where his room is?"

"Of course, sir." Hoffman got up, grabbed the air mattress, and led the way.

A mechanic was just leaving the room carrying a box of airplane parts when Patrick and Hoffman arrived. Patrick looked around. "Brad described it pretty well," he said.

"Best I could do, General," Hoffman said.

"No, no, this is okay, Tom," Patrick said. "Maybe it'll give him a little incentive to finish his training and get out there to make some money to afford his own place." He set the box of food and clothing on Brad's bed, and Hoffman threw the air mattress beside it. "How's he doing, Tom?" Patrick asked.

"You were right—he's a good stick, a good student, and a good worker," Hoffman said. "But I'll be straight with you, General: I sense an attitude about him."

"What kind of attitude?"

"An attitude that he's better than this, like he doesn't deserve the life he's leading," Hoffman said. "I see it in him when he works around here: that he thinks he's too good for all this." Patrick said nothing; Hoffman noticed his grim expression and shrugged. "I'm giving it to you straight, General. I've led aviators and techs for over thirty years. I know what I'm talking about."

"I appreciate that," Patrick said. "Character and attitude matter as much as skill and knowledge—they're all connected. Brad has to pass muster on all of it. I leave it to you to determine if he's good enough for your program."

"Thank you, sir."

Patrick nodded; then, after a short pause, he said, "Brad seems to think you're riding him especially hard."

"Yes, I am," Hoffman said bluntly.

Patrick blinked. "You are?"

"You bet I am," Hoffman said. Patrick had to struggle to quash a rising feeling of anger in his chest; Hoffman obviously noticed it right away. "General, you can't swing a dead cat by the tail around this place without hitting a genuine prima donna. Guys spend millions of dollars on flying toys, and they want me to train them on how to fly them. They don't want to know anything about the aircraft or its systems—they just want to fly a sharp-looking, hair-on-fire badass jet. Unless they're completely unsafe, I'll take their money, train them, and let them fly away. If they're not interested in learning more about the jets they fly, that's their business.

"But I have a great opportunity to avoid all that with Bradley," Hoffman went on. "Frankly, sir, Bradley's on the very cusp of being a prima donna. He's a good pilot, but the problem is: he *knows* he's good. He also knows he's General Patrick McLanahan's son. He does the work and he can fly."

"What exactly is he doing?"

"Every time I page him and he walks into my office and I tell him to do something, I get the hairy eyeball," Hoffman explained. "If the order doesn't involve flying, he gives me the *look*. I get a strong vibe from him almost every time."

"Is he disrespectful?"

"No, not outwardly or verbally—you would have gotten a call from me much earlier if he was," Hoffman said. "He does the same thing with the mechanics and the techs, and they've pointed it out to me. And every time he does it, it makes me want to load him up even more with nonflying crap to do."

"Load him up? Why?" Patrick asked.

"To see if he'll quit, like he quit the Academy," Hoffman said. "From what you've said, sir, Brad is a tough, athletic, and dedicated young man and student. You know I'm an Academy grad, and I still do liaison and orientation activities, so I know the Academy. With his sports and Civil Air Patrol experience, he should have had the Zoo nailed, even if he was getting hazed pretty badly by upperclassmen who knew who his father was. My opinion is that perhaps he didn't want the Academy as badly as he thought . . . or, if I may say, sir: as badly as *you* wanted it."

Patrick choked down a strong twinge of indignation . . . but he knew Hoffman was probably right. "Maybe so, Tom," Patrick said. "It couldn't have been harder than he expected because he was getting ready for it for a year—he knew exactly what to expect."

"My point exactly," Hoffman said. "Brad busted out during Second Beast—that's the field portion of summer camp, ten times as hard as First Beast, which is pretty damned intense. He probably had First Beast nailed, but all of a sudden he's up to his eyeballs in mud and grief and he's not comfortable, so he got in some upperclassman's face. I've seen it a hundred times." Patrick said nothing—because he knew Hoffman was probably spot-on. "You want me to stop bugging Bradley and just treat him like a student, sir? I've got enough other guys around here to do the busywork, and he *is* doing pretty well with the flying stuff, so I can push him a bit more on his ratings and get him some more stick time."

Patrick shook his head immediately. "I'm not going to tell you how to run your business or your training program, Tom," he said. "Truth is, over the years I've probably—no, I *have*—been too easy with him with all the travel and assignments I've had, with Brad living with his aunts and grandmother after Wendy was killed, and maybe he hasn't had to sacrifice as much as other kids. No, you keep on doing what you're doing. Let's see what he does. He said he has his single-engine commercial ticket already, and he's working on his multiengine?"

"Like I said, he knows how to fly."

"And we can keep this conversation between us."

"Tell him if you want, sir," Hoffman said. "Tell him I expect him to be positive, proactive, and engaged. I want him to start acting like he's part of a team. Right now he thinks he's just an errand boy. As long as he feels that way, he always will be. You can't tell someone to be a team player or to be positive and proactive—they've got to want to be that themselves. I think, eventually, he will join the team—we'll just see if he can gut it out long enough. But at least you should know that's he's a good pilot and a good worker. He's just got to ditch the 'tude."

"I hope he does, Tom. I hope he does."

"Same here, sir." They left the storeroom and headed toward the main hangar. "So, any word about your Excalibur proposal?"

"A few requests for additional information, background checks on some of the engineers, and that's about it," Patrick said. "You can probably expect a visit by the FBI or Department of Defense on your background and those of the instructors you propose to use, and maybe some more information on the training program."

"Already have—I turned over five boxes of stuff to the Defense Investigation Agency. No problems that I'm aware of."

"Good," Patrick said. "But the silence is deafening—I haven't heard no, but not a yes either. At least I haven't heard volleys of laughter yet from the Pentagon."

"It's a good plan, sir," Hoffman said. "But DoD is not accustomed to buying *old* equipment, even if the idea makes sense and is doable. But I'll be ready to swing into action when you give the word. I've got a list of pilots ready to go through training, mostly ex-B-1 crewdogs but a few civilians. It's a pretty geriatric bunch, but they're all well qualified and eager as hell."

They walked through the main hangar out onto the parking ramp. Bradley was just climbing down from a ladder after fueling the right wing and was carrying the Jet-A hose and the ladder to the other wing. "When you're done, check the pressure on those tires—I see a little bulge," Hoffman yelled out to Brad. "And don't forget to wash the windows."

"Yes, sir," Brad responded . . . and then Patrick saw it, that little expression that silently said, "Anything else, master?" Hoffman looked at Patrick, who nodded—he had seen it too.

"The 'tude," Hoffman said to Patrick in a soft voice. He shook his head, then smiled wryly and shook hands with Patrick. "I'll see you later, sir," he said in his usual booming voice. "Have a nice flight back." And he left Patrick alone with Brad.

"What did Colonel Hoffman say?" Brad asked.

"Nothing," Patrick replied. "We put your stuff on your bed."

"Thank you," Brad said stonily as he started up the ladder, fuel nozzle in hand. He laid a protective neoprene mat over the wing to guard against any damage to the deicing panels on the wing's leading edge, then uncapped the fuel port and began feeding jet fuel into the wing fuel tank. "Are you heading home right away?"

"We have our Monday department head lunch meeting at eleven o'clock," Patrick said. "Then it's the meeting with the board of directors. Mondays are always pretty busy."

"It's pretty much the same around this place," Brad said morosely. "The pilots fly in and they want it all done snap-snap, and Mr. Hoffman kisses their kneecaps and then barks at me. If he's not giving me yet another menial job to do, I have to read another tech manual and do another test. It's the same routine every day."

Patrick could feel the anger rising in his chest, and he was about to do some barking of his own, but then his intraocular monitor flared to life. The late Dr. Jon Masters had replaced one of Patrick's corneas with a tiny electronic device that acted like a large high-definition computer monitor, allowing Patrick to use a computer and access the Internet anywhere without any other hardware. Patrick scowled at the back of Brad's head, then stepped away to answer the call. "Patrick here. What's up, Kylie?"

"Just got an e-mail from the Pentagon," his assistant, Kylie, said. "I forwarded it to you. The undersecretary of the Air Force for acquisitions wants to see you, Dr. Oglethorpe, and Colonel Hoffman immediately in the national security adviser's office." Dr. Linus Oglethorpe was Sky Masters's new chief engineer, replacing the late Jon Masters, and the head of the Excalibur design project.

Patrick quickly read the e-mail, his excitement rising. "Get us airline tickets for this afternoon, Kylie. I'll double-check with Colonel Hoffman to see if he's free."

"The Pentagon is sending a plane for you, Patrick," Kylie said. "It's already on the way. It'll be here in a few hours. I've sent a text to Colonel Hoffman too—I assume he'll be flying back with you in the Centurion."

An even better sign, Patrick thought. "I'll be back within the hour. Can you throw some clothes and travel stuff in a bag for me, and make sure my laptop has all our latest presentation materials and budget sheets? And check on Dr. Oglethorpe to make sure he's ready to go—you know how he can be."

"Will do, sir," Kylie replied, and she hung up.

Patrick hurried back to Hoffman's office, but his assistant, Rosetta, said he had already left for home to pack and said he looked very excited. Patrick stepped quickly back out to Brad and the Centurion. Brad was busy cleaning the windshield, and he had a portable compressed nitrogen bottle with him ready to help one of the licensed mechanics fill the tires if they needed it. "What's going on, Dad?" he asked.

"We're on our way to Washington to talk about the XB-1 project," Patrick said. "Colonel Hoffman is coming with me. The Pentagon is sending a jet to pick us up in Battle Mountain." Patrick called up a weight-and-balance and flight plan form on his intraocular computer system. "I'd better check the weight and balance with Colonel Hoffman—he's a pretty big guy."

"I think you'll be okay," Brad said. He finished checking the tires a few minutes later. "Just as I thought: the tires were fine," he said.

"Brad, you seem to be doing an awful lot of complaining today, and when I spoke to you on the phone the other day," Patrick said as he worked, accessing the programs using a virtual tactile keyboard on his intraocular display—it was always comical for Brad to watch his father poke and swipe at empty space and see his eyes dart back and forth as he worked. "You may think you're getting a raw deal here, and I've given you your options. Just don't make other people's lives miserable."

"I don't complain to anyone."

"See that you don't," Patrick said. "And it's not just your words but your attitude that gets people down. You have to at least *act* like your work and your study mean something to you. If all folks around here see of you is this bummed-out moaning mumbling Eeyore, you bring everyone down, and that's the impression of you that you'll burn into everyone's brain."

"Is that what Colonel Hoffman said?"

"That's what I've noticed around here myself in the short time I've been here, and I don't like it," Patrick said, "looking up" from his virtual computer to glance at his son. "You know what it's like to be a team player, whether it's Civil Air Patrol or football. You also know that the team needs the support of every member, even if you're not doing exactly what you'd rather be doing. You didn't grumble about being a ground team member in Civil Air Patrol, even if you'd rather be flying; you didn't complain when you were benched or when you played special teams instead of first string."

"But that was different—I knew what I was doing back then," Brad said. "I was usually the leader or captain. Around here, I'm lower than whale poop on the bottom of the ocean."

"You may not remember when you first joined Civil Air Patrol or were a junior varsity football player, but I do," Patrick said. "You always sat in the back of the room, never wanted to get called on, had to be told how to do something a dozen times, and would panic when the others would turn and look at you or whisper about something stupid you said. It's the same now. You're the new guy, and you have to prove yourself all over again, just like you had to do working at Sky Masters."

"Colonel Hoffman doesn't like me," Brad said. "He gives me stupid busywork stuff to do. He knows I'm here to fly, but he gives me menial errands to do instead."

"Brad, remember our conversation about me working for the board of directors of Sky Masters?" Patrick asked. "Just like the board, Colonel Hoffman is the boss—he can treat you any way he likes and tell you to do anything he wants. He's providing flying, simulator, and classroom time in exchange for work. If you don't like the way he treats or teaches you, you're an adult and you have a vote: you vote with your feet. Just politely quit, pack up your stuff, give me a call, and we depart the fix and go home. I think you'd be squandering a great opportunity, but if you're truly unhappy here, you should get out before you get fired or start making others just as miserable as you are. I'll help you figure out what your options are after that.

"Because you're an adult, I'm not going to tell you what to do, just give you my advice: if you're going to stay here, you should work to become a team player and a trusted, valued employee. Start acting like a team member and maybe Colonel Hoffman will treat you better."

Several minutes later, Tom Hoffman came out of the main hangar with a single suitcase. "The wife is infinitely better at packing than I am," he said. "Brad, Jerry Melton is in charge until I get back. Get with him if you have any questions about the calendar. Sondra will be in charge of your flying, ground school, and test calendar."

"Yes, sir," Brad responded. As Hoffman was hurrying past him, Brad caught a glimpse of his father's expression, and he looked back at Hoffman's lone bag. It took only a few moments for Brad to catch on. "Don't you need your laptop on this trip, Colonel?" he asked.

Hoffman shook his head in disgust of his own forgetfulness. "Damn, I'd forget my head if it wasn't screwed onto my neck," he said.

"I'll get it for you," Brad said. Patrick's mood brightened considerably. "I'll grab some bottles of water for you too for the flight back to Battle Mountain. Do you want a Thermos of coffee for the flight, sir?"

"Yeah, coffee sounds good," Hoffman said distractedly as he searched his pockets for something else he thought he might have forgotten. "The Air Force coffee they serve on the plane is probably crap."

"Got your wallet, sir?" Brad asked.

Hoffman touched the rear pocket of his slacks where the wallet should have been. "Oh, cripes. It's probably in the console of my pickup."

"I'll get it," Brad said. "Oh, one thing, sir: the wireless router we're using on the east side of the main hangar is an older dash-G model."

"A what?"

"It's second generation, but the newer ones are much better," Brad went on. "I can get us a newer WIMAX 4G router for practically nothing. It has better range through the metal walls and much faster speeds. It'll extend network coverage even out to the parking lot and the ramp."

"I don't know about routers—all I want is for my wireless to work," Hoffman said gruffly. "Tell Rosetta what you just told me, and tell her I want you to fix it by the time I get back."

"Yes, sir." Brad shot a sly smile at his father, then trotted off.

Hoffman noticed Patrick looking directly at him with a smile. "What are you grinning at, General?" he asked.

"Nothing, you old fart," Patrick said, his whole day suddenly bright and shiny. "Nothing at all."

OFFICE OF THE NATIONAL
SECURITY ADVISER, THE WHITE
HOUSE, WASHINGTON, D.C.

THE NEXT MORNING

"Welcome back to the White House, General," said retired Army general and former chairman of the Joint Chiefs of Staff William Glenbrook, President Phoenix's national security adviser. "You need to get to Washington more often." Glenbrook looked to Patrick exactly how he remembered him back six years ago, tall and burly with a powerful handshake and a ready smile, although now he wore tailored suits instead of Army green.

"Thank you, sir," Patrick said, trying not to grimace as he and Glenbrook shook hands. Patrick had been a special adviser to President Kevin Martindale on new long-range strike technology, and he and Glenbrook rarely saw eye to eye. Patrick had been a strong advocate for the militarization of space; Glenbrook thought the technology was vastly too expensive for its limited capabilities. Profligate spending on unproven, futuristic space technology was one of the reasons stated by critics—and echoed by Glenbrook—for the economic meltdown and the unceremonious end of the Martindale administration.

"Nah, it's Bill around here, Patrick," Glenbrook said casually. "Or sometimes it's 'Say Again,' like when I give the president some advice he didn't expect, which is more often than I care to admit."

"I know the feeling, Bill," Patrick said. "I'd like to introduce you to Colonel Thomas Hoffman, Air Force retired, owner of Warbirds Forever Inc., and to Dr. Linus Oglethorpe, chief scientist and engineer at Sky Masters Inc. These two gentlemen are the architects and foundation of the XB-1 project. Gents, William Glenbrook, U.S. Army, retired, the president's national security adviser."

"Thanks for the introductions, Patrick," Glenbrook said as he shook hands. "When we were in President Martindale's administration I didn't see Patrick that often, squirreled away down in his office in the White House basement or blasting off to Armstrong Space Station all the time, but I could definitely tell when one of his ideas was put into motion—this place became even more chaotic, and back in the Pentagon I had to scramble to figure out what in hell he did." He turned to the towheaded, bespectacled, nerdy-looking man standing behind him. "Gentlemen, meet Dr. Gerald Murth, undersecretary of defense for acquisitions. When your proposal was kicked up from the Air Force to the secretary of defense's office, he was assigned to review it. The secretary of defense was briefed yesterday. Now it's my turn, and I thought you'd want to be here." He waved them all to seats, and an aide brought in a tray of coffee, which Hoffman nearly pushed others out of his way to get at. When they were all settled, Glenbrook waved to Murth. "Dr. Murth, proceed."

"Thank you, General Glenbrook," Murth said in a high-pitched, rather squeaky voice. "If you'll allow me, General?" He turned to look directly at Patrick. "Sir, I have to tell you, I've followed your exploits over the years with a real sense of . . ." He paused, afraid of offending, then resigning himself to speak his mind: " . . . astonishment."

"Interesting choice of words, Undersecretary Murth," Patrick said.

"You must admit, General, that you have a certain . . . reputation," Murth said, obviously enjoying a slight pause before uttering the last word in his sentences, especially if they were meant to be direct and not complimentary. He noticed Patrick's uncomfortable body language and was evidently pleased to have elicited it. "A reputation that leaves senior officials and military commanders I know and respect with a feeling that they have no idea what you will do next, except that whatever it is, it will be . . . bombastic. Globally so." Patrick said nothing. "I must tell you, sir, that when your proposal reached my desk from the Air Force, I was not prepared to be objective. Your reputation and service record fills me with a great sense of . . . trepidation."

"Very honest of you to say so, Mr. Undersecretary," Patrick said. "However, I think we'd all be better served if you left personalities and nonrelevant history out of the evaluation, and let the project stand on its own merits."

"Dr. Murth is well known in the Pentagon for speaking his mind, Patrick," Glenbrook said with a wry smile. "Frankly, I think Dr. Murth is the Pentagon's designated project assassin. But he has the highest recommendation from Secretary Hayes. Proceed."

"I was directed to examine the proposal, despite my . . . reservations," Murth went on. "I was directed to report back to Secretary Hayes with my honest assessment of your proposal and a recommendation on whether it merited any more of the Pentagon's . . . consideration."

"Let's get on with it, Murth," Tom Hoffman said irritably. Murth's head snapped around, and he looked at Hoffman with undisguised surprise and indignation, obviously not accustomed to be spoken to like that. "We've got work to do." Glenbrook's only reaction to the outburst was a thinly disguised smile, the index finger of his left hand on his lips—obviously he was going to let the arguments fly from both sides.

"Yes, of . . . course," Murth said, giving Hoffman an irritated scowl and getting an even deeper, darker one in return.

"You are Colonel Thomas Hoffman, the one who will train the air and ground crews? You are the"—Murth looked him up and down quickly—"flying teacher?"

"Twenty-six years in the Air Force, fifteen years in B-1B Lancers, over six thousand hours' flying time," Hoffman said. "Initial instructor cadre in the B-1, aircraft and simulator instructor, wing and division chief of Stan-Eval. I have an airline transport pilot rating and type ratings in ninety different aircraft. I've trained astronauts in how to fly the Gulfstream modified to fly like the Space Shuttle. FAA master flight instructor in Nevada for the past six years. I can fly and instruct in anything from a Piper Super Cub to a Boeing 787. I'll also be helping train the maintenance and ground crews."

"I'm sure that's a very impressive résumé, Mr. Hoffman," Murth said dismissively. "My experience has been: those that can, do; those that can't . . . teach." Hoffman's eyes and cheeks flared, and Patrick thought he would have to physically restrain him. "Flight instructors are certainly a step above other teachers but then again, you are *just* a teacher. Your military record is unremarkable, and your current business is based in Reno, Nevada—not exactly a world center of aviation."

"Ever hear of the National Championship Air Races, bub?" Hoffman asked. "I instruct in every one of the planes that race at the Reno Air Races, and I take care of a number of them."

"Yes, in fact, I have heard of that event. It's the one where an older pilot killed ten spectators and injured over seventy in a crash a few years ago? Did you train that pilot, Colonel Hoffman?"

Hoffman averted his eyes, but when he raised then again, they were blazing with indignation of his own. "Yes, I did," he said. "He was my friend, and one of the best pilots on the planet. There was a technical malfunction."

"I love that term: 'technical malfunction,'" Murth said. "I

hear it quite often. It tends to invalidate all other actual reasons for . . . mistakes." He looked Hoffman up and down again. "How old are you, Mr. Hoffman?"

"I'm sure you know exactly how old I am, Murth," Hoffman said irritably. "Don't play games with me."

"You wouldn't be considering using age as a reason to deny or invalidate this project, would you, Mr. Undersecretary?" Patrick asked.

"General McLanahan, I don't need a reason to deny approval for this project: all I need is the stroke of a pen," Murth said. "That's my . . . responsibility."

"We're all anxious to get back to work, Murth," Tom Hoffman repeated. Patrick cast Hoffman a warning glance but said nothing. "We have our technology presentation ready to show you if you'd like, or we can answer any questions you may have."

"My staff and I have seen your presentation, and it is quite . . . unbelievable," Murth said. "Frankly, General McLanahan, no one here . . . believes you can do it."

"I assure you, Mr. Undersecretary, we can," Linus Oglethorpe said evenly. Born in England but now a U.S. citizen, Oglethorpe had been Jonathan Colin Masters's understudy and protégé for almost two decades at Sky Masters. He had an impossibly high forehead, blue sparkly eyes behind his thick horn-rimmed glasses, and large ears that protruded Yoda-like from his head. "We invented the process and have demonstrated it with two airframes. The aircraft are better than new, sir."

"All we need are the airframes, engines, avionics, fuel, and weapons," Patrick said. "We charge a flat fee to operate the aircraft under the Air Force's direction. We'll supply the work and the manpower. In two years or less, we'll have a wing ready to deploy."

"Airframes, engines, avionics, fuel, and weapons—isn't

that like building a plane?" Murth asked. "The taxpayers are footing the bill for the whole machine, *plus* paying you a . . . fee?"

"True, Mr. Undersecretary, but the difference is: the taxpayers have *already* paid for all that," Patrick said. "The taxpayers have already purchased the engines, weapons, avionics, and fuel—we're just taking what we already have off the shelf. At our expense, not yours, we're assembling your bought-and-paid-for parts onto airframes that have not just been paid for but have already been fully capitalized and are just sitting in the Boneyard, and we're making them operational for a tenth of what it would cost to build a similar plane. The technology is already there: we've been refurbishing B-1 Lancers like this for years. And you're not paying for the labor to refurbish the planes. After they're assembled, the Pentagon can always train its own crews to man them. But until they're ready, the Pentagon pays Sky Masters a fee to operate them."

"How will we know if any of this really . . . works?"

"We've already got two flying birds, all ready for weapon tests and instructor and ground maintenance training," Patrick said. "Sky Masters pays for the refurbishment, aircrew and maintenance techs training, and upkeep. As I said, Sky Masters developed the refurbishment program years ago, and several mothballed planes were successfully modified using our plans."

Murth looked skeptical in the extreme, and he silently told Glenbrook so. "It's a lot of money," Murth said. "If it fails . . ."

"If it fails, Secretary Murth, the government is not out anything—Sky Masters is investing heavily in manpower and resources," Patrick said. "All we're asking for is access to the hardware; we do the rest. In less than two years we'll have a fleet of heavy bombers that can perform a wide range of tasks at distances far in excess of any other aircraft in the arsenal. If it fails, the government gets its hardware back, and you put it back on the shelf."

"I'm not convinced," Murth said. "I'll meet in private with General Glenbrook and Secretary Hayes and give them my report. They may want to meet with you some time in the future, but I . . ."

At that moment there was a knock on the door to Glenbrook's office. Before he could tell whoever it was to go away, his assistant opened the door . . . and Vice President Ann Page entered the office. "Good morning, gentlemen," she said gaily. All the men in the office shot to their feet, shocked expressions on their faces. "I heard the best of the best was back in town. The president thought I might want to sit in on this meeting." She went over and gave Patrick a warm hug. "Nice to have you back in the White House, Patrick," she said. "The place feels better with you here. The president sends his regards and would like for you and your companions to join him and me for dinner tonight in the residence."

"I'd be happy to, Miss Vice President."

"Excellent, excellent." Patrick made introductions again, and they all found seats. Ann Page motioned to William Glenbrook. "When President Phoenix first took office, he made me his national security adviser, which I greatly appreciated, but I'm glad to have General Glenbrook at the helm of the national security staff. Well, Undersecretary Murth, I understand you have studied General McLanahan's proposal," Ann said. "What do you think?"

Murth was quite taken aback by Page's sudden appearance and her warm welcome for Patrick, but he quickly shook it off. "Miss Vice President, my recommendation to General Glenbrook is the same I made to Secretary Hayes: the plan is a waste of money and resources and should not be approved under any circumstances."

"Tell me why, sir."

"General McLanahan proposes to turn an aircraft designed over forty years ago into a multirole long-range aircraft that can operate and survive in the battlespace of the twenty-first century, ma'am," Murth said. "It is simply not credible. You simply cannot take a vintage car, bolt a big engine and fat tires on it, and turn it into a dragster."

"Excuse me, Undersecretary Murth," Ann said, raising a finger with a smile. "You're far too young to appreciate this, but when I was a teenager, that's *exactly* what my brothers and I did, with everything from Model A Fords to '57 Chevy Bel Airs, and we raced the hell out of those things." She smiled at Patrick. "General McLanahan here is not a gearhead, though—he's a techhead. He probably would've taken my souped-up Model A dragster and made it fly, or even shot it into space. Is that your plan, Patrick—take a Model A dragster and make it fly?"

"The B-1 Lancer is not a Model A, Miss Vice President," Tom Hoffman interjected. "It was far ahead of its time and was the most potent aircraft in the bomber fleet. The general's plan makes it even better."

Vice President Page turned to Tom Hoffman. "I was told you are a plain-spoken and no-nonsense guy, Colonel Hoffman," she said. "So tell it to me straight, sir: What do you think of this whole plan?"

"I told General McLanahan that the Pentagon would never buy it, ma'am," Hoffman said immediately. "It's a good plan, but it won't sell."

"Why?"

"Because the Pentagon wants the latest and greatest, and to hell with operational necessity, budgets, and out-of-the-box ideas," Hoffman replied. "The bean counters like Murth here think that if it's not absolute state-of-the-art, it's a waste of money. I rebuild dozens of World War Two–, Korea-, and

Vietnam-era planes every year, and they are fully certified and able to do the job—they are far better than they were when they were first built, and that's how the XB-1 Excaliburs will be. When General McLanahan approached me with this plan to train crews to fly refurbished B-1 bombers, I signed on immediately. But I told General McLanahan he'd be wasting his company's money because the government would never commit to fielding forty-year-old bombers."

"It's not stealthy, the airframes are of questionable integrity, the basic systems such as flight controls and landing gear are unsupported and prone to unexpected failure, and in order to fly and maintain them Colonel Hoffman here has to recruit aviators and mechanics that are well into their . . . postretirement years, ma'am," Murth said determinedly, showing his displeasure at Hoffman's outbursts. "It's chasing good money after bad. The Russians and the Chinese can fly rings around it. General McLanahan thinks that just because it's less expensive than modern alternatives such as the F-35 or F/A-18, it's better. It certainly is nothing of the . . . kind."

"I see," Ann said. "So tell me, Patrick: we've got Super Hornets, and soon the F-35 Lightnings will be operational . . . hopefully. So why do we need these B-1 bombers?"

"Ma'am, the F-35 and even the F/A-18 Hornet are perfect examples of what's wrong with military procurement: building equipment first and then finding a mission for them," Patrick said. "The F/A-18 is a good carrier-based fighter and bomber, but its short combat radius limits its usability in the Pacific theater without lots of external fuel tanks that rob its performance, a carrier, or basing very close to enemy shores. The Super Hornet was meant to replace the A-6 Intruder, A-7 Corsair, and A-12 stealth bombers and F-14 Tomcat fighter, but it can't do what the others can.

"The F-35 was supposed to replace the F-16 Fighting

Falcon," Patrick went on, "and it has some very advanced capabilities, but its payload is virtually the same as the F-16 and its combat radius is only marginally greater. They are planes that do many roles well, but some roles not as well as the planes they are supposed to replace.

"Now we have a new battle concept: the AirSea Battle. Everyone says AirSea Battle is not specifically designed around a future conflict with China, but unless we go to war with Japan, India, or Australia, there are few other adversaries that require both land- and carrier-based attackers to prosecute. The F-35 and F/A-18 Super Hornet have fantastic technologies, but they can't do the long-range mission in the Pacific without operating from carriers or forward bases, so trying to shoehorn the Lightning or Hornet to do AirSea Battle just won't work."

"So just put cruise missiles on them," Ann said.

"The Lightning can carry the most advanced nonnuclear air-launched cruise missile, the AGM-158A-Extended Range," Patrick responded, "but it has to carry the missiles externally, which greatly decreases its range and destroys its stealthiness—a workable option, if we had enough F-35s, but again we were adapting a weapon system for a mission rather than designing a weapons system *for* a mission. The BGM-109 Tomahawk ship- or sub-launched tactical land attack missile has a greater range, but the ships would need to move in closer to shore to strike targets deep inside enemy territory. Again, workable, but not ideal. The cruise missiles are also subsonic, and of course most only have one warhead. The nonnuclear intercontinental ballistic missile is another option, but launching a large ballistic missile toward Asia would certainly make a lot of unfriendly nations anxious at best and invite a nuclear counterstrike at worst. The answer to me was: build a bomber that can carry multiple cruise missiles and is stealthy enough to come close to or even overfly enemy territory."

"Spoken like a true bomber puke," Ann interjected with a smile.

"Guilty as charged, ma'am," Patrick said. "The B-2 Spirit stealth bomber can certainly do it, but we only have a handful of them surviving after the American Holocaust. The Next Generation Bomber and the Thor's Hammer space-based attack weapon programs were supposed to do the mission, but they were canceled, and even if they were restarted tomorrow, it would take a minimum of five years to build a force large enough to do the job."

"So you thought of refurbishing mothballed bombers to do it?"

"Yes, ma'am," Patrick said. "I took my son, Bradley, for a tour of the Aerospace Maintenance and Regeneration Group at Davis-Monthan Air Force Base a few years ago, and he was blown away by all the shrink-wrapped B-1 bombers stored out there. Sky Masters Inc. has been providing the technology for modernizing B-52 and B-1 bombers for years, and when I took over at Sky Masters, I decided I wanted to get back into the business of rebuilding the bomber force. The Air Force leadership had canceled their B-1 refurbishing program at Palmdale because of budget cuts, and they were all too happy to sell me the entire program. Then we bought a quantity of F136 engines and realized they would fit just fine in B-1 bombers and how much it enhanced the plane's performance and fuel efficiency. Then, after sticking modern engines in the B-1s, we found how easy it was to retrofit modern digital avionics into B-1 bombers as well. The Air Force was willing to give us a bunch of off-the-shelf avionics for little to no cost. Before we knew it, the XB-1 was born. The program practically developed itself."

"Interesting story, Patrick," Vice President Ann Page said.

"Except it's not the entire story, Miss Vice President,"

Murth interjected. "The B-1 isn't stealthy. It can't survive over a modern battlefield, and China certainly has radars and air defense systems that can detect, track, and attack it. The B-1 is . . . obsolete."

"Patrick?"

"It's true, the B-1's radar cross section is ten times greater than the F-35," Patrick said. "But an F-35 carrying two external cruise missiles has a larger radar cross section, and its range is about a *tenth* of the B-1's. The Super Hornet is not yet cleared to carry air-launched cruise missiles, and it would suffer a drastic decrease in performance and range with external stores as well.

"The B-1 with internal stores has just a slightly larger radar cross section than the Super Hornet; it has more powerful radar jammers; it has a much higher ingress speed; it is capable of terrain-following flight, and it can carry as many as sixteen cruise missiles versus the F-35's maximum of two," Patrick went on. "Plus, the F-35 isn't operational yet, and isn't forecast to be so for another four years at best. The XB-1 Excalibur is only an interim solution to AirSea Battle until the Next Generation Bomber or Mjollnir is built, but it can do the job for less money, better than any other alternative and be operational sooner."

"The design is forty years old, and the newest plane is almost thirty years old and hasn't been flown for almost fifteen years," Murth said. "General McLanahan is quoting performance and stealthiness numbers based on 1980s technology. If a Chinese JN-15 or J-20 or a Russian Sukhoi-34 or T-50 gets within range of one, all those sixteen cruise missiles will be lost in the blink of an eye. I strongly urge you to not consider this program, Miss Vice President."

"Thank you, Mr. Undersecretary," Ann said, then looked at National Security Adviser Glenbrook. "Bill?"

"I like the plan, Miss Vice President," Glenbrook said after a moment of silent consideration. Murth's mouth dropped open in surprise. "Frankly, ma'am, we don't have much choice. Look at what's happened out in the South China Sea: we have a handful of bombers, including a B-2 stealth bomber, survivors of the American Holocaust, stationed on Guam with the Continuous Bomber Presence task force, but we were hesitant to use them over the South China Sea for fear of escalating tensions or, worse, getting one mysteriously shot down like we lost the P-8 Poseidon. Carriers launching Hornets would need to move in close to hostile waters to operate, and the F-35 Lightning won't even be operational for three to four years at best. The skipper of that Coast Guard cutter was pleading for air support, and we had nothing to offer him. General McLanahan's plan is the only viable option." He thought again, then nodded. "I will recommend to the president that the Pentagon should go to Congress to seek funds to implement General McLanahan's project."

"Excuse me, sir, but in my opinion there is no way Congress is going to agree to spend almost half a billion dollars on a few forty-year-old flying . . . dinosaurs," Murth said, the dumbfounded expression plastered on his face. "The White House will look . . . foolish."

"In light of what's happened over the South China Sea," Ann said, "I'll recommend that the president request emergency funding to immediately implement the program."

Murth turned his stunned expression to the vice president. "Emergency funding, Miss Vice President?" he asked. "That is not at all . . . reasonable."

"The president and I disagree, Mr. Undersecretary," Ann said. "We want the project to proceed with all possible speed. The White House and Pentagon have some emergency discretionary funds allotted to us precisely for this type of contingency. Some will be used to replace the rotary-wing aircraft on the Coast Guard cutter; some to replace the P-8

Poseidon; something for the families of those lost; and the rest
to procure the refurbished B-1 bombers for use in the Pacific.
We can do this until we get Congress to fund more B-1s or a
new long-range strike aircraft. Thank you very much for your
hard work, Undersecretary Murth." That was an unmistakable
indication that he was free to leave, and the young bureaucrat
nodded and departed without a word.

"Okay, guys, your work is cut out for you," Ann said
seriously to Patrick, Hoffman, and Oglethorpe. "The president
and I just overruled the number four civilian in the Pentagon,
the guy whose job it is to kill programs that don't make sense.
The president would like you to present your proposal to the
national security staff this afternoon. Bring your A-game, boys.
And don't forget dinner in the residence later"—she smiled,
then added as she headed for the door—"assuming you're still
on speaking terms and still want to hang out with him after the
grilling I think you're going to get from him and the national
security staff."

NAVAL AIR STATION FALLON, NEVADA

SEVERAL MONTHS LATER, FEBRUARY 2015

"Ladies and gentlemen, welcome to Naval Air Station Fallon," the U.S. Navy officer said. The auditorium was filled with almost a hundred men and women. On the right were seated persons in a variety of colors of flight suits, from black to dark green to red. Then there was a noticeable gap of empty seats, and then on the left another group wearing flight suits also of various colors, but mostly international orange. The large screen behind the speaker onstage changed to a triangular emblem with two jets, mountains, and a steer's horned head. "My name is Captain Richard Avery, and I'd like to welcome you to Naval Air Station Fallon and the Naval Strike and Air Warfare Center, the Navy's premier air warfare training unit.

"As most of our guests may know, the NSAWC combines three formerly separate schools: the Naval Strike Warfare Center, or 'Strike U,' teaching advanced bombing and gunnery tactics; TOPGUN, which teaches advanced air-to-air combat tactics; and TOPDOME, the Carrier Airborne Early Warning Weapons School, which teaches advanced radar air intercept and control techniques," Avery said. "Every unit getting ready for deployment comes to Fallon for predeployment workup, and we are the only facility in the world where we can take an entire carrier air wing at one time for comprehensive, realistic training.

"We happen to be in between workup sessions right now—the air wing of the *Nimitz* will be coming in a few weeks for their workup, in preparation for their final cruise before decommissioning—so this gives us an opportunity for some realistic training for a rather unusual group of folks," Avery went on. "Frankly, folks, I thought this was a joke at first—I thought, 'we're going to train who?'—but the chief of naval operations assured me this was no joke. So here you are. We're going to run you though a vastly abbreviated fleet air wing workup course to see what you folks can do."

He nodded to the men and women on his right. "Welcome to VF-13, the 'Fighting Saints,' our adversary squadron based here at Fallon," Avery went on. "They fly the F-5N aggressor fighter." The image on the large screen behind him changed to a photo of a sleek twin-engine jet fighter in unusual gray, blue, and brown stripes. "Our aircraft are painted like many of our potential adversaries' aircraft; our crews train and fly exactly how our adversaries would; and as you can see, our aircrews are even encouraged to wear flight suits and use equipment that our adversaries will use, so they would have the same experiences and limitations as our adversaries."

Avery turned to the folks on his left, and he had to smile and chuckle inwardly at the extreme differences between the two groups. Most on the left were significantly older than the men and women of VF-13; their hair was longer and thinner; and for some their midsections were noticeable thicker. "Saints, welcome the men and women of Sky Masters Incorporated, out of Battle Mountain, right up the road from us." The image on the screen changed again to one of a B-1 bomber. "They fly what they call the XB-1 Excalibur bomber, which is a refurbished and modernized B-1B Lancer strategic supersonic bomber. The Air Force is going to deploy a number of these bombers in the Pacific theater in the next few months to support carrier strike group operations and implement the AirSea Battle concept. Your mission over the next week is to provide them classroom and flying instruction on fleet tactics and procedures."

The right side of the auditorium erupted into a low but very noticeable level of bedlam. "Say again, sir?" one of the members of VF-13 seated in the front row asked. "We're going to train civilians?"

"Roger that, Noose," Avery said. To the civilian seated directly opposite of the one making the outburst he said, "General McLanahan, I'd like to introduce you to Commander Chris Kahn, call sign 'Noose,' commander of VF-13. Noose, I'm sure you've heard of Air Force Lieutenant General Patrick McLanahan, retired." Kahn's facial expression changed from confusion to disbelief and back to total confusion, but he managed to pull himself back to the here and now long enough to get to his feet and shake hands with Patrick. "General McLanahan is the vice president of Sky Masters Inc., the company that refurbishes the B-1 bombers. He'll be attending training with the initial cadre of aircrews."

"Yes, sir," Kahn said, still dumbfounded. "Nice to meet you, sir, and I apologize for the outburst." Patrick said nothing, just nodding with a skeptical smile on his face. Kahn turned back to Avery. "Sir, the Air Wing Fallon war games and the Advanced Readiness Program exercises each last a month. How can we train non-Navy crews in just one week?"

"I'm going to leave that up to you and your squadron staff, Noose," Avery said. "It's obviously not a full predeployment workup, but an introduction to Navy terminology, basic procedures, and tactics. The CNO knows it'll take time for the B-1 guys to learn Navy procedures, but he just wants to limit the confusion factor here. The B-1s will be coordinating long-range overwater operations with the carrier strike groups, but we don't envision Hornets flying formation with B-1s." He ignored Kahn's totally confused expression. "The civilians will have access to the Silver State Club, Desert Moon Theater, Sagebrush Bowling Center, Flightline Grill and Bar, and the Fitness Center. I expect you to help in making them feel welcome, Noose. Thank you."

A preliminary schedule for the next day was set up, more introductions were made, and then the meeting broke up so staff members could escort the civilians to their dormitories. Kahn and Patrick shook hands before they departed. "Again, sir, sorry for the outburst back there."

"No problem, Commander," Patrick said.

Kahn nodded, then lowered his voice, looked Patrick square in the eye, and asked, "Masters One, I presume?"

Patrick was confused, but only for a moment, and his eyes lit up as he realized what Kahn was saying: "Welder One-Seven flight of two Super Hornets, I presume?"

Kahn nodded and gave Patrick a crocodile grin. "You've got yourself a bunch of nice hot jets, sir," he said. "But you're on my deck now. See you on the range, sir."

"Bet on it, Commander," Patrick said, and departed.

Kahn made sure to intercept Avery in private after everyone else had departed. "What the hell, Skipper?" he asked directly. "I've got to waste my between-workup time to spoon-feed a bunch of old geezers on the Navy way . . . in just one week?"

"Listen, Noose, I'm not happy about this either," Avery said in a low voice, completely different in tone than when he was addressing the entire group—it was no longer the jovial, welcoming, accommodating host. "But I got this mission directly from the CNO. The Pentagon wants these guys trained and sent out to Guam soonest, and that's what we're going to do."

"This is just plain loco, sir," Kahn said. "Did you get a look at some of those guys? They're just as likely to pass out or fall asleep in the cockpit as they are to fly with bad guys in the area! Is the Navy out of its freakin' mind?"

"I hear you, Noose, I hear you," Avery said, "but I got

my orders, and now you got yours. Work up something so McLanahan doesn't go back to his buddies in Washington and say the Navy blew him off. What happens after they leave here is not my problem." He shook his head. "I just hope to hell the fleet stays out of their way. 'The Gang That Couldn't Shoot Straight' is on their way to the Pacific."

The Socialist Republic of Vietnam's Gepard-class frigate, HQ-013 *Cá mập*, or *Shark,* was on patrol near the Vietnamese-occupied Spratly Island. The frigate was Vietnam's newest warship, Russian designed but license built in Vietnam. It was purpose built for antisubmarine warfare (ASW) with a helicopter with dipping sonar and armed with torpedoes, a variable-depth sonar, four torpedo tubes, and an RBU-6000 multibarrel rocket launcher that sprayed antisubmarine rockets in a dense pattern that were programmed by the fire control officer to detonate at a specified depth. Fast and agile, it was the pride of the Vietnamese navy.

The HQ-013's shallow draft of only fifteen feet made it the perfect vessel to patrol within the reefs, sea mounts, and sandbars near the Vietnam military communications facility of Spratly Island. Only thirty-five acres in size but with a population of almost a thousand—mostly army and navy soldiers—the island was the fourth largest in the Spratly Islands archipelago and the largest of the islands occupied by Vietnam. The island was bisected by a two-thousand-foot-long coral and sand runway that ran the entire length of the oblong-shaped island. A jetty on the southeast side of the island extended past the reef surrounding the island, where the water dropped to almost six thousand feet deep in an almost vertical wall, and a long pier was built at the end of the jetty large enough for ferries and big supply vessels making the fifteen-hour cruise from Ho Chi Minh City and to support the many fishing vessels that plied these waters.

Although the Vietnamese Navy communications detachment there was real and provided a radio and telephone link between fishing vessels and the mainland, in the age of satellite communications the detachment was mostly superfluous— its real mission was to maintain a strong military presence on the island to reinforce Vietnam's claim on it and eleven other islands and cays it occupied in the archipelago. Five other countries claimed islands in the Spratlys, and two other countries, the People's Republic of China and the Philippines, claimed ownership of the entire archipelago.

The captain of the *Shark, Thượng tá* (Captain) Dang Van Chien, was on the bridge sipping a mug of tea. Thin and athletic, the veteran sailor was obviously enjoying being in command of one of his country's finest pieces of military hardware. He could not sit still: if he was not on the bridge marveling at the electronic controls and extensive communications systems, he was in the combat center or the engine room, studying everything and asking to be briefed on how something worked. He knew he was making a nuisance of himself, but he *was* the captain, and he felt it was his responsibility as well as his right to ask his sailors about their specialties.

Dang checked his watch and smiled. They had scheduled a surprise gunnery exercise, and that would start in a few minutes. Only he and a few department heads knew about it. Their target was an old fishing vessel that had been seized by the Border Guards several months earlier for smuggling heroin—its crew had been executed after a one-day trial, and now they were going to destroy their drug-running ship for the benefit of the navy. The target ship should be showing up on radar at any moment.

"Bridge, Combat," he heard a few moments later. "Radar contact, aircraft, bearing three-zero-zero, heading south, range fifty kilometers, altitude one thousand meters, speed three hundred, no transponder."

Low, slow, and with no identification beacon, way out here in the middle of the South China Sea—that usually meant smugglers or foreign patrol planes, Dang thought. But the target ship was off to the south and the airplane was north, so it shouldn't be a factor. "Very well," he responded. "Continue to monitor."

"Bridge, Combat, surface contact, bearing one-six-five, range twenty, speed ten, heading east, friendly beacon code received and verified. Second surface contact, appears to be following the first contact, one hundred meters behind it."

The ship with the electronic radar beacon would be an oceangoing tug towing the target ship, Dang knew. "Any other surface contacts nearby?" he asked.

"No, sir."

"Very well." He checked his watch to note the time, then turned to the officer of the deck. "Action stations," he said. "Prepare to engage surface target. Flank speed." The alarm bells, the gradual acceleration of the *Shark,* and the sound of boots running on the decks and ladders and hatches slamming shut was always exhilarating, and he felt his heart race in anticipation.

The bosun's mate handed Dang a helmet and life jacket. By the time he donned them, the officer of the deck reported, "The ship is at action stations, sir. We are at flank speed, heading one-nine-zero."

"Very well. Combat, range to target?"

"Fifteen kilometers, sir."

"Prepare to engage with the AK-176," Dang ordered. The AK-176 was the multipurpose 76-millimeter gun mounted forward. Able to fire twelve kilogram shells as far as fifteen kilometers, the *Shark* had been fitted with the newest model, able to fire at up to two rounds a second and not requiring a long cool-down period afterward. The gun was also steerable with television and imaging infrared cameras as well as by the AK-630 fire control radar.

"AK-176 is ready, deck is clear, sir," the tactical action officer reported.

"Very well. Make sure you target the right ship—do not kill our tug, *xin*."

"Yes, sir."

"Shoal water ahead, sir," the navigation officer reported.

"Maneuver east," Dang ordered.

"Maneuver east, yes, sir." That put the target off the nose. Dang checked the electronic chart—they would be clear of shoal water in just a few minutes.

"Bridge, Combat, air target has closed to within twenty kilometers, still heading south. It has descended to five hundred meters. They are sweeping us with search radar."

Probably not a smuggler, Dang thought. "Still no transponder?" he asked.

"No, sir."

He wondered if he should cancel their gunnery practice, then decided as long as the plane stayed to the north they were safe. They were close enough that they should see a pretty good show. "Very well," he responded. "Continue to monitor. Let me know if he gets within ten kilometers."

"Yes, sir."

"Clear of shoal waters, sir," the navigator reported.

"Very well. Steer one-nine-five, prepare to engage surface target." The *Shark* responded like the thoroughbred she was. Dang felt the anticipation grow even more as he watched the AK-176's turret turn left to track the target.

"Range to target?" Dang shouted.

"Ten kilometers to target, sir." A moment later: "Bridge, Combat, new surface contact, bearing two-three-zero, range thirty, heading east at twenty-five knots."

"Pretty fast," Dang commented to the officer of the deck. "Comm, Bridge, broadcast on all frequencies in Vietnamese, Chinese, and English our identity and position; advise that we will be conducting gunnery practice shortly; and warn other ships to stay clear of the area within thirty kilometers of Spratly Island. Combat, verify you are not locked onto the target with the beacon."

"Verified, sir. Tug is not being tracked."

"Very well. Officer of the Deck, sound alarm." When the alarm horn stopped, Dang picked up the shipwide intercom handset. "All hands, this is the captain, prepare to fire guns." He switched channels back to the Combat Center. "Combat, this is the captain, batteries released, fire when ready, rate thirty, radar guided."

"Batteries released, fire when ready, rate thirty, radar guided, yes, sir."

The sound of his 76-millimeter gun firing was music to his ears, and he rarely wore ear protection. Dang raised his binoculars to his eyes and was excited to see flashes of fire and puffs of smoke as the rounds hit the fishing vessel. "Cease fire," he ordered. "Good shooting, Combat. Switch to infrared tracking, rate thirty. I do not want to blast our target apart quite yet. Batteries released, fire when ready."

An aide hustled into the commander's office, carrying a message. "Sir, urgent report from one of our patrol planes near Spratly Island."

"What is it?" Admiral Zhen Peng, commander of the People's Liberation Army Navy South Fleet, asked distractedly without looking up from his work.

"A Vietnamese frigate is firing guns south of Nansha Dao," the aide said, using the Chinese name for the Spratly Islands. "It appears to be firing at a target vessel being towed by a tug."

He was about to say he didn't care what the Vietnamese were doing, but then he stopped what he was doing. General Zu Kai had made it quite clear to the general staff and the major headquarters staffs as well: China was going to take control of the Nansha and Xisha Dao. Certainly he would not permit a foreign warship to be firing guns near Nansha Dao.

He looked at a large wall chart across his office, which showed the position of each and every vessel in his command, from the aircraft carrier *Zhenyuan* to the smallest barge, updated hourly. The *Zhenyuan* battle group was back in port and available for action, but even if it sortied immediately—more likely, it would take a day or two at best—it would not reach the Vietnamese frigate for almost two days. He resolved to make sure the group spent more time on patrol and less time in port. The second Chinese carrier group, led by the aircraft carrier *Zheng He,* a former Brazilian aircraft carrier, was even farther away; and a third aircraft carrier group, led by the *Tongyi,* a former Spanish amphibious assault craft and helicopter carrier, was still about a year from deploying, and its main area of responsibility was the East Sea, opposite Taiwan. South Fleet appeared to not be in position to do anything about the Vietnamese ship cruising around in Chinese waters. He thought about his fleet of Xian H-6 bombers with their antiship cruise missiles, but even they would take several hours to generate a sortie—he resolved to start placing more H-6 bombers on alert from now on, loaded and ready for action—but for today they were not available.

There was one small Chinese boat, a Type-062 patrol boat, not far from Spratly Island. Zhen called his senior controller in the command post. "See if the patrol plane near Nansha Dao has contact with P-71."

A moment later: "Radio contact established, sir," the controller reported.

The Type-062 was fast and agile, but it carried just one twin-barreled heavy cannon and one twin-barreled heavy machine gun—no match for a Vietnamese frigate . . .

. . . but maybe it didn't have to be. There was one weapons system he knew about that would do the job. It was not under his command, but it was available and would certainly be effective. "Is that patrol plane near Nansha Dao capable of target datalink?" he asked the senior controller on duty.

"Yes, sir," the controller responded a few moments later. "All our long-range patrol planes can send secure digital target information to our headquarters or to any other authorized user."

That would be perfect, Zhen thought. Maybe his ships couldn't prosecute this target, but perhaps he could assist someone else who could.

"Call in the entire battle staff," Zhen ordered. "I want the *Zhenyuan* and *Zheng He* battle groups to make all preparations to get under way. Then get me General Zu, secure, *immediately*! Our patrol boat is under attack by the Vietnamese Navy south of Nansha Dao, and I want something done about it!"

Major General Hua Zhilun hurried into his command center almost at a run. "Report!" he shouted as soon as he was in the door.

"Datalink confirmed, sir," the senior controller reported. "A navy patrol plane, about fifteen kilometers north of the target. Solid lock."

"No, damn you, *Hǔ Zhǎo,*" Hua said. "'Tiger's Claw.' Status report!"

It took several moments to check all the available batteries, but soon: "No Tiger's Claw batteries available within range, sir," the controller reported.

"*Méiyǒu?*" Hua exclaimed. "None?" But he shouldn't be that surprised: although tensions were high in the western Pacific and Indian Oceans that the DF-21s covered, they did not keep them on alert, but safely stowed in garrisons until ordered to deploy to presurveyed launch points. They were quite mobile, but they still took the crews some time to get them ready to launch. The missiles they had now were armed only with nonnuclear high-explosive payloads, which severely restricted their range. "What else do we have available within the next ten minutes?"

"Stand by, sir," the controller said. A few moments later: "Sir, Battery Two, CJ-20 *Changjian,* Wuzshan, Hainan Dao, reports up and ready," the senior controller said with a smile. "It was participating in a simulated launch drill. The commander reports the missile is armed with a high-explosive warhead only. Awaiting orders."

"That is most excellent," Hua said. The CJ-20 *Changjian,* or "Long Sword," was a new class of long-range antiship cruise missiles being fielded by the People's Liberation Army. Developed from the CJ-10 supersonic land-attack cruise missile, the CJ-20 was fired from a road-mobile transporter-erector-launcher. Like the Dong Feng–21, the nonnuclear version of the CJ-20 did not have the long range or high speed as the nuclear-tipped version, but in this case it was well within range and would do the job. It used the same high-speed radar terminal guidance system as Tiger's Claw and was extremely accurate, even at long range, high speeds, bad weather, and against moving targets.

Hua's expression was deadly serious as he contemplated what they had been ordered to do, but when he looked at the smile of anticipation on his senior controller's face, he couldn't help but smile himself. "Battery released," Hua said in a quiet voice. "Launch when ready."

"*Zhàn wèi!* Battle stations!" the squadron commander shouted as he slammed the telephone receiver down on its cradle. An electronic horn sounded outside his command vehicle. "Firing stations! Report when missile ready. Call up the feed from that patrol plane."

The targeting officer typed furiously on his computer keyboard, and soon a map of the South China Sea south of Spratly Island came into view. Four targets were highlighted on the screen, showing their tracks and speeds. He zoomed the display in so just the three surface targets showed. "What do we have, Lieutenant?"

"The northernmost vessel is the Vietnamese frigate, sir," the targeting officer said. He pointed to the screen. "The target to the southeast is a tug. The third is a target fishing boat that is being fired on by the frigate. The westernmost return is our Type-062 patrol boat."

"Designate the frigate as target one," the commander ordered. "Begin data transfer immediately."

It did not take long. The position, heading, and speed of the Vietnamese frigate was electronically transferred to the flight computers aboard a Changjian-20 cruise missile. The information was checked and rechecked several times in moments. Meanwhile, the thirty-two-thousand-pound CJ-20 missile was being elevated from its transporter-erector-launcher into firing position. The solid-fueled CJ-20 did not need to be fueled—as soon as it was elevated, its gyros aligned, its present position updated by satellite, and its target information received and verified, it was ready to fly.

"Do we have a position from Yaogan-9?" the commander shouted. "I want verification and another line of position of the target's position." Yaogan-9 was a constellation of three ocean-scanning radar satellites that provided an around-the-clock scan of the South China Sea and western Pacific Ocean with radar imagery and targeting information, fed to the entire fleet of DF-21D ballistic antiship missiles and CJ-20 antiship cruise missiles.

"No, sir," the targeting officer reported. "Yaogan-9 appears to be off-line."

"How about *Chángyuǎn de mùguāng*?" the commander asked. *Chángyuǎn de mùguāng,* or Long Gaze, was the over-the-horizon backscatter radar located at Chongqing, Guizhou Province. The system reflected radar beams off the ionosphere, down to Earth, back to the ionosphere, and back to a receiver, allowing radar returns to be picked up thousands of miles away, hundreds of times farther than line-of-sight radar signals. The radar beam could be electronically angled to sweep the ocean and skies, locating ships and aircraft at impossibly long range.

"No contact by Long Gaze, sir," the targeting officer reported. "Long Gaze appears to be down for maintenance."

It was not surprising—over-the-horizon backscatter radar was not new technology, but it was new for China, and it was not perfect. "How about that patrol boat?" the commander asked.

A few moments later: "Negative, sir. Navigation radar only. No datalink."

It appeared that the only targeting cues they would have were from the patrol plane's radar. It was adequate, but multiple azimuths were always preferred. "Very well," the commander said. "Status?"

"Gyro alignment complete," the controller reported. "Missile is elevated, course laid in."

"Very well." The commander reached up to the top of his control console, withdrew a key from around his neck, inserted it into a lock, and turned it to the left, which immediately alerted command posts all across the area by satellite that a missile was about to be launched. Moments later the telephone beside him rang, and he picked it up immediately. After he gave and received authentication codes, he reported, "Prelaunch checks complete, missile is ready, sir."

"Launch when ready, Colonel," General Hua Zhilun ordered.

"Launch order acknowledged, sir," the commander said, and he turned the key off, waited a few moments, then turned it all the way to the right.

At the launch site, an alarm bell sounded, and moments later a CJ-20 cruise missile shot from its storage canister atop the transporter-erector-launcher and blasted off into the night sky. It climbed to ten thousand feet in the blink of an eye, clearing the mountains in the center of Hainan Island with ease. Moments later wings popped out of the missile body, and the CJ-20 began a slow descent to one hundred feet above the South China Sea as it accelerated to almost twice the speed of sound.

"Missile launch detection!" the sensor technician shouted. That immediately riveted everyone's attention, and console operators turned back to their computer screens.

"Origin?" the senior controller, Air Force Captain Sally Martin, asked.

"Looks like Hainan Island, China," the sensor technician replied. "We'll get the precise launch pad shortly. Heading is south-southeast, accelerating, approaching the Mach."

"Alert Pacific Command," Martin said. "Missile departing Hainan Island heading south-southeast supersonic, target unknown." She studied the large monitor in front of her as the computer displayed a graphical depiction of the missile in flight they had detected. Martin was the duty officer in charge of the Air Force's Space Based Infrared System, or SBIRS, a network of high, low, and geostationary heat-seeking satellites that was designed to detect and track ballistic missiles, determine their launch and impact points, track and classify their warheads and determine if any were decoys, and pass targeting information to land- or sea-based missile defense units.

What they had determined once the entire system was in place was that the sensors were so sensitive that they could not only detect and track the white-hot rocket plume during ascent or the red-hot warheads during reentry, but even detect the heat trail behind the rocket motor, which gave them even more precise tracking and targeting data. But this time, there was something strange about this heat trail. Martin turned to her deputy controller, Master Sergeant Ed Ingalls, a fifteen-year veteran of U.S. Space Command. "What do you make of that track, Ed?" she asked. "Are we not getting a good look at it?"

"I'd say it's not a ballistic missile, but a cruise missile, ma'am," Ingalls responded after a few moments. "Rumor had it the Chinese were deploying antiship cruise missiles, along with ballistic missiles. We might be watching one right now. They stay low so that the atmosphere attenuates their heat trail."

Martin's intercom beeped, and she moved the microphone to her lips. "Martin here, go ahead, SPACECOM."

"What do you have, Sally?" the senior controller at Space Command headquarters asked.

"Master Sergeant Ingalls thinks we have a cruise missile, sir," Martin replied. "Speed is over the Mach and accelerating, and it's not rising through the atmosphere. Heading south-southeast."

"Impact point?"

"Stand by." Martin studied the display closer and waited to see what the depiction would show, but nothing was happening yet. "The missile is maneuvering slightly, so the computer's not making any guesses yet, sir," she said. "It looks like it'll pass west of the Paracel Islands, but it could impact anywhere between Vietnam and the Philippines and as far out as Malaysia—it's too early to tell for sure. But my guess would be somewhere in the Spratly Islands. If we have any ships out there, they'd better be notified."

"I'll pass the word to PACOM," the controller at SPACECOM said. "When the computer gives you a definite impact point, give me a shout."

"Wilco, sir."

"Unidentified vessel south of Nansha Dao," Captain Dang Van Chien of the Vietnamese frigate *Shark* heard in Chinese, "this is the People's Liberation Army Navy patrol vessel *Qíyú;* identify yourself!"

"Is this man dense?" Dang muttered aloud. "Comm, you have been sending out those warnings, yes?"

"Yes, sir. For the last ten minutes, in Vietnamese, English, and Chinese."

"Continue," the captain said. "Combat, range to that Chinese patrol boat?"

"Ten kilometers. Heading right for us."

"Secure from gunnery practice, sound action stations, no drill," Dang said. The alarms sounded again, but the skipper didn't feel excitement this time, only dread. He picked up the microphone and changed the channel to the emergency maritime frequency. "Patrol vessel *Qíyú,* this is the frigate *Cá mập* of the Socialist Republic of Vietnam Navy," he radioed in Chinese. "You are on a collision course with this vessel. Alter course immediately." No reply. Dang was now watching the radar repeater on the bridge, and he could see the Chinese vessel was not changing course. "Helm, steady up on course two-two-zero." That would put them head to head, presenting the smallest profile to the incoming ship. "Combat, stand by on the -176, target that Chinese patrol boat, stand by to fire warning shots."

"AK-176 ready."

"Fire a warning shot," Dang ordered. "Radar-guided warning shot, single-round burst, battery released."

"On the way," came the reply, and moments later the AK-176 cannon let loose. In warning shot mode, the fire control system on the *Shark*'s cannon was designed to land a shell precisely one hundred meters directly in front of a radar target.

On the radio again, Dang spoke, "Patrol vessel *Qíyú*, this is your last warning. Alter course immediately!" Still no response. Dang closed his eyes for a moment. *I do not want to do this*, he thought, but he wasn't going to turn and let this little Chinese pipsqueak chase him out of his own waters. "Combat, fire another warning . . ."

"Target turning, sir," the radar officer reported. "Turning south . . . now continuing the turn to the east."

Thank the stars, Dang thought—the last thing he wanted to do was shoot at a Chinese naval vessel, even if it was violating Vietnamese waters. "Very well. Reduce speed to ten knots, maintain this heading until the target is . . ."

And at that moment there was a tremendous explosion on the *Shark*'s starboard side. The ship was thrown violently to the left so steeply that its port rail briefly went into the water. Everyone on the bridge was thrown to the deck even if they were secured in their seats. The bridge filled with thick smoke, and the windows were illuminated from the fires that were erupting on the ship.

An unknown number of minutes later, Dang awoke, lying on the bridge of his once proud ship. He found he was still alive, but he couldn't see a thing, and his throat was burning from the thick smoke that choked his beautiful bridge. Alarm bells were going off and men were screaming all around him. The ship had righted itself, but it was being buffeted by explosions. He crawled over bodies, blood, and broken glass to the starboard side of the bridge. He could see the fires, but the smoke was too thick to make out anything else. He crawled to the port side of the bridge.

"Captain!" someone shouted. Two sets of arms pulled him to his feet, and to his surprise he found his legs wobbly but working. The men supporting him had firefighting masks on—the damage control parties were on the job. They pulled Dang just outside the port side of the bridge where the air was much clearer.

"Report!" he shouted over the roar of the flames and the alert horns.

"I do not know, sir," one of the damage control techs said after pulling off his mask and helmet. "Our damage control station is the bridge, so we reported here immediately. I have not heard anything on the radio."

Dang stepped around the port side of the superstructure aft of the bridge. It seemed as if the entire midsection of the *Shark* was covered in smoke, and a massive explosion or column of fire would blast out of the smoke every few moments. But it appeared the damage was above the waterline, not below, so it was probably not caused by a torpedo. It was just too early to speculate on what hit the *Shark*—he had to see to his crew.

"Whoever is responsible for this will pay dearly," Dang said aloud over the smoke and chaos all around him. "Vietnam is at war with whoever did this, I promise."

SIX

OVER THE WESTERN PACIFIC OCEAN

EARLY THE NEXT MORNING

"Radar contact!" Patrick McLanahan heard on intercom. He was the copilot aboard a Sky Masters XB-1 Excalibur bomber, flying at thirty thousand feet over the Pacific Ocean a hundred miles northwest of the island of Guam. The pilot was Warner "Cutlass" Cuthbert, flying his first of a series of six checkout flights—along with all his other duties, he had passed the academic and simulator checks in record time and was now happily at the controls of the bomber that had always been his favorite. "Surface contact, ten o'clock, one hundred thirty miles."

"Copy that," Patrick said. "Karen, any ID yet?"

"Negative, sir," said the DSO, or defensive systems officer, Karen Wells. Normally the DSO on a B-1 bomber sat in the systems officers' compartment behind the cockpit, but in the Excalibur the manned systems officers' compartment was on the ground back at Andersen Air Force Base on

Guam, and the sensor data from the bomber datalinked by satellite. Wells was a civilian electronic warfare officer, an Air Force veteran of the B-1B and EF-111 electronic warfare aircraft; after leaving the Air Force after twenty-one years, the mother of four grown children had been flying regional airlines until joining Sky Masters Inc. for this project. "No radar . . ." And then she paused. At the same time a radar warning indication appeared on both Patrick's and Cutlass's multifunction displays. "Stand by, sir. It just popped up . . . got it, Golf-band long-range air search. I'd classify it as a Chinese Luhai-class guided-missile destroyer."

"That's the one we're looking for, the one that sank that Taiwanese fishing boat and killed twenty crewmembers," Cutlass said. "Let's get configured to attack, crew." Patrick made sure the cockpit was in "COMBAT" mode, then verified that the crew back at Andersen were configuring their systems. "What are the weapons aboard that destroyer, DSO?"

"Hong-Qian 9, radar-guided surface-to-air missile, maximum range sixty miles, sir," Wells replied.

"That's longer than the range of our Sniper targeting pod," Patrick said. "We have to move in to at least ten miles to get a good visual ID."

"Defense is ready for combat," Wells reported. "SPEAR is in standby."

"Offense is ready," said George Wickham, the offensive systems officer, seated beside Wells in the air-conditioned container that served as their systems officers' compartment back at Andersen. Wickham was a Navy veteran of eight years who retired as an avionics engineer for a major defense contractor before being recruited by Sky Masters—he had never been aboard an airplane except as a passenger, and this was the closest he ever aspired to being in one.

"My plan is to go in, stay at thirty thousand, take a look,

and see how close we get so we can get a positive visual ID," Cutlass said.

"If this is the guy we're hunting for," Patrick reminded him, "he's killed innocent people before. He might try to do it again."

"I guess if he takes a shot at us, we'll know he's our guy then," Cutlass said. He tightened his ejection seat straps. "Everyone, stay on your toes. Patrick, double-check my configuration for low-level . . ."

"Attention, attention, unidentified aircraft, one hundred ten miles northwest of Guam at thirty thousand feet heading west," a voice said in English on a discrete radio frequency, "this is the *Sea Dragon,* a destroyer of the Chinese navy. You are on course to overfly us. Turn away immediately. Stay at least twenty miles away or you will be fired on."

"Sea Dragon, this is Masters Zero-Seven," Patrick radioed back. "Your position is being relayed to the United States Navy and Coast Guard. I suggest you heave-to and prepare to be boarded."

"Kiss our grits, Masters Zero-Seven," came the reply.

"Echo-Foxtrot-band target illuminator!" Wells announced. "Solid lock-on!"

"Clear to engage SPEAR!" Cutlass ordered. "Knock that radar off the air!"

"SPEAR malfunctioned," Wells said. "I'm reinitializing, but it'll take several minutes!"

"Engage the TFRs and let's go low, Patrick!" Cutlass said. Patrick's fingers flew over his touch-screen MFDs, and soon the Excalibur was hurdling toward the ocean at ten thousand feet a minute. "Get SPEAR up and running soonest, Karen!"

"Wing sweep," Patrick said on intercom. "Throttles. Watch your barber-poles." The "barber-poles" were yellow-and-black warning indicators on the performance display, warning of airspeed limitations.

"Thank you," Cutlass said. He swept the wings full aft and pulled the power back slightly to avoid going over Mach one as they did their steep computer-controlled dive.

"Passing ten thousand."

"Range?"

"Coming up on ninety miles," Wickham said.

"Can we forgo visual ID on this guy now?" Cutlass asked. "He's getting ready to shoot at us."

"The rules of engagement call for a visual ID," Patrick reminded him. "Passing five thousand. Clearance plane set to one thousand. Starting to level off."

"And the Rod Pod has a range of thirty miles?"

"Identification range of a ship-sized target is about twenty miles," Wickham said.

Both Patrick and Cutlass monitored the Excalibur carefully as it did its level-off, and they quickly stepped the clearance plane down to five hundred feet. "TFRs are engaged."

"Target illuminator and air search broke lock," Karen reported. "SPEAR still initializing . . ." They heard a new radar warning. "X-band sea-skimmer detection radar has a lock-on," she said. "They can slew the HQ-9 to that radar and use it to direct close-in cannons."

"Range fifty miles. Missiles ready. Check five hundred clearance plane." Five hundred feet was the minimum altitude from which they could launch a missile.

"Five hundred checks," Patrick said.

"Forty miles."

"Target illuminator is back . . . illuminator locked on," Wells said. "With SPEAR initializing, you'll have to do chaff and flares manually, General."

"Copy," Patrick said.

"Thirty miles." The image from the Sniper targeting pod started to reveal the shape of their target—definitely a very large warship, but still too far for positive identification. "Target locked. Coming up on target ID . . ."

"*Missile launch!*" Wells shouted. "Break!"

"Left chaff!" Cutlass shouted, and as soon as he saw Patrick hit the touch screen he threw the Excalibur bomber into a steep right turn.

"Broke lock," Wells said.

"Sniper still locked on . . . twenty miles!" Wickham said. "Positive ID, Chinese destroyer! Wings level, ready on bomb bay doors!" Cutlass rolled wings-level. "Doors coming open." They all heard the rumbling as the middle bomb bay doors opened. "Missile one away . . . missile two away, doors coming closed. Left turn to three-zero-zero and center up for the photo op. Ten miles. Smile for the cameras." Cutlass steered the bomber straight toward their target, angling slightly away so as to not fly directly over it going almost Mach one. Seconds later they overflew the "target" . . .

. . . but it was not a Chinese destroyer but the USS *Sampson,* a U.S. Navy Arleigh Burke-class guided-missile destroyer, one of a group of various cruisers, destroyers, and frigates the XB-1 bombers on Guam had been working with on extended overwater patrols. The story about a Chinese destroyer sinking a fishing boat was all part of the realistic scenario Patrick and Tom Hoffman had built for Excalibur crewmembers. The *Sampson* had been transmitting real signals of Chinese naval antiair and air search radars so the Excalibur crews could get even more realistic training. The missiles they "launched" at the *Sampson* were simulated AGM-65M Maverick ER extended-range attack missiles—the Excaliburs had not yet been cleared to carry any weapons.

"Very cool flyby, Masters Zero-Seven," the skipper of the

Samson radioed after the XB-1 flew past the destroyer. "It's nice having company out here."

"Thanks for the workout, *Sampson,*" Cutlass radioed back. "Masters Zero-Four should be out shortly to take up patrol stations."

"We sure appreciate the eyes," the skipper said. The XB-1 Excaliburs that had arrived at Andersen Air Force Base had been tasked to work with solo or small groups of Navy ships in the western Pacific, scanning out beyond the ships' horizon for aircraft or other ships, identifying them, and relaying the information back to their charges. At altitude, the Excaliburs' active electronically scanned array had a range of over two hundred miles for both surface or airborne targets and could precisely identify targets with great detail.

Cutlass started a climb and turned toward Guam. "Station and oxygen checks, crew," he said, then knocked his helmet with the heel of his hand. "It's easy for me to forget I've only got one crewmember," he said.

"No, Cutlass, you still have a four-person crew—it's just that two of them don't need to do oxygen checks," Patrick said. "They still have to reconfigure their stations."

"Roger that," Cutlass said. "Anything else?"

"It was very good overall, Cutlass," Patrick said, checking his notes on his kneeboard. "Keep an eye on your airspeeds so we're not returning without a Sniper pod. The flight control system should alert you, but it won't retard the throttles for you. Also remember that when SPEAR fails, we have to deploy the 'Little Buddy' towed decoy manually, just like chaff and flares—I was waiting to see if you would have remembered that. It would've helped out fighting off the HQ-9." The ALE-50 towed decoy system was an aerodynamic canister towed behind an aircraft that, because of its design, had a much larger radar cross section than the aircraft, making it a juicier target for radar-guided antiaircraft missiles—it was so effective that many combat pilots dubbed it the "Little Buddy." The improved version of the decoy had infrared emitters that could decoy heat-seeking missiles, and the canister could also be reeled in for reuse.

"I did completely forget that," Cutless admitted.

"Karen gave you a hint when she reminded us about manually deploying chaff. I don't think you'll forget it next time."

"I hope not."

"Masters Zero-Seven, Control," the senior controller came up on the command channel.

"Control, Zero-Seven, go ahead," Patrick replied.

"We need you to RTB as soon as possible," the controller said.

"We'll be on the ground in about twenty minutes. What's up?"

"The you-know-what hit the fan out in the South China Sea, sir," the controller said. "All tactical units have been placed on alert."

Less than twenty minutes later, Cutlass taxied the XB-1 Excalibur to its shelter on the First Expeditionary Bomb Wing parking ramp, and he and Patrick emerged. Security on the ramp had been noticeably beefed up. After turning the jet over to the crew chief and maintenance technicians, they headed immediately for headquarters. They found that it was not much cooler inside the normally well air-conditioned building than outside. "Power go off again?" Cutlass asked.

"Yes, sir," Lieutenant Colonel Nash Hartzell, the deputy wing commander, said. Hartzell wore command pilot's wings, a product of over ten years flying transports all over the world, but the tall, bald, bespectacled officer's real passion was computers. "Guahan Utility District says the fuel oil flow was briefly disrupted by a faulty valve, and once the vapor lock is clear power will be back on. Backup generators are working okay at the command post and security checkpoints."

"That's a common problem here, Patrick," Cutlass explained. "Power and water to the base is provided by the municipal utility district, just like basic phone service is provided by Guam Telephone. We have our own backup sources for essential areas, but this base is so large that we can't build our own power plant." He turned back to Hartzell. "So what's going on, Nash?"

"The Air Force detected a missile launch they suspect was a cruise missile from Hainan Island," Hartzell said. "Several minutes later a Vietnamese frigate was hit by some unidentified weapon. PACOM thinks the launch from Hainan was a Chinese antiship cruise missile."

"Christ," Cutlass exclaimed. "China really seems to be on the warpath these days. Any orders?"

"Just a general alert and a change in Force Protection Condition to Charlie," Hartzell said. Force Protection Condition dealt with the security level on the base; it usually was a response to terrorist threats, but it could be affected by any sort of disturbance or threat. Level "Charlie" was a heightened state of security against a nonspecific threat. "Outer security contractors are being augmented by our own security teams, and inner security has been upped."

Cutlass nodded and thought for a moment, then said, "I want to go to FPCON Charlie Plus," he said. "We've got too many planes out here, and with China firing cruise missiles out of nowhere, we could be next. Restrict all personnel to the base and all flight crews to the flight line. Two forms of picture ID at the gates, search all vehicles, and full alert badge exchange for the flight line. I want all the flight crews, especially the civilians, briefed on the evacuation orbit areas and emergency deployment procedures to Tinian and Saipan." The international airports on the other two major islands of the Commonwealth of the Northern Marianas Islands were used as alternate divert and emergency evacuation bases—the airstrips were too short to fly loaded bombers but were often used by fighters.

"Yes, sir," Hartzell said. "I have to run to issue the orders, sir—the power outage took out the phones too." He hustled off, followed by the commander's staff.

"Things are getting dicey around here, sir," Cutlass said to Patrick as they headed back to the maintenance hangar to debrief their training mission. "I have a feeling we're going to be put on alert, including the Excaliburs."

"I hope you're wrong, Cutlass," Patrick said. "It all depends on what China says and does next. But I don't think this is going to blow over any time soon." He clapped Cutlass on the shoulder. "I hate to do this to you, Cutlass, but after I debrief, I'm heading back to the mainland to launch the last Excalibur. That should be rolling off the line any day. You got one ride under your belt, and you did very well, but I don't know when the next checkout ride will be."

"That's okay, sir," Cutlass said. "I have a feeling I'll be pretty busy on the ground. Things are stirring out there, sir, and I think we're going to be in the middle of it . . . very, very soon. Got time to stay for the alert mission brief?"

"Absolutely," Patrick said.

After Patrick and Cutlass finished their maintenance debrief, they went over to the command center briefing room. Lieutenant Colonel Nash Hartzell was onstage conducting the briefing, with a very large electronic monitor behind him.

There were about fifty crewmembers in the room. Hartzell gave a time hack, then pressed a button that connected the briefing room's monitor to the weather center, and they received a three-day weather briefing. The weather was virtually the same for all three days: warm and humid, with an almost 100 percent chance of thunderstorms in midafternoon. Typhoon season had ended a couple months earlier.

Captain Alicia Spencer, the First Expeditionary Bomb Wing's intelligence officer, took the stage after the weather briefing. "The regional situation is still tense, as I'm sure you've all seen on the news," she began. "Martial law continues in China. Civil unrest is widespread now as is the brutal military crackdown. As a result of the unrest, imports and exports have decreased about twenty percent, and there are widespread shortages of many commodities. The Communist government could collapse at any time—in fact, it may already have collapsed."

Spencer changed the display to show China's coastline, with several icons scattered along the entire length. "Because of the shortages and political instability, all of China's ballistic missile submarines appear to be in port," Spencer went on. "None have been detected in their normal patrol areas in the South or East China Sea or Yellow Sea. Same goes for China's aircraft carriers: the *Zhenyuan* is in home port at Zhanjiang, the *Zheng He* is under way but near its home port of Zhongshan, and the helicopter carrier *Tongyi* is in its home port of Quanzhou and appears to be operational.

"The most alarming movement we've seen in strategic weapons has been the movement of two Dong Feng-21D antiship ballistic missiles from their storage facilities near Guangzhou to new field garrison locations near Huizhou, about a hundred miles east," Spencer went on. "The area from Guangzhou to the coast is heavily fortified with surface-to-air missiles, so it's likely this will be a new deployment area for DF-21s. We believe the movement of these missiles is in response to the announced transit through the South China Sea of the *Nimitz* carrier strike group later this month."

"Not a very good time to be sailing through the South China Sea," Tom Hoffman commented.

"The United States wants the world to know that we're not afraid of whatever is happening in China, and that we expect to freely navigate the world's oceans despite the building tension," Alicia said. "You can bet those crews will be on a hair's trigger alert, but they're going to do it. Obviously this ratchets up the tension even more."

"It's coming up on reelection campaign season," someone else commented. "President Phoenix wants to act tough for the voters, and to hell with the danger to our carriers."

"Okay, okay, enough of the politics," Hartzell said. "Anything else, Alicia?"

"Yes, sir. The last item is that the Russian aircraft carrier *Putin* along with eleven other escort and support ships has put in for what is being described as joint aircraft carrier flight training and underway replenishment training at Zhongshan with the *Zheng He* carrier battle group. They are expected to train closely together and explore interoperability with each other, including flight operations off each other's decks, damage control exercises, joint underway replenishment, and so forth." Alicia took a few questions, then turned the podium over to Hartzell.

"Okay, guys and gals, here's the big picture," Hartzell said. "Task force call sign will be Leopard. Everyone keeps their squadron call signs. Communications plan has changed, so be sure to check the date-time group when you upload flight plans and data.

"Obviously the area around Guangzhou, what used to be called Canton, is looking pretty busy these days," Hartzell went on, "so that's the focus of our alert missions. The XB-1's primary responsibility is to take out the Chinese S-300 surface-to-air missile sites along the coast with AGM-158 cruise missiles, suppress any fighter coverage, and attack land and shipboard antiair radars with AGM-88 antiradar missiles. The B-2 and B-1B bombers will follow, head inland, and attack the DF-21D launch sites at Huizhou with AGM-158s and the DF-21D storage complex at Guangzhou. The B-52s' primary target is the H-6 bomber base at Fushan with AGM-86Ds and -158s, the radar site and naval air base at Guangzhou, and the carrier *Zheng He.*"

"How about the *Putin* carrier?" Lieutenant Colonel Bridget "Xena" Dutchman, the B-52H Stratofortress expeditionary bomb squadron commander, asked. "Mind if we take a shot at it?"

"I haven't heard anyone say no, but let's stick with the Chinese targets first, Xena," Hartzell said. "Now, we can't expect any land-attack Tomahawk cruise missile support for these missions for the time being. Japan has deployed the Tomahawk on its ships, but they're too far away for our sortie. The Taiwanese and Filipino air forces are on high alert, so our route of flight avoids overflying those countries while ingressing—on the way out you can contact them and request overflight or even help with pursuers. Any questions?" There were none. "Okay, alert preflights, update the Mode Two codes and the new communications rundown, report any squawks to Maintenance, and I'll see you at the DFAC for chow. Dismissed."

Patrick met up with the squadron commanders, Hartzell, and Cuthbert at the front of the briefing room. "That takes me back to my old days sitting alert in B-52Gs," Patrick said. "I'm surprised the briefing isn't classified top secret, Cutlass. You're reporting the position of the *Nimitz,* position of submarines, communications plans, and readiness of allied air forces, and the room isn't secure?"

"No, because it's not a real mission briefing, Patrick," Cutlass said matter-of-factly.

"Say what?"

"It's not a real mission, Patrick," Cutlass explained. "You think PACOM is going to allow us to fly a bombing mission over China with a handful of bombers? No way. We give these briefings so the crews stay sharp in real-world procedures, especially handling live weapons. We've practiced alert responses before, but we've never launched with full weapon and fuel loads."

"*What?*"

"The last thing PACAF wants is for us to crash a bomber with a full load of fuel and bombs, Patrick, especially one of the few remaining two-billion-dollar stealth bombers," Cutlass said, surprised at Patrick's disbelief. "The Continuous Bomber Presence is a show of force, sir, nothing more. We brief real-world stuff, but it's all open-source unclassified material."

"So the DF-21 movement, the H-6 bombers, the *Putin* aircraft carrier . . . ?"

"Read all that it in *Aviation Week and Space Technology* a couple issues ago," Hartzell admitted. "The crews get a kick out of the realistic-sounding intelligence briefing, and Alicia does a good job putting it together. We'll probably see something on TV about the Russian carrier soon."

"So the strike missions are . . . ?"

"We don't have any authority to launch and go anywhere, especially with loaded planes," Cutlass said. The squadron commanders were starting to smile at Patrick's stunned expression. "We have the crews build real missions, get intel, write up flight plans, and program all the stuff into the computers on the planes, but they're not meant to be flown."

"So they're not real targets?"

"They look like real targets, and they probably *are* real, but they're not assigned targets from Pacific Command or PACAF—the crews find them themselves," Cutlass said. "They have to update them every week, but that's all practice for mission planning and programming the strike computers."

"Pretty unbelievable," Patrick murmured.

"You didn't think your Excaliburs were the only planes that weren't allowed to launch with live weapons on board, did you?" Cutlass asked. "Sir, except for the air defense fighters, *we've* never launched with live weapons aboard! We've done exercises in various countries, but only with shapes or practice bombs, not the real thing. We're not even allowed to drag our own weapons from stateside—they fly them out on airlifters."

The squadron commanders said their good-byes so they could proceed with preflighting their planes—Patrick could hear a few "Do you believe he thought all this was for real?" comments as they departed.

"Jeez, General, you look disappointed," Cutlass said in a low voice. "I'm very impressed by the Excaliburs and your crews, sir—they're working very hard and are remarkably proficient, given how long they've been out of the cockpit. But they're not going to see any real action. Heck, if things get any worse in China, they'll probably yank us all out of here and send us home, not plan real-world missions. Sorry, sir."

"*Wǎnshàng hǎo.* Good evening, ladies and gentlemen around the world," the broadcast began in English. "I am Tang Ji, foreign minister of the government of the People's Republic of China. Greetings to you all. With me is Colonel General Zu Kai, chief of the general staff of the People's Liberation Army. We will give a short statement on behalf of President Zhou Qiang. It is the president's most sincere desire to reduce recent military activities and rising tensions that have resulted in the unfortunate loss of life. The people and government of China want nothing more than peace, security, and prosperity for all.

"As you may know, the People's Republic of China has historical and legal rights to all the waters enclosed by the first island chain, which are all waters west of the Korean peninsula, the Ryukyu Islands to Taiwan, the western Philippine Islands, and north of Borneo to Vietnamese territorial waters," Tang went on in very good English. "However, we realize that other nations ignore historical precedent and do not agree with this. In the interest of peace, China has not exerted its rights or prevented any foreign vessels from transiting the area and has preferred and sought peaceful negotiations to resolve our issues.

"However, other nations have begun to take advantage of the peace and have sent military aircraft, survey vessels, and then warships into these waters. The survey vessels wish to extract oil and gas from territory belonging to China; and the warships likewise seek to take advantage of China's neutral stance to increase their hostile presence and protect their illegal mining and drilling operations. China was forced to respond.

China deeply regrets the accidental and unintentional downing of American search aircraft during a rescue mission, but it was a direct by-product of the increasing military activities taking place in the South Sea. China has no choice but to respond. General Zu will present China's military response to this urgent security crisis."

General Zu and an interpreter stepped forward to the dais. "Good evening. I wish to inform you that the People's Liberation Army Navy has instituted a defensive patrol regime within the first island chain, particularly of the southern South Sea, or as some of you refer to it the South China Sea. The Chinese aircraft carrier battle groups *Zhenyuan* and *Zheng He* have been dispatched and will conduct surface and air patrols of the area to identify and classify every vessel transiting this area. We will also be stepping up aerial and satellite patrols as well.

"I must emphasize that this is not a cordon or blockade of the Nansha Dao, Xisha Dao, Taiwan, or the South Sea," Zu said. "China will not impede or interfere with any peaceful movement through the area, including that of military vessels. However, for the safety of our personnel and to lower the risk of accidental conflict, we will institute strict policies regarding the actions of certain military vessels transiting the area.

"With regards to aircraft carriers: all foreign aircraft carriers must block all but one of their aircraft launching catapults by the use of parked and chained aircraft while within the first island chain, which includes Nansha Dao and Xisha Dao, and within two hundred kilometers of Chinese aircraft carriers or the Chinese shore. We realize that many navies rely on patrol and supply aircraft, so we will not request any restrictions on the type of aircraft that may be launched or recovered, but in the interest of peace we request that only patrol aircraft launch while in the area. This may seem like a drastic request, but many nations require similar restrictions while transiting their

territorial waters, and for the first time China will now institute
this requirement for a limited time only. Monitoring compliance
of this request will be made by patrol boats, satellite, and patrol
aircraft. We place no restrictions on carriers that use the so-
called ski-jump launching method. Warships of the People's
Liberation Army Navy will also conform to this limitation
when farther than two hundred kilometers from land.

"With regard to subsurface vessels: they represent the
greatest danger to peace and security in the region. Therefore,
China will consider any submerged submarine detected within
the first island chain as hostile, and will act accordingly. China
likewise will not sail any submarine submerged through this
area."

Zu abruptly stepped away from the dais, and Foreign
Minister Tang took his place. "These may seem like
unreasonable and even belligerent demands, ladies and
gentlemen, but I assure you, our goal is to reduce tensions in
the area and restore lasting peace as quickly as possible," he
said. "President Zhou, the Politburo, the general staff, and the
good people of China seek nothing else. We humbly welcome
and solicit your cooperation during this difficult time. *Xièxiè.*
Thank you." Tang bowed, turned with his eyes averted, and
left the dais.

"Why, Zhou and Zu have got to be smoking some wacky terbacky," Vice President Ann Page said with a laugh. "Are they kidding? No submarines in the South China Sea? One usable catapult on our aircraft carriers? Are they serious?" Along with the president and vice president in the Oval Office were Secretary of State Herbert Kevich, National Security Adviser William Glenbrook, Secretary of Defense Fredrick Hayes, and Chairman of the Joint Chiefs of Staff Timothy Spellings. Ann turned to Kevich. "And where is President Zhou, Herbert? No one has seen him in quite some time. Who's in charge out there?"

"The real question is, Ann: What can they do to enforce these restrictions?" President Ken Phoenix asked. "General Spellings, what's China got out there that could threaten us if they decide to carry through with these restrictions?"

"A lot, and growing every day, sir," Spellings said. He read from his secure tablet computer: "As Zu mentioned, they have two carrier battle groups deployed right now. One, the *Zhenyuan,* is a ski-jump carrier, but it carries several advanced aircraft, although not with the same heavier loads as American carriers can carry. The *Zheng He* is a different matter: it's a slant-deck carrier with steam catapults, very much like a Nimitz-class carrier except a bit smaller, and it can carry more aircraft with heavier payloads. They have an amphibious assault aircraft carrier, the *Tongyi,* which is based in the East China Sea and is expected to lead any operations against Taiwan or the Paracel Islands, but it could be swung into action farther south. It is another ski-jump carrier, but it carries mostly helicopters and amphibious assault craft, plus about five hundred Chinese marines. All these battle groups are supported by at least ten vessels, including guided-missile cruisers, destroyers, frigates, replenishment vessels, and submarines. Most of these support vessels are modern ex-Russian ships or indigenously built and stack up well against our legacy ships. They should be activating a third aircraft carrier battle group soon. Bottom line: they definitely geared up to match whatever we can put into the South China Sea.

"The big problem is offensive capability from the Chinese mainland, sir," Spellings went on. "We have a qualitative advantage at sea—maybe slight, but still an advantage—but we start to lose it when it comes to support from shore. China has at least two dozen ballistic- and cruise missile antiship batteries within range of what they call the first island chain. That's equivalent to another ship at sea but with vastly expanded coverage. The missiles are mobile, and they only take an hour to align and launch even if launched from an unsurveyed spot. They also have at least three bases with dozens of long-range H-8 bombers fitted with supersonic antiship missiles.

"And all this doesn't include what we *don't* know about the Chinese military," Spellings went on. "We still don't know for sure what knocked down the P-8 Poseidon or the Sea Eye drone. Military bloggers and some analysts who have reviewed the transmissions from the P-8 think that China may have employed some kind of microwave, nuclear, laser, or cyber weapon that knocked out the P-8's electronics for a short time, similar to our netrusion technology we've used in the past. We just don't know. But if they have a directed-energy weapon that can down any aircraft within a hundred miles or so from their carrier, we could be at a distinct disadvantage. We don't have anything like that in our deployed arsenal right now."

"That's still not going to stop us from patrolling the South China Sea," the vice president said, "and we're going to put our aircraft on our carriers wherever we want. It was a silly statement for Zhou to make. They won't risk a general war by attacking the United States, so when a ship goes through the area unmolested, it makes them look weak."

"I agree with the vice president, sir: China wouldn't dare attack an American aircraft carrier in the South China Sea," Secretary of Defense Fredrick Hayes said.

"I agree too, sir," Secretary of State Herbert Kevitch said. "All that statement will do is drive up the insurance rates for all ships going through the area—that'll hurt their economy the worst because they rely on exports to drive their economy."

"Bill?" the president asked his national security adviser.

"I'm not as positive as the others, sir," Glenbrook said. "If the United States was up to full AirSea Battle strength, I'd be a lot more positive, but we're barely holding on as it is. Like the general said, they have a lot of firepower in that region. If they challenged us, they could make it look ugly."

"It was a bold statement that directly challenges every nation on Earth," President Phoenix said. "It puts everyone on notice." He looked at his vice president. "This makes it even more imperative to get that emergency funding for the full complement of McLanahan's bombers, Ann, and perhaps get more funding for the Navy, Air Force, and Space Defense Force again as well."

"I've got the budget staff working overtime on all that, Mr. President," Ann Page said.

"How many of McLanahan's bombers do we have on Guam now?"

"Eight, sir," Hayes replied. "He has two more ready for deployment and two more being refurbished—that was all last year's emergency funding allowed, and his company couldn't afford to rebuild more with their own funds."

"We'll find the money," President Phoenix said. "In the meantime, Fredrick, you are cleared to send additional forces to Guam per the plan put together by Pacific Command. I want Guam to turn into a fortress: air defense, ballistic missile defense, long-range surveillance, the works. Whatever Guam or the outlying Pacific islands need, I want in place. This is going to turn into another Midway mobilization."

"Do you want to change the profile of McLanahan's bombers, sir?" Secretary of Defense Hayes said. "Right now they just perform over-the-horizon reconnaissance for small groups of surface ships—they're not armed. The other bombers on Guam are armed for ground attack and antiship missions. The wing commander says they've been practicing loading weapons on some of McLanahan's bombers to make sure the remote weapons system works, but they've flown no missions with weapons aboard."

Phoenix thought for a moment, then nodded. "Yes, allow McLanahan's bombers to participate in all the wing's activities, including alerts with live weapons," he said. "I understand his bombers can carry air-to-air weapons as well?"

"Yes, sir."

"Those are authorized as well."

"Yes, sir. McLanahan's XB-1s are equipped with a system called SPEAR that has the ability to not only jam radar and radios but to insert commands and even malicious code into enemy electronic sensors," Hayes said. "Is that authorized?"

Phoenix shook his head ruefully. "My old buddy Patrick McLanahan and his high-tech toys," he said with a smile. "Yes, authorized. How are things working out with the Navy?"

"McLanahan's forces so far have had very little to do with the aircraft carriers or other Navy fighters," Hayes replied. "They perform as part of a Surface Action Group, providing long-range reconnaissance for small groups of cruisers, destroyers, and frigates that aren't part of a carrier strike group—surface ships that don't have their own air assets. They haven't tried coordinating strikes with carrier-based fighters or Navy cruise missile attacks. But as part of the SAG, they seem to be fitting in well. Overall, I'd say the program is working."

"Excellent," the president said. "We'll find the extra money and get more of those Excaliburs out there."

After the meeting broke up, Ann Page stayed behind with the president. He picked up a telephone. "Get General McLanahan on his personal communicator, please."

A few moments later the phone rang, and the president picked it up: "McLanahan here, Mr. President."

"Patrick, I'm going to get you the funding for the rest of the Excalibur program," the president said. "But it may take some time. I wanted to ask you if you could go to your company once again for initial funding for the remainder of the fleet, and perhaps a little more for some of the other planes you said you were working on."

"That is great news, Mr. President," Patrick said. He had returned to Battle Mountain a day earlier to supervise the last of the XB-1s completing refurbishment and preparing to deploy. He was sitting in his office in the main hangar of Sky Masters Inc., which overlooked the final assembly area for the refurbished planes, talking with the president of the United States through his secure subcutaneous transceiver system. Through the large soundproof picture window behind him in his office he could see an XB-1 Excalibur at the head of the line closest to the hangar doors ready to be rolled outside, and an XF-111 SuperVark, a refurbished F-111G Aardvark medium supersonic bomber, was right behind it, still with a small knot of technicians around it finishing details. Like the B-1 bomber, the F-111 bomber was a swing-wing supersonic design, but it was originally intended to operate off aircraft carriers. Finally rejected by the Navy as being too big and cumbersome for carrier duty, the F-111 served an exemplary role in the U.S. Air Force as a medium and strategic bomber and electronic warfare platform, dropping 40 percent of the guided munitions in Operation Desert Storm before being retired shortly thereafter.

"I'll schedule a meeting with the company president and ask her to go to the board and the shareholders and find out, sir," Patrick said. "I'm looking at Excalibur number ten just rolling off the line, and we're putting the finishing touches on the second refurbished XF-111 bomber."

"That's the one I was thinking about, the other swing-wing plane, right?"

"Yes, sir," Patrick said. "It doesn't have the long legs or payload of the XB-1, but it's better than anything else in the Pacific right now."

"Be in a position to put a few together to send out to Guam."

"Yes, sir," Patrick said. "I was watching the address by Foreign Minister Tang and General Zu. I guess they really believe they can dictate terms in the South China Sea."

"Most everyone in the White House seems to think China won't follow through," Phoenix said. "I'm not so sure. Pacific Command came up with a plan to fortify the defenses around Guam and our other Pacific bases in the region, and I've ordered that implemented as well. With all of China's saber-rattling going on, I think Congress will come up with the extra money. But no matter how belligerent China seems to be getting, somebody will squawk when we start talking about raiding their piggy bank."

"If you'd like me to talk with the folks in Congress, sir, let me know," Patrick said. "I've been out of uniform for a while now, but if you think it'll help, I'll be there."

"You've been out of uniform but not out of the news, my friend," the president said. "Everyone around here still winces when they hear your name. But a lot of people still admire and respect you—like me. We might have you come back and do just that."

"Thank you, sir," Patrick said. "I'll even bring one of the Excaliburs. They have a jump seat—we can even offer congressmen and staffers some rides."

"What about me?" the president asked. "I remember when President Martindale said he wanted to be the first sitting president to go into space. I nearly dropped my teeth when he said that. But I'd like to fly low-level in one of your monstrosities. The First Lady would kill me, but I'd sure like to do it."

"I can be at Andrews in four hours, sir—just say the word."

"I think we both have enough work to do without going off on joy rides," the president said. "But when all this is over with, I might take you up on that. Later." And the connection was terminated.

"Kylie, ask Dr. Oglethorpe to come and see me," Patrick called to his assistant. "And get me an appointment with Dr. Kaddiri for as soon as possible." The first call he made was to Tom Hoffman. "I just spoke with President Phoenix," he said. "He wants more Excaliburs and maybe even some XF-111 SuperVarks, but he doesn't have the money and asked if our company can kick in for a few more until they get funding. I'll have to go to the company board and find out how much money we can get advanced to us for more planes and training until the funds from Washington show."

"Excellent, General," Hoffman said. "I'll call my next group of pilots and techs and get them started. They've already been doing academics, so I can have them headed out your way in a few weeks for flight, simulator, and hands-on maintenance training."

"Bring them out as soon as you can, Tom."

"Yes, sir!"

While Patrick was speaking to Hoffman, Linus Oglethorpe arrived in Patrick's office. Oglethorpe was always amazed and amused to watch Patrick talking in midair with no phone or Bluetooth headset in sight. When he was done speaking with Hoffman, Patrick turned to him. "The president wants more Excaliburs and maybe even SuperVarks," he said. Linus punched the air in triumph. "However, he doesn't have the money, so I'm going to ask Helen to kick in. Where are we with the next batch of airframes?"

"We've received two from AMARG this past week, Patrick," Linus said. "Both are in the stage-two inspection hangar ready to start detailed structural inspections. One airframe down at Davis-Monthan did not pass the stage-one inspection, and another is questionable, so you may assume we're down to twenty. The rest have all completed stage-one inspections and are awaiting their train ride up here. We've identified forty-three F-111G and FB-111 airframes that are ready for stage-one inspections."

"Great. I'm going to meet with Helen, hopefully soon, to see if we can get some advanced funds to start, and I'll let you know when we can start shipping them up here." Dr. Helen Kaddiri was the longtime president and chairman of the board for Sky Masters Inc. With multiple doctorates in both business and engineering, the exotic, almond-eyed woman from Calcutta, India, started out in the company as one of founder Jonathan Masters's assistants. Helen's resentment at having to work for the boyish, immature, free-spirited Jon Masters propelled her to quickly move her way up the corporate ladder just to get away from him, and she eventually became company president. "I don't want to wait around for Washington to send contracts and money."

"We shall be like sprinters in the starting blocks at the Olympics, waiting for you to fire the starter's pistol, old chap," Linus said excitedly. "We shall be ready!"

SEVEN

WARBIRDS FOREVER AVIATION, RENO-STEAD AIRPORT, RENO, NEVADA

THE NEXT DAY

Tom Hoffman found Brad McLanahan in the break room, sipping a bottle of water, surrounded by logbooks and paperwork. "Hey, Brad," Hoffman greeted him. "Just get back from another early-morning lesson?"

"Yes, sir," Brad said. He was wearing a white aviator's shirt with epaulets and a captain's four gold stripes on the epaulet tabs, silver civil aviation wings with a silver senior pilot's star, a blue name tag, and a black tie—he looked every bit the professional aviator he had become. "Tom Cook. He wants to get his license on his seventeenth birthday, so he's been taking dawn patrol lessons before school. You gotta admire that kind of drive."

"I appreciate you doing that for him, Brad," Hoffman said. "His grandfather is a good friend. Tom Cook lost his dad in Iraq."

"I know. The kid's pretty tough."

"How's he doing?"

"Unfortunately, typical pattern," Brad replied. "He does real well when he can fly at least once a week, but if he drops to less than four lessons a month, we have to spend flight and ground time going over old stuff, and that's a little frustrating for him. I bought him a PC flight simulator that he can play with at home to stay motivated."

"Good idea."

"If he comes in again this week, we'll do a practice cross-country, and if he does okay I'll sign him off for solo cross-countries, and then if he flies at least once a week, he should have no problem taking his practical before his birthday."

"Sounds good," Hoffman said. "With avgas prices going through the roof, I'm surprised anyone can still afford to fly. With all the junk going on with China and what seems like half of Asia, oil and food prices are going berserk."

"Business really slowed down, didn't it, sir?"

"Personal and some corporate flying have really tanked, and airplane rentals are almost zero, but higher-end corporate and cargo ops are hanging in there," Hoffman replied. "The folks who can afford the warbirds and the big jets are still flying. But the 'hundred-dollar hamburger' fun flights that turned into the six-hundred-dollar hamburger have all but gone away."

"The simulators are getting a good workout, though."

"At least the pilots care enough about staying proficient to come in and get some simulator time when they can't afford to fly," Hoffman said. "Hopefully we'll get a break with fuel prices soon."

"It sure is looking weird," Brad said. "I went to Walmart yesterday—the shelves are looking pretty bare all of a sudden."

"Fewer container ships will risk sailing through the South China Sea with all the shooting going on out there," Hoffman said. "I'll bet it'll start hurting China really bad if their exports dry up any more than they have already. The good news is, a lot of companies are talking about opening manufacturing plants in North America to replace the factories in China. We could actually get a boost in our economy. I'm seeing a lot of corporate execs coming out here looking for land outside Reno to build factories. I see good things ahead for America—we just need to hang in there."

Hoffman held up an envelope. "I do have some good news for you, Brad. This is a first for me, in all my years of instructing: I've never seen an instructor get a tip." He dropped the envelope on the table in front of Brad. "Only fifty dollars."

"Fifty bucks is fifty bucks—I'll take it!" Brad said happily. "The students lay out so much money for lessons, they never think about tipping—they think we're all rich anyway. Who's it from?"

"Jeff Keefe, your multiengine student," Hoffman said. "He passed his check ride, no problems. He was so excited he could fly his own plane home he was dancing on the ramp. He included a card addressed to me with some nice comments about the work you did and the hustle, getting his multi in just one weekend."

"He came prepared, he did everything I told him to do, and he worked his butt off," Brad said. "He was a good student—he only tried to kill me once or twice."

"He says he wants to come back for his instrument rating and maybe his commercial certificate," Hoffman said. "We like repeat business around here." He paused for a moment, then said, "You've been doing a hell of a job around here, Brad. The hard work is much appreciated. I don't think there's an assignment you've turned down."

"I need the hours if I want to get my airline transport pilot rating sometime this decade."

"You're well on your way with that," Hoffman said. "So much so that I've uploaded a new curriculum for you, if you're interested. Take a look."

Brad changed the page on his laptop computer to the new curriculum folder. His eyes grew wide as he read: "You're kidding me, Colonel—this is the flight training program for the XB-1 Excaliburs!"

"Exactly," Hoffman said. "Your dad's bomber refurbishing program has been expanded and put on a crash schedule. He got more funding for XB-1s and even some money for XF-111s, and they want those planes out on Guam fast."

"Cool. So I can fly an Excalibur or SuperVark to Guam?" Brad asked incredulously.

"You still need your ATP to be pilot-in-command," Hoffman explained, "but we got special papal dispensation from the FAA for ferry flights originating at Battle Mountain destined for a military base or outside the CONUS or reverse: if you have more than five hundred hours total time, a commercial certificate, a multiengine and instrument rating, and at least two hundred and fifty hours in multiengine jets, and you complete that course, you can be first officer. You'll have the total hours soon; we'll get you more flights in the Lear 35 and Gulfstream to get the rest of your jet time; and you've done such a good job around here that you deserve a great big attaboy."

"That's awesome!" Brad exclaimed, hopping to his feet. "I can't believe it!"

"The course is not hard, but it's long and pretty in-depth," Hoffman said. "We also have to send you down to Edwards Air Force Base for altitude chamber, life support, flight physiology, spatial disorientation, and ejection seat training, and we may send you to Fallon for the Navy integration training your dad set up, but you'll enjoy the heck out of all that. I'm on my way to Guam in an Excalibur tomorrow, and I'll be out there to do some check rides. It should take you about a week to do the online course, another week for the simulator sessions, a week at Fallon, and a couple days at Edwards, and then I'll come back to do the course in the jet itself and give you a check ride. It'll be a good five weeks of training, but I think you can handle it. Interested?"

"Heck yes, I'm interested!" Brad exclaimed. "I'll start the online course tonight."

"The best news: hours as second-in-command time in the Excalibur count toward your ATP rating," Hoffman added. "That's ten hours per one-way ferry sortie from Battle Mountain to Guam, and if we fly you back on a company airplane and you get stick time on the return, you get more hours. Plus in the XB-1 you get to observe air refueling from the right seat—and if a willing pilot wants to give you some stick time, even behind a tanker, I wouldn't object."

"Cool!" Brad cried out happily. "Thank you, Colonel! I'll knock this course out right away. What an opportunity! Thank you!"

"You deserve it," Hoffman said. "The XB-1 will definitely water your eyes."

"Try it? Absolutely I will, sir!" *Shàngxiào* (Captain) Yao Mei-Yueh replied excitedly. The young, short, slender officer had been standing at attention in front of the commanding admiral of First Naval District South of the *Zhōngguó hǎijūn gònghéguó,* or Republic of China Navy, *Zhōng jiàng* (Vice Admiral) Wu Jin-ping, but after being asked a simple question by the admiral, he could hardly contain himself. "I was afraid we would appear as if we were cowering in front of the Communists!"

"As you were, Captain," the admiral said, barely containing a smile. A few seconds after Yao snapped back to attention, he ordered him to stand easy, and Yao snapped to parade rest. "This is serious business, Captain. Patrols have spotted the *Zheng He* carrier battle group just one hundred and seventy-five kilometers to the south. They have so many patrol planes up that they are disrupting the wind patterns."

"It does not matter, sir," Yao said. "The *Avenger*'s gold crew is the best attack submarine crew in the world. We have four successful simulated torpedo attacks on their ships in the past year, including one on the *Zhenyuan*. We have never been detected."

Admiral Wu liked confident, even cocky young officers, and Captain Yao was all that and more, which was why he was standing there this morning. "I know your operational record well, Captain," Wu said. "This too will be a simulated attack on their battle group, first with simulated torpedo-launched Harpoon missiles fired within fifty kilometers of a ship, and then with torpedoes fired within ten kilometers of an escort . . ."

"Allow me to do a simulated attack on the *Zheng He* itself, sir," Yao interrupted. Wu was not accustomed to being interrupted by a junior officer, and he was about to lash out, but Yao went on: "There would be nothing better than publishing an image of the *Zheng He* in my periscope crosshairs all over the world over the Internet!"

"This is not a game of taking embarrassing pictures of your children at their birthday party, Captain," Wu said angrily, although he certainly liked his spirit, and he had to admit that was a good idea. "We want to gauge their search patterns, study their acoustic patterns and sonar frequencies, and gather as much data as we can on their patrol activities." He paused, then nodded and smiled. "And yes, publishing a picture of their new carrier in the crosshairs of a Taiwanese submarine would certainly be welcome."

"My pleasure, sir," Yao said. "I promise a nice picture for your wall."

"Just keep your attention focused on the task at hand, Captain," Wu said. "I want your submarine back in one piece a lot more than I want a photo on my wall."

"Do you believe the Communists would really attack if they detected us, sir?" Yao asked, his voice a lot more concerned now.

"Assume that they will, Yao," Wu replied. "They are definitely acting more aggressive within the first island chain, although they have not attacked anyone except that American survey vessel."

"And the Vietnamese frigate, sir."

"There is no direct evidence that the frigate was hit by a Chinese missile," Wu said, "although that is what everyone suspects. Assume they will attack if you are detected, and bring your ship back in one piece." He stood from his desk, and Yao snapped to attention. "Good luck, Captain."

"*Shì hǎijūn, shàng jiàng,*" Yao said. "Yes, Admiral." He saluted the admiral. Wu returned his salute, and the young officer departed.

Wu's aide came into the officer a moment later. "The orders, sir?"

"Publish the orders immediately, all secure channels," Wu said. He signed a piece of paper and then handed it to his aide. "The *Avenger* will be under way within twenty-four hours. Deploy the normal decoys and have the usual false radio broadcasts made."

"Yes, Admiral," the aide said, then departed.

In the outer office, the aide signed a custody log for the orders, added the verbal orders issued by the admiral, and then gave the orders to his runner. "Take these orders to Cryptology and have them coded and broadcast immediately," he said. The runner signed the custody log and then placed the orders in a briefcase, and the aide locked it himself. Only he and the officers in charge of the various offices in headquarters that handled classified documents had the combination to that briefcase. The runner departed.

In Cryptology, the briefcase was opened by the duty officer and hand-carried to the first available encoding technician. Two computer programs were used in every encoding process. The first program generated the keys that were embedded in the preamble of the coded message and would be used at the other end to decrypt the message, and the second program used the keys to encode the message, which came out as a long string of numerals. The key generation program used a combination of the date-time group, originating author, recipient, and a random number generator of varying numbers of digits to create a key sequence, which was then passed to the second program so it could begin the encoding process. The computer doing the key generation and encoding was not connected to any other network, so it was impossible for hackers to intercept the key sequence. The key generation was invisible to the technician: all he saw was an error-checking readout that read the key sequence and computed a bit count that was either correct or incorrect. It was not possible to hack the computer itself, so the key sequence generation was totally secure . . .

. . . but inputting the parameters of the key sequence generation on a keyboard and displaying the bit count on the computer monitor *could* be hacked, and in fact it had been done many months earlier by agents of the People's Liberation Army Navy. The regular secure keyboard and monitor had been replaced by unsecure but identical-looking machines that transmitted each keypress and every character on the screen, where agents outside the building could record the information. If the parameters going into the key generation were known, once the hacker received the bit count it was relatively simple for a fast computer to reverse the key sequence generation process and acquire the key sequence. Once the key sequence was known, any message transmitted using that key could be read with ease almost as quickly as the proper recipient could.

This was how, in less than two hours, the information on the planned movement of the submarine *Avenger* had made its way to the People's Liberation Army Navy South Sea Fleet headquarters.

"*What did you say, Admiral?*" Colonel General Zu Kai thundered. "Repeat!"

"It is confirmed, sir," Vice Admiral Zhen Peng, commander of the South Sea Fleet, responded. "The Taiwanese are planning to deploy an attack submarine in the South Sea in order to directly challenge your newly imposed restrictions and stalk the *Zheng He* carrier battle group. They are purposely going to flout your orders. They are even planning on taking periscope photographs of Chinese ships and want to publish them on the Internet to prove that the restrictions are meaningless to them and to insult you and our entire country."

"How did you learn of this, Zhen?" Zu asked.

"I have a network of spies in the headquarters of the First Naval District in Kaohsiung," Zhen replied. "It has managed to infiltrate their computers to a very high degree. It provides us with very actionable intelligence."

General Zu looked at his deputy, Major General Sun Ji, who was listening in on the secure telephone conversation on a dead extension. The concern on Sun's face matched his own. "I knew nothing about this spy network of yours, Zhen," Zu said. "The Reunification Support Bureau of the Military Intelligence Division handles espionage work against Taiwan. Fleet admirals do not run spy networks. One incompetent move by one of your so-called spies could unravel the work of thousands."

"My apologies if I have exceeded my authority, sir," Zhen said. He did not sound truly apologetic in the least. "But my network has been in place since I took command of the South Sea Fleet, and it has provided the People's Liberation Army with much actionable intelligence without any hint of being discovered. I will of course dismantle the network if you order it, sir, but I request that you allow it to continue."

"Stand by, Zhen," Zu snapped. He put the call on hold. "Zhen has been running a spy network in Taiwan and hacking their computers without my knowledge?"

"He is indeed a resourceful and aggressive officer, sir," Sun commented.

"He could have hacked into *my* computer network for all I know!" Zu growled. "I should have the man shot!"

"It might be better if you allow him to continue, with your approval," Sun said, "until we can scan our system and try to trace any hacker trails back to him."

"'Hacker trails'?"

"Hacking a computer network is very much like breaking into a home, sir," Sun explained. "Even the best burglar always leaves some evidence that he has been there. If Zhen tried to hack our system, we will find it. But if you have him arrested before we can do the back-trace, the network will dissolve. We do know he has managed to infiltrate the Taiwanese encryption service, and they have some of the best cybersecurity in the world."

Zu thought for a moment, then nodded assent. "But I want the back-trace to begin immediately," he said. "I want to know the origin of every attempted infiltration of our systems."

"Yes, sir."

Zu hit the hold button again. "Very well, Admiral. I was at first upset that one of my fleet admirals was engaging in unauthorized activity, but the information your network has obtained is indeed valuable, and so now I will authorize it. Just do not allow your network to be discovered."

"Yes, sir," Zhen said. "Thank you. I have a suggestion on what to do about the Taiwanese submarine, sir."

"No suggestion is necessary, Admiral," Zu said. "The acting president and I have issued our orders: anyone violating the restrictions within the first island chain is subject to detention or attack. Those orders have not changed."

"Yes, sir, I understand," Zhen said. "But the nature of the attack should be dramatic and leave no doubt that China means to defend and control the waters within the first island chain."

"What are you talking about, Zhen?" Zu asked.

"I am referring to the BLU-89E, sir," Zhen said. "*Kěpà debō*—'Terrible Wave.' The weapon is still in the inventory of the South Sea Fleet, and it can be deployed on the Y-8 antisubmarine warfare aircraft immediately, and later redeployed on the cruisers escorting the *Zhenyuan* and *Zheng He*."

Sun immediately put down his receiver and accessed a computer terminal in a far corner of Zu's office to look up what the weapon might be . . . and when he found it, his eyes bulged in surprise. He sent the page over to Zu's computer, who appeared to be even more shocked. "Are you insane, Zhen?" he asked.

"The weapon was taken off our ships because the latest generation of torpedoes was much more accurate and higher performance," Zhen said. "But the BLU-89E was standard armament for our cruisers for many years—we even deployed them to the Gulf of Aden with the Somalia task force. If the Nationalists want to openly and brazenly challenge the People's Liberation Army Navy in our own waters, we should employ every weapon in our arsenal."

The sense of shock that General Zu experienced at the suggestion was slowly waning. "Stand by, Zhen," he ordered, and hit the hold button again. "Is he insane?" Zu murmured. "First his own spy network, and now he wants to deploy

'Terrible Wave'? 'Tiger's Claw' and 'Silent Thunder' are not enough for him?"

"Sir, we had deployed 'Terrible Wave' for the last ten years, on both ships and navy patrol aircraft," General Sun pointed out. "Zhen is probably the best qualified commander in the entire navy on how to use them."

Zu thought for a few moments, then picked up the receiver and punched the hold button off. "Authorized," he said. "One weapon only. Report to me for permission to deploy the weapon first."

"Acknowledged, General," Zhen said.

Zu terminated the secure connection. "I had better tell Gao what I have in mind," he said, rising from his seat. "I do not care what he thinks about it, but he ought to be prepared in case it really is employed." He shook his head. "We are about to unleash *Lóng Dehūxī*—the 'Dragon's Breath'— again," he said to his deputy. "It was only seventeen years ago when my predecessor last unleashed it, and it has been only ten years since the Russians did so."

"Sun Tzu said, 'If your forces are superior, attack,' sir," General Sun said. "The Americans are weak and getting weaker by the day, while China is growing stronger every day. The Americans were attacked on their own soil by the Russians, and they did not retaliate with nuclear weapons. They are fearful and undecided. This is the perfect time to assert our authority." He paused for a moment, then said, "Sir, I suggest you contact President Truznyev of Russia. If you want to maintain his cooperation and assistance in keeping the United States off-balance, Russia will be key."

Zu nodded, lost in thought. A few moments later he picked up the telephone again. "Get me President Truznyev of Russia immediately, secure," he ordered. He put down the telephone. "I hope they do not have any subs in the South Sea."

A few minutes later the phone rang, and Zu picked it up. "Colonel General Zu, secure."

There was a slight pause as the secure channel was locked on both ends, and then an unfamiliar voice said, "This is the voice of President Truznyev's translator, General. The president says it is about time someone in Beijing told him what in hell was going on."

"Tell the president thank you for returning my call," Zu said.

"The president says that the rumors of a military coup are true."

"There has been no coup," Zu said. "Acting President Gao Xudong is in charge until President Zhou's condition can be . . . further evaluated."

"Indeed," the Russian translator said. "Even so, I assume I am speaking to the de facto president of the People's Republic of China. So. What can I do for you today, Mr. President—excuse me, Colonel General?"

"You are of course aware of the activities in the South Sea regarding the Americans and Vietnamese military."

"Of course. Very intriguing. Your carrier battle groups obviously possess some advanced capabilities that our intelligence services have not yet revealed. Care to talk about them, General?"

"All will be revealed to you soon, Mr. President," Zu said. "I called because China is prepared to take our struggle over control of the South Sea to the next level, and we are seeking Russia's cooperation."

"In what way, General?"

"The Americans have considerable forces in the Pacific region, and they have recently indicated they are prepared to augment those forces twofold to counter China's deployments," Zu said. "We know Russia's resources in the Far East are limited, but not so in the West. If Russia activated its considerable military and economic influence in the West, America would realize their capability to respond to emergencies on two fronts on opposite sides of the planet are limited, and they could be stymied into inaction. America has fewer ships afloat than any time since after the Vietnam War, and forcing them to respond to a second front in the west could force them to sue for terms to Russia as well as China."

"America is no threat to Russia, at least in our own sphere of influence—namely, eastern Europe and central Asia," Truznyev's translator said. "Our work is already done. Russia does not need to dominate the South China Sea—in fact, limiting access to the South China Sea is not in our interests. You are not helping your cause with Russia by rattling sabers in the South China Sea, General."

"We will do much more than rattle sabers, sir," Zu said.

"Explain immediately, General!" Zu could hear Truznyev's angry voice in the background, a dramatic difference from the emotionless, mechanical tone of the translator.

"Mr. President, China is today claiming all its historic and legal rights in the South Sea," Zu said. "I am determined and honor-bound to lead my country in protecting and defending our rights to the inner island chain, and we will do whatever is necessary. I called you to inform you of my intentions and to ask for your support and assistance in this sacred endeavor."

"I do not give a shit about your intentions or honor, Zu," Truznyev's translator said. Truznyev's very loud voice was clearly discernible in the background, and it was obvious that it was made so. "I will put you on notice right now, you traitorous bastard: if one Russian sailor or airman even gets his hair tousled or has one meal interrupted by Chinese actions, I will drop a hundred megatons of nuclear warheads on your backwater country."

"That was not my intention in the least, Mr. President," Zu said. "I seek nothing but Russia's cooperation in our endeavor. Our efforts are the same exactly, sir: the reduction or elimination of the American naval influence on all the world's oceans. The United States Navy has a presence in every one of the world's oceans; I want to limit that influence in regions that are vital to China, which include the South Sea, Straits of Malacca, and the Indian Ocean."

"General Zu, you are either a crazy megalomaniac or completely deluded," Truznyev said. "The United States unfortunately has the most powerful navy in the world, even after all their austerity measures. If you think your puny two aircraft carriers can take on the navy of the United States of America, you should be institutionalized."

"Alone, no one can take on the United States," Zu said. "But with Russia's cooperation, we can force the United States to negotiate."

"Negotiate what?"

"Power sharing in the Pacific," Zu said. "Unfettered access to all the world's oceans, free of the interference and constant threat of the United States Navy."

"Russia already has unfettered access to any ocean in which she chooses to sail, General," Truznyev said.

"But if the United States decided to take that access away from you, Mr. President, what could you do about it?" Zu asked.

"Russia is not as dependent on the sea as is China," Truznyev said.

"Perhaps not," Zu replied, "but it must sicken you, as it does me, to live under the constant threat of American domination." Truznyev was silent. "Mr. President, this was a courtesy call to inform you that China will act soon, very soon, to put the world on notice that she will defend her sovereign territory against all threats with every weapon in her arsenal. Russia can side with China, as we did on the Gulf of Aden incident, and stand up to the Americans. If you decide not to act, China will still pursue her destiny."

"Russia is not going to side with you just so you can assert some wild baseless claim on the South China Sea and western Pacific, Zu."

"Then perhaps there are other areas where our two nations can cooperate, sir," Zu said. "Russia has vast natural resources virtually untapped in Siberia; China has a large appetite for resources that grows exponentially every year. I believe Chinese investment in several natural gas liquefaction plants, pipelines, cryogenic ships, and port facilities in Siberia would serve both our nations well." Truznyev was silent again. "Mr. President?"

"Tell me more about what you have in mind about the South China Sea, General," Truznyev said. "And I want to know about these other weapons it appears you have employed in the area, the one that took down the American aircraft. And I want to know why I am speaking to you instead of to Zhou, and why you are deploying thousands of troops all throughout your country."

"I think it is time to tell you everything, Mr. President," Zu said, "and I think you will be pleased at the prospects for both of us."

"Incredible weather this morning for this operational tasking, sir," *Hai Jun Da Xiao* (Lower Admiral) Weng Li-Yeh said, smiling proudly as he surveyed activity on his ship down below. Even though this was their first mission after completing trials and a shakedown cruise, his sailors appeared to be in excellent spirits and worked with fluid precision.

"It is indeed most excellent, Admiral," Weng's superior officer, *Hai Jun Shao Jiang* (Rear Admiral) Hu Tan-sun, replied. "You may commence launching when ready."

"*Shì, haijun shàng jiàng,*" Weng replied. He picked up a telephone. "Operations, this is Flag. You may commence air operations as briefed, Captain."

Slowly, activity down below began to increase in tempo. Hu and Weng were watching the activity from the flag bridge of the aircraft carrier *Zheng He,* the People's Republic of China's second aircraft carrier, just recently made combat-ready. Named after a world-traveling Chinese fleet admiral from the fifteenth century, the *Zheng He* was formerly the Brazilian Navy's *Sao Paulo,* which in turn had formerly been the French Navy's Clemenceau-class carrier *Foch.* As the *Sao Paulo,* the fifty-five-year-old carrier had been extensively upgraded and modernized, so even though it was smaller than the *Zhenyuan,* it embarked just as many aircraft, a mix of Chinese and Russian multirole fighters and helicopters. Brazil was in the process of beginning an extensive upgrade of its navy, including an indigenously built carrier, and the two carriers being built by

China were experiencing some construction delays, so China gladly purchased the surplus vessel. Unlike the *Zhenyuan,* the *Zheng He* had an angled deck, which allowed for simultaneous takeoffs and landings, and it used steam catapults instead of the ski-jump ramp to launch aircraft, which allowed launching more heavily armed aircraft.

After the Harbin Z-5 rescue helicopters and Harbin Z-9 antisubmarine warfare helicopters were launched, the crew of the *Zheng He* prepared to launch one of the largest carrier-launched strike aircraft in the world from its deck: the JH-37 *Fēi Bào,* or Flying Leopard. The Leopard was a carrier-based version of the Russian-built Sukhoi-34 fighter-bomber, modified with folding wings and vertical stabilizer, stronger undercarriage to withstand carrier landings, and more powerful Xian WS9 turbofans. It used canards—small moving wings on either side of the nose—for extra maneuverability in dogfights, but its primary purpose was long-range strikes—it could carry almost twenty thousand pounds of a wide variety of weapons, from mines to cruise missiles. The JH-37 was also able to perform long-range electronic submarine searches, radar patrols, electronic warfare, and reconnaissance, using underwing sensor and emitter pods. On this sortie, the JH-37 was carrying six APR-3E rocket-powered torpedoes, three under each wing.

Watching a JH-37 launch was always an exciting event, and many of the off-duty crew came up on deck to watch the magnificent beast taxi up to the catapult shuttle and unfold its long wings and tall tail. There were only six JH-37s in the *Zheng He*'s complement simply because the bombers were so massive that there was no room for more. The nearly ninety-thousand-pound JH-37 took the number three catapult, its left wing hanging far over the port side—no aircraft could use any of the other catapults at the same time as the Leopard because of its enormous size, and landings had to be carefully planned because no aircraft could park on the fantail when the JH-37 came in for landing. Because of its long range and size and because getting it back on board the carrier took so much preparation, the JH-37 was often sent off to land bases until the decks could be made ready. In accordance with the carrier operations restrictions initiated by China, the number one and two waist catapults had aircraft parked on them.

After hooking up to the catapult shuttle and holdback bar, the big Xian turbofans were run up to full military power, the exhaust so powerful that it shook the heavy steel blast deflector behind it. When the catapult was fired and the breakaway holdback bar released, it always appeared as if it was impossible for the big bomber to actually accelerate quickly enough to make it down the three hundred feet of deck and become airborne before tumbling over the edge and splashing into the ocean. But, sure enough, the big bomber rumbled into the sky, shaking the deck with the blast of its big engines, and it was quickly lost from view. In its antisubmarine role, it could patrol as far as three hundred miles from the carrier and stay aloft for six hours.

After the JH-37 was away, the air defense fighters were next. Like the *Zhenyuan,* China's first aircraft carrier, the *Zheng He* had a mix of fighters in its arsenal: two squadrons, each with fifteen JN-15 multirole fighters, China's first domestically produced carrier-based fighter, a reverse-engineered copy of the Russian Su-33 carrier fighter; and one squadron of ten JN-20 advanced air superiority fighters. The JN-20s were definitely the "show" planes of the fleet and were rarely flown except for qualifications, proficiency, or when foreign patrol planes were in the area, so the JN-15s were used for routine patrols.

Along on this sortie but not part of the *Zheng He*'s complement was another aircraft orbiting around the carrier battle group at five thousand feet above the South China Sea: a Shaanxi Y-8 medium four-engine land-based turboprop transport plane, a Chinese-made copy of the Russian Antonov-12 transport, that had launched a few hours earlier. The Y-8 was configured as both an airborne early-warning aircraft and an antisubmarine warfare plane, with a fixed "Balance Beam" air search radar mounted atop the fuselage, a surface search radar on the chin, and a magnetic anomaly detector, or MAD, mounted on a long boom on the tail. The MAD sensed the change in the earth's magnetic field when a submarine moved through it, alerting an operator to its presence. Once alerted, the Y-8 would start a search pattern, dropping sonobuoys to help track the submarine, and once located, it would drop depth charges to try to destroy the sub or vector in carrier-based antisubmarine helicopters to attack. The Y-8 was China's first long-range surveillance and antisubmarine warfare aircraft, purpose-made for patrolling China's long coastline.

For this special patrol, the Y-8 was armed with a special weapon, one that was designed to cement China's claim on the inner island ring once and for all.

Normally the Y-8 would not patrol more than one or two hundred miles from Chinese mainland ports and coastal military bases, but they had special intelligence of a target that had to be located, and they were determined to do so.

Less than two hours later: "Bridge, Combat, the Y-8 has made MAD contact and is beginning its orbit, range one-thirty kilometers, bearing three-zero-zero," the combat systems officer radioed to Admiral Weng.

The range was too great for their helicopters, Weng knew, and it would take them a couple hours to close the distance. "Have the Y-8 maintain MAD contact, but make sure it does not drop sonobuoys," he ordered. "I do not want our friends to be alerted yet. Helm, steer three-zero-zero, best possible speed. Operations, ready a flight of Z-9s to prosecute the target when we are in range. Make sure the crew of the JH-37 is advised and tell them to be ready."

The phone from the flag bridge beeped, and Weng picked it up immediately. "Report," Admiral Hu ordered.

"Right where our intelligence said it would be, sir," Weng replied. "Our intelligence agents reported that the Taiwanese intelligence-gathering submarine *Fùchóu zhe* was going to put to sea yesterday from its base in Kaohsiung and attempt a simulated missile and torpedo attack on the *Zheng He* battle group. I have ordered the Y-8 to maintain contact. The JN-15 fighters are on normal air patrols. I have ordered another flight of antisubmarine helicopters to be ready when we receive the order. The JH-37 is standing by and ready. We should be in position for helicopter and escort ASW operations in about two hours."

"Very well, Admiral."

"Sir, on our present course and speed, we will intercept the *Fùchóu zhe* in Taiwanese waters," Weng said. "Am I approved to continue, sir?"

"There is no such thing as 'Taiwanese waters,' Admiral Weng," Hu said, the derision thick in his voice. "Yes, you will continue. The submarine is in violation of operational restrictions on submerged submarines. An example must be made."

REPUBLIC OF CHINA SUBMARINE FÙCHÓU ZHE (AVENGER), SOUTH CHINA SEA

A SHORT TIME LATER

"We have received the latest position information on the *Zheng He* battle group, Captain," the operations officer aboard the Taiwanese Type 800 submarine *Avenger* reported. He plotted the position on the chart in the con. "About thirty kilometers to the south."

Captain Yao nodded. "We will be in range of their patrol helicopters soon," he said. "Get a last GPS update for the inertial navigation system, then we will go to patrol depth and commence ultraquiet operations."

"Yes, sir." The submarine *Avenger* was at periscope depth now, getting radio messages and updating its position by a GPS receiver mounted on the periscope mast, but in seconds it received a final GPS update and the mast was lowered to avoid detection. The *Avenger* then commenced a steep dive to four hundred feet and began ultraquiet operations. The *Avenger* was a former Israeli Dolphin-class diesel-electric attack submarine, built in Germany, and was already one of the quietest submarines in the world, but on ultraquiet all possible means for extraneous noise was eliminated; the crew was even directed to walk carefully, not slam hatches or drop metal objects, and speak in whispers even on the intercom. Submerged speed was cut in half, which made the days that much longer, but hunting ships was a patient man's game anyway.

Avenger was fitted with ten torpedo tubes, six of which were larger twenty-five-inch tubes capable of firing Tomahawk cruise missiles. Taiwan was not currently allowed to buy any sub-launched cruise missiles from the United States, so the larger torpedo tubes were fitted with liners that allowed them to fire twenty-one-inch diameter torpedoes; it carried a total of sixteen twenty-one-inch wire-guided torpedoes. *Avenger* was also armed with a new weapon system: IDAS, or Integrated Defense and Attack System, which was a torpedo-launched laser- or infrared-guided missile capable of attacking ships, land targets, and even antisubmarine helicopters at ranges out to thirty kilometers—IDAS was the first missile in the world to attack aircraft while the launch platform was submerged. Two of *Avenger*'s torpedo tubes, one forward and one aft, each carried a magazine of four IDAS missiles.

About an hour later the sonar operator whispered on intercom: "Captain, sonar contact, bearing two-five-zero, aircraft, sounds like a patrol helicopter." The passive sonar could pick up any sounds traveling through the water, and computers analyzed the sounds and took an educated guess at what it might be.

"Slow to five knots, turn left heading one-six-zero," Yao ordered. A patrol helicopter's dipping sonar was probably one of the submarine's most dreaded adversaries other than another submarine, and the only way to avoid being detected by its active sonar signal was to get as far away from it as quickly as possible while not being detected. It became a cat-and-mouse game as the helicopter transmitted its signal then moved, and the submarine had to respond with its own move.

"Let us try a simulated IDAS attack on this helicopter," Captain Yao said. "Periscope depth, half standard rate. Stand by on IDAS, simulated attack on airborne target. Flood tube three." The *Avenger* rose ever so slowly to a depth of sixty feet. "Bearing to helicopter?"

"Bearing to helicopter three-five-two."

Yao turned the periscope until the lens was pointing toward

three-five-two degrees, then slowly raised it above the surface. He immediately saw the helicopter, moving away from them. He locked onto the helicopter and hit the laser rangefinder. "Mark."

"Range three thousand two hundred meters."

"Simulate fire two IDAS."

"Simulate fire IDAS . . . one away . . . two away." Had they actually launched the wire-guided missiles, they would take steering cues from the periscope and laser marker to home in on its target.

"Good job," Yao said. "Down periscope. Steady up on two-two-zero, simulate reloading tube three with IDAS. How far until the first escort?"

"Approximately ten kilometers, sir."

Well within the active sonar range of a medium- or large-size escort vessel, Yao knew, but outside their own passive sonar detection range. Stealth was very important now. They made temperature measurements as they ascended and descended, which improved the computer models for determining thermoclines—marked bands of different temperatures through the water that might deflect sound or sonar—so they could pick the proper depth to head toward the target, but it was all educated guesswork. It was akin to a bowhunter stepping quietly through a forest toward where he thought the deer would be, using everything possible—wind direction, foliage, silence—to close in undetected. In the end, it usually came down to patience and luck.

Just then: "Single sonar ping, sir, bearing two-four-zero."

The Communists had made a mistake—he used his active sonar to try to get a fix on them, which instead gave away his own location. "Getting a little anxious, are we?" Yao said under his breath. "Now, it would really help if you . . ."

"Second single ping!" the sonar operator reported, his voice still muted but noticeably excited. "Bearing two-four-seven, heading one-zero-zero, approximate range eight kilometers!"

"Up periscope," Yao ordered. He turned the periscope tube to the proper bearing, then slowly raised it. A few clicks of magnification and he had the destroyer in his crosshairs. "You are mine, *pigu,*" he said in a low voice. He took several photos. "Down periscope," he quietly ordered. "Stand by for simulated torpedo attack, crew," he spoke on the intercom. "Flood tubes two and five, keep the outer doors closed, acknowledge."

"All outer torpedo doors closed and verified, sir."

"Very well. Simulated only, match bearings . . . simulate fire one . . . simulate fire two." The WS-2A5 torpedoes were the standard Taiwanese torpedoes, designed and built in Taiwan but designed after the American Mk-48 torpedo. They were wire guided, with passive sonar detection as primary terminal guidance and active sonar guidance if the wire was cut and for a final range and bearing to the target. The wire transmission was two-way, so not only could the torpedo operator on the sub steer the torpedo through the wire, but the torpedo could send sonar signals back to the sub as it closed on its target. The torpedo swam as fast as fifty-five knots, slowed to forty knots to take a terminal active sonar fix, then sped up again to close in for the kill.

"Make your course two-one-zero," Yao ordered. He turned to his executive officer, *Zun Khong* (Commander) Chein Si-yao. "Now we go after their carrier, Si-yao."

"It is risky, sir," Chein said. Chein Si-yao was far younger and less experienced than Yao, on his first extended cruise aboard the *Avenger.* "The battle group is only eight kilometers away, and several helicopters are airborne. If they start hammering away with their active sonars, they can swarm us."

"We will let them sail past, and then try to come up behind the *Zheng He* for a shot," Yao said. "I am not going to let this opportunity pass. The Communists expect everyone to run away with fear when they sail their big carrier battle group around—they will not expect anyone to pursue them."

"Simulated strikes on Communist destroyer complete, sir," Chein said as the seconds ticked past on his watch. "Successful engagement. Congratulations, sir."

"Thank you, Commander," Yao said, "but I want that carrier next. Continue scan for the *Zheng He*. Range and bearing as quickly as possible."

EIGHT

ABOARD THE PLAN AIRCRAFT CARRIER ZHENG HE

THAT SAME TIME

The phone from the flag bridge rang, and Lower Admiral Weng Li-Yeh, captain of the carrier *Zheng He,* picked it up immediately. "Yes, Admiral?"

"Any sign of that traitor submarine yet?" Rear Admiral Hu Tan-sun, commander of the *Zheng He* carrier battle group, asked.

"We have it narrowed down to less than a hundred square kilometers, sir," Weng replied. "The Y-8 radar operators thought they had spotted a periscope very briefly about a half hour ago, but the sea state is a little choppy so radar reports are not totally accurate."

"How about the diesel detectors?" Hu asked. The Y-8 patrol plane had the capability to sniff the air for telltale signs of diesel exhaust to alert it to the presence of diesel-electric submarines.

"The Y-8 is patrolling too close to the battle group, sir," Weng replied. "Diesel detectors will not be reliable unless they fly farther out. Besides, if the target is trying to do simulated attacks on our group, he will likely be running on batteries only."

There was a slight pause, then Hu said, "How many antisubmarine helicopters can we launch into the area right now?"

"We can launch four, sir," Weng replied. "Four of our escorts have helicopters, but I think only two are configured for antisubmarine operations at this time. A total of six, sir."

"Weng, we had intelligence that the traitors were going to send a submarine after us—we should have had all helicopters configured for ASW." Another pause, then: "Launch all available ASW helicopters into the search area immediately."

"*All* of them? But, sir, the Taiwanese sub will be alerted that we are searching for him the moment he detects multiple sonars. I recommend . . ."

"Weng, we know the traitor is on the way, and we have a good idea where he is," Hu snapped. "The last thing I want is for the traitors to come within torpedo range of this ship—or worse, actually take a shot at us. Launch the helicopters immediately!"

The search for the *Zheng He* did not take long: "Got him!" Yao whispered excitedly. The profile of the carrier was unmistakable through his periscope even at this range. "Bearing one-nine-one." He hit the laser rangefinder. "Range twelve kilometers, speed twenty, heading zero-eight-zero. Transmit target position and the periscope photo of the second engagement to fleet headquarters."

"Transmission sent, sir," came the response a few moments later.

"Very well." He made a fast 360-degree scan of the horizon. There was one escort ship to the west. Yao got a photograph and a position on it. "Periscope down." Twelve kilometers was right at the edge of the torpedo's envelope, and it was perpendicular to their course so it was an even more difficult shot—they had to close in. "Steer one-seven-zero, make fifteen knots, set your depth one hundred meters." He estimated the carrier battle group was probably making no more than twelve knots, so he could close in slowly without going to full underwater speed. The *Zheng He* could probably sail at almost thirty knots when launching aircraft, which was far faster than the *Avenger*'s top underwater speed, but within its protective cocoon of ships it had to slow down so the others could keep up. "Let us get this one, men. I want a picture of a dead Communist carrier on the admiral's wall by tomorrow morning."

"Sir," Chein said, "we are nearing our maximum submerged speed. We are exceeding ultraquiet parameters."

"I do not want to lose this one, Exec," Yao said. "We 'torpedoed' a destroyer with ease—I think the carrier will be just as easy. Proceed."

"*Contact!*" the radar operator shouted. "Periscope, bearing zero-three-five, range twelve kilometers!"

The copilot made a mark on his chart. "We got you now, friend," he said. On the command channel he radioed: "*Jiâ*, this is *Yúying* Three, radar contact periscope, thirteen kilometers northeast of you."

Like a pack of starving wolves chasing down a deer, the six ASW helicopters zoomed to the location, then established a rectangular pattern. On cue, together they seeded the sea with sonobuoys. Once the sonobuoys hit the water they deployed a floating platform with a UHF antenna, then unreeled the main body with a hydrophone six feet under the surface. This first pattern was composed of passive hydrophones that only listened for mechanical sounds . . .

. . . and it did not take long to triangulate a bearing to an underwater target.

"Heavy rotor sounds overhead, sir!" the sonar operator aboard the *Avenger* radioed. "Now several sets of rotors! It might be a swarm, sir!"

"Reduce speed to five knots, come to a heading of zero-six-zero, make your depth two hundred meters," Captain Yao Mei-Yueh ordered. He realized he had gotten too anxious about getting a photo of the carrier and had let errors multiply— sailing too fast, keeping the periscope up too long, and ignoring the threat from the helicopters—and now he might have to fight his way out of this. The farther he got away from the carrier and its escorts, the more likely it would be for the helicopters to break off their search and fly home.

They all heard it a few minutes later: the sound of active sonars pinging all around them. "Make your depth two hundred and fifty," Yao ordered. "Come left zero-four-five, maintain five knots."

"If the Chinese operators are good," Commander Chien said, "they will have our position triangulated within minutes."

"But they are not very good, Si-yao," Yao said. "And if their helicopters are using their dipping sonars, that means they are hovering, not pursuing. Conn, make turns for fifteen knots." He turned again to Chein. "The chase continues, Commander. If they try to pursue, we will just go silent again, wait for them to start banging away with their active sonars, and run again. We can do this much longer than they can."

"The Z-9s report the traitor submarine is dashing, sir," captain of the *Zheng He,* Admiral Weng, said to Admiral Hu, commander of the *Zheng He* carrier battle group. "The helicopters are running low on fuel, and converting the others for antisubmarine duty will take another twenty minutes."

"I told you, Weng, every helicopter in the battle group should have been made ready for antisubmarine duty," Hu said angrily. "We could lose the traitor." He went on, "Get a second JH-37 ready to launch with torpedoes. Have every helicopter stay on station as long as possible with all sonars active. I want a position on that submarine close enough to get the JH-37 in position to attack. I do not care if they employ their sonars while sitting with empty fuel tanks on the surface—I want the Flying Leopard to attack, and I want that traitor's submarine on the bottom *now*!"

"Here they come again," Yao Mei-Yueh said as the sound of the active sonars got closer. "They are just not going to give up. Helm, steer zero-eight-five. Let us put more distance between us and the carrier—that will make those helicopter pilots watch their fuel gauges even closer."

"Should we decrease speed, sir?" executive officer Chein Si-yao asked. "At fifteen knots, we are putting off quite a racket."

Yao shook his head. "I want to get some distance first," he replied. "If we hear those helicopters get closer, we will go back to five knots. But every kilometer we get from that carrier is another chance we will have to escape." The *Avenger* on batteries was very quiet at this depth, even at twenty knots, although at that speed the batteries would not last very long. He flicked a channel switch on his intercom. "Sonar, any sign of pursuit from their surface ships?"

"None, sir," the sonar operator replied. "All escorts appear to be staying with the carrier."

"Very well." Yao smiled. "What good is having destroyer escorts if they are just going to stay with their primary? Are they going to let the helicopters do all the work?" For the first time since they were discovered, Yao felt a touch of relief. They might just make it out of this with their skins intact.

"Contact, sir!" Weng shouted. "One of the helicopters got a momentary contact, bearing only."

"Pass to the Flying Leopard and have him attack immediately," Admiral Hu ordered, "and he had better not miss."

The JH-37 *Fēi Bào* swooped less than five hundred feet over the ocean near the carrier *Zheng He* at patrol speed, then took up a heading east on the same bearing as the sonar contact. Immediately after overflying the gaggle of Z-9 patrol helicopters, the bomber crew began sowing APR-3E torpedoes along the last reported bearing to the Taiwanese submarine, dropping one every ten seconds. When the torpedoes dove underwater, they detached their aerodynamic tailcones and activated passive sonar to search for a target.

Minutes later, one of the torpedoes picked up the sound of the *Avenger* sliding through the sea, less than a half mile away. It locked the target bearing into its navigation system, armed its 150-pound warhead, activated its active sonar, and fired its solid-propellant rocket motor. The torpedo immediately accelerated to almost one hundred miles an hour and closed quickly with its quarry.

"*Torpedo inbound!*" the sonar operator shouted. "*High speed, closing fast! He has acquired with active sonar!*"

"Countermeasures starboard!" Yao shouted. "Helm, hard to port, flank speed! Sound collision!"

But at just a half-mile distance, there was no time for evasive maneuvers—the torpedo closed the distance in less than thirty seconds. It missed the Taiwanese submarine, but its proximity fuze detonated the warhead just a few dozen yards behind the *Avenger*. The massive overpressure instantly deformed the submarine's rudder and several propeller blades, creating a massive vibration throughout the entire vessel. The sub felt as if it was going to roll inverted.

"All stop!" Yao shouted, scrambling for a handhold. "Damage report!" He dashed to the sonar station. "Are we making any noise?"

The sonar operation listened for a few seconds. "Loud cavitation and structural defect noises at this speed, sir," he said finally. He listened again. "Sounds decreasing as we slow, but I can still hear some in the background."

That could be a problem, Yao thought as he went back to the control area. "Damage report."

"Several leaks around the propeller shaft and bearings, and possibly several bent propeller blades," Chein replied, "but Engineering thinks we will have propulsion if we can risk the noise. The rudder has a seven-degree port cant but it is movable. All other compartments reporting no serious damage."

Wounded, Yao thought, but not dead. "How much speed does Engineering think we can make?"

"It depends on how much noise you are willing to make, sir. They think a maximum of fifteen knots."

"At least we can still make it home, if we can evade the Communists," Yao said. "Comm, prepare a message floater, radio our position in relation to reference point *Ânquán*, request

assistance—these helicopters are over Taiwanese waters."
The message floater was a buoy with a satellite transmitter
and antenna aboard that would send a coded message to fleet
headquarters, wait for message confirmation, then sink itself so
it did not reveal the position of the sub that launched it.

"Floater ready, sir."

"Release it," Yao ordered. He waited until the message was
sent and the floater sunk.

"Con, Sonar, helicopter noises on the surface, bearing two-
zero-zero."

"He might have spotted the floater before it sunk itself,"
Chein said in a low voice.

"Helicopter sounds increasing, sir, bearing two-zero-zero,"
the sonar operator said. "He is coming closer."

"It is time to stop being the hunted," Yao said. "Helm, take
us to periscope depth, nice and slow."

It took careful balancing of the ballast tanks to approach
the surface without using forward propulsion and without
broaching, but several minutes later they were stabilized at sixty
feet below the surface. After a careful sonar scan, Yao raised
the periscope and quickly did a 360-degree scan of the horizon,
then turned to the approaching helicopter's bearing. "Target,
aircraft," he announced. He tapped the laser rangefinder
button. "Range eight kilometers. Weapons, ready IDAS in tube
three, stand by to engage. Flood tube three."

"Con, Weapons, IDAS ready."

"Tube three flooded."

"Open outer door on tube three," Yao ordered. He
magnified the image of the Communist helicopter, then locked
it in. "IDAS, aircraft, tube three, shoot one."

"IDAS, tube three, shoot one."

The IDAS missile shot out and ahead of the *Avenger* on a
blast of compressed air from the torpedo tube, and it steered

itself to the target bearing. Once it was about fifty yards ahead of the sub, a booster motor on the rear of the missile fired, propelling the missile upward at over one hundred miles an hour and pushing it above the surface. As soon as it cleared the surface the spent booster motor ejected and the main rocket motor ignited, pushing the missile to almost twice the speed of sound. Seconds later, the missile impacted the Chinese Z-9 helicopter on its rotor mast just above the cockpit. The missile's fifty-pound high-explosive warhead separated the mast from the helicopter, and the stricken helicopter crashed into the sea.

"Direct hit!" Yao shouted. "That helicopter will make enough noise to mask our damage sounds. Down periscope. Secure tube three, then reload IDAS. Helm, make your depth two hundred meters. Make turns for fifteen knots. Steer zero-five-zero." Yao allowed himself to think they might actually get away from the area alive.

General Zu picked up the telephone, knowing exactly what the call was about. He never should have doubted that Admiral Zhen would unleash *Kěpà debō* if authorized. "What is it, Admiral?" he spoke after the secure link was established.

"The Taiwanese submarine has been detected, sir," South Sea Fleet commander Admiral Zhen Peng said. "It is apparently damaged but under way. It used a new missile that has shot down and destroyed an antisubmarine patrol helicopter while submerged."

"How did the traitor submarine get damaged, Admiral?" Zu asked.

"It was attacked by torpedoes from one of our carrier attack planes, sir," Zhen said.

"If it got away from a torpedo, Zhen, what makes you think your forces can destroy it with *Kěpà debō*?"

"It is damaged, sir, so it cannot evade the torpedo as before, and we have a solid position on it with sonobuoys," Zhen replied. "I am confident we can kill it now."

Zu hesitated. This was going to be an extreme escalation, and he was going to be responsible for it—not Zhou, not Gao, no one but himself.

"Sir?" Zhen asked. "Am I authorized to proceed?"

"Stand by, damn you, Zhen."

"Sir, we must act before the traitor submarine gets away," Zhen said. "If it challenges your restrictions and escapes, the world will think we do not have the technology or the will to enforce our own territorial waters."

"I said shut up, Zhen," Zu said. The deputy chief of the general staff, Major General Sun, entered Zu's office, heard his superior's angry retort, and narrowed his eyes with a silent question. Sun was right, Zu thought: no one, not even the Americans, were powerful enough in the region to take on China. This would leave every nation on Earth fearful of taking on China.

"Authorized, Zhen," Zu said. "Make sure it is killed." He slammed the receiver down onto its cradle. "Get Gao on the line immediately!"

A few moments later: "Yes, General?" Gao Xudong responded.

"There is a Taiwanese submarine preparing to attack our aircraft carrier *Zheng He,*" General Zu said. "I have ordered our aircraft and ships to attack. They are authorized to use 'Terrible Wave' to destroy the submarine. Do you understand?" And then Zu explained what the weapon was . . .

. . . and Gao gasped aloud. "*Yi!* By the stars, General!" he exclaimed. "That would be insanity!"

"Perhaps that would be the best deterrent—if everyone thought China was insane," Zu said, a touch of dark humor in his voice. "It worked with Iran and North Korea for years."

"And half the world was poised to destroy both countries if the threat even appeared in the slightest bit to be real," Gao said. "Rescind that order, General!"

"No one is going to retaliate, Gao," Zu said. "America has been attacked many times in the past several years and has never mounted a strategic response."

"Tell that to President Gryzlov of Russia!" Gao exclaimed. "He is still buried under millions of tons of the rubble from his underground command center after the American bombers got done with him—*after* they destroyed most of their land-based intercontinental ballistic missiles!"

"And the Americans threw away what bombers they had left to get Gryzlov, and they still have not rebuilt their bomber force," Zu said. "America is too weak to respond to anything except an attack against their homeland—they will not dare risk a general war for something that happens half a world away."

"But if you are wrong, General, China will suffer," Gao said.

"The plan is already in place, Gao," Zu said. "I will give you a statement that you will issue afterward. Study it—it should appear to be your words, not mine."

"I have a better idea, General," Gao said. "After you employ the weapon, the Americans will certainly call Ambassador Li Peiyan in for consultation, or call me directly. As soon as that meeting has concluded, I will call President Phoenix and gauge his reaction. I should be able to convince him that all these attacks were cooked up by Zhou and that China will pull all our forces back and disengage in the South Sea."

"Disengage? Why would I wish that? The whole objective is to occupy and defend the first island chain, not disengage!"

"General, if you don't allow me to talk President Phoenix down, he could very well retaliate," Gao said. "I don't think he will, but he might, especially if we don't open up a dialogue right away. Now if I can't convince you to stop this lunacy, at least allow me to contact Phoenix shortly afterward, listen to him, and try to convince him that China will back off."

"Back off? China will never back off!"

"Then China is doomed to destruction," Gao said earnestly. "If Phoenix is assured that China only wants peace, we buy more time to build our forces in the South Sea. If we say nothing, or if Phoenix is not convinced, he could be forced to retaliate."

Zu did not feel convinced in the least, but finally he said, "Very well, talk with him. But do not reveal a thing."

"That's the wrong tack, General," Gao insisted. "We should admit everything."

"*What?*" Zu exclaimed. "Why in the world would I do that?"

"General, you have been attacking foreign ships and mobilizing ground forces, and now the president of China has mysteriously disappeared," Gao said. "I have spent a lot of time in America. Americans are the most paranoid people on the planet, especially when nuclear weapons are potentially involved. They will gear up for thermonuclear war within moments of your attack. I don't think they'll retaliate until they get more information, but I guarantee you they'll target each and every ballistic missile launch pad, radar site, command-and-control center, air defense site, military port, and airfield with cruise missiles. They'll blot out the sun with waves of cruise missiles."

"You do not know what you are talking about, Gao."

"I know exactly what I'm talking about, General," Gao maintained. "I urge you not to use special weapons against any ships, but if you insist on doing it so you can send a message that you're taking over the first island chain, you had better be ready for a devastating response from the United States. Their air force and navy may be smaller than it has been in the past eighty years, but I don't think their cruise missile inventory has shrunk one bit." Zu was silent, still unconvinced. Gao went on, "You're chief of the general staff, Zu. You have a large intelligence branch, and you get updates several times a week. What do your experts say?"

"They say that the United States does not have the capability or the stomach for fighting an Asian or Pacific war, Gao," Zu said. "They say they barely have enough resources to defend their Pacific islands. They say they would have to rely on support from friends and allies in Asia while they mobilized, which could take years and devastate the economies and military resources of several countries in the process. They say that the American government is more concerned with internal security and economic recovery than it is about Asia."

"I believe all that is true, General," Gao said. "But mark my words: at the first hint of a Chinese threat against the Aleutian, Mariana, or Hawaiian Islands, real or perceived, the United States will strike with everything they have, including nuclear weapons. *Everything.* We must convince them that China is not on the path to war."

Finally, Gao Xudong sensed that Zu appeared to be thinking about what the acting president was saying. On his end of the line, Zu stubbed out his cigarette. "What do you suggest, Gao?" he asked irritably.

"Allow me to tell them everything," Gao replied, "including about how you downed the patrol plane and search helicopters." Zu's eyes widened at that remark, but he remained silent. "Blame it all on Zhou. I'll convince them that Zhou was insane and ordered all those attacks because he was obsessed with any foreign presence in the first island chain. You were just following orders, or perhaps Zhou bypassed you and went right to Admiral Zhen or whoever it is in charge of naval forces out there, because you resisted the idea of attacking the Americans. Then you have to cancel all the ridiculous restrictions on movements within the first island chain and remove all naval forces to our territorial waters immediately."

"The first island chain *is* within our territorial waters!"

"I agree with you, General, but you know the Americans won't accept it," Gao said. "You must pull the aircraft carrier battle groups to within three hundred kilometers of the mainland—not three hundred from Nansha or Xisha Dao, but from the *mainland*. If you do that, and ask that the United States demilitarizes the South China Sea as well, I think they will agree."

Zu thought about it for several moments, pulling out another cigarette, then throwing it on his desk without lighting up. "Very well," he said finally. "You may speak with Phoenix. Admit everything. Offer to pull our naval forces back. But if they do not agree, or if they ask for more concessions, China retakes the South Sea."

"They'll accept it," Gao said confidently. "They'll be angry as hell, but they'll accept. I just hope Phoenix does not have an itchy finger on the red button."

Although the crashed Z-9 helicopter masked the sounds coming from the *Avenger* heading away from it, it did not cover the sound from the Chinese Y-8 patrol plane coming in from the north. But it did conceal the sound of passive sonobuoys being dropped in its path . . .

. . . and the sound of a single depth charge, a BLU-89E *Kĕpà debō,* or Terrible Wave, being dropped several minutes later.

Resembling an oil barrel with stabilization fins on one end and a sonar dome on the other, the BLU-89E released from the bomb bay of the Y-8 patrol plane and disappeared into the South China Sea. Its sonar activated automatically in passive mode, and it began to steer itself to the damaged Taiwanese submarine as it descended through the ocean. As the submarine began to increase the distance between them—the depth charge was sinking straight down, while the submarine was sailing ahead—it activated its active sonar to get a more precise distance to its target.

"Con, Sonar, loud splash directly above us, could be a torpedo or depth charge," the sonar operator aboard the Taiwanese submarine *Avenger* reported. "No propulsion sounds yet. Possible depth charge."

"No one uses depth charges anymore," Captain Yao Mei-Yueh said half aloud. He was afraid it might be another of the Chinese rocket-powered torpedoes. "All stop. Rig for ultraquiet," he ordered. If it was, he didn't have the steering capability or speed to try to outmaneuver it with countermeasures like the last time. Better to sit quietly and hope the torpedo didn't detect him. He knew the torpedo dropped straight down into the sea, and if it didn't detect any target it simply kept on descending until it buried itself in the sea bottom or self-destructed. "Anything, Sonar?" he asked quietly on intercom.

"Nothing, sir."

Maybe they lucked out again, Yao thought. He decided to wait a few more minutes and then . . .

And then he heard it—the unmistakable pings of a powerful active sonar, *very close*. "*Con, Sonar, active sonar, range two thousand yards, bearing—*"

He never finished that report. The one-kiloton nuclear warhead in the BLU-89E detonated less than a mile behind the *Avenger,* and the red-hot undersea fireball completely engulfed the submarine. The fireball created a bubble of superheated steam that expanded at hundreds of miles an hour, creating a surge of seawater that cracked the submarine into pieces in an instant. When the weight of the seawater exceeded the pressure of the bubble, it collapsed into itself, creating a second surge of ocean water in the opposite direction. As the bubble compressed, it superheated the water once again, creating another rapidly expanding bubble of energy and another fast-moving wall of water, like a living, breathing tsunami.

The explosion was deep enough that all that was detected on the surface was a dome of water and steam less than fifty feet high, and as the steam from the bubble vented into the atmosphere the dome quickly dissipated. A few of the Chinese aircraft carrier *Zheng He*'s smaller escorts were rocked by the sudden reversing ocean surges, and a few watchstanders thought they noticed something that looked like a low cloud or fog bank on the horizon, but nothing more.

But the sudden appearance of the white-hot steam dome in the middle of the cooler South China Sea was detected by the American Space-Based Infrared System heat-sensing satellites, and another report was sent through the chain of command.

NINE

THE WHITE HOUSE OVAL OFFICE, WASHINGTON, D.C.

A FEW HOURS LATER

"It was a deliberate and aggressive act of war on the part of the Taiwanese Nationalists, Mr. President," Li Peiyan, the People's Republic of China's ambassador to the United States said in excellent English. The fifty-year-old former army general looked very stiff, moving his entire body instead of just his head as he addressed President Phoenix and Vice President Page in their Oval Office meeting, and his very large hands were formed into fists and laid atop his thighs, as if expecting to use them at any moment. With Phoenix and Page were Secretary of State Herbert Kevich and National Security Adviser William Glenbrook. "Our aircraft carrier battle group was being stalked by that Taiwanese submarine, and a helicopter was shot down when the sub was discovered. Every nation on Earth has the right to defend itself!"

"That is nonsense, Mr. Ambassador," President Phoenix said. "China has no right to impose restrictions and issue ultimatums on any vessel operating in the South China Sea."

"Mr. President, Chinese vessels have come under fire from Vietnam, Taiwan, and even from the United States . . ."

"That is nonsense as well," Vice President Ann Page interjected. "Our Coast Guard helicopters did not open fire on anyone—they were unarmed, as was our P-8 Poseidon patrol plane."

"Our intelligence reports say otherwise, madame," Li said. "We have a complete list of the weapons that are routinely carried by your aircraft, and they match with what our crews on the scene reported. As for that Taiwanese submarine: it was an obvious challenge to President Zhou's instructions that were designed to eliminate the very threat that existed out there—an attack by a submerged submarine on a Chinese vessel. Do you expect China not to respond?"

"Our analysts tell us that the People's Liberation Army Navy attacked with a *nuclear depth charge,* Mr. Ambassador," President Phoenix exclaimed.

"That is an outrageous lie, sir!" Li retorted. "China has pledged a no-first-use policy . . ."

"Yes, you did—after you attacked Guam with nuclear weapons ten years ago!" Ann interjected.

"I would very much appreciate not being interrupted, madame," Li snapped, looking like some kind of automaton as he stiffly turned to address the vice president. "Mr. President, I have no explanation for that explosion, which our sea-surveillance satellites and carrier battle group vessels also detected. Perhaps that was a nuclear-powered submarine, or it was a diesel-electric submarine carrying nuclear weapons. The blast was relatively small, so perhaps it was not even a nuclear device—we have not yet had a chance to investigate. But the fact is, sir, that a Taiwanese submarine attacked a Chinese aircraft and warship, and our navy responded. The same with the Vietnamese warship—it attacked a Chinese patrol vessel, and long-range weapons were used to defend our ship because the patrol vessel did not have the weapons to defend itself against the Vietnamese frigate. China is not the aggressor here, sir—it is Taiwan, Vietnam, and the United States, and we believe we are being threatened by Japan, the Philippines, Australia, and Indonesia as well. China has a right to defend its territory and its warships."

"China must lift restrictions on warships transiting the South China Sea, and do it *immediately,*" President Phoenix said angrily. "Otherwise China will see itself being matched two to one—for each surface vessel, submarine, or aircraft you station in the South China Sea, the United States and its partners will shadow them with at least double that number."

"That is a serious and dangerous escalation of forces in that region, sir," Ambassador Li said. "Think carefully of what you pronounce, Mr. President. A two-to-one match might be construed as preparation for a blockade of China's port cities or even a general war, sir."

"Think of it as you wish, Mr. Ambassador," Phoenix said. "The South China Sea is not China's sole possession, and it does not have the right to wantonly attack ships and aircraft there, especially peaceful, unarmed aircraft or nonthreatening ships. As for preparation for war, Mr. Ambassador: the United States has been closely monitoring large troop movements all throughout your country, especially along the coasts. It appears to us that you're mobilizing troops for action." He held up a hand just as Li was going to speak. "I don't need to hear your denials or flimsy explanations, sir. Our intelligence is accurate, and I assure you, the United States and its partners around the world that we are sharing our information with are responding accordingly. Our actions will be swift and accurate."

Ambassador Li Peiyan shot to his feet, all semblance of

stiffness instantly gone. "That, sir, sounds like a threat to me," he said, "and that is what I will convey to my superiors. I have already been recalled by my government. Good day, sir, madame." And he strode to the door, which was opened for him from outside the Oval Office by a Secret Service agent.

"Well, that went very well," Kevich said sarcastically under his breath but loud enough to be heard by everyone.

"Get off it, Herbert," Ann Page snapped. "The Chinese just set off a nuclear explosion in the South China Sea, and they nearly sank a Vietnamese warship with a supersonic cruise missile. Do you think they still care about diplomacy and peace? They are not just asserting themselves—they are putting the world on notice that they will use any and all means, including nuclear weapons, to keep warships out."

President Phoenix nodded but remained silent for several moments; then he picked up the phone. "Get me the secretary of defense right away."

While he was waiting, he pulled a card from his pocket, looked at his watch, and did a fast calculation in his head. He didn't have to wait long: "Yes, Mr. President," Fredrick Hayes responded.

"Fredrick, put us at DEFCON Three," the president said, then read off the authentication code he had computed, using the current date-time group.

"Yes, sir," Hayes said, and he read off his own authentication code, which the president checked and verified. Any event involving movement or employment of nuclear weapons required coded verification and a two-man authorization. DEFCON, or Defense Readiness Condition, was a gradual change in military readiness for nuclear war. DEFCON Five was the lowest level of readiness; DEFCON One meant that nuclear war was imminent. The United States had been at DEFCON One immediately following the American Holocaust; on DEFCON

Two after a cease-fire had been negotiated with the Russians
following the American counterattacks; on DEFCON Three
several months later as tensions eased around the world; then
down to DEFCON Four about a year after the attacks, where
it had been ever since. DEFCON Three resulted in ships being
put to sea, leaves canceled, battle staffs formed, contingency
plans put in place, and all available aircraft and ships loaded
and made ready.

"Secretary Hayes has relayed the order to Northern
Command, U.S. Strategic Command, and Air Force Global
Strike Command, sir," National Security Adviser William
Glenbrook reported a few minutes later, "and we are at
DEFCON Three. The posture change is being relayed to
NATO."

"I'm going to need a complete rundown on exactly what
we can bring to bear against China," the president said angrily.
"I'm not going to back down. China will rue the day they
decided to set off a nuke. I want to park an aircraft carrier
battle group opposite each one of their largest military ports."

"That may not be a good idea, sir," Glenbrook said, his
face a mask of deep concern. "We don't dare send a carrier
strike group out there now, sir, until we figure out who's in
charge and get an idea of what they intend to do. Whoever's
really in charge in China—Zhou, or more likely General Zu
himself—has just let the nuclear genie out of the bottle. They
could just as likely hit our carriers with a nuclear carrier-killer
ballistic or cruise missile. That could kill thousands of sailors
and destroy billions of dollars' worth of hardware with just
one warhead."

"I'm not going to let that happen," President Phoenix said.
"I want every known storage facility and launch site for those
carrier-killer ballistic missiles and cruise missiles targeted by
Tomahawk cruise missiles. If we don't have enough cruise

missiles in range to cover all the known targets, I want preparations made to put more ships and subs to sea that can fire Tomahawks. I want as many ballistic missile defense ships and ground systems deployed as possible in the Pacific. I want as many bombers and fighters as possible deployed to bases in the Pacific, armed appropriately with whatever they need to destroy China's air defense and command-and-control system, penetrate their airspace, and take out ballistic missile sites." He paused, expecting the usual hesitant reaction from Herbert Kevich, but he didn't get it this time.

"All that is going to take time, sir," Glenbrook said. "We have only two aircraft carrier battle groups available right now in the Pacific. Under DEFCON Three we can probably get another put to sea in a few months, but the other is in extensive maintenance and won't be available for a year at the earliest."

"Then we need other solutions, Bill," the president said. "We have other ships, cruisers and destroyers, that can fire cruise missiles. We need to figure out a way to get them the same long-range air protection that the carriers have." He thought for a moment then said, "Ann, we need to talk to the leadership in Congress about getting funding for more of McLanahan's bombers, and then to resurrect the Space Defense Force and the carriers I canceled last year. They're the only solutions we have if China is going to continue to throw its weight around like this. We need to brief them on the DEFCON change—that'll be a good time to hit them up for the money. Make it a closed-door classified briefing in the Situation Room—I'm going to tell them everything we know about what China has been up to lately."

"Yes, sir," she said. She stepped over to Phoenix and asked in a low voice, "Want me to leak some details about that nuclear depth charge, Ken?"

"Later, after the meeting with the Leadership—they

might even leak it first," Phoenix replied sotto voce. In a normal voice he said, "Until then, tell the press we know about the explosion and we're investigating. You can tell them we're not getting any cooperation from the Chinese and they have recalled their ambassador."

The phone on the president's desk beeped. "The hot line with Beijing," Phoenix told everyone in the Oval Office, and he picked it up. His surprised expression immediately got everyone's attention. He put the call on hold. "This has to be some kind of speed record," he said. "I don't think Ambassador Li is even out of the White House yet." He put the call on speakerphone, which activated the videoconference function. "I'm here with the vice president, the secretary of state, and my national security adviser. Go ahead, Mr. Gao." Now the others had matching surprised expressions.

"Thank you for taking my call, President Phoenix," acting president of China Gao Xudong said in excellent English. "I just spoke with Ambassador Li, and I felt it most important to speak with you directly."

"That's good, Mr. Gao," the president said, "because as a result of our meeting with Ambassador Li I have ordered additional defensive weapons systems to be delivered to the Pacific theater of operations; I have ordered every known Chinese antiship ballistic missile pad to be targeted by long-range cruise missiles; and I am seeking a meeting with congressional leadership about approving funding for more ballistic missile defense systems. Everyone in this room fears that war with the People's Republic of China is imminent. Tell me I'm wrong, Mr. Gao."

"I called to avert exactly that scenario, Mr. President," Gao said. "President Zhou ordered the attacks on the Vietnamese and Taiwanese warships, including the use of special weapons."

"You mean *nuclear* weapons, Mr. Gao," Ann said. "We had

better be crystal clear about what we're talking about here, don't you agree, sir?"

"Quite so, Miss Vice President," Gao said. "I agree completely. Yes, President Zhou had authorized the use of the long-range antiship cruise missile and the nuclear depth charge. He wanted to prove to the world that China was prepared to use all means necessary to protect and defend China's sovereignty of the South China Sea."

"You speak of President Zhou in the past tense, Mr. Gao," Phoenix observed. "What has happened?"

"The president was forced to undergo medical treatment because of a deteriorating mental health condition that called into question his ability to make rational decisions on behalf of the people of China," Gao said. "He was obsessed with keeping all foreigners, especially foreign warships, out of the first and second island chains, and he even decided to use nuclear weapons. His orders against the Taiwanese submarine had already been issued, but after I learned of the president's orders, I notified the Politburo. They took the president away immediately. Unfortunately we were not in time to stop the depth charge attack on the submarine, but I believe we have stopped many more such attacks from happening. General Zu is cooperating completely. The Politburo appointed me president until the National People's Congress can convene and elect a new president."

"So you're saying that Zhou was working alone, without any authority from the Politburo or Secretariat?" Secretary of State Kevich asked. "You are acknowledging that the People's Liberation Army Navy attacked the Vietnamese warship and Taiwanese submarine, but the orders were given by Zhou without authority of the Politburo or Central Military Committee?"

"Exactly, Secretary Kevich," Gao replied.

"What about the P-8 Poseidon patrol plane and the Coast Guard helicopters?" Phoenix asked. "Did he give the orders to have them shot down as well?"

"Unfortunately, President Phoenix, he did," Gao replied without hesitation. "The patrol plane and the first helicopter were downed by an experimental high-power microwave weapon called 'Silent Thunder' mounted aboard the aircraft carrier *Zhenyuan* that temporarily cripples electronic signals. It is similar to weapons employed by the United States and Russia. Zhou was told that the P-8 aircraft had the capability of launching antiship cruise missiles, and he immediately ordered it to be brought down. The second helicopter was shot down by a carrier-based fighter because your helicopter was out of range of Silent Thunder. Zhou is plainly insane, Mr. President."

"This is extraordinary," Phoenix said, shaking his head in utter shock. "How in the world can anyone trust China ever again, Mr. Gao?"

"The heart of the matter here, sir, is countries who claim they have the right to explore for resources in the South Sea, and the militarization of the South Sea," Gao said. "The issue of which country is permitted to explore for oil, gas, and other minerals in the South Sea is important for China. It is not fair for one or more countries deciding on its own to explore for oil and gas without consulting the other nations who claim that right. Similarly, countries who place armed troops on disputed islands in the South Sea without consulting others, or who used armed aircraft and warships to patrol within a nation's territory, are not right and such actions lead to distrust, hostility, and conflict. If the practice is not stopped, we could see an arms race in the South Sea on a massive scale."

"What is China's position, Mr. Gao?" Phoenix asked.

"Our position, sir, is that all the waters and islands within the first island chain belong to China," Gao said matter-of-factly.

He correctly interpreted Phoenix's and Page's exasperated expressions. "However, unlike Zhou Qiang, there are those of us who understand that many other nations claim this territory as well under the United Nations Convention on the Law of the Sea. Our claim is based on historical and legal fact, which no one seems to care about or wants to discuss. But notwithstanding Zhou's actions, there are many leaders in China who are patient and confident that a solution will be found. All must understand that hostile aircraft and vessels inside the two-hundred-kilometer economic exclusion zone represent a serious threat to all nations and must be kept away."

"The UNCLOS treaty allows for unrestricted passage of any ship or aircraft outside of a country's territorial waters—that's twelve nautical miles," Ann Page said. "China is a signatory to that treaty, sir."

"I believe the twelve-mile limit was instituted because at the time that was the maximum range of shore bombardment guns aboard most warships," Gao said. "In this age of cruise missiles and supersonic flight, twelve miles is a pittance, a matter of just a few seconds. Surely you understand that any military activity that might be considered hostile must take place outside the two-hundred-nautical-mile limit. This would include submerged submarines, armed aircraft, spy planes, and warships that are configured for battle, such as aircraft carriers with ready flight decks."

President Phoenix looked at the vice president in surprise. "You seem very well prepared to discuss such a wide-sweeping policy, Mr. Gao," he said.

"It is a matter of great importance to my people, sir," Gao said. "Think of this, Mr. President: our *Zheng He* carrier battle group steams in toward New York, Washington, San Francisco, or New Orleans. We have forty supersonic stealth strike aircraft, dozens of nuclear cruise missiles, and guns that can fire a shell twenty miles with great precision. Eleven nautical miles off the coast it is considered hostile and is prohibited, but at thirteen miles it is not? I think the populations of all our coastal cities would be thankful if carrier battle groups stayed at least two hundred nautical miles away, not just twelve. Would you not agree, sir?"

President Phoenix nodded to the vice president. "Yes, I would," he admitted.

"That is most excellent, sir," Gao said. "I realize it will take many weeks or months—hopefully not longer—to get an international treaty signed, but I think it should be possible for our two nations to agree to this as a signal to all nations to work toward peace. Hostile aircraft and ships should stay at least two hundred nautical miles from our respective shores."

"I'd like to discuss it with my entire national security staff, sir," Phoenix said, "but if we are in agreement, I think such a restriction can be put in place while we consult with the Senate on a formal treaty."

"Thank you, sir," Gao said. "This has been a most unfortunate and, frankly, terrifying episode, Mr. President. I felt as if events were threatening to spin completely out of control. I hope we can plan a way forward that increases communication and cooperation between our countries so this never happens again."

"I feel the same way, Mr. Gao," Phoenix said. "*Zàijiàn,* Mr. Gao."

"Good-bye to you too, sir," Gao said. "*Xièxiè.*" And the connection was terminated.

Phoenix replaced the receiver on its cradle, then looked up at the others. "What do you make of that?" he asked.

"It makes me even more distrustful of the Chinese, sir," Ann Page said. "They set off a nuke in the South China Sea, then expect us to just sign a piece of paper and back away?

Why should the United States back away? We haven't been attacking anyone in international waters!"

"I know, Ann, but it's a start—we're less likely to start a war on the high seas if all the warships stay away from each other," Phoenix said. "Herbert?"

"I am extremely relieved and optimistic to hear from Gao Xudong, and grateful to him for his very complete explanation and for formulating a plan of action so quickly. It certainly eases my concerns."

"I'm still not convinced, Herbert," Ann said. "Just a few days after Tang and Zu announce strict rules about movement in the South China Sea, Gao completely reverses them?"

"It makes sense if what Gao said about Zhou is true," Phoenix said. "If Zhou was calling all the shots without getting permission, he and Zu could have easily brought China to the brink all by themselves."

"I don't know Gao that well, sir," Kevich said. "But he is Western educated, highly intelligent, and well respected all around the world. He appears to me a very capable vice president and will probably make a good president."

"But does he have the stones to stand up to General Zu?" Ann asked.

"That I do not know, Miss Vice President," Kevich said, his forehead wrinkling at the vice president's salty language. "But he would not be allowed to reveal all he did without cooperation from the general staff. His admissions and presenting that plan were extraordinary, and he would never have been authorized to do it if the military wasn't on board." Ann Page still looked doubtful but said nothing.

"Bill?" the president asked.

"I'm with the vice president on this one, sir—this stinks to high heaven," National Security Adviser Glenbrook said. "I think we should press ahead with everything you wanted to do before we got that call from Gao: beef up defenses in the western Pacific, send as many bombers and fighters as possible out there, and get ready for a fight."

"That would not send a very cooperative signal, General Glenbrook," Kevich said.

"The Chinese *admitted* they set off a nuke in the South China Sea—that doesn't sound very cooperative either, Mr. Secretary," Glenbrook said acidly. "We can still comply with everything Gao suggested: aerial patrols, transiting the South China Sea, exercises, port calls, and keep two hundred miles from port—except we build up our presence and defenses in the western Pacific, and do it quickly. Maybe China won't be so ready to set off a nuke if we have a few fighter and bomber wings and a couple aircraft carrier battle groups nearby."

"I still think that would be overly provocative, sir, given the admissions and conciliatory tone of President Gao's call," Kevich said.

President Phoenix thought about it for a few moments, then said, "I agree, Bill. Continue on with arming the western Pacific, but we'll limit the patrols to unarmed aerial patrols and announce when we sail ships through the South China Sea. We can still look cooperative and continue beefing up our footprint out there." To the vice president: "When that dispatch from Gao comes in, Ann, read it over and brief me on the high and low points. You can tell the press that we're in direct contact with the highest levels of the Chinese government on a resolution to this incident." Phoenix shook his head ruefully. "When the word of that nuclear depth charge attack gets out, I don't know what's going to happen. I just hope there's not a massive international panic."

"Do you think he believed me, General?" Gao asked. He was in General Zu's office on the computer that served as the videoconference hotline terminal to several capitals around the world. "He did not seem angry or confrontational at all."

"I told you, Gao, the Americans do not want a fight in Asia," Zu said, lighting a cigarette. "Since World War Two, the Americans have failed to win an Asian war, even with a powerful army and nuclear weapons and against vastly inferior forces." He nodded his head to Gao. "But I have to admit: you were right, Gao," he said. "Talking with the Americans and even admitting attacking their aircraft seems to have mollified them—you even had that spineless drone Phoenix speaking Mandarin! I thought he would take an hour cursing and swearing at us, and instead he was speaking Mandarin—*awful* Mandarin, but still Mandarin!"

Zu thought for a moment. "This should give us an opportunity to build our naval forces without fear of an American mobilization and blockade," he said. "We should be completing the purchase of the French aircraft carrier *Clemenceau* shortly, and we can begin assembling its battle group and air wing. Then we will have three aircraft carrier battle groups within the first island chain, and the Americans will be lucky to sail just one. Our domination will be complete!"

THE WHITE HOUSE SITUATION ROOM

A FEW HOURS LATER

The Situation Room exploded in a storm of shouts and exclamations of disbelief and absolute shock from the civilian attendees; the Speaker of the House of Representatives, Joseph Collingsworth, shot to his feet. "China did *what,* Mr. President?" he cried. Along with the president, vice president, the secretaries of defense and state, the national security adviser, and the chairman of the Joint Chiefs of Staff, there were a group of senior congressional leaders of both political parties and the chairpersons and ranking members of the congressional military committees in attendance.

"All indications point to precisely that," President Ken Phoenix said. "A Taiwanese attack submarine wanted to challenge China's restrictions in the South China Sea; it approached one of China's aircraft carrier battle groups; it was discovered and was attacked and destroyed with a nuclear depth charge. The yield was less than one kiloton—about one-twentieth the size of the bomb that was dropped on Hiroshima, and far smaller than the ones launched against our air and ICBM bases in the American Holocaust."

"*This is outrageous!*" Diane M. Jamieson, majority leader of the U.S. Senate, exclaimed. Jamieson was the long-serving senator from Nevada who had served on several military committees in both the House and Senate and had as much knowledge of defense matters as almost anyone else in the room. "I don't care what the yield was, Mr. President—the Chinese are again using nuclear weapons! What have we done in response? What is the DEFCON?"

"Right after we had confirmation that it was a nuclear depth charge, I ordered our forces to DEFCON Three," Phoenix replied. "Since then we were able to place two more Ohio-class ballistic missile submarines out to sea last night, one in the Pacific and the other in the Atlantic Ocean." A slide changed on the large electronic monitor at the head of the conference table, showing a map of the world marked with icons for submarines and aircraft. "That makes a total of three ballistic missile subs and one cruise missile sub in the Atlantic, and four ballistic missile subs and one cruise missile sub in the Pacific. In addition, we have three B-2A Spirit stealth bombers and three B-52H Stratofortress bombers, dispersed to various air bases in the continental United States, being loaded now with nuclear gravity and standoff weapons to be placed on around-the-clock alert. The bombers already deployed to Guam only have conventional weapons, but we're considering arming them with nuclear weapons as well. The aircraft carriers already at sea won't be loaded with nuclear weapons, but the three that are in port getting ready for deployment can be armed."

"That's *it*?" Jamieson remarked, her blue eyes wide with disbelief. "That's our nuclear strike force? I know most of our bombers and land-based ballistic missiles were destroyed in the American Holocaust, but where are all the submarines?"

"Normal patrols these days are usually six or seven subs total, split between the Pacific and Atlantic Oceans, Senator Jamieson," Secretary of Defense Fredrick Hayes said. "We're lucky to be able to deploy the other two. The remaining subs are either undergoing maintenance, coming back from patrol, or getting ready to go out on patrol. The ones getting ready for patrol can be accelerated to get them out faster, perhaps in a day or two. Others may take as long as a month."

"A *month*?" Joseph Collingsworth blurted out. Although a member of the House of Representatives almost as long as Jamieson, Collingsworth was relatively new to the top leadership position in the House and was not as knowledgeable of military or foreign affairs. "I didn't realize what a sorry shape our military was."

"Since we got into office we've been pushing for more military spending, primarily in long-range strike and space, Congressman," Vice President Ann Page said. "But with tax receipts down, unemployment still high, and nondiscretionary spending through the roof, there's no money available for the military unless other programs get cut first."

"You can solve this problem right away without cutting entitlement, education, research, and health-care programs, Miss Vice President: raise the marginal top tax rate to what it has been during any period we are at war or needed to raise money for defense or infrastructure; eliminate the Medicare salary cap; and support cap-and-trade carbon emissions legislation," Senator Jamieson said. "Cap-and-trade alone would raise one hundred billion dollars a year, along with reducing greenhouse gases and encouraging development of antipollution technology."

"Let's get back to the issue at hand, ladies and gentlemen," President Phoenix said, trying very hard not to sound exasperated. "My response to the Chinese use of a nuclear weapon was to raise the DEFCON level, place more nuclear-armed subs and bombers on alert, and prepare other assets such as tactical fighter aircraft and other warships to employ nuclear weapons. I have been in contact with acting president Gao Xudong of China, who explained that former president Zhou had ordered the use of a nuclear weapon but is no longer in charge. This has been verified by our ambassador in Beijing. We also agreed to limit naval activity in the South China Sea to outside the two-hundred-kilometer economic exclusion zone in order to reduce tensions. Any other suggestions?"

"Let's start with kicking China out of the United Nations

Security Council and slapping a trillion-dollar sanction on them!" Senator Jamieson said.

"The ouster of a permanent member of the Security Council requires a unanimous vote of the permanent and temporary members of the Council and a two-thirds vote of the General Assembly," Secretary of State Kevich said, "and in my opinion Russia would veto. However, Congress could pass a nonbinding resolution to that effect. China has agreed to pay the costs for environmental cleanup, rescue, recovery, and replacing the damaged and destroyed warships."

"That's *it*?" Senator Jamieson asked incredulously. "China sets off a nuke in the South China Sea, and all the United States can do is gear up its scant military forces for war?"

"China has the second-largest economy in the world, Senator," Phoenix said. "Their GDP is growing while ours is shrinking, and it's possible that in five years their GDP could surpass ours. They hold twenty percent of U.S. debt, and we import twenty-five percent of what China produces. They have the largest military in the world, and it grows both in numbers and quality every year, while ours shrinks. It's difficult to fight numbers like that."

"I never would have believed we'd come to this point," Jamieson said. "You're saying we're powerless to do anything?"

"We're not powerless," Phoenix replied. "This is what I want Congress to do: approve my budget, which provides the Department of Defense an additional two hundred billion dollars a year for the next six years. With it I will reactivate the Space Defense Force constellation of space-based weapon platforms to provide the United States with proven, reliable, responsive global strike capability. I will also speed up development of a next-generation long-range bomber force and put the canceled Ford-class supercarriers CVN-79 and -80 back into accelerated production."

"*Your* budget, Mr. President?" Jamieson asked derisively. "The budget that eliminates four cabinet-level departments, cuts everyone else's budgets by twenty percent, and eliminates hundreds of programs meant for education, research, environmental protection, health, and retraining? Your budget was soundly rejected by both houses of Congress, sir. It's never coming back."

"It's the only budget that's been put on the table, Senator," Ann said. "Congress hasn't passed a budget in over five years."

"When we get a budget that doesn't force the lower and middle class to pay for military hardware and tax breaks for the rich, Miss Vice President, we will," Collingsworth said.

The president looked at each of the faces around him, saw no compromise in sight, and nodded. "All right, Majority Leader, Speaker," he said finally. "I think this situation with China is serious enough that something needs to be done immediately, so I'll agree to support a temporary ten percent income tax hike . . ." As a smile began to break out on Jamieson's face the president raised a hand and quickly added, ". . . on *everyone*, Senator. Across the board." The smile began to disappear. "Shared sacrifice, Majority Leader?" Jamieson finally nodded. "And the funds go completely to bolstering defense: long-range strike, aircraft carriers, and military space, all the things we should have been building up over the past five years."

"And the marginal tax rate, cap-and-trade, and Medicare salary caps?" Collingsworth asked. "The last time we had a large military or infrastructure building program, the marginal top tax rate was seventy percent. A ten percent hike is a good start, but it's not enough."

"That discussion we'll save for some other time," the president said, a touch of weariness in his voice. "Do we have a deal, Miss Majority Leader, Mr. Speaker?"

The two congressional leaders looked at each other, and

their eyes said it all: they had finally gotten the president to go back on his pledge not to increase taxes—he was toast in the next election. Jamieson turned to the president and nodded. "We have a deal, Mr. President," she said.

"Good. If there are no other suggestions on what we might do with China, I'd like to thank you for coming. Please remember all the information I've passed along to you today is classified secret and is not to be released to the public in any way. Thank you again." Phoenix got to his feet, and the others did likewise. He shook hands with each member of Congress and his national security staff, then departed, followed by Ann Page.

Back in the Oval Office, the president poured himself a cup of coffee and sat at his desk, staring out the windows. "Do you believe Jamieson and Collingsworth?" Ann asked behind him. "China sets off a nuke in the South China Sea and shoots down two American aircraft with a microwave weapon, and all they want to do is argue over entitlement spending and cap-and-trade? They control both houses of Congress, but they still can't agree on a damn thing!"

"They're ideological partisan politicians with a strong progressive agenda, Ann," the president said. "National defense is not high on their priority list except as a big chunk of the budget they hope to raid to pay for other programs. The South China Sea might as well be on the planet Mars."

"We should have talked before you agreed on a tax hike, sir," Ann said. "We both pledged never to raise taxes. The other side is going to rake us over the coals for that."

"I know, I know, campaign season starts up soon, and I'm starting it by going back on a promise," Phoenix said. "But when the world finds out that China used a nuclear weapon again, the United States won't be the only country building its military. I'm just relieved Jamieson agreed to earmark the

3

new income for defense—that's huge for her." The president remained silent for several long moments, sipping his coffee. Then he spoke: "Leak it."

"Excuse me, Mr. President?"

"Leak it," Phoenix repeated. "Leak a few of the details of the Chinese nuclear depth charge, long-range antiship missiles, and the high-power microwave weapon. Do it over a period of a few weeks. Refuse to comment on reports from foreign media outlets or blogosphere rumors, but acknowledge to a few outlets that we're looking into these reports."

"Aren't you afraid of creating a panic, Ken?" Ann asked. "Once folks learn China set off a nuclear warhead in the South China Sea and can hit a ship with a missile hundreds of miles over the horizon, trade through that area will disappear. No shipping company in their right mind will sail a cargo vessel or tanker through the South China Sea. A third of the goods that travel by sea go right through that region."

"Yes, I realize that," Phoenix said quietly. He turned to Ann. "Congress won't act because they're not focusing on the military threat from China—everyone thinks we're linked so tightly together that there's no threat against the United States from China. But the United States was linked with Japan just as tightly until Japan invaded China in 1937 and we cut off oil and steel exports to Japan in 1941, which resulted in the Pearl Harbor attack. If there's a panic, it won't be because we leaked some information—it'll be because China attacked foreign warships and aircraft and wants to turn the South China Sea into their own private lake."

Ann Page studied the president for a few moments. "You've changed over the past few weeks, Ken," she said finally. "You're still the same president, but . . . the man has changed, I think. You're silently getting pissed off at all the antics being pulled off around the world, and you want so badly to do something about it, but you don't quite have all the tools . . . yet. So you're pissed off."

Phoenix looked at his vice president for a long few moments, then shrugged and asked, "So?"

"So nothing," Ann said, smiling. "I like it. I like pissed off."

TEN

SHANGHAI, PEOPLE'S REPUBLIC OF CHINA

AUTUMN 2015

The afternoon protest was just getting under way. For the past several weeks, idle dock workers at the Wangma Jiazhai piers in northeastern Shanghai would gather, organizers would whip them up by giving speeches with a bullhorn, then the angry crowd would march down Wuzhou Avenue to the Government Administration Building a few kilometers away to protest the continued high food prices, layoffs, inflation, and perceived government indifference to the precipitous economic collapse that was gripping China. Their numbers started out modest, just a few hundred, but now the protesters numbered in the thousands, large enough to block the Shanghai Ring Expressway during rush-hour traffic, which made everyone angrier still. The signs and banners that the protesters brought at first were still there but in much greater size and numbers, and more and more protesters were bringing tools, chains, and other implements from the docks.

The protests started two months earlier, following the news reports of the Chinese use of a nuclear depth charge in the South China Sea. At first every country involved denied it, but soon independent tests confirmed low levels of plutonium contamination in the sea. Even so, the public outcry was not as loud as might be expected: China said it reacted because of a perceived submarine attack on its carrier battle group, which Taiwan did not deny; the contamination levels were not very high and still dropping; minimal damage had been done to the seabed and nearby coral formations; and China had pledged to compensate all involved for the deaths and damage done.

However, the matter was far from over. Unseen by the public was the astronomic climb in insurance rates for cargo ships transiting the South China Sea, East China Sea, and Yellow Sea—any body of water in which a Chinese warship was patrolling or within range of a Chinese air base. It was simply too risky for most private companies to insure a vessel traveling anywhere near mainland China, and the companies that did write insurance policies charged hefty premiums. As a result the cost of everything, from clothing to electronics, nearly doubled overnight. Unsold goods started to pile up in warehouses and on piers. The Chinese government tried to subsidize workers' salaries, but soon the layoffs began, and in a few months hundreds of millions throughout the entire country were unemployed. There was double-digit inflation, and not on a yearly basis, but a *monthly* one.

It was immediately apparent that this protest march by unemployed dockworkers was different. In all other marches the city police were on hand to protect stores and commuters, and there was rarely any violence, but this time the protesters noticed that the closer to the Government Administration Building they got, the more they saw soldiers and armored vehicles in the streets. By the time they were within two blocks of the administration building, the avenue was completely blocked by soldiers armed with automatic weapons. In the center of the avenue was a truck with a large rectangular panel atop it mounted on a pedestal that resembled a blank white billboard.

Over the protesters' chants a voice over a loudspeaker said, "Attention, all protesters, attention, this is Major Li Dezhu, commander of the 117th People's Armed Police Force from the Zhimalou barracks. You are hereby ordered by the Shanghai Municipality Office of Safety, the mayor of Shanghai, and the Ministry of Security to disperse and go home immediately. You can be assured that your grievances against the government have been heard and will be addressed by your government leaders. There is nothing that can be accomplished by your presence here, and these protests are disrupting the movement of your fellow citizens. Go home to your families immediately."

"We are not leaving!" a protester with a bullhorn shouted back. "The monthly unemployment money we receive will not pay for even two weeks' worth of food! Our landlords are threatening to turn us out into the street if we do not pay the rent!"

"No one will be rendered homeless during this financial emergency," Li said. "The National People's Congress is voting to appropriate more unemployment funds. All that can be done is being done! There is nothing you can do here at this time, and you are disrupting traffic! Now go home!"

"You tell us the same every day!" another protester shouted. "But no one in Beijing listens to us! Let us in to talk with the mayor and city council!"

"You have been warned!" the major said. "Disperse immediately and go home! The use of special crowd control systems has been authorized! Disperse immediately!"

"We are not leaving until the mayor speaks to us!" a protester shouted. "If he will not come out to talk with us, we will go in!" The mob started to surge forward.

Li brought a portable radio to his lips, keyed the microphone button, and spoke, "Level green, *jihuó*."

At that moment the first one hundred protesters at the head of the mob stopped and began patting their arms and face, as if their skin was being pelted with windblown hot sand. The ones farther back in the crowd still marched forward, colliding with the stopped ones in the front, and then the ones moving forward had the same strange feeling on their bodies. But now confusion started to turn into panic as more and more of the mob was affected. People started to run in every direction, mindless of who they ran into. Despite the strange sensation, many of the mob still marched forward.

"Level yellow," Li ordered.

Now the sensation of being hit by a sandstorm turned into the feeling of standing in front of an open furnace. Shouts of pain and fear quickly changed to screams of panic. Persons were no longer trying to brush away sand—they were trying to protect themselves from the searing heat, although they saw no fire and their skin did not seem to be damaged. Some tried to put out the fire they felt by throwing themselves on the ground and rolling. There was no tear gas, no sounds of bullets or shotguns, but people were falling to the ground as if shot. Finally the crowd stopped advancing, and they bolted left and right to get away from whatever they were being exposed to . . .

. . . and as they ran behind buildings or darted down adjacent streets, the feeling of being set afire disappeared.

"Get over here!" several of the protesters shouted to their comrades who were still writhing in pain out in the open, and as they ran for cover the pain stopped. "What is going on? What is happening?"

"I saw something like this on television," another worker said. "I will bet it is that large sign in the middle of the street."

"A sign? What does that have to do with anything?"

"It is not a sign—it is a microwave transmitter," the other man said.

"A *microwave*? Are you joking?"

"Remember that major said something about 'special crowd control systems'? I will bet that is what he was talking about. The police are using microwaves on us! The microwaves heat the fluids in our bodies without burning the skin."

"How are we going to shut that thing down?"

"I think it is directional—I did not see any of the police standing beside it affected, and as soon as we ran behind this building the pain stopped," the other said. "I think if we rush it from the sides it will not affect us, either."

Using handheld radios and runners, the protesters quickly organized. While a large group remained on the avenue chanting and shouting as a diversion, two groups circled several blocks around on either side of the police guarding the microwave transmitter. As darkness began to fall, all at once they rushed the police from two sides. Within moments they had overwhelmed the police and torn down the microwave transmitter. Standing victorious over the subdued police, grabbing weapons, they turned toward the administration building . . .

. . . and at that moment machine guns mounted on armored vehicles on both sides of the avenue opened fire, mowing down protesters like a scythe cutting wheat. Several dozen protesters tried to rush the armored vehicles but were blasted apart long before they could reach them.

"I met with Acting President Gao and the chief of the Politburo late last night, in response to the rioting that took place last night in Shanghai and that has been erupting throughout our country over the past few months," Colonel General Zu Kai said, reading from a script he held in front of him. He was broadcasting a radio and television message from the broadcasting center inside the central government building in Beijing. "Over three-dozen police were killed last night in Shanghai, and since the protests began last year there have been over a thousand police killed. The president and the Politburo chief want the violence to end, and they informed me that it was time to act to prevent any more senseless deaths by these criminal murderers.

"President Gao informed me that the office of the president, the National People's Congress, and the Politburo agreed to be subordinated to the military on a temporary basis," Zu went on. "Under our constitution, the military may from time to time be permitted to step forward in order to ensure peace and security, and that is what I have been ordered to do. Here is what I have been directed to put into place and enforce, with the use of our military forces, in all of the cities, provinces, and independent municipalities in China.

"A curfew has been put in place from dusk to dawn, and anyone violating it without an official work or transit permit will be arrested," Zu continued. "Food rationing will begin immediately. Looters will be shot on sight, and food hoarders or anyone engaging in black market sale of food or medicine will be arrested. The military will assist local and provincial police forces in controlling crime and distributing commodities."

Zu put the script down, removed his glasses, and looked directly into the camera. "I know this is a difficult time for our country, my fellow citizens," he said. "China has not faced such a severe economic drawdown in a generation. The government is doing everything possible to reopen factories and regain full employment. Acting President Gao will address the government's efforts shortly.

"But I wish to say that it is my duty to see to it that order is maintained while our economy and our way of life are restored, and I demand every citizen's cooperation. Riots have torn our cities apart, and the violence must end. My military forces will work closely with local and provincial authorities to maintain order, but we need your help to see to it that the violence ends. If you see looters or black marketers, inform the police or a soldier. If you hear of a riot or protest being organized, tell us right away so that we may ensure peace. That is all."

"Slipway doors are open," Tom Hoffman said. He was in the pilot's seat of a newly refurbished XB-1 Excalibur bomber, but he wasn't flying the plane and had not done much flying at all on this trip, because Brad McLanahan insisted on doing most of it. But this was the first time Brad was going to try aerial refueling for real. He had done it from the right seat plenty of times in the dozen simulator sessions they had accomplished, and he got to watch Hoffman do the first real one just west of Hawaii, but now it was his turn.

They had a third crewmember along on this trip. Sondra Eddington was a few years older than Brad and was one of the first persons to go through Tom Hoffman's accelerated flight training program at Warbirds Forever, except she had a bit more money saved up than Brad and could afford an apartment, a car, and attend the University of Nevada–Reno for her bachelor's degree in business and a master's in business adminstration instead of having to stay in a storeroom and work at the company.

After a corporate stint for a few years flying everything from Piper Cheyenne turboprops to Gulfstream bizjets, the tall, blond, blue-eyed pilot returned to Warbirds Forever by special invitation from Tom Hoffman to be part of the Excalibur project. She had already ferried several Excaliburs to Guam, but on this hop she was the relief pilot, spending most of her time in the bunk reading or napping and fixing the others cups of coffee or Ramen noodles. Now, in preparation for air refueling, she was strapped into the jump seat between the pilot and copilot, wearing her helmet plugged into oxygen and intercom, gloves, and a parachute. In an emergency, after the two pilots safely ejected, her task was to make her way aft to the entry hatch, blow the nose gear down, and jump—not an appealing prospect, especially if the jet was not straight and level, but her only option.

"Okay, remember your sight picture, Brad," Hoffman said. "You're on the right side, but it'll look exactly the same from over there."

"Yes, sir," Brad said. He looked eminently confident and relaxed at the controls of the big jet.

"Masters One-Four, Cajun Two-One, how do you read your boom operator, sir?"

"Loud and clear," Brad responded.

"Loud and clear up here, too. I have you in sight. Cleared to precontact position, Two-One is ready."

"One-Four is cleared to precontact." All the director lights on the belly of the KC-10 Extender aerial refueling tanker ahead of them flashed briefly, and then two green lights began flashing, verifying that he was cleared to precontact position. The tanker's flying boom was already lowered and the nozzle extended slightly.

"Very smooth, gradual control inputs," Hoffman coached Brad in a quiet voice. "You'll find it much easier than the simulator. You don't even have to move the stick. It's like moving the planchette on an Ouija board—you just barely touch the stick and *think* about moving it, and it moves. No rush. Nail your airspeed, then make fine corrections. The Excalibur is very slippery, so you won't need many throttle adjustments once you're in sync with the tanker."

The boom started to get larger as Brad crept up and forward. "Don't focus on the nozzle, Brad," Hoffman said. "Keep your scan going—director lights, nozzle, window bow, tanker belly. Keep scanning. You're looking for that precontact picture: aft row of the director lights right at the top of the window bow, nozzle centered, director lights telling you to come on in, checking for closure rate or elevation warnings, then repeat. Nice and easy."

Now Hoffman was starting to see Brad clenching and unclenching his hands and swallowing hard—the first sign of nervousness he'd seen Brad have past the first few simulator sessions. "Nice easy grip on the stick, Brad—don't fight her. You got this. The B-1 is the easiest plane to air refuel but the slipway is in front of you, not behind as it is on most planes, and you tend to get the feeling that nozzle is coming right through the windscreen. The boomer won't let that happen, believe me. Don't focus on it. Relax. Scan."

Brad forced himself to relax, and soon his hands were starting to make the tiny adjustments needed to form the sight picture he had practiced so many times in the simulator. Now he was making only quick glances at the approaching nozzle, and even though he knew this was for real and not a simulation, he got into the rhythm of forming the sight picture and using a quick and easy scan to . . .

. . . and before he knew it, *there it was*, the perfect picture of the landmarks on the tanker and the cockpit windscreen bow, and he heard, "Stabilize precontact, One-Four."

"Roger, stabilized precontact," Brad responded, pulling off just a tiny bit of power to stop the forward motion. Before he knew it he saw the boom come down a bit, the nozzle extended, and he heard and felt the satisfying *CLUNK!* as the nozzle extended and slammed home inside the receptable, without even touching the slipway.

"Contact, Two-One," the boom operator said.

Hoffman checked his multifunction display. "Contact," he reported.

"Contact, One-Four," Brad replied.

"Taking fuel," Hoffman reported. "We're not going to take on much fuel, but just be aware that if we were taking on a normal onload you'd have to make very slight power changes as the gross weight increases."

Now the director lights on the tanker's belly had changed: Brad's job was to keep the boom aligned with the yellow centerline and respond to the director lights, which would tell him if was too high or too low or too close or too far away. Brad found that the lighter his touch on the control stick, the easier it was to stay in the center of the refueling envelope.

They took on just a token amount of fuel—Hoffman had already accomplished the first refueling that would be sure to take them all the way to Guam, and Sondra had gotten a few practice contacts from the left seat as well—and then he had Brad do a few practice disconnects and reconnects, including contacts while in a turn, as if they were doing a refueling anchor pattern—a racetrack pattern designed to keep the aircraft in a particular geographic location—instead of a long straight refueling track. Just before Brad made it to precontact position on the fifth practice try, Hoffman keyed the microphone button and said, "*Breakaway, breakaway, breakaway!*" Brad immediately chopped the throttles to idle and started a brisk but not too rapid descent, while the tanker pilot gunned his throttles and started a fast climb and the boom operator yanked the refueling boom up and back to its maximum retracted position on the tanker's tail.

"Thanks for the work, Two-One," Hoffman radioed. "You had a newbie doing those contacts and the breakaway from the right seat."

"Nice job, copilot," the boomer radioed. "Catch you on the flip side, guys. Cajun Two-One is clear."

"Great job on your first contact, Brad," Hoffman said. "I think you're going to have the Excalibur nailed."

"Like you said, sir," Brad said, "the lighter the touch on the stick and throttles, the easier it is."

"Kinda seems like I've done this a few times before, eh, Brad?" Hoffman deadpanned. He patted the top of the instrument panel. "It may seem like the B-1 is a big muscular roaring monster, Brad, but she's really more like a sweet intelligent woman: you be respectful and aware and don't try to muscle her around, and she'll respond just as sweetly. Try to push her around and she'll bite back." He turned over his right shoulder. "Sondra, I'm going to clear off for relief, grab a protein bar, and then I'm going to take a nap for a half hour. Sound good?"

"Yes, sir," Sondra replied. She took off and stowed her parachute, folded up her jump seat, let Hoffman squeeze past, then pulled herself up into the pilot's seat and strapped in. "Pilot's up on intercom," she reported. She put her hand on the control stick and gave it a quick shake. "I've got the aircraft."

Brad shook his control stick and felt Sondra's resistance on it, and he knew she had control. "You've got the airplane."

"I've got it." She disconnected the autopilot and made some gentle turns, getting the feel for the aircraft—Brad knew she almost never used the autopilot. "How's it going, Brad?" she asked.

"Great, Sondra."

"Sounded like you got a little nervous there during the first hookup, but you worked your way through it. Nice job."

"Thanks."

"I'm really impressed by how fast you've moved through the colonel's flight training program," Sondra said. "I thought I did it quick, but you blew me away."

"I wasn't doing a full load of credits at UNR while doing flight training," Brad said.

"No, but I felt a little sorry for you—having to put up with the boss while you trained full-time," Sondra said. "But you did good." She paused for a few moments, then said, "So what's next, Brad? You're a multi- and instrument flight instructor and commercial pilot; you're checked out in a few warbirds; and now you're getting checked out in an XB-1 bomber. What else?"

He looked over at Sondra and gave her a smile. "To be honest, Sondra: I want to do what you're doing," he said. "My dad suggested this way back before I started the program, and now I've met someone who's done it: commercial, CFI, CFI-I, and you have a degree in business and a master's in aviation maintenance management. He said all that plus maybe an A and P license would make me competitive for working at Sky Masters, plus the fact that I've worked there and the bosses know me."

"Pretty good advice," Sondra said. "But to tell you the truth, I did all that stuff for one thing: to meet guys."

"Say what?"

"To meet pilots." Brad gave her a skeptical expression. "Pilots are hot. You probably don't think so, but I do. All the pilots I've ever met know they have a skill that less than one percent of the people in the country possess. The jerk pilots have this cocky swaggering deal going on that turns me off, but the cool pilots keep the swaggering to a minimum, fly the plane, and complete the mission." She looked over at him. "I haven't figured out which you are yet," she said, a slight smile just visible behind her microphone. "When you first arrived at Warbirds Forever, I thought you were the biggest jerk I've ever seen. You're starting to come around."

"Thank you . . . I think," Brad said.

Sondra gave him a big smile. "That was a compliment," she said. "So, tell me: What's it like being General Patrick McLanahan's son?"

Brad shrugged. "A mixed bag, I guess," he said. "All I really know about my dad are the stories or opinions other people tell. He never talks about what he did in the Air Force. Every now and then I see him get this look, like he's remembering something bad that happened a long time ago. He'll hear a heavy jet fly nearby or see a warbird taxi out, and he'll stop what he's doing and get that faraway look. It's not sadness or post-traumatic stress disorder or anything like that—at least I don't *think* it is—but it happens, and I ask him later to talk about it, and he won't."

"I think your dad is quite hot," Sondra said.

Brad's head snapped around in surprise. "*What?*"

Sondra smiled, looking straight ahead. All the time they were talking, the Excalibur bomber didn't wander one iota in altitude or heading—it was as if she had engaged the autopilot. "The strong silent type," she said dreamily. "In a room full of pilots you'd never know he'd be the guy in charge . . . until it was time to get to work or until he spoke, and then you'd get it."

"But he's twice your age!" Brad exclaimed, probably too vociferously.

After a few long moments, she shrugged. "Not a complete disqualifier," she said finally. She looked over and smiled at Brad's shocked expression. "I see where you get it from."

"Get what from?"

"You got the skills and the cocky attitude, Brad," she said, "but you don't show it—in fact, you work hard to hide it." She gave him a smile, then added: "Not a complete disqualifier."

"Disqualifier for what?" But she never answered him, only wore that slight little smile and steered the Excalibur as if it was on rails until Hoffman came up a half hour later and switched with Brad so he could take a break.

*

A few hours later they were painting the island of Guam on radar. "Guam Center, Masters One-Four," Brad McLanahan radioed, back in the copilot's seat but flying the Excalibur, "level at one-four thousand, forty miles east of BAGBE intersection, information Romeo for landing."

"Masters One-Four, Guam Center, welcome," the controller responded. "Descend and maintain eight thousand eight hundred, cleared for the GPS Zulu runway two-four left approach. Winds three-zero-zero at ten gusting to seventeen."

After doing aerial refueling contacts, flying a GPS approach with the Excalibur seemed like child's play to Brad. He used the same techniques as during air refueling: light touch on the stick and throttles, remain relaxed, and maintain the sight picture while keeping the needles centered and the airspeed under control. Hoffman made sure the checklists were done, and they rode the ILS beam nice and steady. The satisfying *SQUEAK! SQUEAK!* of the main landing gear touching the pavement was almost a surprise.

"Welcome to Guam, son," Patrick McLanahan said as Brad, Tom Hoffman, and Sondra Eddington climbed down the Excalibur's long entry ladder after parking the Excalibur outside of its tent. He gave Brad a big hug. "How was the flight?"

"Great!" Brad exclaimed, "except my butt thinks my legs have been cut off." He unzipped his flight suit to his waist. "Whew! Is it humid out here!"

"We should be getting our usual three P.M. thunderstorm any time now, so it'll feel better," Patrick said. He handed each of them a bottle of water, then asked Hoffman, "How did he do, Tom?"

"Chip off the ol' block, sir," Hoffman said. He added with a smile, "But don't worry: we'll make him better."

"Thanks, buddy," Patrick said. They headed to maintenance debrief, all chugging cold water. By the time they reached the maintenance hangar, the skies had darkened, and moments later the clouds that had appeared as if out of nowhere disgorged sheets of rain. "You can almost set your watch by the afternoon thunderstorm," he said.

"And the same for the power outage," Colonel Warner "Cutlass" Cuthbert said, trotting into the maintenance hangar. "Blackout, usually caused by a tripped breaker at the municipal power station or transformer farm from a lightning strike or surge. Our backups should be kicking in any minute. The computers are all on uninterruptable power supplies, so you can still debrief, but air-conditioning and lights are out. Shouldn't last long."

Just a few minutes into the maintenance debriefing the lights and power came back on, but the afternoon deluge had already cut down on the humidity. After the debriefing, Cutlass gave Sondra a set of keys. "Would you show Brad here where his father's tent is? He'll bunk in there with him. You can take him by the flight line and show him the other bombers. Don't forget your flight-line IDs. Be back at the command center in an hour for the mission briefing."

"Yes, sir," Sondra said. Brad grabbed his backpack and computer case and followed.

In a few minutes they were slowly driving in a four-door crew pickup truck down the flight line at Andersen Air Force Base, examining the rows of B-52H, B-1B, and XB-1 bombers, KC-135 and KC-10 tankers, and F-22 Raptor and F-15 Eagle fighters in their parking spots. They were stopped frequently for ID checks. Vehicles with carts loaded with munitions of every description, and roving security and munitions maintenance vehicles drove up and down the line as well. "It looks like chaos, but it's all pretty well orchestrated so no bottlenecks occur that create a safety or security situation," Sondra said.

They stopped at an XB-1 Excalibur bomber about halfway down the line. A security guard checked their IDs and waved them past a simple yellow nylon rope barrier. "Be sure to only enter and exit here, where the guard is," Sondra said. "The guards will jack you up if you cross over the rope, and they are authorized to shoot if they think you're a suicide bomber or something."

"I remember the security briefing," Brad said.

They walked underneath and found Ed Gleason pre-flighting his jet inside the forward bomb bay. "Hello, Sondra," Gleason greeted them.

"Hello, sir," Sondra said. "Ed, I don't think you've met General McLanahan's son. Ed, this is Bradley McLanahan. Brad, meet Lieutenant General Ed Gleason, retired, one of the most experienced B-1 drivers at Sky Masters. He graduated number one in his Air Force Academy class, flew F-15E Strike Eagles as a second lieutenant, flew B-1s as a young captain, and commanded flying wings until finally becoming Twelfth Air Force commander. We're lucky to have him." Brad shook his hand.

"Sorry about the Academy, son," Gleason said.

Brad rolled his eyes in exasperation. "Does everyone on Guam know that I dropped out of the Air Force Academy?"

"*I* know now," Sondra said. That really turned Brad's face sour, but she gave him a smile that perked him right back up. "Brad is a flight instructor at Warbirds Forever, and he just completed his first Excalibur ferry flight as second in command. I think he did pretty well. Colonel Hoffman even got him some air refueling stick time from the right seat. No dings on the Bone."

"We'll get you trained as an aircraft commander before you know it," Gleason said. "You going to show Brad around the bird, Sondra?"

"Yes, sir."

"Great. Nice to meet you, Brad."

"Same here, sir." They shook hands again, and Gleason departed, leaving Brad and Sondra alone.

"As you know, Brad, we can put three different payloads in each of the three bomb bays, or we can move the bulkhead between the forward and center bays to accommodate larger weapons.

"The primary mission for this bird is suppression of enemy air defenses, both against surface ships and on land," she went on. "The forward bomb bay has a rotary launcher with four AIM-9 Sidewinder missiles and four AIM-120 AMRAAM radar-guided air-to-air missiles, which I think all the Excaliburs carry now." They moved to the intermediate bay. "Here we have a rotary launcher carrying six AGM-158 Joint Air to Surface Standoff Missiles. JASSM has a one-thousand-pound warhead, a range of over two hundred miles, and an imaging infrared terminal seeker along with inertial navigation system and GPS. We can retarget it with the AESA or with target information received by satellite. The aft bomb bay has a three-thousand-gallon fuel tank, which all the Excaliburs carry because of the long overwater legs, even though we have our own tanker support."

They exited the bomb bay, and she motioned to two clusters of missiles mounted externally under the fuselage. "These are my favorites: the AGM-88 HARM, or High-Speed Anti-Radiation Missile," Sondra went on. "We have two clusters of two missiles each on the external hardpoints. HARM can detect, home in on, and destroy enemy radars from as far as thirty miles—it can kill any target within range in less than a minute. They're programmed to detect every known radar in the Chinese or Russian military."

"Do they fly the Excaliburs armed with JASSMs?" Brad asked.

"They'll fly them for proficiency or weapon checkouts, but not on patrols," Sondra said. "Only the birds with the air-to-air missiles are allowed to fly patrols."

"The patrols sound a little boring."

"Most of the time we fly airborne radar overwatch for Navy patrols," Sondra said. "We can send our radar data directly to the Aegis ships, or we just pass on radar or visual information to ships that can't collect datalinks or digital imagery. They can get boring, but finding and classifying a ship out ahead of a Navy formation is pretty cool. We air refuel every two hours or so, which gives us plenty of fuel for a divert base, so we stay busy."

"Wish I could fly those patrols," Brad said.

"I don't see why you can't," Sondra said. "If you fly with Colonel Hoffman, Ed Gleason, or your father, you'll be flying with an instructor, so those hours count toward your ATP, and once you get that you can get checked out as an Excalibur aircraft commander. You probably need all the security clearances and background checks we had to get to be part of this task force. Tell them you want some patrols. Colonel Cuthbert can get you all the clearances, and you're good to go."

They drove to the housing area, not far from the flight line. Brad saw rows and rows of white tents on a coral and sand lot. "My dad lives in a tent?" Brad exclaimed.

"He insisted on living like the other crews and maintainers live—if he gets uncomfortable, he knows how everyone else feels," Sondra said. "Besides, these things are pretty nice." She punched in a code on the door—no tent flaps here—and showed Brad inside. It was surprisingly spacious. There was room for two folding beds, two dressers, and two desks.

"I didn't see any power lines coming in here," Brad observed.

"The tents are all solar powered," Sondra said. "A group of six tents shares a big battery, and there are solar collectors on each tent and on each battery enclosure. The battery can be topped off by base electrical power, but that's rare—the solar cells do a pretty good job."

"Not much privacy."

"The task force patrols and works on the flight line twenty-four-seven," Sondra said, "so everyone is pretty busy. We work a five-days-on, two-days-off rotation, but to tell the truth, everyone makes themselves available on off days because there's not much to do out here—the hotels and casinos are all but shut down, and lying around on the beaches gets old fast. Privacy isn't really an issue—you make your own privacy. The sound of planes taking off is a bother, bunking so close to the flight line, but you get used to tuning it out." She looked at him carefully, gave him a little smile, then reached out and touched his hand. "Besides, Brad, whatever would you do if you had a little privacy?" she asked.

He stepped over to her and gave her a light kiss on the lips, which she seemed to enjoy. "I'd come up with something," he said in a soft voice.

"Oh, I'm sure you could, stud," Sondra said, heading for the door. "I'm sure you could. C'mon, we have the mission briefing."

"Am I allowed to attend?" Brad asked.

"They'll tell you if you're not, but I don't see why not—we all have the same security clearance," Sondra said. "It'll get your mind out of the gutter."

"It wasn't there before I met you," Brad said. She smiled but said nothing.

ELEVEN

OVER THE SOUTH CHINA SEA

SEVERAL DAYS LATER

"Anytime I get to fly is a great joy," the weapons officer of the carrier-based JH-37 Flying Leopard attack plane, Lieutenant Du Weiqing, said on intercom to the officer seated beside him, pilot Lieutenant Commander Bo Xueji. The JH-37 was based on the aircraft carrier *Zheng He* operating in the northern South China Sea one hundred and fifty miles southeast of Shantou, on routine patrol. It was armed with four *Ying Ji* (Hawk Attack)-83 missiles, which were sea-skimming ramjet-powered antiship weapons, plus two advanced PL-12 active/passive air-to-air missiles on wingtip pylons. "But these overwater patrols are so damned boring."

"I agree," Bo said. "But would you rather be back at the ship doing yet another additional duty?"

"*Bùyòngle, xièxiè,*" Du said. "No, thank you. I got 'volunteered' for two more of them yesterday."

"Which ones?" Bo asked.

"Water survival instructor and assistant flight deck safety officer," Du said morosely.

"Ah, just more opportunities to excel," Bo said.

"Of course." Du put his eyes up to the hood over his attack radar. "I have surface radar contact, twelve o'clock, ninety kilometers," he reported. He entered commands into his targeting computer, then activated the JH-37's electro-optical camera. The MFD on the forward instrument panel showed a large replenishment ship. "Looks like a U.S. Navy oiler," Du said.

"How far are we from Xisha Dao?" Bo asked.

Du called up an electronic chart on one of his MFDs. "Two hundred and ten kilometers," he replied.

"All warships are supposed to be three hundred kilometers from shore, from other warships, or Nansha Dao or Xisha Dao," Bo said. "He is in violation of the agreement!"

"It is just an oiler, not a warship."

"It is a U.S. Navy vessel, and it is in violation of the agreement," Bo said. "Send the contact information to the carrier and advise we are going to make contact." Bo began a descent, allowing the Flying Leopard to accelerate past the speed of sound.

"Target image transmitted to the ship," Du said a few minutes later. "Operations orders us to make contact with the vessel and ask about their intentions."

"I will *certainly* make contact," Bo said. He leveled off at one thousand feet above the sea and nudged the power up slightly to maintain supersonic speed, and they closed the distance quickly. Still going over Mach one, they overflew the oiler. Bo started a hard left bank. "Do I have your attention now, my friends?" he asked.

"Unidentified aircraft going supersonic, this is the replenishment ship USS *Laramie,*" came the call on the international maritime emergency channel. "You just overflew us going supersonic! That's not permitted! Back off!"

"USS *Laramie*, this is *Qiánfeng* Three-Three," Bo radioed back. "You are sailing too close to Xisha Dao and are in violation of international agreements. State your intentions!"

"*Qiánfeng* Three-Three, we are an unarmed support vessel proceeding to port in Kaohsiung, Taiwan, for refueling and resupply," came the reply. "We are a solo vessel and not a warship, and there are no restrictions on our movements. Do not overfly us again! We see you have some kind of missiles under your wings, so we will assume you have hostile intentions. Stay clear."

"Assume anything you like, American bastard," Bo said on intercom. "You cannot just sail around anywhere you like, especially not around a Chinese island."

"Operations says they are dispatching a frigate to intercept the American," Du said. "They order us to maintain contact until we reach return fuel state. They are launching another Leopard to relieve us."

"As long as we are up here, why not practice some antiship missile attacks?" Bo said. "It will give us something to do."

"Good idea," Du said. "Master arm switch is off and switch cover is down."

"My master switch is off as well," Bo said, decelerating below the Mach to stay within antiship missile launch parameters.

Du ran his checklists and directed the pilot to fly in different directions, practicing attacks against the oiler from different aspects. It was easy to acquire and target the big oiler from the side, but a bit more challenging to get it from the stern and even harder from the bow. Du tried it with and without the radar and with and without the electro-optical sensor.

"This guy is totally dead," Du said after their fifth pass. He took his eyes out of the radar hood, checked the navigation and systems readouts, made some flight log entries, and then pulled out a bottle of water and looked outside to relax his eyes. "About fifteen minutes before we have to head back to the ship. We can make one or two more passes and then . . . *What in the world is that?*" he suddenly shouted. Bo followed his weapons officer's gaze out the cockpit canopy. There, not a hundred meters away off their left wingtip, was an immense light gray bomber aircraft! "Where did that come from?"

"It's an American B-1 bomber!" Du said. He noticed the American flag painted on the tail, but at the base of the vertical stabilizer it had a U.S. civil aircraft registration number, N-03SM. The wings were swept at about forty degrees. They could see what looked to be a sensor pod under the fuselage on the right side. "How long has he been sitting out there?"

"I never saw anything until just now. Radio contact in to base and ask for interceptors." While Du radioed back to base, Bo switched to his secondary radio, which was usually set to GUARD, the international emergency channel. "Unidentified American B-1 bomber aircraft," he radioed in halting English, "this is *Qiánfeng* Three-Three. We are conducting military patrol operations in this area. Identify yourself immediately."

"This is Masters Zero-Three," Tom Hoffman replied, piloting the XB-1 Excalibur bomber. "We're just going to hang here for a while, check out a few things, and take some pictures. We won't bug you."

Although his English was better than most of the pilots in his squadron, Bo was having difficulty understanding the American. "United States Air Force bomber, be advised, we are conducting hazardous military flight operations in this area. You are ordered to exit this area immediately. Acknowledge."

"We're not an Air Force aircraft, just a civilian job," Hoffman said. "We are conducting routine patrol and crew checkout operations in this area. We were told you overflew an American ship going supersonic, and we were sent to check you out. I think it's time for you to go away and fly back to your carrier."

"Masters Zero-Three, your request will not be followed," Bo said, his eyes bulging in disbelief. "This is a People's Liberation Army Navy military operation. No interference will be tolerated! Exit this area immediately or you may be intercepted by fighter aircraft and fired upon without warning. Acknowledge!"

"Look here, boys," Hoffman said. "It's a nice day for flying, so why don't you just relax and we'll just have a nice pleasant cruise out here—no reason to start getting all belligerent. Besides, we're almost inside Taiwan's air defense zone, and I don't think they'd appreciate armed bombers flying around so close to their shoreline."

"No interference will be tolerated!" Bo shouted on the radio. "Leave immediately! Acknowledge!"

"A JN-15 is en route," Du said on intercom. "About ten minutes out. A JN-20 from the carrier *Zheng He* is being readied. We are to head back to the carrier to speed up the intercept."

"Turn tail and run, with this bastard on my ass?"

"The fighters will chase him away," Du said. "He is just trying to irritate us."

"Well, he is doing a good job," Bo said irritably. He forced himself to relax. "That guy has a civilian registration number. Could it be possible for civilians to . . . ?"

"*Qiánfeng* Three-Three, Operations," came a radio call from their home base, "advise you . . ." And just then the transmission cut out.

"Operations, do you copy Striker Three-Three?" Du radioed. But as he spoke, his own words were repeated back to him, but delayed about one second . . . and he found it impossible to keep on speaking. He tried his best to ignore his own voice, but it was simply not possible to keep on speaking while his own voice was stepping on him!

"Say again, Three-Three," the operations officer on the *Zheng He* radioed. "You were . . ." But the transmission was again cut off.

"We are being meaconed," Du said. "Someone is interfering with our radios, injecting a different signal onto our channel."

"Could it be from that American bastard flying next to us?" Bo asked.

"Operations, this is *Ying* Seven-One leader," came a new voice on the command frequency, "we are tied on radar with *Qiánfeng* Three-Three and the American aircraft and will take over the intercept. Break. *Qiánfeng* Three-Three, *Ying* Seven-One flight of two, inbound, we have you on radar, we will join in two minutes."

"Three-Three, acknowledged," Bo responded. "Seven-One, be advised, use caution, our radios are being meaconed, and I think the American is doing it."

"We have not picked up anything yet," the leader of the JN-15 formation, *Hai Jun Shao Xiao* (Lieutenant Commander) Wu Dek Su, said. "We are tied on radar with the American aircraft. Advise you return to base."

"Acknowledged," Bo replied. He scowled at the B-1, still steady as a rock on his left wingtip. When he turned left to head back to the carrier, the American B-1 started to turn with him, then quickly descended and was lost from view. "Bastard. Just out for a little cruise, eh?"

"We were done for the day anyway," Du said.

"Seven-One, tied on visual," Wu radioed a few moments later. "I will take him on the left side. Take the high perch."

"Two," the wingman replied.

In moments the JN-15 fighters had positioned themselves

around the American B-1 bomber, the leader off the left side of the nose in good view of the pilot, and the other two hundred feet above and five hundred feet behind the bomber, in a good position to watch all the players and to react if the bomber tried any evasive or dangerous maneuvers. "Operations, *Ying* Seven-One, visual confirmation, the aircraft is a large four-engine strategic bomber resembling an American Air Force B-1B Lancer bomber," Wu reported on the command channel. "American civil aircraft registration number November dash Zero Three Sierra Mike. American flag painted on the tail, but no other markings. I see what appears to be a targeting pod under the nose on the right side, but otherwise no external weapons or devices visible. Request instructions."

"Stay in formation and monitor," came the reply from the operations controller aboard the carrier *Zheng He*. "Continue warnings on UHF GUARD. Get him out of this area immediately."

"Acknowledged." On the universal GUARD emergency channel, Wu said, "American B-1 bomber, this is *Ying* Seven-One flight of two JN-15 fighters, warning, warning, warning, you are interfering with military flight operations vital to the defense of the People's Republic of China. You are ordered to turn east immediately and remain clear of this area. Do you understand? Acknowledge immediately please."

"Hawk Seven-One, this is Sky Masters Zero-Three," Tom Hoffman replied, using the English translation for *Ying*. "I read you loud and clear, but we're not going anywhere. You and your pals can just go pound sand. This is international airspace and we're entitled to fly in it just as much as you are. We'll stay away from your ships but we're not going anywhere. Now *zou kai, go niang yang de*!" adding "Go away!" plus a few expletives to his response.

"The American bomber aircraft commander refuses to

leave the area!" Wu radioed back to the Chinese controller. "He uses profanity and dares us to attack him! Request permission to fire warning shots!"

"Stand by, Seven-One, stand by," the operations controller responded. Several moments later: "Negative, Seven-One, negative, do not fire, repeat, do *not* fire. A single-ship JN-20 is airborne and will intercept in three minutes. If the American bomber does not respond to the presence of our fighters, we may take action. Remain in close formation and monitor position from the carrier group."

As much as it galled him to do so, Wu stayed off the radios and remained in formation with the B-1 bomber, occasionally nudging closer and closer to make out any other details of the aircraft and to see if he could scare the pilot away just by flying dangerously close to him. The B-1 pilot didn't appear fazed at all when the JN-15 moved closer. He was also galled by the fact that the Hollywood JN-20 pilot was going to be allowed to chase the B-1 away, not the JN-15s.

"*Ying* flight, this is *Laoying* One-One, tied on radar," the JN-20 Challenger's pilot reported. It was the JN-20 squadron's commander, *Hai Jun Zhong Xiao* (Commander) Hua Ji, himself—he should have known the boss would take this intercept, Wu thought. "Say status."

"Eagle One-One, this is Hawk Seven-One flight of two, still in close formation with the American bomber, airspeed accelerating now that the Striker is heading back to the ship," Wu reported. "The JH-37 crew reported some kind of meaconing and interference and suspect it might be from the bomber's radar, but we are not experiencing any problems."

"Acknowledged," Hua replied. "Switch to the target's right side and I will come up on the left."

"Seven-One flight, acknowledged. Hawk flight, lead is switching to the right side."

"Two."

The JN-15 pilot pulled off a tiny bit of power, then steered below the bomber. With the big plane above him now, he could clearly see the Sniper targeting pod mounted on an external stores station, the three bomb bays, and the other external stores stations, all empty. When he flew all the way around to the other side, the pilot smoothly put the power back in, then slowly climbed until he was even with the copilot's window on the right side of the bomber. The bomber's copilot immediately pulled out a small camera and started snapping pictures.

"Masters Zero-Three, this is *Laoying* One-One," Hua radioed on GUARD, "confirm you are not armed and not radiating."

"I'm not confirming anything, One-One," Hoffman said. "I didn't clear any of you jokers in. Someone could get hurt—by accident, of course."

"Do not make any aggressive moves, Zero-Three," Commander Hua said. "I have you in sight and will close on your left side."

"You're *not* cleared in, One-One," Hoffman said irritably. It definitely sounded like he was getting agitated. Maybe he was getting ready to bug out. "Stay clear. I am unarmed and flying in international airspace. You guys don't own this territory. *Líkâi,* prick!"

"Zero-Three, you are flying in an area where Chinese military operations are under way," Hua said, infuriated that the American was using such foul language on an open radio frequency. "It is you who is doing dangerous acts. If you will not depart the area immediately, we have no choice but to shadow you until you do."

"Suit yourself, bozos," Hoffman said. "Hope you didn't fill up your piddle pack already."

Hua pulled his JN-20 Challenger fighter up to the B-1

bomber, taking digital photos of the aircraft from its left side as he got closer, then maneuvered beside and no more than a few yards away from the bomber. The bomber pilot took a few photos, then gave Hua an obscene finger gesture, putting his thumb between his index and middle finger.

"Why do we not blast this guy with our afterburners, like the American fighters did to our JH-37?" Lieutenant Commander Wu radioed on his command channel. There had been a confrontation between a land-based JH-37 and fighters from the American carrier *George H. W. Bush* in the south part of the South China Sea, where the U.S. Navy F/A-18 Super Hornet fighters tried to chase the JH-37 away with a tactic called a "handstand"—a Hornet pilot pulled directly above the JH-37, then pulled up steeply and hit its afterburners, pushing the Chinese bomber into an almost uncontrollable dive.

But the maneuver resulted in the release of a supersonic antiship missile that steered directly at the *Bush*—whether accidental or intentional still had not been revealed. The missile was destroyed just seconds before hitting the supercarrier, but the resulting damage of the exploding missile killed fifteen, injured thirty-seven, and destroyed eight aircraft; the *Bush* was out of commission for almost two years. Although the incident was almost five years ago, it still left a deep scar for most Chinese sailors and airmen.

"Hey, One-One, back away," Hoffman radioed a few minutes later. "You're crowding me. The guy on my right is moving in too close too."

"Sounds like the American is getting nervous," Wu radioed.

"Maybe if he gets nervous enough, he will leave," Hua said. "See how close you can move in."

"My pleasure," Wu said, and he expertly maneuvered even closer to the B-1 bomber, rattling the bomber's right wing with exhaust from his engines. "How do you like that, my friend?"

Just then the B-1 bomber started a gentle right turn until it was heading southwest—away from Taiwan's air defense identification zone, but in the direction of the Chinese mainland, less than two hundred and fifty miles west.

"Careful, Seven-One," Hua radioed.

"It is not a problem, One-One," Wu said. "I can stay with him easily. But he is heading toward the mainland."

"Not for long," Hua said. On the GUARD channel he radioed: "Masters Zero-Three, this is Eagle One-One, you are not permitted to come within three hundred kilometers of our coastline. Alter course immediately."

"I don't think so, *húndàn,*" Hoffman replied, adding another expletive. "You guys don't own this airspace or the ocean. We're unarmed. Get off my wing."

"Masters Zero-Three, this is your last warning," Hua radioed. "If you come within two hundred kilometers of our mainland base, you will be fired on." He checked his navigation displays—less than two minutes before they broke the two-hundred-kilometer line. On the command channel Hua radioed: "Operations, Eagle One-One, verify, am I cleared to engage the bomber inside the . . . ?"

And at that instant Hua caught a glimpse of a large fast-moving object that zoomed past him, no more than a hundred meters above him. Then a loud crashing *BANG!* and a violent rush of turbulence surrounded him, and he was forced to peel away from the B-1 bomber so he wouldn't collide with it. "*What was that?*" he radioed on his command channel.

"A large aircraft, going supersonic!" one of the JN-15 pilots replied.

Then Hua saw it as it performed a steep climbing left turn: it was *another B-1 bomber,* its wings swept all the way back, going almost too fast to keep in sight! It was gone in the blink of an eye over his left shoulder. "It is another American B-1 bomber!" he shouted. "A *second* bomber! Operations, do you copy? Another American B-1 bomber!"

"Eagle One-One, maintain contact with the second bomber!" the controller responded after an agonizingly long silence. "We do not have radar contact! Maintain contact! Hawk Seven-One flight, maintain contact with the first bomber, and do not lose contact! Acknowledge!" All the pilots affirmed their orders.

Hua activated his radar as he started a hard left turn to pursue the second B-1 bomber. "Operations, One-One, lost visual, attempting radar lock," he radioed. "Request launching the alert-five fighters."

"Hawk Eight-One flight of two will be airborne in five minutes, One-One."

Hua swore to himself as he checked his radar display—and realized it was being jammed! "Operations, One-One, I am receiving intense electromagnetic jamming!" he radioed. Usually the JN-20's superior active electronically scanned array radar was very difficult to jam because it shifted frequencies very quickly, but whatever jammers or radars were on the B-1 were much more powerful and faster than his. "Seven-One flight, say status."

"The first B-1 bomber is turning away from the mainland and heading north," Wu responded. "We are turning with him, but we will be at required recovery fuel state in five minutes. We are being . . ." And then the radios completely cut out—not jammed or meaconed, but completely silent.

"Seven-One flight, how do you hear?" Hua radioed. But his radio was silent as well, and his radar was still being jammed. Without radios or radar he had no way of knowing where the JN-15s were, so they were required to execute lost communications procedures and return to the carrier. Damn the decision of the air wing commander not to use external fuel tanks, Hua thought—any flight farther than two hundred kilometers, when the carrier was farther than two hundred kilometers from a suitable abort base on land, had to have drop tanks. The air wing commander thought the external tanks spoiled the performance of his jets too much . . .

. . . and at that moment he received a "MISSILE LOCK" warning on his radar threat receiver from his seven o'clock position and less than ten kilometers—he was being tracked by an enemy fighter! Hua immediately put in full afterburner, ejected decoy chaff and flares, and executed a hard climbing left turn. *Where did the fighter come from?* The enemy fighter zoomed past him, just below and to his left, heading north . . . and Hua caught a glimpse of the B-1 bomber! The American bomber had an *air-to-air missile?*

Hua tightened his left turn and pulled around behind the B-1 bomber. He had no clearance to attack, but his radios were inoperative, and he had just been highlighted by an enemy aircraft, and that was all the provocation he needed to attack. He armed his missiles and cannon. The B-1 had slowed considerably, and it was fairly easy to see him off in the distance. Even if his radar wouldn't work, his PL-12 missiles could home in on the bomber's exhaust and . . .

At that moment the jamming abruptly ceased. "Eagle One-One, Eagle One-One, this is Operations, how do you hear?"

"This is One-One, loud and clear now, Operations," Hu responded. "Jamming has ceased. I have been locked on by enemy radar from the B-1 bomber, and I may have evaded a missile launch. I have radar lock on the second bomber. It is heading north, altitude seven thousand meters, airspeed . . ."

And at that moment the radar locked onto something else—six more targets, approaching from the north at high speed!

"Attention, attention, People's Liberation Army Navy

fighter aircraft, this is *Jiàn* Four-Seven-Four flight of six, *Chung-kuo Kung Chuan,* Republic of China Air Force," a voice over the emergency GUARD channel said in Mandarin. "You have violated the Air Defense Identification Zone of the Republic of China. You are ordered to turn off all emitters, reduce speed, and lower your landing gear. You will be visually identified and escorted to T'ainan Air Base. The use of deadly force has been authorized. Comply immediately!"

Hua felt the almost overwhelming urge to reply with threats of his own, or even lock them all up with his fire control radar—the JN-20's AESA radar could track twenty targets and attack six simultaneously—but he choked the anger down and mashed the microphone button of his command channel: "Operations, One-One, I have radar contact on six Taiwanese fighters, repeat, six fighters, type unknown, same altitude, airspeed one thousand two hundred," he radioed. At that speed they had to be fighters, probably American-made F-15s or F-22s. "Request instructions."

The wait was agonizingly long. When the Taiwanese fighters were about seventy kilometers away, almost within range of radar-guided missiles, Hua heard, "Eagle One-One, Hawk Seven-One flight, *yèyīng,* repeat, *yèyīng.* Hawk Eight-One flight will be airborne and will provide cover. Acknowledge."

"One-One acknowledges," Hua responded. "Seven-One flight, disengage, fly southwest, descend to eight thousand, join on me." *Yèyīng,* or "nightingale," was the code word to direct airborne aircraft to return to the carrier as quickly as possible. He had to admit it was a good decision, and he turned hard left and headed southwest away from the Taiwanese. He knew the Taiwanese fighters would not pursue him or order him to surrender again, and a glance at his threat warning receiver verified this—the fighters set up two combat patrol orbits, one at five thousand meters' altitude and the other at ten thousand. Although the JN-15 was equivalent in performance and firepower to the American-made F-15, and the JN-20 was a generation ahead of anything else in the sky, three versus six were not good odds. Hua really wanted to take on the Taiwanese, but it had to be on *his* terms, not theirs.

"The report has been verified, sir," Vice Admiral Zhen Peng, commander of the South Sea Fleet, said by secure telephone. "Both the JH-37 and JN-20 crews reported that their radars and radios had been completely shut down after making contact with the American bombers, and that the American bomber locked onto the JN-20 fighter with an air-to-air missile tracking radar. It is a serious and potentially devastating escalation."

"We knew about the B-1 bombers on Guam, of course," Colonel General Zu Kai said in his office at People's Liberation Army headquarters. "But they appear to have capabilities we did not anticipate."

"We must do something about them, General," Zhen said. "Long-range bombers with advanced electronic countermeasures and air-to-air weapons threaten all our air patrols. Our carrier-based fighters roamed over the South Sea freely because the American carrier-based fighters do not challenge us—they either do not launch fighters while they transit, or they keep them close to their carriers. And the B-1 bomber can carry every air-launched weapon in the American inventory, including antiship cruise missiles, torpedoes, and mines. If it can sneak up on our carriers as easy as it sneaked up to our patrol planes and screen itself from our fighters . . ." "I know, Zhen, I know," Zu interrupted. "I have been so focused on deploying troops to the western provinces to root out antigovernment rebels, and more troops in the cities to put down riots. I thought things had quieted down in the South Sea. Now this. The Americans are sailing through the South Sea, but not the shipping companies. Something must be done. But what?"

"There is only one solution, sir: destroy the American aircraft on Guam," Zhen said.

"We tried that once before, remember?"

"Our weapons are a hundred times better than they were back then, sir," Zhen said. "The American fighters on Guam patrol out only fifteen hundred kilometers or so—that is well short of the maximum range of our nuclear-tipped AS-19 cruise missiles launched by H-6 bombers. Our ballistic missile and cruise missile submarines are better too."

"A nuclear attack on Guam would certainly trigger a nuclear response," Zu said. "Nuclear weapons will not be used."

"Sub- and air-launched conventional cruise missiles can overwhelm Guam's air defenses and do the job," Zhen said. "I have also instituted another system that will assist an attack."

"What are you talking about, Zhen?"

"It is called *Nèizài de dírén*, sir—'Enemy Within,'" Zhen said. "It is our most ambitious computer hacking project to date, far more extensive and successful than the hacking program against Taiwan." Zu swallowed nervously—he knew that Zhen would not stop at just one self-initiated spy program.

"Explain."

"'Enemy Within' is a project to hack into the computer systems controlling utilities on the island of Guam, sir," Zhen said. Zu had to struggle to contain his absolute shock and surprise, even on the telephone. "My teams have managed to hack into every municipal computer and server on the island, as well as a number of corporate and personal networks. They are far less protected from hacking and computer virus infection than military computers."

"What does that accomplish, Zhen?"

"The American air base on Guam gets its power, water, and telephone from the municipal utility company, sir. I can shut down all the utilities to the base instantly, on command. I have been doing it for years. The Americans think it is circuit breakers tripping from lightning, or operator error. The power goes out because I direct it. I can do the same to municipal telephone, radio, satellite, and Internet."

Zu was absolutely stunned. A navy admiral, under his command, secretly hacking into a foreign utility? "What good does any of that do, Zhen?" Zu asked after shaking himself out of the sudden feeling of dread. "Surely the military base has backups."

"Yes, sir, they do, and quite extensive," Zhen said. "Their Patriot missile batteries, command post high-frequency and satellite communications, and security divisions are completely self-contained and do not rely on municipal power, and individual computers and servers have battery backups. But emergency generators cannot power everything, and in many systems it takes time, from several seconds to several minutes, for backup power to kick on and the systems to reboot and start working again. Even a short period of time can be exploited." Zu rolled his eyes in exasperation, even though inside he was fairly trembling. "More importantly, sir, their long-range civil radars, computer networks, and normal air-to-ground communications are all powered by the municipal grid. A disruption will not completely blind or deafen them, sir, but we can confuse them long enough."

"Long enough for what, Zhen?"

"To destroy Andersen Air Force Base, sir," Zhen said. "Or at least destroy enough aircraft on the ground and cripple the base to make it unusable for their few surviving heavy bombers."

Zu blinked in surprise. "Are you serious, Zhen?"

"It can be done, sir," Zhen said. "I have a plan formulated that can do the job."

"What if it is done, Zhen? After the Americans retaliate, they will just move them somewhere else—Japan, the Philippines, Australia . . ."

"If those countries chose to support them," Zhen said. "Those countries would know that they would become Chinese military and economic targets. In any case, the American bomber force would be crippled and almost completely wiped out."

"I do not know if China will continue to be such a great economic power in the world if this damnable recession continues," Zu said. "If America reacts with a nuclear attack, it could completely destroy our country."

"America is still crippled and weak, sir," Zhen said. "I do not think they will risk nuclear war."

"They have placed more ballistic missile submarines on patrol, Zhen," Zu said. "That is their most potent weapon. Every one of our military bases would be destroyed if we attacked Guam."

"I do not think so, sir," Zhen said. "I do not believe the Americans want a war with China. If they retaliate, it will be with conventional cruise missiles launched against our missile bases, airfields, and command-and-control facilities, just like eighteen years ago, and I think we can disperse our weapons well enough to survive. Our surface-to-air missiles and air defenses can take care of any attack against fixed installations." Zu was silent. "Sir, the Americans are forcing us to respond to their provocations, sir, and the main provocation right now is their bomber base on Guam. It must be attacked, but not with nuclear weapons. A pinprick would be sufficient."

Zu remained silent so long that Zhen thought he had hung up. Then: "Do you have a plan, Admiral?" he asked. He knew he hardly needed to ask—Zhen seemed to be a fanatic with his dangerous but audacious plans, but so far they all seemed to have worked.

"Of course, sir," Zhen said. "I have been updating the plan daily since its creation, depending on new intelligence reports, and I have reserved weapons, crews, and aircraft as much as I am allowed. The plan is ready to put into motion at any time."

"Very well," Zu said. "Submit it to me immediately." He terminated that phone call, then called his deputy, General Sun. "Get me Phoenix in Washington on the 'hot line' and a translator immediately."

"This is President Phoenix," the president said, speaking slowly for the benefit of the Chinese translator. "Who is calling, please?"

"*How dare you, Phoenix?*" Zu exclaimed—actually the translator's voice was professionally calm and even toned, while Zu's voice in the background was loud and shrill. In the Oval Office listening on dead extensions were Vice President Ann Page, National Security Adviser Glenbrook, Secretary of State Kevich, Secretary of Defense Hayes, and Chairman of the Joint Chiefs of Staff General Timothy Spellings, all who had been summoned to the Oval Office after the message was received that Zu wanted to speak directly with the president. The president and his advisers had just been briefed on the confrontation over the South China Sea. "Your B-1 bombers swarmed and threatened a patrol aircraft belonging to China! I demand an explanation!"

"First of all, General Zu, you will address me as 'President Phoenix' or 'Mister President,'" Phoenix said. "Second, why am I talking to you? I should be speaking with Acting President Gao or Defense Minister Cao, not the chief of the general staff."

"First of all, Phoenix, I will address you any way I please," Zu shouted. "Second, under martial law I speak for the Chinese government. The government and the Politburo have subordinated themselves to me during this emergency—an emergency that your bombers have taken to the brink of general war! Now explain yourself! Why are my patrol planes being harassed like this?"

"Because your patrol plane intercepted, overflew with menace at supersonic speed and low altitude, and then proceeded to perform mock missile attacks on a solo, unarmed naval support vessel," Phoenix replied. "The crew of the USS *Laramie* requested help, and the Excalibur reconnaissance aircraft were the closest available."

"You refer to the B-1 bombers!"

"The bombers are refurbished surplus B-1 bombers, configured by a private contractor for long-range reconnaissance," Phoenix responded, not revealing by agreement with the national security staff that the XB-1 Excaliburs were armed with air-to-air missiles. "They are used for long-range reconnaissance in support of small groups of surface vessels."

"But they locked onto our patrol plane and fighters with antiaircraft radar, disrupted radio communications, and shut down our navigation radars . . ."

"You mean, your fire control radars, the radars used to direct guns, bombs, and missiles—it appeared as if your patrol planes and fighters were getting ready to attack," Phoenix said. "General, I thought both sides were going to stay away from each other's ships and shorelines. Why was that patrol plane harassing our support ship?"

"We agreed that we would stay two hundred nautical miles from each other's shores, including the disputed islands in the South Sea," Zu replied. "Your warship was well within that distance. You violated the agreement!"

"We agreed to keep warships away," Phoenix said. "The *Laramie* was not a warship, but a naval support vessel, carrying nothing but food, cargo, and fuel—not even ammunition," the president said. "It was unarmed, by itself, and heading away from the Paracel Islands. It was no threat to China in the least."

"So that is the way you wish to have it, is it?" Zu responded. "You are quick to make agreements, then parse your words and stretch reality when it suits you."

"General Zu, we have made repeated requests for a formal

meeting between President Gao and myself to draft a formal agreement on the status of military forces in and around the South China Sea," Phoenix said. "We've heard nothing from you. In the meantime you have deployed millions of ground troops through-out your country, attacked civilians, and used nuclear weapons on foreign navies. Now we're seeing more long-range bombers being readied, your aircraft carriers deployed outside your largest port cities along with two Russian carrier battle groups, and we've detected Chinese submarines heading east. The situation is getting grave, General. The last thing the United States wants is war, but all we see in China is preparation for war."

"And China sees more and more bombers and fighters deployed to Guam and Saipan, more nuclear ballistic missile submarines launched, and warships that were laid up being made ready to sail," Zu said. "It is the United States that is looking for war, Phoenix!"

"All that preparation was in response to your nuclear depth charge attack and your antiship cruise missile attack," Phoenix said. "General, I don't want war, but I will respond to mobilization for war. Now I strongly suggest that you turn those submarines around and stand those H-6 bombers down."

"I am not going to take orders, suggestions, or anything else from you, Phoenix," Zu said. Zu's voice in the background sounded as if he was going to explode. "Those bombers you have on Guam are aimed right for our ports and cities, and China will not tolerate their presence. Remove them at once! When China sees some evidence that the United States is searching for peace, China will reciprocate. Otherwise we will take all necessary steps to protect our country. Be forewarned."

"Do not try to threaten us, General Zu," Phoenix said. "I want peace, but I will respond to all direct threats against my country." But the call had already been terminated.

Zu slammed the "hot line" receiver back onto its cradle. "*Bastards!*" he shouted. "I want to blow that island into the next decade! I want to make Guam glow like a lightbulb!"

"It appears as if the Americans are going to push back," Zu's deputy, General Sun Ji, said. He looked quizzically at his superior officer. "Sir? Why did you . . . ?"

"I need time to implement Zhen's plan," Zu said, thinking furiously.

"What plan?"

"He has a plan to attack the island of Guam," Zu said. Sun did not disguise his skeptical expression. "The bastard even said he has hacked into the municipal utilities and can disrupt power and telephone on the air force base."

"I would not believe a word he says, sir."

"But all his plans have worked so far," Zu pointed out, "and so far no one has retaliated against us."

"Except by not trading with us, General!" Sun said. "Exports are down twenty percent, and imports are down fifteen percent. There are already fuel shortages, and the unrest in the country is spreading. No one needs to militarily retaliate against us, sir—it is happening in the marketplace!"

"I am not concerned about that, Sun," Zu said. "When people tire of paying higher prices for goods, they will come back." Sun didn't believe that, but he did not show his disagreement. "But something has to be done about the American arms buildup on Guam."

"You are not thinking about another nuclear attack on

Guam, are you, sir?" Sun asked. "After the Russian attack on the United States, I do not feel they will sit back and allow another attack without massive retaliation."

Zu thought for a moment, then he said, "Get Gao in here."

Gao Xudong appeared in Zu's office in less than an hour. "What now, General?"

"I want you to negotiate a complete demilitarization of the South Sea with the Americans," Zu said. Sun was shocked but did not change his expression. "Our ships stay within our territorial waters. No armed aircraft overflying the South Sea. This will be between America and China, but we will invite other nations to participate. We will later discuss coordinating exploitation of the natural resources of the South Sea so as to avoid confrontation."

Gao was openly skeptical. "Why the sudden change of heart, General?" he asked.

"You told me yourself: China is reeling from the lack of trade and domestic unrest," Zu said. "We cannot stay in martial law indefinitely. We must do something. The Americans say they do not want war—let us see if they are honest. You work out the details."

Gao's expression turned from skepticism to hope. "I will open a dialogue right away, General," he said. "I think the Americans will be happy to cooperate, and they will certainly encourage other nations to as well." He exited Zu's office smiling and fairly bouncing from anticipation.

Sun looked at his superior officer in confusion. "Sir? What is the plan here? You wish to demilitarize the South Sea? How is that even possible?"

"I have no idea, Sun," Zu said. "I just need time to implement Zhen's plan to attack Guam."

"Have you studied this plan yet, sir?"

Zu turned to his computer and opened a classified documents folder. "There it is," he said. "I knew he would have his plan to me instantly. I want you to study it and give me your thoughts."

TWELVE

FIRST EXPEDITIONARY BOMB WING, ANDERSEN AIR FORCE BASE, GUAM

A FEW HOURS LATER

Patrick McLanahan climbed down the boarding ladder of his XB-1 Excalibur bomber into the warm, tropical air, instantly feeling sweat pop out underneath his international orange flight suit. His copilot, Colonel Warner "Cutlass" Cuthbert, was waiting for him on the ramp. "What a flight, Patrick!" he exclaimed when Patrick joined him a few moments later. He handed Patrick a bottle of cold water. "And we got to see JN-15s and JN-20s up close! Amazing!"

"It was excellent, Cutlass," Patrick said, gladly accepting the bottle of water and almost downing it all in one swig. "The machines did great."

Tom Hoffman joined them a few moments later, his XB-1 parked in the shelter right next to Patrick's. "Now I see where you get this reputation of yours, General," he said. "Where did that high-speed pass come from? We didn't brief that."

"With a freakin' JN-20 on your tail, I had to do something," Patrick said. "I improvised."

"Well, it impressed the hell out of me, General," Hoffman said. "I'd hate for you to be shot down by a JN-20, but thank you for stepping in."

"You're welcome. And I see you've been brushing up on your Chinese swear words."

"I wasn't going to do that on an open frequency, General, but when they started moving in like that, it pissed me off," Hoffman said. "It reminded me of the EP-3 incident again." In 2001, a U.S. Navy EP-3 electronic intelligence aircraft had been patrolling near Hainan Island, China, when it was intercepted by two People's Liberation Army Air Force J-8 fighters. One fighter collided with the EP-3 during a high-speed pass, causing the fighter to break into pieces and causing damage to the EP-3's radome and one propeller. The EP-3 managed to safely land on Hainan Island. The crew was detained for ten days then released. The EP-3 was dismantled, examined by Chinese intelligence experts, and then the pieces shipped back to the United States.

Patrick, Cutlass, Hoffman, and his copilot, the veteran Air Force pilot Ed Gleason, performed a postflight inspection of their XB-1 Excalibur bombers. On the First Expeditionary Bomb Wing's parking ramp, underneath large Kevlar fabric tent shelters, were eight XB-1 Excaliburs. Two were being readied for patrols over the South China Sea; and two were being readied for patrols over the Strait of Malacca, a thin vital waterway in Malaysia between the South China Sea and the Andaman Sea where most sea traffic between the Pacific and Indian Oceans traversed. Two shelters were empty because those XB-1s had already taken off for South China Sea patrols. Farther down the line were the active-duty bombers of the Continuous Bomber Presence, nestled in revetments instead of tents, and the KC-10 Extender, KC-46A Provider, and KC-135 Stratotanker aerial refueling tanker aircraft, and on the other side of the ramp were four F-15C Eagle and two F-22 Raptor fighters, who like the bombers rotated to Guam from stateside units.

After their walkaround postflights, the flight crews met with their maintenance teams and crew chiefs in a debriefing tent and went over every system in the aircraft, discussing malfunctions and any unusual indications or activity. It took over an hour, but it was a vital part of every mission, just as important as the flying itself. After making sure the data dumps and systems and cockpit recordings were safely retrieved, the crews headed to the DFAC, or dining facility, to sit and talk about the mission.

"I'll tell you, General, I'm very impressed with your XB-1s," Cuthbert said over yet another bottle of ice-cold water. "I was a little skeptical, even after the test flights. But the old gals look like they're doing well. I'll be interested to see if the data dumps discover any problems, because I thought I saw some twitchiness in the exhaust gas temperatures on our number three engine, and the left main landing gear seemed to take a long time to report down-and-locked, but otherwise those bad girls look good."

"Thanks, Cutlass," Patrick said. He checked his handwritten notes on his kneeboard tablet computer. "I think I wrote something about the number three EGT and the landing gear too. The left main seemed pretty noisy during retraction too, a lot of grinding noises—too many for my taste." He checked messages on his tablet. "There is a list of things being reported by my guys back at Battle Mountain they want us to check—the maintenance crews should have this list already. I'll make sure after we get done. The number thirteen plane should be ready to deploy in a couple days."

"I've got their tents set up already," Cutlass said.

"Pretty darn nice shelters and quarters, Cutlass," Gleason remarked. "When I heard we'd be staying in tents, I wasn't so excited to come out here, but those definitely ain't my daddy's tents."

"Bulletproof Kevlar, air-conditioned, solar-powered, and high-speed Internet access in every one," Cutlass said. "Some of the crews out here prefer them to our standard brick-and-mortar dorms."

Patrick finished checking messages on his tablet. "I thought I'd be able to take a nap," he said, "but there's a video teleconference scheduled in twenty minutes with PACAF. Tom, Ed, can you make sure the maintainers got that list of things to check from Battle Mountain before you hit the rack?"

"Sure, General," Hoffman said, "but I don't need no stinkin' nap. Heck, I'd love to take another patrol."

"Same here," Gleason said.

"Let's give the other guys some stick time, okay?" Patrick said with a smile. "We can't hog all the flights." He checked the sortie schedule to make sure he'd be available to sit in on the preflight briefing for the next XB-1 patrol launch, then he and Cutlass headed toward the First EBW command center to take the video teleconference.

"Well, that certainly didn't take long, gents," General George Hood, commander of Pacific Air Forces, said on the video teleconference a few minutes later. "I've already heard from Admiral Luce at Pacific Command, and he's already heard it from CJCS and CNO. The Chinese are hopping mad. General McLanahan, did you or someone in your patrol do an intentional high-speed near miss with a Chinese JN-20 fighter this morning—and, may I remind you, the first call came in to the White House at zero-five-hundred hours?"

"That was me, General Hood," Patrick said. "Colonel Hoffman's plane had been intercepted by two JN-15s and a JN-20 from the carrier *Zheng He,* and I thought they were crowding him a little too closely, trying to force a confrontation. I decided I needed to break up that formation."

"You flew over the JN-20 going *supersonic*?"

"Yes, sir. It was clear in a million and I had all the players in sight."

"That was a harebrained thing to do, General, with all due respect," Hood said. Patrick McLanahan had been retired from the Air Force for many years, but he still had an enduring reputation that garnered respect from even the most senior active-duty Air Force officers. George Hood was definitely one of them: even though he had a higher rank than Patrick when he was on active duty, Patrick McLanahan's actions all over the world on behalf of the United States of America, his unstoppable drive—and, frankly, his sheer audacity—led Hood to address Patrick as equals. "The Chinese say *we* were trying to force a confrontation."

"Of course they did, General Hood," Patrick said. "They were definitely crowding Colonel Hoffman, and in my judgment they wanted to either chase him out of there or force him to do something belligerent so they could attack."

"All right, all right," Hood said. "I assume you have helmet-cam video and radar data downloads of all this?"

"Yes, General," Patrick said. All their flight helmets were fitted with a high-definition video camera that shot everything the crewmembers saw, and also recorded all intercom, radar, and radio transmissions; the offensive and defensive systems suites' datalink provided detailed position and performance data to ground stations as well.

"Transmit it to me as soon as you can," Hood said. "Okay, here's what PACOM ordered: first, obviously, no more high-speed passes. Second: single-ship patrols from now on." Patrick's eyes narrowed with concern; Cutlass's mouth dropped open in surprise. Hood saw all this on his video teleconference monitor and held up a hand. "I know what you're going to say, boys. I set up two-ship patrols for a reason, and I'll keep on lobbying PACOM, but for now let's do what they say until we get some more sorties under our belt."

"Yes, sir," Cutlass said, but he obviously did not like that order.

"Third: no more jamming unless you get illuminated with an uplink or missile-guidance signal."

"All this puts us at a decided disadvantage, General Hood," Patrick said.

"That's the way it's got to be for now," Hood said. "Just to clarify, General—what are the airborne patrols armed with?"

"The forward bomb bay is loaded with a rotary launcher with four AIM-120C AMRAAM and four AIM-9X air-to-air missiles, and the aft bomb bay has a three-thousand-gallon fuel tank. The planes also carry chaff, flares, a Sniper targeting pod, and the Little Buddy." Chaff was used to decoy radar-guided missiles; flares could decoy heat-seekers.

"Good. No other stores are authorized for the airborne patrols," Hood said.

"The JH-37 we intercepted was carrying antiship missiles as well as air-to-air missiles, sir," Patrick said, "and they were practicing attack runs on that Navy oiler."

"Frankly, General McLanahan, I wouldn't be surprised if your bombers there were recalled," Hood said. "Your stunt back there could have pushed China to the breaking point. You might have to be sacrificed to keep China happy."

Hood paused for a moment, then added, "I'll be honest

with you, gents: I think Pacific Command thinks of you guys as not much more than window dressing. Now the White House is afraid that intercept might shove the Chinese over the edge. Sending you home might be the only thing that keeps your stunt from morphing into an international incident, General McLanahan."

SEVERAL DAYS LATER

The White House photographers just finished taking their pictures of the president of the United States and the acting president of China sitting down in the Oval Office together and shaking hands just before their meeting. Vice President Ann Page and many members of the Cabinet stopped by to meet Gao, who warmly greeted them. Finally, the two leaders sat down in their seats in the Oval Office, the president with a cup of coffee and Gao with tea.

"I wish to thank you for agreeing to this informal meeting, Mr. Gao," President Phoenix said. "I'm sorry we couldn't make it an official state visit; I'm sure you understand."

"Of course, Mr. President—I was only appointed president by an unelected body, so I am not technically a head of state," Gao Xudong said. "But you are very kind to receive me. It is indeed an honor to be in the White House."

"The honor is mine for you taking time out of your day to leave New York on the eve of your address to the United Nations and meeting us," Phoenix said. "And thank you for providing the State Department with a draft of your address. That is of course what prompted my request for a meeting."

"I am happy to do so, Mr. President," Gao said. "I understand you have concerns about my address?"

"I wanted to clarify some details in your speech, sir," Phoenix said, "and I was hoping to persuade you to make some changes to the text of your address to reflect the actual situation."

"Such as, sir?"

"First of all, sir, the aircraft carrier *Gerald R. Ford* is not being based in Australia," Phoenix said. "It is taking part in regularly scheduled exercises with Australia, Indonesia, the Philippines, and New Zealand."

"It has not left the area of the southern South Sea and eastern Indian Ocean for many months, and it has put into ports in Australia several times," Gao pointed out. "And your Marines are definitely based in Australia. The United States first deployed just five hundred Marines—that number has grown to over five thousand."

"I'm not perfectly familiar with all the details, sir, but I assure you, the *Ford* is not based in Australia," Phoenix said. "We no longer have carriers stationed in other countries, all due to the economic slowdown and cuts in military spending." Gao said nothing. "But now that you mention bases for carriers, we couldn't help but notice that the Russian *Vladimir Putin* carrier battle group has been on an extended visit to China. Are you basing Russian carriers at Chinese ports now, sir?"

"The Russian navy has been kind enough to train our carrier aircrew, maintenance personnel, and many other specialties," Gao explained. "China is also contemplating building a nuclear-powered aircraft carrier, and Russian expertise would be of great importance."

"I see," Phoenix said. "You also say in your speech that the bombers that are stationed on Guam are armed with nuclear weapons. They are most assuredly not armed with nuclear weapons."

"Our intelligence suggests otherwise, sir," Gao said rather sternly. "An in-person inspection of your aircraft and facilities on Guam would be in order to verify that there are no forward-deployed nuclear weapons."

"That would be acceptable," the president said. Gao raised his eyebrows in surprise at the response. "We would also like to verify the existence of nuclear weapons aboard your warships in the South China Sea."

"As you know, sir, China is under martial law at the present time," Gao said. When he noticed Phoenix's expression turn to one of deep skepticism, he added, "But I think that can be arranged."

"Very good," Phoenix said. "You also say that we are conducting armed airborne patrols of the South China Sea. That also is not true. Only the aircraft on the ground are armed and are on quick-reaction alert." He paused for a moment, then said, "China seems to be quite anxious about those aircraft on Guam, Mr. Gao. Guam is an important military base, and access to the Pacific is extremely important for the United States and our allies, as it is with China and her allies. The Continuous Bomber Presence program has been in effect since shortly after 9/11, sir—almost fifteen years. China has never expressed any concerns about the bombers on Guam before now."

"The nearly tripling of the size of the bomber task force, the addition of more fighters and radar aircraft to the task force on Guam, and the aggressive way the B-1 bombers were used near our aircraft recently all contribute to my government's concern, Mr. President," Gao said. "If your goal is to intimidate the People's Republic of China, Mr. President, you have succeeded."

"That was not my intention in the least, sir," Phoenix said. "We have also noted in your speech, Mr. Gao, that the United States is now 'stationing' two carrier strike groups in the South China Sea. That also is not true. We conduct regular patrols through the entire western Pacific and South China Sea, but we have not stationed any carriers there. Per our agreement, the transit times and duration of each passage is communicated well in advance to your government, and the carriers are configured so as to not have a ready deck for fixed-wing aircraft."

"Perhaps that can be modified in my address, sir," Gao said, although he clearly didn't like it and didn't seem too committed to do it. "But our intelligence analysts have noted an increase in the number and frequency of those patrols."

"Mr. Gao, those patrols were increased after the loss of our patrol plane, patrol helicopter, and rescue helicopter last year," Phoenix said. "Surely you can understand our deep sense of caution after those tragic losses."

"Of which China has freely admitted and done everything possible to prove our sincere regret and mitigate the losses to those involved." There was an uncomfortable pause in the Oval Office; then, a few moments later, Gao said: "President Phoenix, the B-1 bombers patrolling the South Sea—they appear to be different from the ones on ground alert. Can you tell me about them?"

"Seems to me you already have a great deal of information, sir," Phoenix said.

"I am not trying to be coy, Mr. President," Gao said, the stiffness of his posture accentuating the edge in his voice. "You have spies in China; we have spies in the United States. It is the nature of the world we live in. But the information we gather only leads to more questions."

"If I can answer your questions, Mr. Gao, I will; otherwise I will collect the answers right away."

"Thank you, sir," Gao said. "We have noted that some of the B-1 bombers have civil registration numbers on them instead of serial or bureau numbers, and some are painted differently. The crews also wear different flight suits than the others. If I may be so bold, sir, but they appear to be civilians or perhaps nonmilitary operators. CIA, perhaps?"

"Contractors," Phoenix said. Obviously China has spies that were uncomfortably—and possibly dangerously—close to Andersen Air Force Base, he thought, close enough to distinguish subtle differences like registration numbers and flight suit colors. That was very ominous and needed attention. "Civilian contractors, familiar with the aircraft, run under Air Force supervision."

Gao's face was the most expressive than it had been the entire meeting. "Indeed. Not military or government?"

"The purpose of those civilian B-1 aircraft is strictly long-range surveillance," Phoenix said. "They don't even have weapons operators aboard. They are there to augment our fleet of Global Hawks and other unmanned aircraft. They are much more flexible and responsive than many other sensor platforms."

"That is very interesting, sir," Gao said. "Not CIA?"

"Not CIA."

Gao didn't seem like he believed Phoenix, but when he searched Phoenix's face he didn't sense any attempt at evasion or untruth. "Very interesting," he said. "But you understand that the presence of long-range strike aircraft such as B-1 bombers only increases our deep concern over your intentions, sir."

"That's why I'm telling you about them," Phoenix said. "They are there to support the Continuous Bomber Presence task force and take the patrol burden away from them. Since we have so few Air Force personnel these days who know about B-1 bombers, we rely on contractors."

"So these . . . private aircraft, they are not being armed?"

"No."

"Is it possible to arm them, Mr. President?"

Phoenix leaned forward and looked Gao directly in the eye. "I think that depends on the nature of the threat, Mr. Vice President," he said. He sat back in his chair after a brief but tense pause. "Truthfully, I don't know if they can carry weapons, but right now I've ordered them to just patrol."

"Would not the Global Hawks be a better aircraft for overwater patrols, Mr. President?"

"Everyone wants a Global Hawk these days, Mr. Gao,"

Phoenix said. "There just aren't enough to go around. Besides, the Pacific is a big body of water. We got a good deal on refurbished B-1 bombers. It turns out they're perfect for this mission."

Gao nodded, still with a slightly surprised look on his face. "Refurbished strategic bombers operated by civilian contractors," he muttered. "Very interesting indeed."

"I'd like to get back to the issue of militarizing the western Pacific and South China Sea," President Phoenix said. "Namely, your new aircraft carriers and the DF-21D antiship ballistic missile sites popping up around the region. You have two carrier battle groups in the South China Sea, and a third we understand, the former Spanish amphibious assault ship, is being readied for deployment in the East Sea. Your DF-21D ballistic missiles cover the entire region, including the Philippine Sea, Celebes Sea, Adaman Sea, and Strait of Malacca."

"You seem to possess a great wealth of information as well, Mr. President," Gao observed.

"That seems like a lot of firepower being deployed in a very short period of time, sir," Phoenix said. "Why?"

"I am sure you know the reasons as well as I, Mr. President," Gao said. "It is for the very same reasons you have such a large and powerful navy: you have long coastlines, and foreign trade and open lines of communication are essential to you, as it certainly is with China. At the risk of offending you by appearing to lecture you, sir, China has always been vulnerable from the sea. China is surrounded by natural barriers from every direction but the east, and most every foreign invader has attacked from the sea. And in the modern era, China relies more than ever on maritime trade."

"But the ballistic missiles?"

"Purely defensive in nature, sir," Gao said. "We are decreasing the size of our army, but it is still large and takes many resources. Our military budget is slowly expanding, and we are trying to modernize, but it will take years, perhaps even generations, to do so. We must rely then on technology for our defensive requirements. Half our population lives within three hundred kilometers of the sea. Our population centers are vulnerable to attack from the sea, even with a large army behind them."

"The Dong Feng–21 has been described to me as a 'carrier killer,' Mr. Gao," the president said. "Is that your intention—to kill aircraft carriers?"

Gao made what could have been a stiff chuckle. "I have seen your aircraft carriers, sir," he said. "A missile that you launch from the back of a truck does not appear to me to be a match for a vessel that weighs almost one hundred thousand tons. No, sir, America's aircraft carriers are not a target for China's missiles."

"Mr. Gao, we've been studying the DF-21D for almost ten years," Phoenix said. "It's based on a mobile medium-range ballistic missile. It has a maximum range of almost two thousand miles and a five-hundred-kiloton nuclear warhead. You've deployed dozens of them along your coast and several in foreign countries. You cannot pretend they're insignificant."

Gao appeared to remain motionless for several moments, then bowed his head slightly. "My apologies, sir," he said, although his voice did not sound contrite in the least. "I do not intentionally make light of this very serious topic, and I again apologize for not treating you with the proper respect." Phoenix did not say or do anything in response. "Allow me to speak plainly."

"Please," Phoenix said stonily.

"First of all, sir, the Dong-Feng missiles deployed currently are not armed with nuclear warheads," Gao said. "They have a sixteen-hundred-kilogram high-explosive warhead and a range of only seven hundred kilometers. These are not 'carrier killers,' as you say—against a ship that size they may do some damage, but will not sink it."

"But you can put a nuclear warhead on them, correct?" Phoenix asked.

Now it was Gao's turn to look the president in the eye and say, "As you said, Mr. President, it depends on the nature of the threat." Phoenix rewarded him with a hint of a smile and a nod. "Mr. President, let us again speak plainly. We both have vital national matters that require the protection of our armies and navies. We rely on free movement of the sea for our economic well-being. That imperative is not going away any time soon.

"Therefore, I am sure you know well that the People's Republic of China has no intention of taking down our missiles or decommissioning our carriers," Gao went on, "no more than the United States would beach its nuclear submarines or dry-dock its carriers. Our nations must protect themselves. It is lamentable that our forces confront each other as they did yesterday, but that is the nature of the world and of the current geopolitical and military posture in which we find ourselves."

"Sounds like you're resigned to accepting the current state of affairs, Mr. Vice President," Phoenix said.

"I try to be realistic and pragmatic, sir," Gao said. "America used its prosperity and status after World War Two to build a great navy with which to secure the seas so as to expand trade throughout the world. China is merely doing the same. We must export goods, so we must have unfettered access to the world's oceans—and thus a military force capable of guaranteeing that access."

"That is a very honest and forthright view of the situation, Mr. Gao," Phoenix said. "So why don't you say that in your speech tomorrow? Why accuse the United States of trying to start a war with China by stationing a few aircraft on an island a thousand miles from China? Why invent half-truths about our naval forces?"

"Because the people of the world and the politicians who will listen to my speech do not care about pragmatism," Gao said. "Pragmatism does not increase defense budgets or inspire boys and girls to become sailors or airmen or work on the docks or in the factories. My speech is designed to show the people of the world that China faces danger and we need to do something about that danger. I want to focus the world's attention on what is happening around China's shores, and to put the world on notice that China is developing the modern resources to protect itself. China is no longer an isolated third-world country with old outdated ideas, tactics, politicians, soldiers, and weapons. China is on the rise."

"Sounds very ominous and fatalistic, sir," Phoenix observed.

"Not at all, Mr. President," Gao said, a slight smile forming on his lips. "I enjoy watching American football when I visit your country. When the receiver and the safeties are racing down the field, occasionally there is contact between them." For the first time in their meeting, Gao raised both hands, extended his index fingers, and tapped the sides of each together. "No one meant to contact the other—they are both intent on watching the ball in the air. Usually no one is hurt, play is continued, and a touchdown, and interception, or an incompletion results. It is when one player decides to intentionally play the man and not the ball that a penalty has taken place."

"Our job is to make sure no one commits a foul."

"Exactly, sir." Gao smiled again, proud of the president accepting his football analogy. "Contact I believe is inevitable. America's imperative is domination and control of the seas; China's imperative is no obstacles to continued worldwide growth and prosperity. They appear to be conflicting. But contact does not have to lead to disaster." He paused for a moment, then said, "May I ask, sir: What do you think of our proposal?"

"Complete demilitarization of the South China Sea?" Phoenix asked. "I'm all for it, Mr. Gao. But what do the bombers on Guam have to do with the South China Sea?"

"They can obviously patrol with ease over the South Sea," Gao said, "and each represents significant firepower directed at China. Reducing their numbers on Guam to the level before the tensions began, six maximum, or at least withdrawing them to Hawaii, would go a long way to reducing tensions in the region.

"At the same time you withdraw the bombers, China will withdraw its two aircraft carrier battle groups and its helicopter carrier battle group to our territorial waters, which I mean within twelve nautical miles of the mainland," Gao went on. "We will no longer patrol around the Paracel or Spratly Islands. We still reserve the right for our warships to transit the region, and port visits and exercises would not be protested if announced in advance, but we will not patrol it with surface vessels or submarines."

"That is certainly a good start, sir," Phoenix commented, the surprise on his face obvious. "What about air patrols?"

"We still reserve the right to conduct air patrols of the South China Sea," Gao said, "but they will be conducted solely for reconnaissance, customs and fisheries, and search and rescue, and the aircraft will be unarmed. We would like to see the United States use patrol aircraft other than B-1 bombers or P-8 Poseidon aircraft, because they can be armed with offensive weapons, but if you guarantee that the aircraft will be unarmed, and we are allowed to visually inspect them for verification on a short-notice basis, that will be sufficient. Of course, China will continue to research the ecological damage to the South China Sea and pay any cleanup or restoration costs, as well as costs associated with recovering the Taiwanese submarine and repairing the Vietnamese warship." There was a rather long silence, then: "Naturally, in the spirit of cooperation, we expect the United States to follow all these guidelines as well," he said.

"I will certainly discuss this at length with my national security staff, Mr. Gao," Phoenix said, "but it sounds very promising. I would like to see details, of course, but I think this is a very good place to start."

"Excellent," Gao said. "I will have Foreign Minister Tang, Defense Minister Cao, and General Zu draw up details. The plan will need to be ratified by the Central Military Committee and the Politburo, but I think you can expect swift agreement." Gao got to his feet. "Now I must go."

Phoenix stood, somewhat surprised. "We haven't talked about Taiwan or the disputed islands in the South China Sea, Mr. Gao," he said.

"It must wait for another time, I am afraid," Gao said. "But I will say this: they belong to the People's Republic of China." He looked at Phoenix's suddenly stony expression. "I know you do not accept this. You believe the South Sea belongs to the entire world and that Taiwan should be an independent country, but those are not the views of my government or most of my people. These issues will someday be resolved." He tapped his forefingers together again. "Contact, infrequent and not deliberate, but no penalties. That is our mission." Gao gave Phoenix a slight bow of his head, and they shook hands. "Thank you for receiving me today, Mr. President. Good-bye." The door of the Oval Office was opened from outside by a Secret Service agent, and Gao departed.

Phoenix returned to his desk, and Vice President Ann Page entered the Oval Office a few moments later. "How did it go?" she asked.

"Very well," Phoenix said. "What an interesting meeting. He doesn't sound at all like any Chinese politicians I've ever listened to. He's part of the new breed of politicians, probably the first generation that didn't fight in a civil war or was subjected to a cultural revolution. Did you read his proposal on demilitarizing the South China Sea?"

"Yes," Ann said. "I think it's a big step in the right direction."

"I hate to pull those extra B-1s from Guam," Phoenix said. "But, unfortunately, our good buddy Patrick McLanahan got in China's face, and I think withdrawing some of those planes and going down to a maximum of six long-range bombers on Guam at any one time will go a long way to defusing tensions out there."

"I feel we're giving up too much, but I agree: I don't think things will get better if we keep the status quo," Ann said.

"Very good," Phoenix said. "Let's get a meeting set up with the national security staff and the congressional leadership, and we'll look at that proposal. I'll give Patrick and the colonel in charge of that task force a heads-up that they should start packing up some of their bombers for a flight home."

ANDERSEN AIR FORCE BASE, GUAM

SEVERAL DAYS LATER

"It was fun while it lasted," Sondra Eddington said as she began packing her clothes in a suitcase. "But it'll be nice to get stateside again. I can't wait to do some skiing. Ever been heliskiing at Ruby Mountain near Elko, Brad?" She got no response. "It's the most incredible experience. They fly you up to the tops of these ridges, where the snow is powder dozens of feet deep and hasn't been touched by another living creature, and they drop you off and you ski down. It'll blow your mind. I flew the helicopter for a couple years but thought I'd never try skiing it, but when I finally did, I was hooked. You've got to come with me this season— you'll love it." Still no response, so she looked over at Brad and noticed him looking at her. "What?"

"I am just getting to know you," Brad said in a quiet voice, "and now we're going to leave."

"Hey, we'll see each other again," Sondra said. "I work for your dad, remember—that is, if they keep the Excalibur project going. If you finish up your certificates and ratings and get your degrees, maybe you'll get hired on at Sky Masters."

"That's the plan."

"Besides," she said, taking his hand and pulling him toward her, "we still have to unload and pack up the weapons on the birds, and that'll take a couple days at least with no flying. We'll have a few days to hang out at the beach, get some sun, and learn more about each other." And she leaned forward and kissed him gently on the lips. "How does that sound, stud?"

"Sounds great," Brad said.

"Good," she said. She waved a hand at the door to her tent.

"Now get out of here and let me finish packing before I get too distracted and we start doing something we'll be embarrassed about if someone walks in."

"Yes, ma'am," Brad said, and he left.

"Siren One-Eight flight, Spyglass, radar contact aircraft, bearing two-eight-five, range two-eighty, altitude thirty-one thousand, heading eastbound at four hundred knots," the radar controller aboard an E-3C Sentry AWACS (Airborne Warning and Control System) radar aircraft radioed. The E-3C Sentry had a thirty-foot rotating radome mounted atop its fuselage that provided three-dimensional air and surface search, IFF identification interrogation, and over-the-horizon communications relay, and it could share its radar imagery with other aircraft, ships, and battle management areas through JTIDS, or the Joint Tactical Information Distribution System. "Looks like a formation of two aircraft. Squawking a civilian mode three code, negative mode Charlie."

"Roger, copy," Lieutenant Colonel Jimmy "Juju" Maili, the leader of the flight of two F-22A Raptor fighters on patrol west of Guam, replied. Maili was also the commander of the 199th Expeditionary Fighter Squadron of the Hawaii Air National Guard based at Joint Base Pearl Harbor–Hickam, Honolulu, Hawaii, in charge of the four Raptors deployed to Guam. The two Raptors were flying loose formation with a KC-135 Stratotanker, making sure the fighters had plenty of fuel during their long-range patrol. "Brewski, why don't you get topped off, then I'll top, and we'll go check it out."

"Two," replied Major Robert "Brewski" Carling, Maili's wingman. "Break. Esso Three-Six, Siren One-Nine, clear me to precontact position, please."

"Roger, One-Nine, you are cleared to precontact position," replied the pilot of the KC-135. With Maili still on the tanker's right wingtip, Carling smoothly slipped down off the tanker's left wing and slid expertly into precontact position beneath the refueling boom. After making contact and topping off his fuel tanks, he went back up to the tanker's left wingtip, and Maili was cleared in. A few minutes they were all topped off, and they left the tanker and headed west.

"Your bogeys are at twelve o'clock, two hundred miles, still at thirty-one thousand, still at four hundred indicated airspeed," the AWACS radar controller reported. "Still squawking just mode three."

"Any report from Guam Oceanic?" Maili asked. While out of direct radar contact, civil aircraft used satellite position reporting to Guam Oceanic Control to keep track of their flights and deconflict with other aircraft.

"Several airliners are transiting the area," the controller reported, "but they're all in the upper thirties or forties. These guys are fairly low. Their squawk code doesn't match any assigned codes."

"Roger," Maili responded. Not unheard of, but not common either.

It took another thirteen minutes for the Raptors to close the distance, and Maili set up for a visual identification, putting Carling high and to his right while he turned left to close in on the formation. They used night-vision goggles to fly formation and for the visual identification. The NVGs had an effective range of about five miles for detection and two miles for identification, so he had to be patient. He spotted the formation right at five miles. "Tied on visual," Maili reported. "You got me, Brewski?"

"Two," his wingman responded. "Tied on visual with the bogeys too. Weird-looking aircraft so far."

"Moving in," Maili said, and he maneuvered in and above the formation. He wished the Raptor had a nice powerful forward-looking infrared and a searchlight for these identifications, but the NVGs did the job. "Okay, guys, who do we have here tonight?" He slid in closer and was soon able to get more detail . . .

. . . and suddenly he realized he was not looking at two planes in formation, but *several*! "Spyglass, Spyglass, One-Eight, this is not two aircraft, it's . . . shit, it's two formations of *six* aircraft, repeat, two formations of six in 'V' formations, twelve in all! They are large swept-wing jets and . . ." And the closer he got, the worse it got: "Spyglass, One-Eight, the two jets at the ends of each 'V' look like tankers, and they . . . *they are tanking fighters*! I see two . . . no, I see *four fighters with each tanker*! I count at least sixteen fighters up here, Control!"

"Do you have an ID on the large jets, One-Eight?"

"I don't recognize them yet," Maili said. "They look like old Stratojets, like big fighters, but I can't . . . wait, I recognize them now—they're H-6s! Control, I think they're Chinese H-6 bombers! And the fighters they're dragging look like J-20s!"

"Are you positive, One-Eight? Can you get a positive ID?"

"Stand by." Maili swerved left and descended until he was below the southernmost formation. "Okay, it looks like they have two engines, one in each wing root, elevator midway up the vertical stabilizer, and . . . holy shit, Spyglass, they are carrying large missiles under the wing, repeat, three large missiles under each, they are *all* carrying missiles except the tankers! These guys are loaded up to their eyeballs! I cannot identify the missiles, but they are big and mean-looking! Request instructions."

"Juju, this is Brewski," Carling radioed. "Several of the fighters that were on the tanker are breaking off and climbing, heading northeast. I'm going to lose them in a second."

"You still got me visual, Brewski?"

"Affirmative."

"I'm coming up." Maili turned away from the formation heading northeast and started a climb. "Join on me."

"Two," Carling acknowledged.

"Siren One-Eight flight, Control, we have contact with the aircraft that broke away," the radar controller reported. "Four bandits, eleven o'clock, eight miles high, accelerating past six hundred knots." A few moments later Maili's radar warning receiver lit up. "Siren flight, Siren flight, we have music," the controller said, using the brevity word that he was picking up enemy radar. A few moments after that: "Siren flight, eyeball, repeat *eyeball*!" "Eyeball" was the brevity word meaning that the controller determined that the AWACS was the enemy fighters' target!

"Light 'em up, Brewski," Maili said, activating his AN/APG-77 attack radar and electronic countermeasures system.

"Two." Because they had the AWACS radar plane giving them vectors, that was the first time in the entire engagement that they had turned on their own radars . . .

. . . which meant that now for the first time the Chinese J-20 fighters realized that the Raptors were there. "Siren flight, be advised, several high-speed aircraft breaking off from the formations and turning northeast! Four . . . now six bandits, repeat six bandits, at your six o'clock, fifteen miles, accelerating!"

"What the hell is it, Nash?" Warner "Cutlass" Cuthbert shouted as he trotted into the battle staff area. The alert siren was wailing outside. "What's the alert?"

"AWACS reports they made contact with what appears to be twelve Chinese H-6 bombers, heading east toward Guam," Lieutenant Colonel Nash Hartzell responded. "Four of them appear to be tankers. The other eight are each armed with six large missiles under their wings. They also report that the tankers were each refueling four fighters believed to be Chinese J-20s. Four fighters broke off from the formation and appear to be heading for the AWACS. Six other fighters are pursuing the Raptors."

"Holy Jesus," Cutlass breathed. "Scramble the alert fighters and . . ."

And at that moment, all the lights in the command center went out, and the siren outside stopped. "A power outage? *Now?* The weather is clear and a million!" Cutlass exclaimed. He picked up the telephone—dead. "What the hell is this?" He pulled a portable radio from a holster on his belt. "Security tower two, this is Alpha. What do you see?"

"Power's out all over the place, sir," the sergeant stationed on one of the security towers near the front gate replied. A moment later the emergency lights in the command center came on, followed a few moments after that with more lights coming on when the diesel-fired emergency generator finally kicked on. "Lights are out in town too. Front gate is secure."

"Tell the flight-line security teams that we're going to

launch everything we have," Cutlass said. "I want positive ID on anyone who steps on the flight line, but get the aircrews and crew chiefs to their planes as quickly as you can."

"Got it, sir."

Patrick McLanahan trotted into the command center, followed by Bradley, both in flight suits. A few moments later Ed Gleason, Sondra Eddington, Tom Hoffman, and several other Excalibur crewmembers came in as well. "What's going on, Cutlass?" Patrick asked.

"We've got Chinese bombers inbound, Chinese fighters going after our AWACS, and right in the middle of it we lose power and phones," Cutlass said. Their faces went blank in absolute disbelief. Cutlass found walkie-talkies and gave them out. "I need you guys to run out to the flight line and get the munitions loading crews away from the other Excaliburs. As soon as the munitions crews are clear, form a crew and get an Excalibur airborne. We'll launch as many Excaliburs as we can."

Patrick turned to Brad. "You stay here, Brad," he said.

"Heck no," Brad said. "I'm going with you!"

"It's too dangerous," Patrick said. "This is not a ferry flight."

"And it's not a combat mission either—it's an evacuation," Brad said. "I'm going." Patrick was going to argue, but others were hurrying all around him, and he nodded and ran outside, with Brad right behind him. They piled into the back of a six-pack pickup truck just in time before the driver sped off.

THIRTEEN

OVER THE PACIFIC OCEAN, FIVE HUNDRED MILES WEST OF GUAM

THAT SAME TIME

"*Fox three,* Brewski!" Jimmy Maili shouted on the command channel. All four Chinese fighters were locked on solid on his APG-77 radar, and the fire control computer had selected the best targets. With the press of a button, the left main weapon bay door opened and an AIM-120D AMRAAM was ejected into the slipstream and homed in on its target, followed a few seconds later by another from the right-side weapons bay. He could see tiny sparkles in the distance and assumed it was the Chinese pilots ejecting flares when they got the missile launch warning.

"Siren flight, bandits still at your six o'clock, eleven miles," the AWACS radar controller reported. The Raptor's multifunction cockpit displayed a God's-eye view of the engagement, combining the AWACS's radar information with their own radar data to give a complete picture of the battle.

"I'm breaking off to engage the trailers, Juju," Carling said.

"Nail 'em, Brewski," Maili said.

Carling deactivated his radar, then executed a tight climbing left turn, using the Raptor's thrust-vectoring engine exhaust nozzles to pull the jet's nose around even harder. With the AWACS in the area supplying real-time radar information to each Raptor, it was possible for the F-22s to attack using AWACS radar data, thereby not revealing themselves to the enemy by turning on their own radar. Carling switched into radar-emulate mode, and the fire control computer selected the best targets. "One-Nine, fox three," he announced, and he issued the attack order. The left main weapons bay opened and an AMRAAM shot off into the darkness. Once the AMRAAM got closer to its quarry as shown by the AWACS information, it would activate its own radar and infrared sensors and take over the kill by itself.

"One-Eight, splash one," Maili radioed. "Looks like the second missed. Jamming is heavy."

"One-Nine, splash one," Carling reported as he saw the blinking coffin-shaped box appear around the first bandit. But he also noticed that the targeting cues around the other bandits had disappeared. "Lost radar data from the AWACS," Carling radioed. He activated his AN/APG-77 radar to start searching for the Chinese pursuers . . .

. . . and found them all around him! Like sharks closing in on a baby seal, the Chinese fighters had surrounded him. Carling shut off his radar, rolled inverted and dived five hundred feet, executed a hard right turn, waited a few heartbeats, then rolled wings-level and executed a hard barrel roll. If the bandit to his north tried to follow him down, he should be right in front of him when he finished the roll . . .

. . . and when he turned on the radar again, there he was, less than four miles in front of him! Still inverted he radioed, "One-Nine, fox two!" he radioed. The fire control computer had already selected an AIM-9X Sidewinder heat-seeking missile from the left-side weapons bay and sent it into space. Carling immediately deactivated his radar . . .

. . . but as he did he heard, "One-Nine, bandit, five o'clock high, eight miles!" from the AWACS controller. "Additional bandits now eleven o'clock nine miles and seven o'clock ten miles!" Carling immediately snapped into a tight climbing right turn, chasing after the closest target behind him . . .

. . . but that was what the other Chinese J-20 fighters were waiting for. As soon as he made the turn he exposed his hot exhausts to the fighters off to his left, and two J-20s launched a volley of PL-9C heat-seeking missiles. The automatic countermeasures system aboard the F-22 reacted instantly, firing decoy flares and warning the pilot, and Carling executed a hard right diving break to escape the incoming missiles. But as soon as he did he presented a perfect radar target for the eastern bandit, who fired two radar-guided PL-12 missiles. Carling's Raptor exploded after a direct hit.

Meanwhile, Maili had killed another of the three remaining J-20s pursuing the AWACS plane. The two remaining Chinese fighters split up, both turning away from the AWACS. "Brewski, looks like the J-20s up here are turning your way." No reply. "Brewski, how copy?"

"Negative radar contact with One-Nine, Siren leader," the controller radioed. Maili swore into his oxygen mask. "Warning, bandits, seven o'clock, fifteen miles and closing, numerous targets. Bandit at ten o'clock, six miles, still turning, heading southwest. His wingman is at your two o'clock, heading southeast."

"Spyglass, it looks like they can't see me with my radar off," Maili said. "How's that datalink looking?"

"It's clear right now, One-Eight," the controller said. "Vector left heading two-eight-zero, target will be at twelve o'clock, six miles. Intermittent heaving jamming on all frequencies," the controller said. "The bomber formation is at your five o'clock, thirty miles—the heaviest jamming seems to be coming from them. But it's getting less the greater distance you get."

Unfortunately, Maili thought as he turned to the new heading, it also meant that the bombers were getting that much closer to Guam. As soon as he rolled onto the new heading he saw a "SHOOT" indication on his multifunction display. He pressed the launch button, and an AMRAAM flew out of the left main weapons bay. A few seconds later he saw a bright flash of light off in the distance, followed by a brief trail of fire, then nothing except another blinking coffin on his display.

"Vector left heading zero-five-zero," the controller said. "Bandits will be at your twelve o'clock, nine miles. Additional bandit at your two o'clock, six miles high." The threat warning receiver blared. "Bandit at your two o'clock is descending, appears to be diving on you. Two bandits at your twelve o'clock, eight miles, accelerating, climbing, range to Spyglass inside fifty miles."

Shit, Maili thought, and he pushed the throttles to zone one afterburner. The datalink was intermittent again, so he activated his radar, found the two J-20s closest to the AWACS plane, locked them up, and fired two AMRAAMs in quick succession . . .

. . . but not before the Chinese J-20s fired four PL-12 radar-guided missiles at the AWACS plane. The PL-12s were some of the world's most advanced air-to-air missiles. They had four different modes of guidance, and they used them all on this engagement:

They first got the initial target position from the J-20s' attack radar at launch. When Maili's AMRAAMs hit home and the J-20s' radars went down, they switched to inertial guidance mode to navigate themselves to a predicted point in space where their target might be. As they got in closer they switched on their own radars, discovered their target, and closed in for the kill. As soon as they activated their terminal guidance radars the AWACS radar plane began sending out jamming signals, dropping chaff and flares, and maneuvering as best as the big plane with its thirty-foot-diameter radome atop the fuselage could do, but the PL-12s used their fourth terminal guidance mode and homed in on the jamming signals themselves. Two of the missiles missed . . .

. . . but the two remaining PL-12s were more than enough to do the job. They ripped into the Sentry's fuselage, and their fifty-pound shaped-charge warheads and laser proximity fuses did their job, tearing the plane apart in seconds and sending it crashing to the sea.

Maili saw the fireball off in the distance and knew he was too late, and he thought of that big plane and the over twenty crewmembers killed, but now was the time to figure out his next moves. He made a quick assessment of his situation: he had two AMRAAMs and one Sidewinder remaining. He was getting low on fuel, but that didn't matter because they were all heading to the same place—the island of Guam. Turning for home wouldn't do him any good if there was no home to go to.

Maili was determined to take out as many Chinese bombers as he could. He still had four hundred and eight rounds of twenty-millimeter ammunition for his cannon, and he was even determined to kamikaze into another bomber if he couldn't get their formation to break up and turn away.

He turned in the direction that he believed the formation was located and activated his AN/APG-77 radar, and sure enough he painted the two V-formations just thirty miles to his southeast—they had not bothered to stray off their original course or altitude. He immediately locked up the lead bomber in the northernmost formation and fired, hoping that the sight of their leader going down would prompt the others to turn around or at least break up the . . .

. . . and at that instant his radar picked up other air targets flying eastbound, going fast and accelerating, already approaching the Mach just seconds into their flight . . . *cruise missiles, supersonic cruise missiles!*

"Warning, warning, any vessel, any command post on freq," he cried on his command channel and the international emergency GUARD frequency, "this is Siren One-Eight, United States Air National Guard, cruise missiles inbound heading toward Guam, if you hear me, take cover!" He knew he was hundreds of miles from Andersen Air Force Base and well over their horizon, and without the AWACS plane acting as a communications relay for his Joint Tactical Information Distribution System no one else was receiving his radar imagery, but he just couldn't remain silent while . . .

. . . and then he saw an immensely bright flash of light and felt a tremendous whipsaw effect as his F-22 Raptor was blown apart by several Chinese PL-12 missiles hitting him simultaneously, and then he felt nothing at all.

In the cockpit, Bradley switched the auxiliary power unit control switches to "RUN" and the battery switch to "ALERT," then hopped into his seat and began strapping in. Down below, Patrick hit the "ALERT START" button on the alert control panel on the nose gear door, which immediately started both auxiliary power units and would initiate the engine start sequence on all four engines, then raced up the entry ladder. As he did a crew chief arrived, pulled the wheel chocks, and quickly checked for streamers, open access panels, or other ground maintenance safety items. Planes were taking off from runway two-four left and right—the night air was thick with the smell of jet exhaust, and the noise was deafening.

The crew chief donned his intercom headset. "Crew chief is up, sir!" he said. "Chocks are pulled! Bomb bay doors and all four engines are clear!"

"Roger," Brad replied. "Bomb bay doors coming closed!" and he hit the switches to close all three sets of bomb bay doors. Meanwhile Patrick entered the cockpit and hurriedly strapped in.

"I'm up," Patrick reported.

"APUs are started, engine start sequence under way, bomb bay doors are closed, and chocks are pulled," Brad said. "I'm strapped in and my seat is hot."

"Same here," Patrick said. They both monitored the engine start, looking for any sharp upward spikes of engine temperatures that might indicate a hot start. As soon as all four engine temperatures stabilized Patrick radioed, "Cleared off, chief! Clear the taxiway."

"Crew chief clearing off. Good luck, sir." Patrick hit the taxi lights and pushed in power, and the Excalibur was on the move. He could see the crew chief with his fluorescent orange batons guiding him out onto the ramp—Patrick and Brad were by far the first ones out of the parking area.

Brad made sure the radios were configured. "Andersen tower, Masters Zero-Three," Patrick spoke, "taxiing from the shelters, request immediate takeoff clearance." Brad's hands continue to fly around the cockpit, making sure switches were properly configured for takeoff.

"Masters Zero-Three, Andersen tower, winds two-seven zero at eleven, cleared for takeoff, any runway."

"We'll take two-four left," Patrick said—their shelters were right at the end of runway two-four left, so it was a short taxi. On intercom he asked, "How am I looking, Brad?"

"I think I got everything, Dad," Brad said, "but check it first!"

"Not enough time," Patrick said. "Wing sweep, flaps, and slats are set—we're going. Anything we missed we'll take care of in the air." At the end of the runway he made sure the flight controls were clear, checked around the cockpit quickly for anything obvious he could have missed, then smoothly pushed the throttles up to military power, checked the nozzle swing, pushed it up into zone one afterburner, checked gauges again, then into zone five. The Excalibur surged down the runway like a cheetah in full pursuit, and it leaped into the sky.

Patrick raised the landing gear, retracted flaps and slats, then swept the wings back to cruise climb settings. "After takeoff checklist, Brad," he said, and Brad immediately called up the proper page on one of his MFDs and made sure the computer had checked off each item in sequence.

"Checklist complete," Brad announced.

"Thank you," Patrick said. "Call up the northern emergency evacuation anchor—we'll wait there and join up with everyone else once they make it off."

"Roger." Brad quickly recalled and loaded the proper waypoints. Guam used several emergency orbits, called anchors, for everything from runway closures to typhoon evacuations. The northern anchor was twenty miles south of the island of Tinian; Tinian International Airport had a concrete and asphalt runway long and strong enough to land XB-1s. Saipan International Airport a few miles north of Tinian had a runway just as long as Tinian's, but it was made of asphalt only and would not support even a lightly loaded XB-1.

"Switch number one radio to the command post."

"Roger," Brad said.

"Control, Master Zero-Three."

"Zero-Three, Control," the senior controller replied. "Read you three-by."

"You are weak and barely readable," Patrick said.

"We're on portable radios—power on most of the base is still down," a new voice that sounded like Colonel Warner "Cutlass" Cuthbert said. "I need you to stay within five miles of Andersen so we can stay in contact."

"Wilco," Patrick said. "Are you in contact with the Patriot missile batteries?" There were four Patriot antiaircraft missile batteries nearby: three on Guam itself in the northern part of the island, one on the base, and one in the south, plus one battery on Tinian.

"The Patriots are up and self-contained, and they have your Mode Twos," Cutlass responded. The Mode Two was a coded transponder used to identify individual military aircraft.

"How many made it off?"

"The alert birds all made it—one B-1B, one B-52H, one B-2A, three XB-1s, two F-22s, two F-15s, and three KC-135 and one KC-10 tankers," Cutlass said. "I put them in an orbit northwest of FISON intersection at ten thousand feet. We don't have Center radar operating, so we're trying to deconflict all the planes down here on paper and with the Patriot surveillance system."

"How many more made it?" Patrick asked.

"None of the other B-52s are going to make it within the next thirty minutes," Cutlass said. "We might get most of the XB-1s and B-1Bs off in thirty minutes, but that'll be cutting it close. General, I'm going to put you up at twenty-five thousand feet right over the runway, and I'll have you do a racetrack facing the west. I'll keep the fighters with the alert bombers until someone spots something, and then I hope we can chase them down. Hopefully you can spot the H-6s or whatever they throw at us. We're getting Wells and Wickham into the remote systems operator's trailer to operate your weapons."

"Copy that," Patrick said. He applied climb power and began a steep ascent to his new patrol altitude. On intercom he said, "Okay, Brad, let's fire up the radar and find those bastards." Patrick set up a triangular search pattern over the central part of the island so there was only one leg that the XB-1's AESA radar would not be looking west.

"Hoffman and Eddington are airborne in One-Four," Cutlass said. "They're going to be at twenty-one thousand feet, flying an opposite pattern as you so we always have at least one radar aimed westward."

"Copy that," Patrick said. Brad had called up a "God's-eye" view of the area around them on one of the center MFDs, and they could see all the planes orbiting around the island. The Joint Tactical Information Distribution System combined radar data from all the aircraft and from the Patriot radar into one, so Patrick and Brad could "see" the other planes even though they might not be directly scanning them with their own radar.

Just a few minutes later they saw an extremely fast target moving in from the west. "I see something!" Brad shouted. "Moving fast, descending, heading right for us!"

"Give me a heading of two-niner-zero, Patrick," George Wickham, the remote offensive systems officer said. "Solid lock. Weapons coming hot, I'm warming up your AMRAAMs. Masters One-Four, take heading three-zero-zero, your weapons are coming hot too, stand by. Cougar Seven flight of two and Buffalo Two-Five flight of two, inbound high-speed bandits at your seven o'clock high, see if you can spot them."

Patrick had just barely completed the turn to the northwest when the forward bomb bay doors opened, and two missiles on streaks of fire blasted off into the night sky a few seconds apart, followed by two more several seconds later. They could see other streaks of fire from below them too as Hoffman and Eddington's missiles went off in search of targets. The AESA radar data from the two XB-1s was being fed to the fire control computers of the F-22 Raptors and F-15 Eagles, helping their missiles to lock onto targets that were behind them, and seconds later their missiles were in the air as well, tracing huge arcs through the night sky as they turned to pursue their quarry.

In less than thirty seconds, it was over—no more Chinese cruise missiles were detected and no more AMRAAM missiles were commanded to launch, and the forward bomb bay doors closed. "What happened?" Brad asked. "Did we get them?"

"I don't know," Patrick said. He keyed the microphone button: "Control, Masters Zero-Three, how copy?" No response. "Zero-Three remote, Masters Zero-Three, Wick, how do you hear?" Still nothing. "This is not good."

"Maybe we're out of range," Brad suggested.

"We'll find out soon enough," Patrick said. "One-Four, this is Zero-Three," he radioed on the secure command channel. "Any contact from Cutlass?"

"Negative, Zero-Three," Tom Hoffman responded. "Nothing from the Patriot engagement control centers either."

"I'm going to fly over the base and take a look with the Sniper pod," Patrick said.

"Roger. We'll stay up here."

The entire island looked completely dark. Patrick could see a few lights on the base, but it too was mostly dark. He descended to a thousand feet aboveground, mindful of Mount Santa Rosa, Mount Barrigada, and other high hills and obstructions around the base, slowed to approach speed, sweeping the wings forward and lowering flaps and slats to get a good look.

"One-Four, this is Zero-Three, I see several impact points," Patrick reported. Brad seemed to be frozen in his ejection seat as he watched the horrific Sniper pod images on his multifunction display. "Looks like direct hits on the command center, several on the aircraft parking ramp, fuel farm, and transformer farm. Several aircraft on fire. One crater down about five thousand feet on runway two-four left, but it's off to the side between the runway and taxiway and I think it's passable or avoidable. Runway two-four right took a couple hits—I think it's out of commission."

"Bastards," Hoffman responded.

On the secure command channel McLanahan spoke: "Break. Task Force Leopard, this is Masters Zero-Three, how copy?"

"Loud and clear, sir," replied Lieutenant Colonel Franklin "Wishbone" McBride, the most senior member of the alert birds and task force commander, flying as aircraft commander aboard the B-2A Spirit stealth bomber.

"Did you contact PACAF yet, Wishbone?"

"Negative," McBride said. "I wanted to get all the alert birds in their orbits and settled down, and then I was going to send a B-1 to look over the runway which you've already done, get everybody back on the ground, then ask for instructions. We copied your report about the base, and we could see your Sniper video over JTIDS. Looks like we can still use runway two-four left okay."

"What are you talking about, Wishbone?" Patrick asked. "We've got missions to fly. I'm down to just Sidewinders for air-to-air, but we've still got JASSMs and HARMs. Let's get on it. We're wasting fuel."

"What missions, McLanahan?" McBride asked, forgetting to address the retired general with more respect. "I was there when Cutlass explained it to you: the missions on our computers *are not real.*"

"Cutlass is probably dead, McBride," Patrick said. "Is that real enough for you? I looked at some of those targets—they looked real enough to me, and when a SAM comes up we'll be shooting at the real thing."

"You're insane, McLanahan!" McBride exclaimed. "You can't fly that jet all the way to China and back! It's illegal! You have no authorization! Those planes don't belong to you!"

"You're wrong there, McBride—they *do* belong to me," Patrick said. "The Air Force just rents them from me. And I've never been told by the Air Force that our missions aren't real. Are you going to fly the strike mission or not, McBride?"

"*There are no strike missions, McLanahan!*" McBride cried. "Don't you get it? It's all for show. Now get off the radios and let me coordinate getting our asses back on the ground!"

"Call up the strike plan, Brad," Patrick said on intercom. Brad had it loaded in seconds. "Masters aircraft, head for ARCP number one. Check in." The ARCP, or Air Refueling Control Point, was common to all the strike plans for all aircraft.

"Zero-Five copies," Ed Gleason responded.

"Zero-Nine, wilco," Sondra Eddington replied.

"One-One, roger," replied Sam Jacobs, one of the young nonexmilitary pilots hired by Sky Masters for the Excalibur project.

"One-Four, roger," Tom Hoffman replied.

"*What in hell do you think you're doing?*" McBride exclaimed. He obviously saw the XB-1s leaving their assigned parking orbits on his JTIDS display. "Get back in your damned anchors, *now*!"

"Masters flight, switch to KBAM Uniform," Patrick ordered.

"Two."

"Three."

"Four."

"Five."

"Punch in Battle Mountain's UHF tower freq for me, Brad," Patrick said.

"Done."

"Masters flight, check."

"Two."

"Three."

"Four."

"Five." Everyone had figured out what Patrick had in mind.

"Why'd you do that, Dad?" Brad asked.

"Because I knew all the Battle Mountain guys would know the frequency, but I'm betting the Air Force guys won't," Patrick explained. "I don't want to listen to McBride yelling at us."

"So we're going to bomb China, Dad?"

"Unless you don't want to do this, Brad," Patrick said. "I didn't have any time to ask you. Like you said, you came along just to do an evacuation, not a combat mission. I don't even know if you know how to work the offensive systems—we won't have the remote systems operators working with us."

"I think I can work it."

Patrick looked over at his son. "Are you okay with all this, Brad?"

"I think so, Dad," Brad said in a low voice. "I mean, I want to be there for you, and if I say no you'd have to turn around, land, and find somebody else to go—or maybe they wouldn't let you take off again. I'm . . . I'm just . . ."

"What, son?"

"I'm just afraid if I chicken out," Brad said. "I mean, I've never been in combat before except in the Cybernetic Infantry Device, and that thing kicks butt so bad it's really not fair to call it combat." The Cybernetic Infantry Device was a manned robot that gave its pilot incredible strength, speed, vision, and attack capabilities, akin to an entire armored infantry platoon; Brad had been checked out in it and had gotten to use it to ambush and capture terrorists who were out to kill his father. "I'm just worried I'll wimp out on you."

"Everyone is worried about that, Brad, no matter how experienced you are," Patrick said.

"Even you, Dad?"

"Of course," Patrick admitted. "I'm leading my son and four other crews and four other bombers into battle against the largest army and the fourth-largest air force in the world. You don't think I'm scared of that? But I think of what we saw back at Andersen Air Force Base, and I think of what the Chinese did and what they've done in the past, and I know I need to do something." Brad fell silent. Patrick keyed the mic button: "Masters flight, I know you might think this is loco. If you don't want to risk it, you can head back to Andersen with the others."

"We're not leaving, General," Ed Gleason said. "We're lucky we weren't on the ground when those bastards hit us. I'm not going back without a little payback."

"Three," Sondra radioed.

"Four," said Jacobs.

"Five," Hoffman replied. "Goes double for me."

"Thanks, guys," Patrick said. He looked at the flight plan. "I've got one hour and twenty minutes to the start-countermeasures point. Check over your equipment and weapons and let me know any problems, and study your targets and threats and let's talk about it. And thanks again for leaning into this with me."

"What the hell happened?" President Ken Phoenix asked as he strode into the Situation Room. "What do you have, Bill?"

"Two formations of twelve Chinese H-6 bombers, consisting of four aerial refueling tankers and eight cruise-missile-carrying bombers, attacked Andesen Air Force Base on the island of Guam," National Security Adviser William Glenbrook said. He motioned to the large wall-sized electronic chart. "The bombers were accompanied by eight J-20 advanced fifth-generation fighters that shot down two F-22 Raptors and an E-3 Sentry radar plane."

"*What?*" the president exclaimed. "My God . . . !"

"The bombers then launched supersonic cruise missiles believed to be AS-17s from a range of about five hundred miles," Glenbrook went on. He looked directly at the president, reading the unspoken question in his face. "The cruise missiles were not nuclear tipped, Mr. President, but they destroyed the air base's command center, fuel storage, electrical grid, put one runway out of commission, and destroyed or damaged a half-dozen aircraft on the ground. The air-to-air missile-armed bombers, fighters, and the Patriot missile batteries installed on Guam probably kept the losses down significantly, but the air base is definitely crippled. We are investigating to see if there's been any damage to other airfields in the vicinity."

"Jesus," Phoenix breathed. Then he said decisively, "Go to DEFCON Two." DEFCON Two was just two steps away from going to all-out nuclear war: it instructed units to load all nuclear-capable aircraft and ships with nuclear weapons, deploy and disperse assets to alternate operating bases, man command centers and emergency reconstitution sites, increase security at all bases to a wartime posture, and move key military and government personnel and equipment to remote locations to be able to operate in case of attack.

"Secretary Hayes has authenticated the order, and we are at DEFCON Two," Glenbrook reported a few minutes later. "He is en route to Andrews right now to board the E-4." The E-4B was the National Airborne Operations Center, or NAOC, a modified Boeing 747–200 loaded with extensive communications and control equipment to be able to direct U.S. forces worldwide in case ground-based command centers were destroyed or rendered ineffective. Formerly based at Offutt Air Force Base in Nebraska before the base was destroyed by a Russian cruise missile, the four E-4B aircraft were dispersed and moved to other bases around the United States following the American Holocaust; one was always based in the Washington, D.C., area for use by the president, vice president, or secretary of defense. "The vice president is en route to Site-R." Site-R was the Raven Rock Military Complex, an underground communications and alternate command center in Pennsylvania just a few miles north of Camp David, Maryland.

"How in the hell did those bombers get within range of Guam?" the president asked. "Didn't we have air patrols up?"

"The Chinese bombers were intercepted by two F-22 Raptor fighters when they were six hundred miles away from Guam," Glenbrook went on. "While they were making visual identification, they were jumped by the J-20 fighters. Several Chinese fighters were shot down, but our guys were simply outnumbered. They blew past the Raptors and took down the AWACS radar plane, and at that point the Chinese fighters had the advantage. The J-20 is probably equal to the Raptor in every way."

"Did *any* of our planes survive?"

"Yes, sir," Glenbrook replied. "Initial reports say we still have one B-2A Spirit stealth bomber, one B-52H Stratofortress bomber, one B-1B Lancer bomber, five XB-1 Excalibur bombers, two F-22A Raptors, two F-15 Eagles, and four tankers," Glenbrook said.

The president's mouth dropped open in complete shock. "You . . . you mean . . . that's *it*?" he asked.

"Those are all the long-range strike and air defense aircraft we have in the entire western Pacific theater, sir," Glenbrook said. "We have a handful of F-22s and F-15s still in Hawaii, another handful in Alaska, and the six XB-1 bombers are preparing for deployment in Nevada. Sir, under DEFCON Two, I suggest moving the *Nimitz* carrier strike group west of Hawaii. The Chinese crippled Guam—Honolulu could be next."

"*Honolulu!*" the president exclaimed. "No way in hell I'm allowing any planes to get within cruise missile range of Honolulu!"

"What do you want to do, sir?" Glenbrook asked.

"What are our options?" the president asked. "Where are the carriers?"

"The closest one available is the *Ford,* currently in the Java Sea," Glenbrook said, referring to information on his tablet computer. "The *Nimitz* is in the western Pacific, but you ordered it back to assist in the defense of the Hawaiian islands. Two Ohio-class ballistic missile subs are also in the western Pacific."

Glenbrook stopped, and the president's eyes widened in shock. "That's *it*?"

"With the threat from China after they released that nuclear depth charge, we didn't dare send any carriers or subs into the South China Sea," Glenbrook said. "The bombers on Guam

were the only other force we put together other than the few
fighters we have deployed in Japan and Korea, and even they
were there just as a show of force."

"Now we don't even have that," the president said. He
looked at Glenbrook in astonishment. "Are you saying that the
only option we have right now is . . . an attack with *sea-launched
ballistic nuclear missiles?*"

"Unless we send in the Pacific carriers, sir," Glenbrook said.
"But we'd have to send them in within a few hundred miles of
shore, well within the range of their antiship ballistic missiles
and supersonic cruise missiles. They could get overwhelmed.
And if we lost even one carrier, the loss of life would be
tremendous—almost double that of 9/11."

"My God," Phoenix said. "I'm actually going to have to
consider a *nuclear attack* on China." He thought for a moment.
"How about limited attacks on targets far from population
centers?"

"We have contingency plans available for small-yield
nuclear missile attacks on isolated targets in China—long-
range radar installations, mobile ballistic missile launch pads,
nuclear weapon storage facilities, coal mines, oil fields, that sort
of thing," Glenbrook said. "General Conaway can brief you on
those. But I think the better option would be to attack their
ballistic missile submarine bases and land-based ICBM silos to
minimize the threat to the United States, and then deal with
the mobile nuclear missiles as best we can. We would have to
coordinate those plans with our Pacific allies—they're more
vulnerable to mobile missiles than we are." He paused, then
added, "There are two more options."

"What are they?"

"The first: threaten to attack and destroy their cities,"
Glenbrook said.

"That's insane—they know I would never do that unless

the United States was attacked with nuclear weapons," the president said. "What's the other option?"

"Agree to terms," Glenbrook said. "No military forces in the South China Sea. China has complete and unfettered control. We don't interfere with their domination and control of the islands or resources in the South China Sea, what they call the first island chain."

"What the hell does that give us, Bill?"

"Time," Glenbrook said. "Time to rebuild our naval, long-range air, and space forces."

"It sounds like surrender to me, Bill."

"We have few options, sir," Glenbrook said. "Either we use our strategic nuclear forces to destroy China's ability to attack us and our allies with nuclear weapons . . . or we bargain for terms."

"And hope they don't attack us anyway," the president said. "Schedule a meeting with the national security staff right away. I need everyone's input on this."

"Unidentified aircraft inbound!" the radar controller shouted into his intercom. "Bearing zero-eight-zero, range two hundred kilometers, speed two hundred kilometers an hour! Multiple targets inbound!"

"Issue an air defense alert to all batteries," the commander of the air defense sector ordered. "Multiple unidentified aircraft approaching at medium speed. Report when all systems ready. What is the target's altitude?"

"Altitude is steady at one thousand meters, sir," the controller reported. "Sir, all batteries report ready to . . ." And at that instant the controller's digital radar scope seemed to waver and freeze for a few seconds . . .

. . . and when it came back, the screen was *filled* with targets, thousands of them, all reporting the same airspeed, direction of flight, and altitude! "Sir, I am being jammed!"

"Shut down, damn you!" the commander shouted. "Transfer intercept to S-300 primary sector engagement control! Alert all radar units to switch to agile frequency mode if they are getting any jamming!"

The first volley of ten AGM-158 Joint Air to Surface Standoff Missiles, two from each XB-1 Excalibur launched simultaneously, took advantage of the jamming and spoofing from the bombers' SPEAR electronic data intrusion system and plowed into the heart of the Chinese coastal radar network sixty miles southeast of the city of Guangzhou, destroying the large long-range radars and fixed air defense radars and surface-to-air missile emplacements arrayed along the coast.

Still ten minutes from crossing the coast, the formation of XB-1 bombers had fanned out along a sixty-mile front, line abreast, heading in at six hundred miles an hour. They would take turns turning on their AESA radars to update the tactical situation and to look for fighters or other air traffic. They had descended to four hundred feet above the water, high enough to avoid most obstacles like ships but low enough to avoid long-range radars.

Patrick and Brad were in the center of the attacking line, aimed directly at the People's Liberation Army Navy base at Zhongshan. Brad found himself grasping at the glare shield around the top of the instrument panel at every bump of turbulence or when some light flashed by. He had never gotten airsick before, but he had never flown at almost the speed of sound just four hundred feet above the water either—if they survived this, he thought, I have a lot of cleaning up to do. "You okay, Brad?" Patrick asked.

"I think so," Brad said weakly. A threat warning appeared on his MFD. "SA-N-12, twelve o'clock, thirty miles."

"Touch the warning box," Patrick said. A smaller window opened on the MFD with a diagram of the Excalibur showing the weapons remaining. "Now touch the 'HARM' icon, and touch again to confirm. It should give you a request for consent."

"Yes."

Patrick reached over to his left instrument panel, opened a red safety cover, and flipped a switch. "Pilot's consent on."

Brad did the same on his right instrument panel. "Consent switch up."

"Hit the 'ENGAGE' box, then watch your eyes." Brad hit the screen, and seconds later there was a tremendous flash of light as a HARM missile shot from its launch rail and sped off into the dark sky. Patrick looked over and saw Brad rubbing his eyes. "I warned you. That missile motor is pretty big. Your eyes should be okay in a minute." Seconds later, just as his eyes cleared, the "SA-N-12" warning went away. "Good shooting."

"It's just like a video game," Brad said. Another warning sounded. *"Missile launch!* SA-11, one o'clock!"

"Unreel the decoy," Patrick said. Brad touched a computer soft key on the screen, which deployed the ALE-50 towed decoy from a canister in the tail. Patrick glanced out the right windscreen. "See that bright light that looks like a really bright star? That's the SA-11."

"You can see it coming at us?" Brad exclaimed.

"We're not sure if it's homing on us—it could be one of the other Excaliburs," Patrick said. "Watch that spot on the windscreen. If it doesn't change positions, it's heading for us."

"I don't see it moving . . . it's gone!"

"The motor burned out. Now it's coasting in on us. Give me a burst on the AESA." Brad activated the radar with a nervous touch on the screen. "Left chaff, now," he said calmly, and as Brad hit the touch screen, Patrick threw the bomber into a tight right turn. Brad thought his head was going to snap off his neck! "Check trackbreakers and SPEAR!"

Brad had to refocus his eyes on the proper MFD. "Trackbreakers active!" he said finally. "SPEAR active!"

"Right chaff, *now!*" Brad fumbled but finally hit the soft key, barely in time before Patrick started another hard break. "I think it missed."

"It missed us, but it got the decoy," Brad said. "The ALE-50 is down. Should I send out the other one?"

"Better hold it for our egress," Patrick said. "Looks like we're feet-dry."

"Huh?"

"Back over land," Patrick said. "One more squeak of AESA." Brad activated the radar until they got a nice clear radar image that was almost photograph quality, then switched it to standby. "Well, well, looks like we have our first ship at one o'clock. Looks like a big one. Can you make it out on the Sniper?"

Brad activated the Sniper targeting pod and zoomed in on the target. "It's big, that's for sure. Can't tell if it's a carrier or what."

"Designate it and let's see how she sails with a JASSM in her," Patrick said. Brad touched the image on his screen, selected an AGM-158, and confirmed the selection. The middle bomb doors came open. "Missile away!"

As they flew closer, it was apparent now that the target was not a warship, but a container ship. "You have a few seconds," Patrick said. "Scan left and right and see if there are any better targets.

Brad swiped his finger on the Sniper image left, which tracked the camera in the same direction. "There!" he shouted. "That *definitely* looks like an aircraft carrier!"

"Designate it," Patrick said. "It'll ask if you want another launch or redesignate the missile in the air. Select 'RE-DESG.' Good . . . right on time. Switch to the missile seeker." Brad did, and he got to watch the JASSM plow right into the aircraft hangar opening on the left side of the carrier. "I don't know if that was the Chinese or Russian carrier," Patrick said, "but you nailed it." A tremendous fireball erupted off in the distance, and on the Sniper image it appeared as if the carrier listed almost all the way to the right like a toy boat caught under the faucet in the tub as more explosions erupted.

"Good shooting, Brad," Sondra radioed. Her Excalibur was ten miles to the south. "We're releasing on Fushan air base now. Give us a couple seconds before you launch."

"Roger," Patrick replied. He saw the brief indication of Sondra's AESA radar being activated, then the alerts that two

JASSMs were in the air. He waited a few seconds, then said, "Clear to release on Fushan, Brad."

"Roger." Brad touched the green triangle around Fushan air base, selected and confirmed two JASSMs, and let them fly. At the same moment, Brad saw a blinking box around one of the other Excaliburs. "What does that mean, Dad?" he asked.

Patrick looked, then took a deep breath. "Blinking coffin box—Jacobs got hit," he said. Patrick threw the Excalibur into a hard right turn. "Get your head back in the game, Muck," he told himself half aloud. "Two more JASSMs and three HARMs left. Let's see if we can find where they supposedly moved those DF-21Ds around Huizhou."

"Fighters inbound!" Brad shouted excitedly. Two airplane icons appeared to their north, both with triangles on their nose indicating the approximate detection range of their radars. "J-15s. They're heading right for us!"

"Keep on looking for the DF-21s," Patrick said. "I'll keep an eye on the fighters." But it was obvious the fighters were headed right for them. "Their radar isn't painting us, but they're still heading in—they must be tracking us with infrared," he said. He selected both aircraft icons, then selected and confirmed one AIM-9X for each bandit. "Forward bay doors coming open." Two missiles dropped free of the forward bomb bay and streaked off into space. Both fighters peeled off in different directions after obviously detecting the missile launches.

"Got it, Dad!" Brad shouted. There in the Sniper image on Brad's MFD were what appeared to be two transporter-erector-launchers, sitting in an open field barely concealed by trees. "I'm going to select them . . ."

"Hold on," Patrick said. "That looks fishy. They're just sitting out in the open. Scan around a little." Brad moved the camera left and right, and, sure enough, several hundred yards farther east there was another set of two launchers, but these appeared to be concealed with camouflage netting, they had more vehicles surrounding them, and there were warm spots on the engine compartment and in various places around the vehicle—Brad could even see a few persons walking nearby.

"But which one is it?" Brad asked. "They both look real."

"You're the gunner today, Brad," Patrick said. "Choose one and . . ."

The "MISSILE WARNING" alert sounded. Distracted by the DF-21 discovery, Patrick had allowed the two J-15 fighters to close in directly behind them! *"Chaff! Flares!"* he shouted, and as soon as he saw Brad's finger touch the screen he yanked the stick left and back and hit the afterburners, starting a rapid climb into their pursuers. They felt a loud hard thrumming on the left wing, and seconds later they got a "FIRE NO. 1" warning message on their MFDs. "Fire on number one!" Patrick shouted. He pulled the throttles out of afterburner, retarded the number one engine throttle to cutoff and hit the fire extinguisher button. Seconds later, the fire warning went out.

"What do I do? What do I do?" Brad shouted.

"First, *relax,*" Patrick said. "Check the engine instruments. I'm going to try to find that fighter."

"Say your status, Zero-Three," Sondra radioed.

"Got one on my tail somewhere," Patrick said.

"On the way."

Patrick activated the AESA radar briefly, but there was no sign of the Chinese fighter. "No sign of him," he said. "Do you still have the DF-21s locked up?"

Brad checked his displays, and sure enough the Sniper pod was still indicating it was locked on. "Yes!"

Patrick made a slight left turn until they could see the image of the DF-21. "Nail them," he said, and seconds later the last two JASSMs were in the . . .

And at that instant a thunderous *BRRRAAAPPP!* sound could be heard that seemed to run up the length of the left side of the Excalibur from tail to nose. The pilot's side window and left windscreen exploded, showering Patrick first with glass and then with triple hurricane-force winds. His body was being shoved left and right like a rag doll held outside a moving vehicle by the massive wind pressure.

"Dad!" Brad screamed. His flight training immediately took over, and he put his hands on the control stick and throttles, pulled back power, pushed the wing-sweep level forward, and started a climb. It sounded as if he was standing inches away from a freight train thundering past him at full speed. He couldn't tell the extent of his father's injuries, only that he was helpless and wounded, and he was just inches away and couldn't do anything for him. "Oh, God, *Dad!* . . ."

Brad then saw it on his MFD—the J-15 was back, lining up for another missile shot. Brad tried to turn into the fighter, but it was as if the controls were half frozen, and he had no maneuverability. They were almost inside the radar cone . . . the "MISSILE WARNING" was blaring, now blinking . . . they were well inside the radar cone now . . .

. . . and just then a coffin box appeared around the J-15, then disappeared.

"Looks like your tail is clear, Zero-Three," Sondra radioed. "You guys okay?"

"We got one engine shut down, and we got hit up the left side," Brad said. "I don't know if Dad got hit, but he's out."

"Roger," Sondra said. Brad couldn't believe how calm she sounded, and that helped him start to get control of his shaking arms and knees. "I've got you in the NVGs. I'll come up on your left side. You just fly the airplane. Head east."

The farther east they headed, the more radar warnings they got, and soon the radar warnings were almost constant—

and then the indications of fighters approaching from both the north and south began.

Sondra pulled up alongside Brad's stricken bomber, and Lisa Mann, her copilot, examined the damage. "You're leaking fuel, you might be getting an engine fire on number two, and you might not be able to fully sweep your wings all the way forward," Mann said.

"What do we do, Sondra?" Brad asked.

"You just fly the airplane, Brad," Sondra said. "Your job is to stay on my wing."

"But those fighters! . . ."

"Stay on my wing," Sondra repeated. "If we get hit, remember your ejection procedures."

"But what about my dad!"

"Brad, don't think about that," Sondra said. "Stay on my wing, and if we get hit, remember your ejection procedures."

"But I can't just eject without doing something!" Brad said. "Maybe I can pull his ejection lever right before I pull mine."

"Just stay on my wing, Brad," Sondra repeated. Now there were at least a half-dozen fighters screaming in on them from three sides. They were going to be enveloped any second. There was a tremendous flash and a brief mushroom of fire down below . . .

. . . and then, one by one, the enemy fighter icons began to disappear, and the radar warnings ceased.

"Masters flight, this is Spirit Three-Zero on GUARD," Lieutenant Colonel McBride radioed on the international emergency frequency. "Switch back to the command channel." Brad switched the number one radio back to the secure command channel. "Masters flight, Task Force Leopard, check in."

"One," Brad replied.

"Two."

"Three."

There was a slight pause in memory of Sam Jacobs, and then Tom Hoffman replied, "Five."

"We'll be inbound past you in a second," McBride said. "Your nose is clear."

"Negative, negative!" Sondra responded. "Three-Zero, I've got fighters inbound from the east. They look like they're on your tail!"

"They are, but they're Republic of China fighters, not People's Liberation Army," McBride said. "They're going to clear a path for you guys while the rest of Task Force Leopard takes care of the targets you guys didn't get. There's a tanker waiting at the second ARCP in case you need it."

"You guys followed us out here? Why didn't you say something?"

"You nuts had your radios turned off or tuned to some other freq, and you never answered us," McBride said. "That's okay—there was a lot of screaming and yelling from Honolulu all the way to Washington that you missed out on, but since we couldn't stop you, we figured we'd better join you. The Taiwanese were more than ready to help, and the Philippine and Vietnamese air forces are patrolling as well in case any more PLAAF fighters want to play."

"Thanks, guys," Brad said. "You really saved our butts."

"You didn't think we were going to let you come out here and get all the glory, did you?" McBride said.

Brad looked over at his father, pinned to his ejection seat, covered in glass and blood, his head being jerked back and forth uncontrollably by the strong slipstream, and there was nothing he could do to help him. He certainly didn't feel like he was getting any glory right now.

EPILOGUE

OFFICE OF THE CHIEF OF THE GENERAL STAFF, PEOPLE'S LIBERATION ARMY HEADQUARTERS, BEIJING, CHINA

THREE DAYS LATER

"The plan is simple, sir," Admiral Zhen Peng, commander of the South Sea Fleet of the People's Liberation Army Navy, said. "First, we must complete the destruction of the island of Guam. Our first attack did not do enough damage. But many of the Patriot air defense systems were destroyed and have not yet been replaced, and of course the bombers that carried air-to-air missiles are no longer there. We still have a quantity of AS-19 nuclear missiles ready to load on our surviving H-6 bombers, and they can make short work of the air base on Guam." General Zu Kai said nothing, only staring into space, an almost burned-out cigarette in his fingers.

"Second, we punish every nation that assisted the Americans on that attack against Guangzhou," Zhen went on. "Taiwan, the Philippines, and Vietnam must pay for their involvement. A series of strikes against their most important air and naval bases must be undertaken immediately. Third, we threaten immediate nuclear retaliation for any nation that dares to attack us again. We should have responded to the attack on Guangzhou with an attack against the Aleutians or Hawaii, but no matter—we will make it clear to the Americans that their most important Pacific bases will become nothing but charred ruins if they . . ." And the connection was suddenly cut.

"Another thing that does not work around here," Zu said half aloud. He walked over to his bulletproof office window. He could see several plumes of black smoke and winks of fire off in the distance, probably from more protests. The daily numbers of civilian casualties were no longer counted in the hundreds from these clashes—they were now in the thousands. And yet not only did the protests not stop, they only grew and multiplied.

There was a knock on the door. "Come," Zu ordered, and his deputy chief of the general staff, General Sun Ji, entered. "I was speaking with Admiral Zhen a moment ago, and we were cut off," Zu said. "Get him back on the line for me."

"I am afraid that is impossible, sir," Sun said.

"Why?"

"Zhen has been arrested for treason and dereliction of duty, sir," Sun said. "He has been sentenced to summary execution."

"*What?*" Zu thundered, shooting to his feet. "Who ordered this? I did not order it! Was it that popinjay Gao? I will beat that man senseless with my own bare hands *before* I throw him in prison! I said, who ordered Zhen's arrest, Sun?"

"I did, Zu," a voice from the outer office said, and to Zu's complete surprise, Zhou Qiang entered the office.

"*You!*" Zu cried. "I thought you were dead!"

"Next time you want someone dead, Zu, do it yourself to be

sure the job is done properly," Zhou said. "Zhen will not be the only one receiving summary execution tonight."

"Why, you *bastard*!" Zu shouted, and he whipped open a desk drawer, picked up a NORINCO Model 77B that he always had stashed away there, aimed, and pulled the trigger . . . and nothing happened.

"You should always check yourself to see that your personal weapons are loaded, Zu," Zhou said. Zu's eyes bulged in disbelief when he turned to the only man who had access to his office and desk at any time—his deputy chief of staff, Sun Ji, who was standing behind Zhou, his hands behind his back, smiling. Sun motioned behind him, and several soldiers came in, put Zu in handcuffs, and pulled him out.

"I am glad that nightmare is over," Zhou said. He turned to Sun. "You will take over as chief of the general staff. I will be sure to recommend the position to the Central Military Committee."

"Thank you, sir," Sun said.

"I will leave you to deal with the Russians as to the sinking of their precious aircraft carrier *Vladimir Putin* by the Americans in Zhujiang Bay," Zhou said. "Frankly, I hope they choke on it. What did they expect by making a deal with a megalomaniac like Zu?"

"Had I been asked, sir, I would have advised Zu against dealing with the Russians," Sun said. "They cannot be trusted."

Zhou studied Sun for a few long moments, then said, "Neither can you be trusted, Sun." General Sun blinked, but stood with his hands behind him at parade rest. "Maybe no one can be trusted these days. When no one can be trusted, perhaps China's response should be to do what it has always done in its thousands of years of history: retreat into itself. Lock itself away from the modern world, whether that modern world is seventeenth-century Portugal, nineteenth-century England, or twenty-first-century America." He shook his head. "I am going home, Sun. Tomorrow is the first day of China's future. Remember that." Sun snapped to attention as Zhou shuffled out of the chief of the general staff's office and departed.

After Sun heard the outer office door close, he relaxed from his brace, went over to Zu's desk, sat down in his chair, and put his feet up on the desk.

"You are a senile, hopeless, tottering old man, President Zhou," General Sun said. "You need to be thrown out into the gutters along with the Politburo, the Central Committee, and all you other political has-beens. If you cannot keep up with the modern world, you should be eliminated." He found one of Zu's cigarettes and a lighter and lit up. "And I am just the man to make that happen."

SACRAMENTO OLD CITY CEMETERY, SACRAMENTO, CALIFORNIA

THAT SAME TIME

The honor guard finished folding the flag that had draped the ceremonial casket, and the captain of the honor guard clutched the flag between his two palms. They were in front of the McLanahan family columbarium at the historic cemetery in downtown Sacramento, the cemetery that held the remains of nearly two hundred years of McLanahans.

But instead of the captain handing the flag to a family member, he handed it to President Kenneth Phoenix, who was accompanied by Vice President Ann Page. The president took it and clutched it to his chest, and Ann touched it and held it. Together they turned and walked over to the front row of family members seated closest to the empty casket. He stood in front of Bradley, bent at the waist, held out the folded American flag, and said in a soft voice, "Bradley, Nancy, Margaret, on behalf of a grateful nation . . ."

And then he stopped. Choking back a sob, Phoenix pressed the folded flag again against his chest . . . then suddenly dropped to his knees on the artificial grass carpeting surrounding the casket. The Secret Service agents accompanying the president surged forward, afraid he might be sick or just overcome with grief, but Ann Page warned them away with a silent, angry scowl.

"Bradley, I ask you one more time," President Phoenix quietly implored, his head bowed. "Allow me to take your father's remains to Washington. He deserves to join our country's greatest heroes in death. He deserves to be honored

by every loyal American soldier, sailor, airman, and marine
in Arlington National Cemetery. It wouldn't be forever. Let
him be honored by our country until your passing, in a special
national memorial columbarium, and then he can be brought
back here for final rest with you and your mother. It is the least
we can do for America's greatest aviation hero."

Bradley sobbed for several long moments, comforted by his
aunts, then shook his head. "No, Mr. President," he said. "Dad
wouldn't have wanted it that way. I don't know much about my
dad, but I do know this: he didn't think of himself as a hero.
He was a crewdog, plain and simple. I don't know what that is,
but that's what he was. That's all I know about him. He saw the
objective, planned the mission, and executed the plan. He didn't
expect praise, commendations, or medals—all he wanted was
results, and then to be allowed to go home."

"Jesus, Bradley," Ann Page said. "Your father was one of
the most inspirational figures of the twentieth and twenty-first
centuries. You can't just . . . just *bury* him. Think of our country.
We need heroes, Brad. Your father is the perfect example of
what every American should aspire to become."

"Maybe, Miss Vice President," Bradley said, "but my dad
wouldn't buy that for an instant, and you know that." Ann
lowered her head in silent assent. "Dad did stuff because it
needed to be done, because the fight was on and he had to get
in there and engage. When the fight was over, he broke off
and headed for home. That's all I know about Patrick Shane
McLanahan, but I think that's all I need to know. I think that's
all the world needs to know about him too."

Bradley stood before the president of the United States
and held out a hand, and President Phoenix took it, got to
his feet, and stood beside him. Together they walked to the
open columbarium chamber. Bradley inserted the urn into the
crypt. Phoenix took the columbarium cover from an astonished

cemetery worker, and together Bradley and the president of the United States secured the cover to the columbarium in place.

"God rest the soul of Lieutenant General Patrick Shane McLanahan," the president of the United States said in a loud voice. "God rest all our souls."